The Backwoodsman
Or,
Life On The Indian Frontier

By

Ed. Sir Lascelles Wraxall

Double9
BOOKS

The Backwoodsman
Or,
Life On The Indian Frontier
by Ed. Sir Lascelles Wraxall

ISBN: 978-93-60460-46-4
Published by

DOUBLE 9 BOOKS

2/13-B, Ansari Road
Daryaganj, New Delhi – 110002
info@double9books.com
www.double9books.com
Tel. 011-40042856

ABOUT THE AUTHOR

Sir Lascelles Wraxall went to school at Shrewsbury and was a Dyke scholar there. On May 26, 1842, he left from St. Mary Hall, Oxford, but he didn't finish his degree there. He took over as third baronet from his uncle, Sir William Lascelles Wraxall, in May 1863. He lived most of his life on the continent after 1846. During the year 1855, he worked for nine months as a first-class assistant commissary in the Turkish force at Kerch in the Crimea. He was given the rank of captain that job. His book Camp Life: Passages from the Story of a Contingent (1860) talks about what he went through during this time. He put out a paper called "A Visit to the Seat of War in the North" before he went to the Crimea. It said it was a translation from German, but it was probably his own work. Wraxall kept being interested in things related to the military. In 1856, he published A Handbook to the Naval and Military Resources of European Nations. In 1859, he wrote The Armies of the Great Powers. And in 1864, he wrote Military Sketches, a book mostly about the French army and its leaders but also including parts about the Austrian army, the British soldier, and "The Chances of Invasion."

CONTENTS

CHAPTER I
MY SETTLEMENT

My blockhouse was built at the foot of the mountain chain of the Rio Grande, on the precipitous banks of the River Leone. On three sides it was surrounded by a fourteen feet stockade of split trees standing perpendicularly. At the two front corners of the palisade were small turrets of the same material, whence the face of the wall could be held under fire in the event of an attack from hostile Indians. On the south side of the river stretched out illimitable rolling prairies, while the northern side was covered with the densest virgin forest for many miles. To the north and west I had no civilized neighbours at all, while to the south and east the nearest settlement was at least 250 miles distant. My small garrison consisted of three men, who, whenever I was absent, defended the fort, and at other times looked after the small field and garden as well as the cattle.

As I had exclusively undertaken to provide my colony with meat, I rarely stayed at home, except when there was some pressing field work to be done. Each dawn saw me leave the fort with my faithful dog Trusty, and turn my horse either toward the boundless prairie or the mountains of the Rio Grande.

Very often hunting kept me away from home for several days, in which case I used to bivouac in the tall grass by the side of some prattling stream. Such oases, though not frequent, are found here and there on the prairies of the Far West, where the dark, lofty magnolias offer the wearied traveller refreshment beneath their thick foliage, and the stream at their base grants a cooling draught. One of these favourite spots of mine lay near the mountains, about ten miles from my abode. It was almost the only water far and wide, and here formed two ponds, whose depths I was never able to sound, although I lowered large stones fastened to upwards of a hundred yards of lasso. The small space between the two ponds was overshadowed by the most splendid magnolias, peca-nut trees, yuccas, evergreen oaks, &c., and begirt by a wall of cactuses, aloes, and other prickly plants. I often selected this place for hunting, because it always offered a large quantity of game of every description, and I was certain at any time of finding near this water hundreds of wild turkeys, which constitute a great dainty in the bill of fare of the solitary hunter.

After a very hot spring day I had sought the ponds, as it was too late to ride home. The night was glorious; the magnolias and large-flowered cactuses diffused their vanilla perfume over me; myriads of fireflies continually darted over the plain, and a gallant mocking-bird poured forth its dulcet melody into the silent night above my head. The whole of nature seemed to be revelling in the beauty of this night, and thousands of insects sported round my small camp fire. It was such a night as the elves select for their gambols, and for a long time I gazed intently at the dark blue expanse above me. But, though the crystal springs incessantly bubbled up to the surface, the Lurleis would not visit me, for they have not yet strayed to America.

My dog and horse also played around me for a long time, until, quite tired, they lay down by the fire-side, and all three of us slept till dawn, when the gobbling of the turkeys aroused us. The morning was as lovely as the night. To the east the flat prairie bordered the horizon like a sea; the dark sky still glistened with the splendour of all its jewels, while the skirt of its garment was dipped in brilliant carmine; the night fled rapidly toward the mountains, and morn pursued it clad in his festal robes. The sun rose like a mighty ball over the prairie, and the heavy dew bowed the heads of the tender plants, as if they were offering their morning thanksgiving for the refreshment which had been granted them. I too was saturated with dew, and was obliged to hang my deerskin suit to dry at the fire; fortunately the leather had been smoked over a wood fire, which prevents it growing hard in drying. I freshened up the fire, boiled some coffee, roasted the breast of a turkey, into which I had previously rubbed pepper and salt, and finished breakfast with Trusty, while Czar, my famous white stallion, was greedily browsing on the damp grass, and turned his head away when I went up to him with the bridle. I hung up the rest of the turkey, as well as another I had shot on the previous evening, and a leg of deer meat, in the shadow of a magnolia, as I did not know whether I might not return to the spot that evening, saddled, and we were soon under weigh for the mountains, where I hoped to find buffalo.

I was riding slowly along a hollow in the prairie, when a rapidly approaching sound attracted my attention. In a few minutes a very old buffalo, covered with foam, dashed past me, and almost at the same moment a Comanche Indian pulled up his horse on the rising ground about fifty yards from me. As he had his bow ready to shoot the buffalo, the savage made his declaration of war more quickly than I, and his first arrow passed through my game bag sling, leather jacket and waistcoat to my right breast, while two others whizzed past my ear. To pluck out the arrow, seize a revolver, and dig the spurs into my horse, were but one operation; and a second later saw me within twenty yards of the Redskin, who had turned his horse round and was seeking safety in flight. After a chase of about two miles over awfully rough ground, where the slightest mistake might have broken my neck, the Indian's horse began to be winded, while Czar still held his head and tail erect. I rapidly drew nearer, in spite of the terrible blows the Redskin dealt his horse, and when about thirty paces behind the foe, I turned slightly to the left, in order, if I could, to avoid wounding his horse by my shot. I raised my revolver and fired, but at the same instant the Indian disappeared from sight, with the exception of his left foot, with which he held on to the saddle, while the rest of his body was suspended on the side away from me. With the cessation of the blows, however, the speed of his horse relaxed, and I was able to ride close up. Suddenly the Indian regained his seat and urged on his horse with the whip; I fired and missed again, for I aimed too high in my anxiety to spare the mustang. We went on thus at full gallop till we reached a very broad ravine, over which the Indian could not leap. He, therefore, dashed past my left hand, trying at the same moment to draw an arrow from the quiver over his left shoulder. I fired for the third time; with the shot the Comanche sank back on his horse's croup, hung on with his feet, and went about a hundred yards farther, when he fell motionless in the tall grass. As he passed me, I had noticed that he was bleeding from the right chest and mouth, and was probably already gone to the happy hunting-grounds. I galloped after the mustang, which soon surrendered, though with much trembling, to the pale face; I fastened its bridle to my saddle bow, led both horses into a neighbouring thicket, and reloaded my revolver.

I remained for about half-an-hour in my hiding-place, whence I could survey the landscape around, but none of the Indian's comrades made their appearance, and I, therefore, rode up to him to take his weapons. He was dead. The bullet had passed through his chest. I took his bow, quiver and buffalo hide, and sought for the arrows he had shot at me as I rode back. I resolved to pass the night at the ponds, not only to rest my animals, but also to conceal myself from the Indians who, I felt sure, were not far off. I was not alarmed about myself, but in the event of pursuit by superior numbers, I should have Trusty to protect, and might easily lose the mustang again.

I reached the springs without any impediment, turned my horses out to grass in the thicket, and rested myself in the cool shade of the trees hanging over the ponds. A calm, starry night set in, and lighted me on my ride home, which I reached after midnight. The mustang became one of my best horses. It grew much stronger, as it was only four years old when I captured it; and after being fed for awhile on maize, acquired extraordinary powers of endurance.

CHAPTER II
THE COMANCHES

The summer passed away in hunting, farm-work, building houses, and other business, and during this period I had frequently visited the ponds. One evening I rode to them again in order to begin hunting from that point the next morning. If I shot buffaloes not too far from my house, I used to ride back, and at evening drove out with a two-wheeled cart, drawn by mules, to fetch the meat and salt it for the probable event of a siege. As I always had an ample supply of other articles for my garrison and cattle, and as I had plenty of water, I could resist an Indian attack for a long time. Large herds of buffalo always appear in the neighbourhood, so soon as the vegetation on the Rocky Mountains begins to die out, and the cold sets in. They spread over the evergreen prairies in bands of from five to eight hundred head, and I have often seen at one glance ten thousand of these relics of the primeval world. For a week past these wanderers had been moving southwards; but, though their appearance may be so agreeable to the hunter in these parts, it reminds him at the same time that his perils are greatly increased by their advent. Numerous tribes of horse Indians always follow these herds to the better pasturage and traverse the prairie in every direction, as they depend on the buffalo exclusively for food. The warmer climate during the winter also suits them better, as they more easily find forage for their large troops of horses and mules.

At a late hour I reached the ponds, after supplying myself *en route* with some fat venison. Before I lit my fire, I also shot two turkeys on the neighbouring trees, because at this season they are a great dainty, as they feed on the ripe oily peca-nuts. I sat till late over my small fire, cut every now and then a slice from the meat roasting on a spit, and bade my dog be quiet, who would not lie down, but constantly sniffed about with his broad nose to the ground, and growling sullenly. Czar, on the contrary, felt very jolly, had abundant food in the prairie grass, and snorted every now and then so lustily, that the old turkeys round us were startled from their sleep. It grew more and more quiet. Czar had lain down by my side, and only the unpleasant jeering too-whoot of the owl echoed through the night, and interrupted the monotonous chorus of the hunting wolves which never ceases in these parts. Trusty, my faithful watchman, was still sitting up with raised nose, when I sank back on my saddle and fell asleep. The morning was breaking when I awoke, saturated with dew; but I sprang up, shook myself, made up the fire, put meat on the spit and coffee to boil, and then leapt into the clear pond whose waters had so often refreshed me. After the bath I breakfasted, and it was not till I proceeded to saddle my horse that I noticed Trusty's great anxiety to call my attention to something. On following him, I found a great quantity of fresh Indian sign, and saw that a large number of horses had been grazing round the pond on the previous day. I examined my horse gear and weapons, opened a packet of cartridges for my double-barrelled rifle, and then rode in the direction of the Leone. I had scarce crossed the first upland and reached the prairie when Czar made an attempt to bolt, and looked round with a snort. I at once noticed a swarm of Comanches about half a mile behind me, and coming up at full speed. There was not a moment to lose in forming a resolution—I must either fly or return to my natural fortress at the springs. I decided on the latter course, as my enemies were already too near for my dog to reach the thicket or the Leone before them, for though the brave creature was remarkably powerful and swift-footed, he could not beat good horses in a long race.

I therefore turned Czar round, and flew back to the ponds. A narrow path which I had cut on my first visit through a wall of prickly plants led to the shady spot between the two ponds, which on the opposite side were joined by a broad swamp, so that I had only this narrow entrance to defend. The thicket soon received us. Czar was fastened by the bridle to a wild grape-vine; my long holster-pistols were thrust into the front of my hunting-shirt; the belt that held my revolvers was unbuckled, and I was ready for the attack of the savages. Trusty, too, had put up the stiff hair on his back, and by his growling showed that he was equally ready to do his part in the fight. The Indians had come within a few hundred yards, and were now circling round me with their frightful war-yell, swinging their buffalo-hides over their heads, and trying, by the strangest sounds and gestures, either to startle my horse or terrify me. I do not deny that, although used to such scenes, I felt an icy coldness down my back at the sight of these demons, and involuntarily thought of the operation of scalping. I remained as quiet as I could, however, and resolved not to expend a bullet in vain. The distance was gradually reduced, and the savages came within about a hundred and fifty yards, some even nearer. The boldest came within a hundred and twenty yards of me, while the others shot some dozen arrows at me, some of which wounded the sappy cactuses around me. The savages continually grew bolder, and it was time to open the ball, for attacking is half the battle when engaged with Indians.

I therefore aimed at the nearest man—a powerful, stout, rather elderly savage, mounted on a very fast golden-brown stallion—and at once saw that the bullet struck him: in his fall he pulled his horse round towards me, and dashed past within forty yards, which enabled me to see that the bullet had passed through his body, and he did not need a second. About one hundred yards farther on he kissed the ground. After the shot the band dashed off, and their yell was augmented to a roar more like that of a wounded buffalo than human voices. They assembled about half a mile distant, held a short consultation, and then returned like a whirlwind towards me with renewed yells. The attack was now seriously meant, although the sole peril I incurred was from arrows shot close to me. I led Czar a few paces in the rear behind a widely-spreading yucca, ordered Trusty to lie down under the cactuses, reloaded my gun, and, being a bit of Indian myself, I disappeared among the huge aloes in front of me, pulling my stout beaver hat over my eyes. I allowed the tornado to come within a hundred and sixty paces, when I raised my good rifle between the aloes, pulled the trigger, and saw through the smoke a Redskin bound in the air, and fall among the horses' hoofs. A dense dust concealed the band from sight, but a repetition of the yells reached my ear, and I soon saw the savages going away from me, whereon I gave them the contents of the second barrel, which had a good effect in spite of the distance, as I recognised in the fresh yells raised and the dispersion of the band. The Indians, ere long, halted a long way off; but after awhile continued their retreat. I understood these movements perfectly well: they wanted to give me time to leave my hiding-place, and then ride me down on the plain. Hence I waited till the Comanches were nearly two miles off, and watched them through my glass as they halted from time to time, and looked round at me. I was certain that we now had a sufficient start to reach the forest on the Leone without risk. My rifle was reloaded, and my pistols were placed in the holsters. I stepped out of my hiding-place and mounted my horse, which bore me at a rapid pace towards my home. The enemy scarce noticed my flight ere they dashed down from the heights after me like a storm-cloud. I did not hurry, however, for fear of fatiguing Trusty; but selected the buffalo paths corresponding with my direction, thousands of which intersect the prairies like a net, and at the end of the first mile felt convinced that we should reach the forest all right, which now rose more distinctly out of the sea of grass. So it was: we dashed into the first bushes only pursued by five Indians, where I rode behind some dwarf chestnuts, dismounted, and prepared to receive my enemies. They remained out of range, however, and in a short time retired again.

My readers will naturally ask why some thirty Indians allowed a single hunter to emerge from his hiding-place, and why they did not compel him to surrender by a short siege? The Comanches are horse Indians, who can only effect anything when mounted, and hence never continue a pursuit into a thicket. They never undertake any martial exploit by night; and, moreover, the Indian, when he goes into action, has very different ideas from a white man; for while the latter always thinks he will be the last to fall, every Redskin believes that he will be the first to be hit. At the same time, these tribes set a far higher value on the life of one of their warriors than we white men do, and they often told me that we pale-faces grew out of the ground like mushrooms, while it took them eighteen years to produce a warrior. The tribes are not large; they consist of only one hundred and fifty to three hundred men; they have their chief and are quite independent of the other clans, although belonging to the same nations. The Comanches, for instance, reckon thirty thousand souls, spread over the whole of the Far West. In consequence of the many sanguinary wars which the different tribes wage together, it is frequently of great consequence to a clan, whether it counts ten men more or less, and hence the anxiety felt by the savages about the life of their warriors. The Northern Indians have assumed many of the habits of the white men, and are advancing gradually towards civilization; they nearly all carry fire-arms, wear clothes, till the ground, and their squaws, children, and old men, live in villages together. Our Southern Indians are all at the lowest stage of civilization, are generally cannibals, have no home, follow the buffalo, on whose flesh they live, and have assumed none of our customs. At times they may get hold of a horse-cloth or a bit, which they have taken from a hunter or stolen from a border settlement, but in other respects they are children of nature; they go about almost naked, and only carry weapons of their own manufacture. Their long lance is a very dangerous weapon, owing to the skill with which they use it; and the same is the case with their bows, from which they discharge arrows at a distance of fifty yards, with such accuracy and force, as to pierce the largest buffalo. The lasso (a plaited rope of leather) is another weapon which they employ with extraordinary skill; they throw the noose at one end over the head of an enemy, then gallop off in the opposite direction, and drag their captive to death. There are but very few foot Indians in the South; they generally live in the mountains, as they are always at war with the horse savages, and would be at a disadvantage on the plains; but they are by far the most dangerous denizens of these parts, as the most of them are supplied with fire-arms, and try to overpower their enemy treacherously at night. The

Weicos form the chief tribe of these foot Indians, and are pursued both by the mounted Redskins and the white borderers like the most dangerous of wild beasts: on their account I have often spent the night without fire, and have been startled from my sleep by the whoot of the owl, which they imitate admirably, as a distant signal to one another. In the conduct of the horse Indians there is something open and chivalrous, and I never hated them for chasing me; we contended for the possession of the land, which they certainly held first, but which nature assuredly created for a better object than that a few wild hordes should use it for their hunting and war forages. It always seemed to me an honourable contest between civilization and savageness when I was attacked by these steppe-horsemen, and I never felt that blood-thirsty hatred which beset me when I noticed the Weicos and Tonkaways creeping about like vipers. I more than once all but fell victim to their cunning, and it is always a pleasant memory that I frequently punished them severely for it.

CHAPTER III
A FIGHT WITH THE WEICOS

As I mentioned, my fort stood on the south side of the Leone river, and in front of it lay one of the richest and most fertile prairies, which ran to the bank of Mustang Creek, a small stream running parallel to the Leone, beneath the shade of lofty peca-nut trees, magnolias, cypresses, and oaks, to join the Rio Grande. The prairie between the Leone and this stream was about five miles broad; and often, when I had spent the day at home, I rode off to pass the night there, in order to shoot at daybreak as much game as my horse could comfortably carry, and be back to breakfast. I had found, in a coppice close to the stream, a small grassy clearing, where Czar was always comfortable. Around it stood colossal primæval oaks and magnolias, in whose shade many varieties of evergreen bushes, such as myrtle, laurel, and rhododendron, formed an impenetrable thicket, as they were intertwined with pendant llianas and vines the thickness of my body. In this thicket I had built a sort of hut of buffalo hides, in which I hid away a frying-pan, an old axe, and a coffee-pot. At this spot I passed many a hot summer night, for I found there a cool, quiet bed, which the sun never reached, for myself and my faithful companions, and ran no risk of being betrayed by my camp-fire and disturbed by the Indians.

After one of these hot days, I rode Czar out of the fort, and Trusty, released from the chain, sprang joyfully at my horse's head, delighted at getting into the open country again, and the prospect of fresh deer or buffalo kidneys. We went slowly toward the thickly-wooded bank of the creek, which bordered the prairie ahead of us like a purple strip, through large gay fields of flowers, with which the prairie is adorned. Blue, yellow, red, and white beds, in the most varied hues, succeeded each other, and filled the air with the sweetest and most fragrant perfumes. Wherever the eye turned it fell on herds of deer, that were sheltering themselves from the burning sun under isolated elms and mosquito trees, and rose on our approach to be ready for flight. Further on grazed many herds of migratory buffaloes, from which the prairies at this season are never quite free, and, here and there, antelopes were flying over the heaving sea of grass and flowers. As I rode along, my eye was certainly rejoiced by this abundance of game, but I did not change my direction on that account, because I was not any great distance from the thickets in advance of the forest on Mustang Creek, where I could approach the game with much less trouble. These wooded intervals, which run for about a mile into the prairie, consist of dwarf plum-trees, four feet in height, partly separate, partly in clumps, which are closely interlaced with wild vines, but always leave small openings between, and here and there are overshadowed by a densely-foliaged elm. You are obliged to wind between these clumps till you reach a broad open grassy clearing, which extends between these thickets and the high woods on Mustang Creek.

I had hardly reached these advance woods, ere I saw a very large stag standing in the shadow of an old elm-tree, driving away the flies with its antlers, and feeding on the fine, sweet mosquito grass, which is much more tender in the shade than when it is exposed to the burning sunbeams. The beautiful creature was hardly sixty paces from me, and I seized my rifle, which was lying across the saddle in front of me. In a moment Czar, who was well acquainted with this movement, halted, buried his small head in the grass, and began seeking the green young shoots which are covered by the dry withered stalks. I shot the deer, and as I saw that it could not go far I allowed Trusty to catch it, which always afforded him great delight. I rode up, threw the bridle before dismounting over the end of a long pendant branch, and then dragged the deer into the shade to break it up, and cut off the meat I intended to take with me. I had knelt down by the deer and just thrust in my bowie knife, when Trusty, who was sitting not far from me, began growling, and on my inquiring what was the matter, growled still more loudly, while looking in the direction behind me. I knew the faithful creature so well that I only needed to look in his large eyes to read what he wished to tell me. They had turned red, a sure sign of his rising anger: but I believed that wolves were at hand, which were his most deadly enemies, because he had fared badly from their claws now and then before I could get up to free him from his tormentors. I ordered Trusty to be quiet, as I heeded the dangers which had beset me for years much less than I had done at the beginning of my border-life, and bent down again over the deer, when Trusty sprang, with furious barks, toward the quarter where he had been looking. I quickly rose, and on turning round saw two perfectly naked Indians, armed with guns, leap out of the tall grass about sixty yards from me, and dash away like antelopes. My first step was to seize my rifle, which was leaning against the tree, but the savages took an enormous bound over one of the clumps of plum-trees, and disappeared from sight. In a few minutes I had unfastened Czar, and rushed after the Indians through the many windings between the close-grown bushes. They had gained a great start, and had increased it by leaping over clumps, which I was compelled to ride round; still I kept them pretty constantly in sight, and reached the open prairie in front of the creek, at the moment when the savages had crossed about half of it. I gave Czar a slight touch of the spur, and urged him on with the usual pat on his powerful hard neck; he leaped through the grass as if he hardly touched the ground, and I was obliged to set my hat tightly on my head for fear of losing it, for the pressure of the atmosphere was so great that I could hardly breathe. The Indians ran like deer, but the distance between us was speedily lessened, and I was only sixty yards behind them, when they were still fifty from the forest. I stopped my horse, leaped off, aimed with my right-hand barrel at the savage furthest ahead, and dropped him. In the meanwhile the other Indian reached the skirt of the wood, and sprang into the shade of an old oak, at the moment when the bead of my rifle covered him. I fired and saw him turn head over heels. At this moment Trusty came panting over the prairie, who had remained behind as I had leapt over some clumps which he was obliged to skirt; he saw the first Indian leap out of the grass, like a hare which has been shot through the head, and his legs seemed too slow for his growing fury; a loud shout urged him on still more, and in a few seconds he and the savage disappeared in the tall grass. A frightfully shrill yell, which echoed far and wide through the forest, proved that the Indian was feeling Trusty's teeth, and the heaving grass over them showed that it was a struggle for life or death. Loading my rifle detained me for a few minutes at the spot whence I had fired; then I ran up to Czar, who had strayed a little distance, and rode to the battle-field. The contest was over; the savage was dead, and Trusty's handsome shaggy coat was spotted with blood. He was standing with his fore paws on his enemy, and tearing out his throat. A dog like Trusty was invaluable to me, and for my own preservation I dared not assuage the creature's savageness; besides, the man was dead, and it was a matter of indifference whether the buzzards devoured his body or Trusty tore it piece-meal. In the meanwhile I fastened the dead man's short Mexican *escopeta*, hunting-pouch, and necklace to my saddle; then I called Trusty off, mounted Czar, and rode back to my deer, as I did not dare venture into the forest, where a large number of these Weicos were very probably lying in ambush. The two had come down from the mountains to the banks of Mustang Creek, whither the great quantity of game of all descriptions had attracted them; on hearing my shot, they crept up unnoticed, had got within distance of me, and in a few seconds would doubtless have settled me, had not my faithful watcher scented them, or remarked their movements in the grass.

On coming within sight of my deer, I saw that a dozen buzzards had collected, some on the trees, others circling slowly in the air, and watching with envious glances three wolves, which had already begun greedily to share my deer. Although I hardly ever expended a bullet on these tormentors,

I was annoyed at their impudence, for though they saw me coming, they did not interrupt their banquet. I shot one of them, a very old red she-wolf, took the loins and legs of the deer, hung them to my saddle, and rode home to pass the night.

My dogs inside the fort announced to the garrison the arrival of a stranger, and they were no little surprised to see me return at so unusual an hour. The gate was opened, and after Czar had been relieved of his rather heavy burden, I led him once more into the grass to let him have a good roll; and after he had been put into the stable with a feed of Indian corn, I described the events of the day at the supper-table. My news aroused the apprehensions of my men, for they knew the vengeful spirit of these Weicos, and we therefore resolved to keep watch during the night. We were still smoking and talking at midnight, when the dogs, of which I had fourteen, began making a tremendous row. They all ran out through the small apertures left for the purpose in the stockade, and stood barking on the river bank at some foe on the other side, at the spot where my maize field in the forest joined the river. It was a pitch dark and calm night. We listened attentively, and could distinctly hear the trampling of dry brushwood in the field. It might be occasioned by buffalo, which had broken through the fence, and were regaling on my maize. But these animals rarely move at night, and there was a much greater probability of Indians being there. We gently opened the gate. I took my large duck gun, which held sixteen pistol bullets in each barrel, and crawled down on my stomach to the river bank, where I lay perfectly quiet. When I arrived there, one of my dogs was yelping, and I distinctly heard the twang of a bow-string. I noticed the quarter very carefully; the river was only forty yards across, and the direction was shown me still more plainly by the crackling of brushwood. I shot one barrel there, upon which human cries and a hurried flight were audible; then I sent the second after it, and fresh groans echoed through the quiet forest and mingled with the roar of my two shots. I remained lying in the grass, as I might be easily seen against the starry sky from the other bank, which was thirty feet lower. The leaping and running through the maize retired farther and farther toward the wood, and scarce reached my ear, when suddenly a wild war yell resounded in the forest, which was answered by countless wolf howls on the prairie behind me. This was the last outbreak of fury on the part of the Indians, of whom I never saw anything more beyond the various bloody traces which they left in the field. We found several arrows sticking in the river bank, whose form led me to conclude that the assailants were Cato Indians. The damage I received from this nocturnal visit only consisted in the trampled maize and a harmless wound which one of my dogs had received from an arrow in the leg. The morning was spent in following the trail of the savages to the prairie on the other side of the forest, where a number of horses had awaited these night-wanderers and borne them away. In the afternoon I rode again to Mustang Creek with one of my people—to the spot where the second Indian had disappeared on the previous day. The entrance into the wood and the roots of the old oak were covered with blood. I sent Trusty on ahead to see whether the road was clear, and if we could penetrate into the gloom of the forest without danger. We cautiously followed the dog, who kept the blood-marked trail and reached the river, on whose bank the Weico was sleeping the last sleep. He was cold and stiff my bullet had passed through his brown sides. The wounds were stopped with grass, and his *escopeta* lay ready cocked close to him. He was a very young and handsome man, and death had chosen him a glorious resting-place under the dark arbour of leaves. The rapid, crystalline, icy stream laved his small, handsomely-shaped feet, and on a pillow of large ferns reposed his head, round which his raven silky hair fell, while the mossy bed beneath him was dyed by his blood, till it resembled the purple velvet of a lying-in-state.

We stood silently before this painfully-beautiful picture, and even Trusty seemed to feel that this was no longer an object for wild passion, for he lay down quietly in the grass. Death had reconciled us: the dice had fallen in my favour, and if they had been against me, I should not have found such an exquisite grave: my bones would have been bleached for years by the sun on the open prairie, and greeted with shouts of joy by passing Indians. Feelings which are rarely carried into these solitudes, and still more rarely retained there, gained the mastery over me. I could not leave this noble creation of nature to the wolves and buzzards. We therefore fastened a heavy stone round his feet, and another round his neck, and gently let him down into the clear water, where he found his last solitary resting-place between two large rocks. Taking his few traps, more as a reminiscence than as a booty, we returned to our horses, which we had left in the first thicket. They greeted us with their friendly neighing and impatient stamping while still a long distance off, and away we galloped over the open prairie, up hill and down hill, after a flying herd of buffalo, at one moment leaping across broad watercourses, at another over aged trees uprooted by storms, until several of these primæval monsters had kissed the blood-stained ground. Our melancholy thoughts had been dispersed by the light prairie breeze, and, merry and independent, like the vultures in the blue sky overhead, we returned heavily laden to our fort, whose inhabitants, down to the dogs, gave us a most hearty welcome.

CHAPTER IV
HUNTING ADVENTURES

It is scarce possible to form an idea of the abundance of game with which the country near me was blessed in those days. It really seemed to be augmented with every year of my residence, for which I may account by the fact that the several vagabond hordes of Indians—who prefer the flesh of deer, antelopes, and turkey to that of buffaloes, whose enormous mass they cannot devour at once, while the smaller descriptions of game could be killed in the forests and coppices, without revealing themselves to the enemy on the wide prairie—that these Indians, I say, more or less avoided my neighbourhood, while, for my part, I had greatly reduced the number of wild beasts, especially of the larger sort. I consumed a great quantity of meat in my household, owing to the number of dogs I kept, but I really procured it as if only amusing myself. There were certainly days on which I shot nothing. At times I did not get sight of a buffalo for a week, or the prairie grass was burnt down to the roots, which rendered it extremely difficult to stalk the game, while just at this period, when the first green shoots spring up, the animals principally visit the open plains, whence they can see their pursuers for a long distance. For all that, though we had generally a superabundance of meat, and too often behaved with unpardonable extravagance, I have frequently killed five or six buffaloes, each weighing from a thousand to fifteen hundred pounds, in one chase, lasting perhaps half-an-hour, and then merely carried off their tongues and marrow-bones. Often, too, I have shot one or two bears, weighing from five to eight hundred pounds, and only taken home their paws and a few ribs, because the distance was too great to burden my horse with a large supply of meat. I could always supply our stock in the vicinity of my fort, although at times we were compelled to put up with turkeys, or fish and turtle, with which our river literally swarmed.

Bear-meat formed an important item in our larder—or, more correctly speaking, bear's-grease—which was of service in a great many ways. We employed it to fry our food, for which buffalo or deer fat was not so good; we used it to burn in our lamps, to rub all our leather with, and keep it supple; we drank it as a medicine—in a word, it answered a thousand demands in our small household. This is the sole fatty substance, an immoderate use of which does not turn the stomach or entail any serious consequences. The transport of this article, though, was at times rather difficult, especially on a warm day; as this fat easily becomes liquid, and will even melt in the hunter's hand while he is paunching a bear. This is chiefly the case with the stomach fat, which is the finest and best; that on the back and the rest of the body, which at the fatting season is a good six inches thick, is harder and requires to be melted over a slow fire before it can be used in lamps.

These animals were very numerous in my neighbourhood. In spring and summer they visited the woods, where with their cubs they regaled upon wild plums, grapes, honey, and young game of all sorts, and at times played the deuce in my maize-field. In autumn the rich crop of peca-nuts, walnuts, acorns, chestnuts, and similar fruits, kept them in our forests; and in winter they sought rocky ravines and caves, where they hybernated. Very many took up their quarters in old hollow trees, so that at this season I had hardly any difficulty in finding a bear in my neighbourhood. Trusty was a first-rate hand at this, for he found a track, and kept to it as long as I pleased; and at the same time possessed the great advantage that he never required a leash, never went farther than I ordered him, and never followed game without my permission. When a bear rose before me it rarely got fifty paces away, unless it was in thorny bushes, where the dog could not escape its attack; for, so soon as the bear bolted, Trusty dug his teeth so furiously into its legs, and slipped away with such agility, that the bear soon gave up all attempts at flight, and stood at bay. It was laughable to see the trouble the bear was in when I came up; how it danced round Trusty, and with the most ridiculous *entrechats* upbraided his impudence; while Trusty continually sprang away, lay down before Bruin, and made the woods ring with his bass voice. Frequently, however, the honest dog incurred great peril during this sport, and his life more than once depended on my opportune arrival.

In this way I followed one warm autumn day a remarkably broad bear trail on the mountains of the Rio Grande. Trusty halting fifty yards ahead of me, showed me that it stopped at a small torrent, where the bear had watered on the previous night. I dismounted, examined the trail carefully, and saw that it was made by a very old fat bear; it was in the fatting season, when the bear frequently interrupts its sleep and pays a nocturnal visit to the water. At this season these animals are very clumsy and slow, and cannot run far, as they soon grow scant of breath; they soon stop, and can be easily killed by the hunter—always supposing that he can trust to his dog and horse, for any mistake might expose the rider to great danger. I ordered Trusty to follow the trail; it ran for some distance up the ravine, then went up the bare hill-side, which was covered with loose boulders and large masses of rock, into the valley on the opposite side, in the middle of which was a broad but very swampy pool, girdled by thick thorny bushes. Trusty halted in front of this thicket, looked round to me, and then again at the bushes, while wagging his long tail. I knew the meaning of this signal, and that the bear was not far off. I ordered the dog on, and drew a revolver from my belt; feeling assured that the bear would soon leave the underwood and seek safety in flight. Trusty disappeared in the bushes, and his powerful bark soon resounded through the narrow valley. It was an impossibility for me to ride through the thicket, hence I galloped to the end of the coppice, and saw there the bear going at a rapid pace up the opposite steep hill, with Trusty close at its heels. I tried to cross the swamp, but Czar retreated with a snort, as if to show me the danger of the enterprise. By this time Trusty had caught up to the bear at the top of the hill, and furiously attacked it in the rear. The bear darted round with extraordinary agility, and was within an ace of seizing Trusty, but after making a few springs at the dog, it continued its hurried flight, and disappeared with Trusty over the hill-top. I had ridden farther up the water when I heard my dog baying; I drove the spurs into my horse, and with one immense leap, we were both in the middle of the swamp up to the girths; then, with an indescribable effort, Czar gave three tremendous leaps, which sent black mud flying round us, and reached the opposite firm ground with his fore feet, while his hind quarters sunk in the quivering morass; with one spring I was over his head, when I sank in up to the knees, and after several tremendous exertions, the noble fellow sprang ashore, trembling all over. Trusty's barking, as if for help, continually reached me as I galloped up the steep hill-side; I arrived on the summit at the moment when the bear sprang at Trusty, and buried him beneath its enormous weight. My alarm for the faithful dog—my best friend in these solitudes, made me urge Czar on; he bounded like a cat over the remaining rocks, and I saw Trusty slip out from under the bear in some miraculous way, and attack it again on the flank. I halted about ten paces from the scene of action, held my rifle between the little red fiery eyes of the bright black monster, and laid it lifeless on the bare rocks. The greatest peril for dogs is at the moment when the bear is shot, for they are apt to attack it as it falls, and get crushed in its last convulsive throes. I leapt off Czar, who was greatly excited by the sharp ride, went up to Trusty, who was venting his fury on Bruin's throat, examined him, and found that he had received three very serious wounds, two on the back and one over the left shoulderblade, which were bleeding profusely, though in his fury he did not seem to notice them. I took my case from the holster and sewed up his wounds, during which operation he lay very patiently before me, and looked at me with his large eyes, as if asking whether this were necessary. Then I took off my jacket and set to work on the bear, stripped it, and put the hide as well as a hundred pounds' weight of the flesh on Czar's back. If my readers will bear in mind that the sun was shining on my back furiously, and that I was on a bare blazing rock, they will understand that I was worn out, and longed for a cool resting-place. The bear weighed at least 800 lbs., and it requires a great effort to turn such an animal over.

I was a good hour's ride from the shade of the Leone, and only half that distance to the mountain springs I have already described. I therefore selected the latter, although they took me rather farther from home. I walked, although I made Czar carry my jacket, weapons, and pouch, and reached my destination in the afternoon, with my two faithful companions at my heels. Czar had a hearty meal after I had bathed him in the pond, and poor Trusty, whose wounds had dried in the sun, and pained him terribly, felt comfortable in the cool grass, and did not disturb the linen rag which I moistened every now and then. Nor did I forget myself; I rested, bathed, and after awhile enjoyed the liver and tongue of the old vagabond, until the evening breeze had cooled the air, and I reached home partly on foot, partly on horseback.

Nature seems to have selected the buffalo before all varieties of game for the purpose of bringing to the door of the man who first dares to carry civilization into the desert, abundant food for him and his during the first years, so that he may have time to complete the works connected with his settlement, and have no trouble in procuring provisions. When this time is passed, nature withdraws this liberal support from him; in the course of a few years he must go a long distance to obtain this food as a dainty, which he grew quite tired of in the early years, for the buffalo is not frightened by the pioneer's solitary house and field, but as soon as several appear, the animals depart and are only seen as stragglers.

The woolly hides of the buffaloes supply the new-comer in the desert with the most splendid and comfortable beds. When laid over the roof they protect his unfinished house from rain and storm; he uses their leather for saddles, boot-soles, making ropes of all sorts, traces, &c.; its meat, one of the most luxurious sorts that nature offers man, seems to be given to the borderer as a compensation for the countless privations and thousand dangers to which he subjects himself. Buffalo's marrow is a great delicacy, and very strengthening. The fat can be used in many ways, and the horns converted into drinking cups, powder flasks, &c.; in a word, the whole of the buffalo is turned to account in the settler's housekeeping.

These animals are hunted in several ways. With an enduring, well-trained horse, you ride up to them and shoot them with pistols or a rifle, for a horse accustomed to this chase always keeps a short distance from the buffalo, and requires no guidance with the reins; but this mode of hunting can only be employed on the plains, for in the mountainous regions the buffalo has a great advantage in its sure footing over a horse that has to carry a rider. In such regions, and in wooded districts, you stalk the animals, which is not difficult, and if you keep yourself concealed you may kill several with ease, as they are not startled by the mere report of a rifle. On the prairies, too, where the grass is rather high, you can creep up to them through it, and if it be not sufficiently tall to hide you, you make use of some large skin, such as a wolf's, and covered with this, crawl up within range. This, however, is always a dangerous plan, for if you are noticed by a wounded buffalo, you run a great risk of being trampled to death by it. On these crawling hunts, I always had Trusty a short distance behind me, who moved through the grass quite as cautiously as myself, and when it was necessary, I set him on, and had time to run to my horse, while Trusty attacked the buffalo and pinned it to the spot.

I always preferred riding after buffaloes, for this is one of the most exciting modes of hunting I am acquainted with, as it demands much skill from the rider and agility and training on the part of the horse. Horses that have been used to the sport for any time are extremely fond of it, and at the sight of the buffalo become so excited that there is a difficulty in holding them in. The revolver is the best weapon to use. You have the great advantage with it of firing several shots without reloading. I always carried two in my belt, which gave twelve shots, and also two spare cylinders. I also had my double rifle with me, which lay unfastened between me and the saddle cloth. The American revolvers are admirably made, and carry their bullets very accurately for a hundred yards; but at longer distances they cannot be depended on, as it is difficult to take aim with them. It requires considerable practice to kill a buffalo at a gallop, for you may send a dozen bullets into it, and yet not prevent it from continuing its clumsy-looking though very rapid progress. The buffalo's heart lies very deep in the chest behind the shoulder-blades; it can be easily missed through the eye being caught by the hump on the back; and besides, it requires very great practice to hit with a pistol when going at full speed. If you shoot the buffalo at the right spot, it drops at once, and frequently turns head over heels. The animal is in the best condition in spring, when it has changed its coat. At this season its head is adorned with long dark brown locks, and its hind-quarters are covered with shining black hair. So long as old tufts bleached by the sun are hanging about it it is not in prime condition, and the experienced hunter never selects such a quarry.

On a spring morning—I need not add a fine one, for at this season the blue sky rarely deserts us for more than a few hours—I rode at daybreak down the river toward the mountains; a cold, refreshing breeze was blowing, which had an invigorating effect upon both men and animals. Czar was full of playfulness. He often pretended to kick at Trusty, his dearest friend, who was trotting by his side, shook his broad neck, and could hardly be held in. Trusty ran ahead, every now and then rolled in the tall grass, kicked up the earth behind him, and then looked up at me with a loud bark of delight. I too was in an excellent humour; the small birds-of-paradise, with their long black and white tails and crimson breasts, fluttered from bush to bush. The humming birds darted past me like live coals, and suddenly stopped as if spell-bound in front of some flowers, whence they sucked the honey for a few seconds with their beaks, and then hummed off to another fragrant blossom. Countless vultures described their regular circles over my head; above them gleamed against the ultramarine sky the brilliant white plumage of a silver heron, or the splendid pink of a flamingo; whilst high up in ether the royal eagles were bathing in the sunshine. The prairie was more beautiful this day than I had ever seen it; it was adorned by every designation of bulbous plants, the prevailing flora in the spring.

Lost in admiration of these natural beauties, which words are powerless to describe, I reached the hilly ground near the mountain springs; and first learned from Czar's tugging at the bridle, and his repeated bounds, that I had come in sight of a herd of about forty buffaloes, that did not appear to notice me yet. Probably they were engaged with that portion of the beauties of nature which most interested them; for, at any rate, they all had their huge shaggy heads buried in the fresh young grass. I was never better inclined to have a jolly chase than on this day, and the same was the case with Czar and Trusty. I let loose the reins, drew a revolver, and dashed among the astounded herd, looking for a plump bull. Surprised and disturbed, these philosophers turned their heads towards the mountains, raised their tails erect, and started in their awkward gallop, with the exception of one old fellow, the very one I had selected for the attack. He looked after the fugitives for awhile, as if reproaching them with their cowardice; shook his wild shaggy mane several times, and then dashed furiously at me with his head down. I was so surprised at this unexpected attack that I did not fire, but turned my horse to fly. The buffalo pursued me some thousand yards, keeping rather close, while his companions halted, and seemed to be admiring the chivalric deed of their knight. At length he stopped, as he had convinced himself that he could not catch up to me, and stamped with his long-haired front legs till the dust flew up in a cloud around him. I turned my horse and raised my rifle, to make more sure of hitting the bull, as his determined conduct had imbued me with some degree of respect. I fired, and wounded him in the side a little too far back; at the same instant he dashed ahead again, but then thought better of it, and tried to rejoin the flying herd. I now set Trusty on him, who soon brought him at bay, and I gave him a bullet from the revolver. Again he rushed at me, and again fled. In this way, pursuing and pursued in turn, I had given him five bullets, when he left the herd in a perfect state of mania, and dashed after me. I made a short turn with my horse; the bull rushed past; I turned Czar again towards the buffalo; and as I passed I put a bullet through his heart at the distance of three yards. The monster fell to the ground in a cloud of dust, and raised up a heap of loose sand which it stained with its dark blood.

To my surprise I noticed that Trusty did not come up to the fallen buffalo, but rushed past it, loudly barking, to the thicket at the springs, whence I saw an immense panther leap through the prickly plants. I galloped round the ponds and saw the royal brute making enormous leaps through the tall prairie grass toward the mountains. Trusty was not idle either, and was close behind it. I spurred Czar, and kept rather nearer the mountains, so as to cut off the fugitive's retreat and drive it farther out on the plains, while my hunting cry incessantly rang in its ears. It had galloped about a mile, when we got rather close to it; it altered its course once more, and climbed up an old evergreen live oak, among whose leafy branches it disappeared. I called Trusty to heel, stopped about fifty yards from the oak to reload my right-hand barrel, and then rode slowly round, looking for a gap in the foliage through which to catch a glimpse of this most dangerous animal. The leaves were very close, and I had ridden nearly round, when I suddenly saw its eyes glaring at me from one of the main branches in the middle of the tree. I must shoot it dead, or else it would be a very risky enterprise; and Czar's breathing was too violent for me to fire from his back with any certainty. I cautiously dismounted, keeping my eye on the panther, held a revolver in my left hand, brought the bead of my rifle to bear right between the eyes of the king of these solitudes—and fired. With a heavy bump the panther fell from branch to branch, and lay motionless on the ground. I kept Trusty back, waited a few moments to see whether the jaguar was really dead, as I did not wish to injure the beautiful skin by a second bullet unnecessarily, then walked up and found that the bullet had passed through the left eye into the brain. It had one of the handsomest skins I ever took; it is so large that I can quite wrap myself up in it, and now forms my bed coverlet. When I had finished skinning it and cut out the tusks with the small axe I always carried in a leathern case, I rode back to my buffalo, with the skin proudly hanging down on either side of my horse. On getting there I led Czar through the narrow entrance into the thicket, where I came upon a freshly killed, large deer, one of whose legs was half eaten away. It was the last meal of the savage beast of prey, and I was surprised it had left its quarry. The noise of the buffalo and the horse galloping, Trusty's bass voice, and the crack of the revolver in such close vicinity, must have appeared dangerous to it, and it had fancied it could slip off unnoticed.

My buffalo was very plump; it supplied me and Trusty with an excellent dinner, and for dessert I had the marrow-bones, roasted on the fire and split open with my axe, which, when peppered and salted, are a great delicacy. A little old brandy from my flask, mixed with the cold spring water, was a substitute for champagne; my sofa was the body of the deer, covered with the skin of its assassin.

CHAPTER V
THE NATURALIST

Years had passed since the first establishment of my settlement, but it was still the greatest rarity to see a strange white face among us; and though I visited the nearest town more frequently than at the outset, it led to no settled intercourse. I rode there several times a year, taking to market on mules my stock of hides, wax, tallow, &c., and brought back provisions, tools, powder, and lead. On these occasions I received the letters which had arrived for me in the interval, posted my own, took my packets of books forwarded from New York, and then my intercourse with the world was at an end for six months. The mules and horses certainly left traces during these rides in the clayey soil, but they were soon destroyed by heavy rains or trampled by herds of passing buffaloes, and thus hidden from the most acute eyes. Moreover, on these journeys I never kept the same road, as I always guided myself by the compass, and altered my course according to the seasons, as I had to pass spots which were inundated at certain periods, and others where water at times was very scarce. The first two-thirds of the country was a wretched sandy region, without grass, on which stunted oaks grew here and there, very mountainous and dry, where no one would dream of settling or undergoing the perils of a pioneer for the sake of the land. Nearer to me no one ventured to come, as many attempts had been made to settle on this fertile soil, but had all turned out unhappily; the last of them entailing the destruction of a family of nineteen persons: on my hunting expeditions I often saw their bones bleaching in the sun. As I said, no change had occurred in my position, save that my mode of life was safer and more comfortable; the country alone still remained a solitude, which no isolated visitor could enter without staking his scalp.

Hence I was greatly surprised one morning when the sentry came into my house and informed me that a white man was riding alone along the river, mounted on a mule, which is the most unsuitable of animals in the Indian country. I ran with a telescope to the turret at the south-east end of the fort, and not only found the watchman's statement confirmed, but also that the man had not even a weapon; unless it was hidden in two enormous packs which dangled on each side of his mule. The rider drew nearer, at one moment emerging on the ridges, and then disappearing again in the hollows. At length our growing curiosity was satisfied, and a white man, a German, saluted us with an innocently calm smile. On my asking how he had come here alone and unarmed, he said cheerfully:—"Well, from the settlement. I was able to find your mule-track quite easily. Mr. Jones accompanied me for a whole day, and during the last four I have seen nobody." It soon came out that his name was Kreger, and that he was a botanist who had come to examine the Flora about us, which had not yet been collected. For this purpose he brought with him two enormous bundles of blotting-paper, which hung on his Lizzy—so he called his gallant charger—and, like woolbags in a battery, might have protected him against Indian arrows, if he had had any missiles to reply with; but he only had a pistol in his trowsers' pocket, which would not go off, in spite of all the experiments we made with it. Everybody had warned him of the danger to which he exposed himself on his journey to me; and the last pioneer he passed, a Mr. Jones, had tried to keep him back by force, but he had merely laughed, and declared that an Indian could not touch him on his Lizzy.

There are men who wantonly rush into perils because danger has something attractive for them, and who seek them in order to have an opportunity of expending the energy they feel within them; there are others who incur danger in order to display themselves to the world as heroes, though their courage is not very genuine; lastly, there are men who expose themselves calmly and delightedly to great dangers, because they are entirely ignorant of them, and cannot be persuaded of their existence till they are surprised and destroyed by them. Such a man was our new acquaintance, Mr. Kreger: we all tried to make him understand how madly he had behaved, and that it was only by a miracle he had escaped the notice of the Redskins, which must have entailed his inevitable death, during his long solitary journey to us, and while sleeping at night by a large fire. He merely smiled at it all, and said that it could not be quite so bad, while making repeated applications to his snuff-box. As regarded his intentions of making his excursions from my house, I told him it was impossible; because when I went out hunting I did not waste my time over plants, and he, as no sportsman, would be a nuisance to me; on the other hand, we could not think of letting him wander about alone, the danger of which I confirmed by telling him various adventures of mine. For all this, I received him hospitably; gave him a place to sleep in, and a seat at table; showed him where to find corn for Lizzy, where he could wash his sheets—in a word, made him as comfortable as lay in my power.

I had long intended to explore more distant countries than those I had visited during my sporting excursions, especially the continuation of our plateaux to the north, and had made my arrangements for this tour, when Mr. Kreger surprised us by his advent. On the day after his arrival we took a walk round the fort and the garden, during which he broke off the conversation every moment, and plucked some rare plant to put in his herbal, which he called his cannon; and laughed at the revolver in my belt and the rifle I carried. I told him that I intended to make a journey, in which, if he liked to accompany me, he would be able to make his researches, as my hunting on this trip would be restricted to my meat supply. He was delighted, and agreed to come with me; to which I consented on condition of his riding one of my horses, and I recommended the mustang, whose powers of endurance I knew and tried to prove by telling him how it came into my possession. But it was of no avail, for none of my cattle possessed the qualities of his Lizzy; and he offered a bet that no one could catch her. For the sake of the joke, the mustang and the mule were soon saddled; a mosquito tree on the prairie, about half a mile from the fort, was selected as the goal; and away we started through the tall grass. It was really surprising how fast Lizzy went, cocking up her rat-like tail and long ears; she accepted with pleasure the shower of blows that fell on her, and reached the goal only twenty yards behind me. I laughed most heartily at the amusing appearance of our naturalist, and expressed my admiration at his mule's pace; but remarked at the same time, that for no consideration in the world would I ride her in the country I intended visiting, because I was well acquainted with the obstinacy of mules, and knew that when called on to show their speed they refuse to do so, and neither fire nor sword could induce them. All such remarks, however, produced no change in Kreger's invincible faith in his favourite; and, as if he had assumed a portion of Lizzy's obstinacy through his long friendly relations with her, he irrevocably adhered to his resolution of only entrusting his carcass to her during the impending excursion.

Our preparations, which were very simple, occupied us about a week; they consisted in removing Czar's shoes, and rubbing his hoofs frequently with bear's grease, for the Indians follow the track of a shoed horse as wolves do a deer's bleeding trail; in grinding coffee, and forcing it into bladders, and in plaiting two new lassos, for which I fetched two new buffalo hides, in which chase the botanist accompanied me, and felt a pride in having given me an indubitable proof of his Lizzy's powers, for she followed close at Czar's tail during the entire hunt. Mr. Kreger assisted me in making the lassos. The hide is fastened tight on the ground with wooden pegs, a very sharp knife is thrust into the centre, and a strip about the breadth of a finger is cut, until the whole hide is transferred into one very long line, which, though not so long as the one with which Dido measured the ground to build Carthage on, attained a very great length. This strip was then fastened between trees, the hair shaved off with a knife, after which it was cut into five equal lengths, and these were plaited into a lasso about forty feet long, which was once more fastened between trees, with heavy weights attached to it, and thus stretched to its fullest extent. When such a line has been dried in the open air, it is rubbed with bear's grease, through which it always remains soft and supple, and will resist a tremendous pull. The one made by Mr. Kreger, though not plaited so smoothly and regularly, was useful, and afforded him great pleasure as a perfection of his Lizzy's equipment. One end of this lasso is fastened round the horse's neck; it is rolled up, fastened by a loop to the saddle, undone when the animal is grazing, and bound round a tree or bush.

The day for our start arrived, and the morning was spent in saddling our horses and arranging our baggage in the most suitable way for both horse and rider, a most important thing in these hot regions, for the horse's back is easily galled, and then you are compelled to go on foot, which is very wearisome and fatiguing in a country where there are no roads. The naturalist at length completed his equipment of Lizzy, who looked more like a rhinoceros than a cross between a horse and a donkey. In front of the saddle hung the two bales of blotting paper over the large bearskin holsters, which, in addition to two pistols I had supplied, were crammed with biscuit, coffee, pepper and salt, snuff, &c. Over the saddle hung two leathern bags, fastened together by a strap, on which the rider had his seat. Behind the saddle, a frying-pan, coffee-pot, and tin mug, produced a far from pleasing harmony at every movement of the animal. Over the whole of this a gigantic buffalo hide was stretched, and fastened with a surcingle round Lizzy's stout body, so that, like a tortoise, she only displayed her head and tail, and caused a spectator the greatest doubt as to what genus of quadruped she belonged. In order to complete the picture, Lizzy had two enormous bushes of a summer plant, which we call "Spanish mulberry," stuck behind her ears, as a first-rate specific to keep the flies off. I had repeatedly told Kreger of the absurdity of covering Lizzy with this coat of mail, in which she would melt away. But he said that I too had a skin over my saddle, and he wanted his to protect him at night against rain and dew. On the back of this monster our naturalist mounted, dressed in a long reddish homespun coat, trowsers of the same material, though rather more faded, with Mexican spurs on his heels with wheels the size of a dollar, and a broad-brimmed felt hat, under which his long face with the large light-blue eyes and eternally-smiling mouth peeped out. Over his right shoulder hung his huge botanizing case, and over his left a double-barrelled gun of mine loaded with slugs; his hat Mr. Kreger had also adorned with a green bush, and sitting erect in his wooden Mexican stirrups, he swung his whip, and declared his readiness to start. I rode Czar, and the only difference from my ordinary equipment was that I had a bag full of provisions hung on the saddle behind me; this and a little more powder and lead than usual, was all the extra weight Czar had to carry, and too insignificant for him to feel. With a truly heavy heart I bade good-bye to Trusty, and most earnestly commended him to the care of my men. I could not take him with me to an unknown country, where I might feel certain of getting into situations where I must trust to the speed of my horse, and Trusty might easily get into trouble. The firearms I left at the service of my garrison, and consisting of nearly fifty rifles and fowling pieces, were carefully inspected. We then rode off, and soon heard the gate of the fort bolted after us.

It was the afternoon when we rode down to the river-side and waded through the stream. For the stranger this river is most beautiful and charming, for at its greatest depth it is so clear, that, were it not for its motion and the leaves, brushwood, &c., floating on it, it would be doubtful to say whether it contained any water or not. This is noticed more especially with horses which have to cross such a stream for the first time; generally they object, and look down at the water, whose depth they are unable to gauge. You see the stones at the bottom as clearly as if there were no water, and can distinctly watch the slightest movements of the countless fish and turtle with which the streams in my neighbourhood swarm. At the same time the banks are covered with the most luxurious vegetation, and the gigantic vines cross it from the tops of the trees, and are in their turn intertwined with other creepers so as to form a hanging wood over the darting waters. Most of these creepers adorn the woods with a magnificent show of flowers, and some trees are so overgrown with them, that none of their own foliage is visible. The stream in these rivers is so violent that it is very dangerous to ride through them, especially at spots where the water is deep enough to reach the horse's girths, and the danger is heightened by the extremely slippery soap stones which cover the bottom.

I rode first into the river, and Lizzy followed obediently after me, though it cost some persuasion to make my companion refrain from riding a few yards lower down in order to pluck some specimens of the beautiful aquatic plants growing on the surface, for he fancied it was no depth, while he and his Lizzy, heavily laden as they were, would have sunk, and never reached the bank again alive. I remember, while hunting, swimming on horseback through places where the current was extremely violent, and carried away my dog, which reached the bank eventually, bruised by the rocks and bleeding terribly. We reached the opposite side without any difficulty, and followed a deep-trodden buffalo path into the forest; which runs with a breadth of several miles along the river. After you have been riding ever so short a time in the sun, you feel the benefit of the gloomy and impenetrable shade of such a forest in an extraordinary degree; the air beneath the leafy aisles seems quite different; it is not only cool and refreshing, but appears to have been purified in its passage through the leaves, for these forests grow on elevated ground, where no swamps or standing waters poison the air with the exhalations of putrified vegetable matter, as is the case on the banks of the Mississippi and other eastern rivers of America. There is not a more majestic or imposing sight than such a forest; trees of the most gigantic size grow in the wildest confusion, strangest shapes, and most varied hues, so closely together that you cannot understand where all their roots find room. You see, perhaps, twenty varieties of the oak, among which the burrel oak is the handsomest and largest; it is eight feet in diameter, and its stem measures forty feet to the first branches, while its crown attains a height of one hundred and fifty to two hundred feet. On the river banks cypresses stand side by side for miles, so close together that there is hardly room for a man to pass between them. The black walnut, the tulip tree, the peca-nut, several sorts of elms, the mulberry, maples, ashes, planes, poplars, &c., press against each other, and wherever death makes a gap and restores one of these giant trees to the earth, young shoots start up from its dust in the opening through which the blue sky is visible, and soon fill up the room. Countless varieties of smaller trees flourish in this gloom, and force their way between the colossi of vegetation, for instance, the wild cherry, wild plum, a small chestnut, and several species of nut trees; beneath these the bushes and cactuses spread with an incredible variety, and relieve the gloom with their magnificently coloured perfumed flowers, which seem to maintain an eternal rivalry with the blossoms of the llianas swinging from tree to tree in the airy height. Finally, the earth itself, beneath the darkest bushes, is covered with a dense carpet of delicate plants, which, although hidden from every sunbeam, are not the less worthy of being sought by the fervent admirer of the masterpieces of nature; they gleam like subterranean fires in the shade, and diffuse their perfume far around in this palace of foliage.

The queen of the whole virgin forest, however, is the magnolia. It raises its haughty head one hundred and fifty feet above a silver grey, smooth trunk, spreads its branches regularly far around, and is so closely covered with its broad, dark green, smooth and shining leaves, that its branches are rarely illumined by a sunbeam. Among this dark mass of foliage, which is unchanged throughout the year, it puts forth in spring its large snow-white roses, with orange petals, in such profusion that you can hardly see whether white or green is the fundamental colour. Far around it spreads a perfume of vanilla which is so strong that it is dangerous to sleep under the tree unless a breeze be blowing. The flowers last a long time, and as the pearls fall one by one on the ground, their place is taken by a bunch of berries, redder and more fiery than any colour on an artist's palette. They gleam far and wide through the majestic forest like candelabra in a cathedral.

Our path ran with a hundred windings through the solemn silence; it seemed as if every living creature that had sought this sanctuary, or fled from the heated plain, were silently revelling in its beauty and gratefully reposing in its coolness; not a bird or insect could be heard, not even the sound of a falling leaf interrupted the tranquillity, and only the footfalls of our animals and the snorting of Czar echoed through the forest. Too soon for us, too soon for our horses, we reached the end of our path, where it entered the prairie on the other side, after we had walked the greater part of the distance, because the crossing creepers frequently compelled us to bow our heads under them, as the makers of the path did, for we saw their brown shaggy hair floating in all directions. We followed the path into the prairie, which begins about two miles from the forest. On either side of the path deer sprang out of the bushes, and flocks of turkeys darted backwards and forwards with long, quick steps in front of us. The former I left undisturbed, but I shot one old fat turkey-cock, and hung it on the saddle behind me.

The sun was rather low when we rode through the wide prairie, and we could only advance slowly because the grass at many spots came up to my horse's back; our cattle were very worn, and poor Lizzy panted painfully under her harness, while the perspiration poured from her in streams. The sun was setting when we reached a small affluent of the Leone, where I knew of a good camping place, at which I determined to spend the night. We unloaded our animals, which I soon completed, as I merely undid the belly-band, pulled saddle and all over Czar's croupe, removed the bit, and then gave him a few taps on his damp back, as a sign that he could go wherever he pleased. My companion was much longer in removing all the articles of his household from Lizzy's back; and when he had finished she was a gruesome sight. White foam and dust had matted her long hair, her ears hung down and almost touched the ground, and her generally melancholy face was rendered still more so by the bushes waving over it. I really felt sorry for the poor wretch, and bluntly told Mr. Kreger that I would not ride a step farther with him unless he left the buffalo hide here. He was also convinced by his Lizzy's wretched appearance, that she could not carry this weight for long, and we agreed, that I should tan the hide of the first deer I shot, and let him use it. Lizzy was led into the grass and tied to a bush, and we arranged our bivouac for the night. Kreger fetched dry wood and water. I lit the fire, set coffee to boil, spitted strips of the turkey breast and liver, rubbed the meat in with pepper and salt, and put it to roast. Then I laid my horse-rug on the grass, with the saddle, holsters, and saddle-bag on it, hung the bridle and lasso on a branch, and took my seat in front of the fire on my tiger skin, while watching the naturalist, who was making a thousand arrangements, as if we were going to remain at least a month here.

It had grown dark. Supper was over. We fetched our animals and took them to water. Lizzy was hobbled in the grass near our camp, and Czar lay down behind a bush, but kept his head up for a long time, as if looking for somebody. It was Trusty, his playmate, that he missed; nor did I feel altogether comfortable under my rug. I dreamed nearly the whole night of Indians, and continually woke, when I made up the fire and lay down again with my rifle on my arm. The botanist, on the contrary, slept like a top, packed up in his buffalo hide, with his head on an open bundle of blotting paper; at the same time he snored nearly the whole night, which did not help to improve my rest. Before daybreak Czar got up, shook himself, and walked up to Lizzy, who still lay half dead in the grass, as if to wish her good morning. I roused my companion. We led the cattle to water, and while I got breakfast I advised Mr. Kreger to make some botanical researches, which he did. He came back with such an armful of plants, that I told him I thought he had better not take more than one specimen of each, as otherwise, by the end of our journey, Lizzy would be unable to carry the load. He laid the plants in the blotting-paper, bound his bundles, and ere we started, I rolled up the buffalo hide with the hair outwards, and thrust it between two branches of a thickly-leaved tree, where it would remain until our return.

CHAPTER VI
MR. KREGER'S FATE

We had a good day's journey to our next bivouac, and I was acquainted with the country so far. We rode rather sharply in spite of the tall grass, and at mid-day reached another small affluent of the Leone, where we granted ourselves and our cattle a few hours' rest. During this time I went down to the river side and shot a large deer, whose hide I conveyed to our resting-place, along with some of the meat and the skull. After scraping the skin quite clean, I split the skull, took out the brains, made them into a thin paste with water, smeared the skin on the inside with this, and then rolled it up tight and gave it to Mr. Kreger to carry, promising to get it ready for use next day. Brains dress skins famously, and this is the way in which the Indians prepare them. After lying in this state for four-and-twenty hours, they are washed clean, hung up in the shade, and, while damp, pulled over the sharp edge of a plank or the back of a bowie knife till they are quite dry, which makes the skin as smooth and soft as velvet. In order to prevent a skin prepared in this way from turning hard when exposed to the wet, it is spread over a hole in the ground in which rotten wood is kindled, and it is smoked on both sides till it becomes quite yellow. My botanist employed the halt in exposing the plants plucked in the morning to the sun, while he collected fresh ones. The greatest heat was past, and it was about 3 p.m. when we set out again. The country here became more broken, the prairies were not so extensive, and here and there were covered with clumps of trees and bushes. The grass was not so tall as on the flat prairies, which considerably accelerated the pace of our cattle. Lizzy especially seemed to feel the difference between yesterday and to-day, and trotted lightly and cheerfully by the side of Czar, who on such tours always ambled, a pace which is very pleasant for the rider, does not tire the horse, and gets over the ground wonderfully quick. This pace is natural to barbs. I knew my Czar's sire, who was one of six stallions presented by the Emperor of Morocco to Taylor, the President of the United States.

At nightfall we reached Turkey Creek, as I had christened it from the great number of those birds I found here. It was still light enough to choose a good spot for our bivouac, where we were near water; we were tolerably hidden, and had very good grass for our cattle. This evening, however, Czar was hobbled, that is to say, a short line round his neck was hooked to a padded ring he always wore on his near forefoot, so that he was obliged to keep his head to the ground or his foot in the air, and hence could only walk. This was an invention of my own, suggested by the fear of losing my horse, and when fastened in this way, he could not be unexpectedly scared and driven off. I prefer it to binding the two feet, for this often lames a horse, and to tying it up with a lasso, because the horse can easily entangle its feet in the latter and be seriously injured. In this manner I could leap from my horse in the most dangerous neighbourhood, and renders it in an instant incapable of bolting.

Lizzy was again picketed, and we kept a watchful eye on the animals during the two hours they were grazing; for I had nearly reached the end of my *terra cognita* and the border of regions which had never yet been visited by Pale-faces. Ere we went to sleep, the logs were covered with ashes, the cattle fastened to trees close to us, and we lay down to rest after supper, but I could not sleep so soundly as when I had Trusty by my side; the slightest sound disturbed me, and it was always a long time ere I fell asleep again. About midnight I started up and fancied I had been dreaming about a storm; I looked up and saw that all the stars had disappeared; at the same moment the surrounding landscape was lit up by a flash of lightning, and a violent thunder-clap rolled down the valley. I sprang up, blew the fire into a flame, laid wood on it, and woke the snoring naturalist, who asked, in great alarm, about the cause of being disturbed. I advised him to do as I did, then broke off an armfull of bushes, laid them in a heap, put my pistols and bags on it with the saddle over them, covered them with the horse-rug, and laid the jaguar skin over all; after which I helped Kreger to put his traps in safety, in which he greatly missed the buffalo hide.

While we were occupied with these preparations, the thunder rolled almost uninterruptedly, and the incessant flashes kept the tall trees brilliantly illumined. From the north we heard a sound like a distant waterfall, and the turmoil soon rose to the mournful howling of the tempest which is only to be heard in these regions. I was well acquainted with the approaching spirit of the storm, for I had often met it; hence I went up to Czar, put on his head-gear and threw the bridle over my shoulder, giving Kreger a hint to do the same with Lizzy. But he had quite lost his head, and ran first to his heap of traps and then to the mule, when the storm burst over our heads in all its fury, and made the primæval trees crack in their very roots. It swept the earth and carried away with it an avalanche of dust, leaves, and branches; our fire stretched out long tongues of flame over the ground, and sent its sparks whirling through the coal-black night into the gloomy wood. The groans of the hurricane were blended with the deafening peals of thunder, which at every second made the earth tremble under our feet, and I had the greatest difficulty in making Kreger understand that he should come to me. I had selected a young white oak, whose branches were interlaced with creepers, to shelter myself and Czar, and had got out of the way of two lofty planes which were singing their death plaint.

The fury of the storm still increased; blast followed blast crash followed crash; the crowns of the two planes bent more and more, and with a shock resembling an earthquake, they suddenly fell across our fire, which scattered in all directions like a bursting shell, and hurled logs and brands over our heads. Czar started back, and in his terror would have broken half-a-dozen lassos, had I not been prepared for this, and followed him with the bridle, while Lizzy dragged my companion, who would not loose the lasso, for a long distance through the grass.

The first drops of rain now fell, and I knew that the greatest fury of the storm had passed. I led Czar back under the oak, held my rifle with the hammer down under my armpit, shouted to Kreger to follow me, and stood as erect under my broad-brimmed hat as I could. The rain fell in torrents, so that in a few minutes we had not a dry thread on us; a stream flowed between our feet, and the storm chilled us to the marrow. We stood silent, like herons; and though it was so dark that we could not see each other, we were contented at being still alive, and having our horses with us. It rained nearly till morning, which was never more heartily greeted than by us two; and, ere long, a clear blue sky cheered us. The greatest difficulty was to light the fire again. My traps had remained perfectly dry, as they were protected by the bushes underneath, and the storm had been unable to touch them; I had the means of making fire, but dry wood was not so easy to procure: still I succeeded in getting some out of a hollow old oak, and the botanist's blotting-paper helped to kindle the flame. It was scarce blazing ere we laid arms-full of dead wood from the fallen trees upon it, and soon produced such a heat that it dried us in a very short time. Kreger's traps had become rather wet, but the damage could be easily repaired; and we did not the less enjoy our breakfast on that account. The sun came out with its warming, cheering beams, and lit up the ruin which the storm had created during the night, while a calm glad smile on the face of surrounding nature seemed to contradict the possibility of it being capable of any such wild passion.

We were ready to start at a tolerably early hour, but an obstacle offered itself which threatened to take us far out of our course. The usually insignificant stream had swollen into such a rapid torrent, and spread so far over its banks, that we could not hope to cross it. I could not forgive myself the oversight of not crossing the stream over night, which is an established rule with travellers and hunters in this country, for the waters often rise fifteen to twenty feet in a few hours, and the hunter who incautiously bivouacs on the bank runs the risk of being so begirt by the swelling tide as to be unable to escape its fury. Not only men are exposed to this, but also the quadruped denizens of these parts, and I repeatedly saw drowned buffaloes and stags being carried away by such swollen rivers. However, as a rule, the inundation only lasts a few hours, because the small streams have but a short course, and are only swollen by the mountain torrents.

I had no intention to stop here, and preferred riding up the stream in order to try and find a ford where we could cross without danger. We rode for a good two hours along the bank. The trees continually grew scantier, and the road more difficult through scattered boulders and rocks. Between these, huge ferns sprang up, and with the fallen trees, frequently blocked the way, so that we had to make a long circuit to fetch the river again. At length we reached a spot where the stream was more contracted, and an old cypress lay across it, which had been probably levelled by some storm. I went across the trunk, cut a long bough and sounded the ground on the opposite bank; it rose at a steep pitch from the water, and was firm, so that I had no doubt but that our animals could easily clamber up it. I took the packages off Czar, carried them across, then fastened the lasso to my horse's bridle ring, and crossed the stream with it, shouting to him to follow me. The bank on his side was rather steep, which fact he had discovered by feeling with his fore feet, but he leaped with all four feet into the stream, bounded up the other bank, and set to work on the grass, which had been freshened by the last night's rain. Kreger followed my example, but Lizzy would not venture the leap; I therefore went across, suddenly seized her hind quarters, and pushed her into the stream, which she entered headforemost, but soon reached the other side uninjured.

We loaded again, and rode down the stream opposite the spot where we had spent the night. It was mid-day by this time, and though the heat was not oppressive, our animals required a rest. We dined, and mounted again at about two o'clock. From this point the country was quite strange to me, and it was necessary to make sure of the direction in which we proceeded. I compared the compass let into my rifle-butt with the one I had in my pocket, and we rode at a quick pace toward the north-west.

All traces of the rain disappeared about four miles from our last bivouac, and hence the hurricane had been limited to the course of Turkey Creek. This is often found to be the case. Such storms at times are not more than a mile in breadth, but dash with equal fury for thousands of miles over hill and valley, so that nothing remains standing which does not bow to the ground before them.

The country again became flat, but very pleasant for ourselves and our horses. The prairies are frequently covered for miles with post oaks, that is to say, oaks growing so close together, that their foliage is interlaced, and hardly allows the sun a peep at the ground, covered with fine short grass. Large and small clumps of trees of this sort are scattered over these grassy plateaux, and give the country an appearance as if human hands had been active here years agone, and these are the remaining and border lines of former grounds and gardens. Riding under this roof of foliage is extremely pleasant: you are not checked by any obstacle, or diverted from your course, and the horses move lightly and quickly over the short grass. It was at the same time a fine day, the wind blew freshly, and hence we resolved to ride late, as we were in the moon's first quarter, which promised us light for some time after sundown. About six in the evening we crossed another small stream, which probably also flows into the Rio Grande, where we could have spent the night very comfortably; but we only filled our gourds, let our steeds take a hearty drink, and rode on, as we could at all events pass the night now without water. At about nine o'clock we reached, with pleasant conversation, the end of the post-oaks, through whose middle a clear stream wound. We greeted it gladly; for it is always disagreeable to camp without water near at hand. Our animals were soon unpacked, a small fire was lit in the thickest bushes, and at about eleven o'clock we lay down, with Czar and Lizzy by our side, hoping for a better night than the last. We slept gloriously, and awoke the next morning invigorated and in the best spirits.

The sun had just risen over the horizon when we mounted and rode over the plain, after taking, with the help of the compass, the nearest direction to the forest rising in the blue distance above the wide prairie. According to my calculation, it was about ten miles off. The prairie was very flat, and only a few mosquito trees grew on it here and there, which sufficed to estimate distances, for that is a difficult job without such marks. I told Kreger it would be better for us to push on, now the road was good, for a feeling of anxiety involuntarily oppressed me on this broad plain, where we could be so easily observed from the woods that formed a semicircle round it. I spoke to Czar every now and then, and we had nearly reached the middle of the prairie when my horse gave a start, and tried to break into a gallop. I attempted to pacify him, but he soon began snorting, and could not be held in.

I had examined the prairie on either side of us, and when I looked behind, to my horror I saw a band of Indians coming after us at full speed, in front of a cloud of dust. My next glance was at the forest ahead of us, to calculate how far it still was, and then my eyes fell in terror on the mule at my side. The band of Indians consisted of at least a hundred, and hence must belong to a powerful tribe, possessing the best horses and weapons. I turned deadly cold when I looked at Kreger, who as yet had no idea of our peril, and was carelessly whistling. I made the utmost efforts to remain quiet, or at least to appear so, in order not to terrify my companion, and begged him to urge on his mule, while I loosed the rein of my snorting steed, and allowed it to make a few forward bounds. Whether Kreger noticed a change in my countenance or voice I do not know, but he looked round, and noticing the approaching savages, with the ejaculation, "Great heavens, Indians!" he drove his enormous spurs into his mule's flanks, and pulled his bridle so tight, that the excessively sharp bit lacerated the wretched Lizzy's mouth, Kreger had turned deadly pale. He looked wildly around him, and showered blows with his whip on Lizzy's hind-quarters. At his first movements I foresaw what would happen, and tried to make him understand that if he let go the reins Lizzy would be sure to follow Czar, and we should be able to reach the forest, where the Indians could not hurt us. He did not hear—he did not see. A picture of horror, he stared fixedly before him, and Lizzy, putting her head between her legs, began kicking out behind. The danger grew every minute, for the yell of the cannibal horde, borne on the breeze, was already echoing in our ears. I rode up to Kreger and tried to drag the reins out of his hand; but it was of no use; no prayers, no remonstrances, reached his ear. It was almost impossible for me to hold Czar in any longer, for at one moment he reared, at another bounded onward.

The Indians during this time had drawn so near that I could hear their several voices, and distinguish the bright colours with which their faces were painted. Our life was in the greatest danger. My horse was terribly excited, and any slip on its part would infallibly entail my death. Once more I shouted to Kreger to be reasonable, and let go the reins, but he did not hear me. Minutes pressed. I let Czar go, and flew like the wind away from the hapless man, who was left to his fate, and my staying longer would be of no avail. I quieted my horse, and looked back at my unfortunate companion.

The horde was now close behind him; in a second a dense cloud of dust surrounded him and the savages, while a yell of triumph, whose cause I could guess only too well, reached my ears. I pressed closer to Czar, patted his neck, and away we flew like light. I looked round again; a dense mob of Redskins was after me, and by their inhuman yells they gave me to understand that I was to be their victim also.

The distance between us, however, had been increased. I drew a fresh breath, and my passion soon dispelled my feelings of pity and its sister fear. The forest rose rapidly before me, and my safety only depended on this question: Was there a stream on this side the wood? Firmly resolved even in that event to force Czar in, I clung closer to him with my knees and gave him a cheery chirrup. Like a swan he flew over the grass towards the woods, whose single trees I already distinguished. There was no river on this side, and I soon reached the dense foliage, and led Czar snorting and champing in, while my pursuers, now few in number, stopped a long way from me on the prairie. I took out my handkerchief and waved it at them to annoy them, for I would but too gladly have avenged my unhappy comrade; but they turned round, and I went along the buffalo path into the forest, dragging Czar after me.

For about an hour I walked through the gloomy shade, cutting my way among the numerous creepers, till I reached a stream whose banks were quite forty feet above the water. The forest on both sides of the path where it led down to the river was so overgrown with thorns that it was impossible to go up or down the river side, especially with a horse; nor would it do to stay here all night with Czar, as there was nothing for him to eat; and in event of pursuit I could be easily tracked. Hence I soon made up my mind, mounted Czar, hung my pistol-belt and saddle-bags over my shoulders, took my rifle in my right hand, and forced him to follow the path down to the stream. It was so steep that walking was impossible, but the faithful creature, once on the steep, half slipped, half fell into the river, as the bank was very smooth and slippery. The waves, as he fell in, broke over the saddle-bow; but the horse at once raised the whole of its back above the surface, and snorting and puffing, passed the crystalline flood.

In spite of the rapid current, we reached the other side, when the path again ran up the bluff; but had it been a few yards lower down, the horse would never have been able to climb the steep; the bank, as it was, was very high and precipitous, but my steed's strength was equal to the emergency, and burying its delicate feet in the soft loose soil, it sprang up the bank, forcing me to cling round its neck lest I should slip off behind. I had noticed from the prairie that the forest grew lower down the stream and gradually ended, which led me to the conclusion that further on the banks would not be so steep, though the river might be broader; hence I rode down the waterside, for the wood was not so close and impenetrable as at the spot I had recently left, for about three miles in this direction, and found a spot where the bank was not so steep, and I could easily lead Czar to water, while at the same time wild oats three feet in height, grew close by. Hence I resolved to spend the night here.

I led Czar into the nearest thicket, unsaddled and hobbled him, and lit a small fire, partly to dry my clothes, partly to make a cup of hot coffee, for I had turned chill, and felt quite worn out. I had chosen my bivouac so that I could see for a long distance along the road I had come, and kept my weapons in readiness, so that I might sell my life as dearly as possible were I pursued. The scene of horror I had witnessed so lately, the probably frightful death of the naturalist, rose vividly before me, and though I had accustomed myself to society again for a very short time, I now felt very lonely, and reproached myself for having ever consented to let Kreger ride a mule on this journey, when I knew the great danger. That he had fallen a victim to this error there could be no doubt; still I resolved to make certain of his fate.

Night set in; the fire had burnt low; Czar lay close to me, and I threw myself over his neck, patting him for his pluck and fidelity: he was very tired, and frequently gave a sigh, nor did he stir the whole night through. I remained awake till near morning, and although I dozed now and then, I was soon aroused by the hoot of an owl, the yell of a wolf, or the mournful cry of a panther, and I then listened to the sound of every falling leaf and every leaping squirrel. The night was cool too, the ground under me rather damp, and the dew very heavy, so that I really awaited daylight with longing. Czar, however, would not get up, and I let him lie, for I knew that he needed rest, and I might very possibly be obliged to trust to his powers during the day. I had drunk a cup of coffee, and eaten a slice of venison by the time my faithful comrade rose. I led him down to the water, and saw a number of turkeys taking their morning draught at the river side, but dared not fire for fear of betraying myself. It was about ten o'clock when I started down the stream again to find a convenient ford. The forest grew thinner, the shores flatter, and I soon found a deeply-trampled buffalo path which conveyed me without difficulty across the river, for though it was very wide it was quite shallow. Within half an hour I was again on the same prairie where Czar had saved me yesterday, and where the poor botanist had probably met his fate. I cautiously examined the whole plain with my glass, and could not see anything except a few herds of buffalo, and a number of deer grazing carelessly among them. I rode up the forest side to the path, where I found my previous trail, which was crossed by later hoofmarks, and then proceeded cautiously in the direction of the spot where I had left my companion.

While still a long way off, I saw the fearful sight before me. The sun lit up his bloody corpse stretched out on the grass. I rode up to him, and found that he was lying on his back, without his scalp, and covered all over with lance and arrow wounds. None of his clothing had been left him; the only things I found were my destroyed pistols and double-barrelled gun, from which I removed the locks; even the blotting-paper had been taken, though for what purpose was a mystery. I would have gladly dragged the body to the wood and buried it, but the distance was too great to do so without help. I therefore bade him a silent farewell, and turned my horse to the ford where I had crossed the river that morning.

CHAPTER VII
A LONELY RIDE

My route led me from here through a very fine country, consisting of undulating plateaux, covered with splendid mosquito grass, and picturesquely broken up by post oaks; here and there a single conical mound, whose top was covered with a thicket, rose some hundred feet from the plain. It was still early in the evening when I neared one of these mounds, and let my horse refresh itself in a rippling stream at its base. The stream came straight down from the thicket on the mound, and the spot pleased me so well, that I resolved to pass the night there. I rode up the hill to the wood, whose tall trees chiefly consisted of holm oaks, with a thick undergrowth of rhododendra and azaleas. A creeping bignonia was remarkably beautiful as it clambered to the tops of the trees and spread over them its scented blossoms like a shower of fire. The shady green of this wood was relieved by flowers of the most varied hues, one of which I can still remember that is rightly called "the traveller's delight." The flowers of this plant hang in clusters two feet long, rivalling the purest blue of the sky above them, and greet the approaching traveller with a perfume which the fabled East could not surpass. The sources of the stream welled up in the centre of the copse, and were girdled by beds of flowers which, as regards colour and form, could not have been better arranged by an artist.

Here I encamped and hobbled Czar, who mercilessly plucked many a beautiful flower and champed it between his teeth with the tender grass. I then took my rifle in order to see whether there was any dangerous animal in the wood, which was about a thousand yards in diameter. I had crept through it and met nothing except a few old does that had their fawns hidden here, and when I stepped out on to the prairie I saw a herd of large male antelopes grazing about a thousand yards from me. This graceful animal, though frequent in our parts, is rarely killed by the sportsman, for it is the most shy of animals. Great curiosity alone brings it at times in the vicinity of the watching gun, and hence I tried to attract the bucks grazing ahead of me. I chose a spot covered with rather tall grass, lay down on it with my cocked rifle by my side, but drew my ramrod out and fastened my handkerchief to it. I then whistled so loudly that the sound reached the antelopes. All looked round towards me at once, and I raised one foot in the air and lowered it again a minute after. I saw that they had noticed it and were leaping about; I then raised the pocket-handkerchief and lowered it again, upon which the herd got in motion, led by one of the largest bucks. They came near me in a large circle, but I continued my telegraphic motions till the antelopes, urged by their fatal curiosity, came within shot, and their leader fell bleeding among the flowers, giving the flying herd a sad parting glance with its large beauteous eyes. I jumped up and fired my second barrel after the fugitives. Clap! I heard the bullet enter the mark, and another buck fell on the grass after a few more bounds.

Hunting is the most cruel sport to which a man can devote himself; I repented of my second shot, for I could make no use of the animal, as a few pounds of the meat amply satisfied my wants. The charm lay solely in the query, "Can you hit or not?" If this doubt be removed, it is all over with the passion, and no one would go out sporting for the pleasure. I must naturally see where the animals were hit, for that is the real enjoyment to know how near you have gone to the right spot, and hence I walked up to the bucks to choose the best of the meat for my consumption at the same time. The one first shot was the plumpest, and carried a pair of large beautiful horns which I regretted I could not take with me. The antelopes do not shed their horns like stags; they are formed more like goat's horns, and annually grow further out of the head: they are brown and bent back at the point like chamois horns. The form of the antelope much resembles that of the deer, but it is rather lighter on the legs and of a brighter hue; its weight does not exceed 120 lbs. The eye of this graceful creature is certainly one of the loveliest that nature has given to any of her creatures, and I have often turned away from the look of a dying antelope because I could not endure the reproach that it expressed.

I cut off the best lumps of game and went back to the dark shade, in which Czar greeted me with a whinny of delight, and rested on my horse-rug, refreshed by the delicious perfumes of hyacinths, jonquils, daffodils, and narcissuses, that surrounded me. The night was warm, and I required no fire after I had finished supper. I slept splendidly, with Czar at my side, and the sun was high when I awoke, to find my horse browzing on the grass within reach of his tether. I washed Czar clean, which I never neglected when I had the chance, and rode out of my arbour down the side of the hill, whence I could survey the country before me for many miles.

A glorious picture was spread out. The sun was not very high yet, so that the shadows over the landscape were rather long, and the light mist gave the distance that reddish-blue tone which renders a landscape with a rich bold foreground so exquisite. I remained for some time at the spot, examining the road to the hills whither I was going, but which were still too far for me to reach them on this day. Up to these blue mountains the ground appeared to be much the same as I had ridden over yesterday; rich in arable land, supplied with the most luxuriant pastures and abundance of wood, and watered by magnificent streams. This earthly paradise awaited men to raise the unlimited treasures which it promised to bestow so bountifully. It was a saddening thought, that these boundless plains were entirely uninhabited, for the nomadic hordes of savages cannot be called such. From where I stood to the north pole, with the exception of a few trading ports of the fur companies, no white man had yet erected his cabin. Westward the enormous regions were unpopulated almost to the Pacific, and even eastward the distance to the first settlement was so great that I felt very solitary, and for the first time was overpowered by a sort of yearning for the social life which I had left in vexation. Still these feelings took no deep root in my breast; they were soon driven away by the joys of hunting, which can only be found in their full extent far away from the civilized world.

For two days I wandered through these gardens of nature without being checked by any material obstacle. On the third day I reached the mountains, and at evening found myself at the height where the limestone leaves off and the red granite begins. To my surprise I saw a splendid spring flowing from a narrow fissure in the granite, with sufficient grass growing near it to give Czar his supper and breakfast. I stopped here for the night, and had a glorious view from this stony height. The misty blue outlines of the Rocky Mountains were only just visible; between them and myself I looked down on the most fertile valleys, which were begirt by lofty mountains. The precipice behind me was overgrown with splendid cactuses, which were just opening their cups after sunset, and diffusing their fragrance. The moon had risen; it illumined the large snow-white clustering flowers of the yucca which grew in the rock fissures, and spread over the whole scene a silvery light, which, though inferior to that of the day in brightness, was far superior to it in pleasantness.

It was a rather cool night, so that from time to time I made up my fire with the dry wood of old mimosas, the only tree that finds nourishment on these stony heights. Many of these grew round my fire, which when it flared up, displayed the beautiful pink flowers with which these trees are literally covered, so that the delicate pendulous leaves can scarce be distinguished. Rarely did a sound disturb the surrounding silence; now and then the yelp of a white wolf reached my ear through the cold damp fog from the valley below me, or the hoot of an owl was repeated by the echoes among the rocks.

Day awoke me from a refreshing sleep as the sun was gilding the summits of the mountains that emerged from the sea of fog at my feet, round which the large eagles were circling. Greatly invigorated, I bade adieu to my pleasant resting-place, and led Czar over the rocks to the nearest valley, which soon received us under its shady trees. I traversed the valley for about two hours in a northern direction, following the course of a clear stream which ran through, with a thousand windings, like a mighty snake, and was framed in on both sides by thick bushes and old overgrown trees.

About mid-day, as I was following one of these windings, I suddenly found myself a few paces from a camp of Cato Indians, and a general "ugh" reached my ear, as the men, about thirty in number, sprang up, and we gazed at each other in surprise, watching for a signal of peace or war. My presence of mind did not desert me; and knowing that these savages, when they have their wives and children with them, prefer a peaceful understanding, I waved a good morning to them with a pleasant smile, and rode, holding my rifle and watching every movement of the men, to the next bend in the river, while the savages looked after me with open mouth, as if petrified. When I had got round a curve and was protected by the bushes, my first idea was to give Czar the spur and gallop away, but this would only have been a challenge to the Indians to pursue me; hence I made him amble, as well as he could manage it in the tall grass, and hastened to get out of this unpleasant company. It was highly probable that the savages would follow me, if only to get hold of my fine horse; hence I was obliged to calculate my next steps. I had but the choice of two ways—either to throw out the savages by riding in the water and on stony ground, where they could not follow my trail, and then concealing myself at some easily defended spot—or else to ride quickly away from them so far that they could not follow me on their wretched horses. The former was difficult and dubious, as the Indian's eye surpasses the nose of the best pointer, and hence I chose the other, trusting to my horse's speed.

I cut off a slice of the antelope's leg, which was hanging on my saddle, about enough for supper, and left the rest behind, not to give my horse any unnecessary weight; then I set Czar at a sharp trot where the grass was dry, and when I reached barren ground made him amble—a pace at which he could do his mile in three minutes when put to it, though he took eight minutes when not hurried, and could go on for hours without a rest. I followed the course of the water, and at the end of some hours reached a gorge where the river ran through perpendicular rocks, and where my horse had scarce room to pass. I could see the water for nearly two miles ahead; the current was wilder and swifter here, and on looking down at its surface I noticed several spots where the water rippled and foamed as it ran over rocks and stones. On both sides of the pass the granite walls rose many hundred feet, so that it was impossible to scale them; and though, farther to the right and left, buffalo paths ran up them, the Indians must be well aware of this fact, and were probably lying in ambush for me there, as they must have noticed from my course that I was quite a stranger to the country. There was only one choice for me, and I quickly made up my mind. I put my holsters over my shoulder, placed in them those articles which must not be wetted, and guided Czar into the river, in which he floated down with me at a tremendous pace past the rock walls. I was not at all afraid about swimming him for an hour; the sole danger of the undertaking consisted in the large masses of rock over which the stream broke, and against which we ran in less than ten minutes. The river bed was here rather wider, and hence fortunately the stream not so violent, or else we should probably both have found a watery grave. Czar raised himself by his forefeet on the rock, which was not covered by more than a foot of water, but his hind-quarters sank as he did so, for he found no bottom, and the waves dashed over my saddle. The current had turned us against the rock, when I pressed Czar with my thighs, and with a frightful effort he worked his way along to the end of the rock, where I felt that he had a footing, though it only consisted of a few boulders. I was compelled to cross this dam, as I could not go back, and the uncertain ground threatened every moment to bury us between its rocks. My horse, first slipping off the smooth stones, and then leaping up again, struggled in vain to find a footing in the rapid stream, and I saw that any hesitation would be certain destruction. I therefore dug both spurs into the flanks of my brave steed; he leaped desperately out of the foaming waves, sprang on the rocks before us, and scrambled over them into the river on the other side, where he sank up to the nostrils, and the waves met over my head. My alarm lest Czar had injured himself was alleviated by his speedy return to the surface, and as he blew the water from his nostrils we followed the stream to a wall of rock, where I noticed that the water was calm at the right hand end. I steered for this point, and we swam unimpeded through this channel into the deep water till the valley opened again before us, and my brave horse trod on the sand. I led him into the grass, examined him carefully, and found that he was slightly grazed on the near foreleg and the knee, but this caused me no apprehension. I let him rest in the shade for half an hour, as he was greatly excited, gave him all the white sugar I had brought expressly for him, and which was now wet, and then continued my journey along the river, as the grass, which must have been burnt here late in winter, and the fresh grown crop had not yet sprung up, did not impede Czar's speed.

The valley constantly grew wider, and trended to the west. I left it at about 6 P.M., and followed a stream which ran from the north. Going along it till nightfall, I reached its source in the mountains, and was at least forty miles from the Indians, when I unsaddled Czar, and hobbled him in the soft grass. I felt quite secure here, for I was no longer frightened about pursuit by the Catos, and it was not probable that accident would lead other Indians here at so late an hour, when they never march except for some special reason. My bivouac was in the only coppice far and wide, in which the springs bubbled up at the foot of a very tall cypress. All around me was a glorious meadow, and, further north, rose barren rocks, on which only a mimosa, a yucca, and varieties of brambles and cactus grew. Czar was tired, and soon came to me, holding up his hobbled leg, begging me to set him at liberty; and when I had thrown the lasso over his neck, he stretched his delicate limbs on the grass. I too fell back on my saddle, and slept so soundly till morning, that I did not once look after the fire, and on waking did not find a spark among the ashes. It was soon lighted again and breakfast prepared, before which I had a bathe in the spring. Then I lit a pipe, washed Czar all over, and left the well-head, going toward the mountains in the north.

The road was so steep and fatiguing that I dismounted; still, I seemed to be on a path at times trodden by buffaloes, which was continued when I reached the top, where a wide tableland covered with rich vegetation was expanded before me. This plain, only interrupted by a few hillocks, was about twenty miles in diameter: it was covered with very high grass and small patches of mosquito trees, elms, dwarf oaks, and yuccas. The ground was quite black and very rich, and this earth was in some places fifteen feet deep, as I could see by the numerous channels cut by rain storms. I did not see a trace of spring water. This country is entirely dependent on the rains, which are frequent in these mountains, as well as the peculiar nature of the soil, which long resists evaporation of the humidity. On all sides I saw herds of grazing buffalo, but, though my mouth watered for a slice of hump and a marrow bone, I did not like to distress my horse, or go too far away from him while stalking. More antelopes were feeding here together than I had ever seen, and the same was the case with deer. I rode quietly on through the tall grass, resolved only to shoot some animal I could ride up to, and succeeded in doing so toward evening, when I saw something dark moving in the grass, which I recognised as a black wolf. In a second I was off Czar's back, as I should be very glad of such a skin, and was just about to fire, when I saw, on the other side of a ditch I had not observed in the tall grass, a very large bear running away. Owing to the high plants, I could not fire, and, forgetting my former resolution, I leapt on Czar's back, and flew after the fat fellow. His road led through a number of low mosquito trees, so that I was obliged to bend down over my horse's neck to escape being caught in the branches. I was close to the bear, but it coursed so rapidly under the branches, that I could not give it a shot from my revolver. At length we emerged from the trees, and I flew a few yards after the bear, when suddenly Czar made such a leap to the right, that I must have been thrown, had it not been for the heavy holsters that kept me on. I turned the horse round again, and then noticed that the bear had disappeared in a gap before me; and on drawing near, I found a *cañon*, going down a hundred feet sheer, and about twenty feet wide at this part. It was a gully washed out by the rain, which I had not observed owing to the tall grass. I dismounted, and walked to the spot where the bear had disappeared: saw that the bushes had been uprooted about thirty feet lower down, but could not discover a trace of the bear. What I had been told by old hunters now appeared to me probable—that a bear will, in a case of need, put its head between its legs, and roll like a ball from some height, without hurting itself; which can be explained by the remarkable elasticity of its bones, and the thickness of the fat over its body, I owed it solely to the agility of my horse, that I had not followed the bear down the precipice, and I willingly resigned the delicate ribs which, in imagination, I had seen roasting at my camp fire.

I continued my journey over the grassy plateau. The sun poured its last vertical beams on the dry soil, which was intersected by deep cracks a foot in breadth. This bursting of the ground during great heat is very common on plateaux where the earth is very rich, and often endangers the rider, as the fissures, being covered by the long grass, are difficult to detect. There was not a breath of air; my horse became very warm, and looked in vain for water in the deep dry ditches. I also pined for a fresh draught, for the water in my pouch had become quite warm, and Czar could not swallow it when I poured some into his mouth. My horse rug was so hot that I was hardly able to sit on it, and the barrels of my rifle almost blistered my hand. I stopped several times in the shade of an isolated tree to draw a little breath, but this did not advance my journey, and I could not possibly spend the night here without water. How far I still had to ride to the next stream I did not know, but I was aware that I might travel for days in these mountains without finding a spring or a stream. The sun was on my left hand when I reached the end of this plateau, but, instead of perceiving the longed-for sign of water, a poplar tree, I saw before me almost impassable hills covered with loose stones, that rose behind one another like sugar-loaves. I could only reckon on an hour's daylight, and it was highly probable that I should have to pass an unpleasant night. So far as I could see northward, the hills were piled on each other, without offering a prospect of water, hence I turned my horse westward, on the chance of reaching the valley which ran along parallel with the plateau. I was obliged to dismount, for in the hollows between the hills the torrents had torn deep ravines in which old trees washed down were piled up and became very dangerous to pass. The rocks over which I wearily climbed were red hot and burnt my feet, and at the same time I suffered intolerable thirst. I had shared the last water in my flask with Czar. My mouth was very dry and my tongue clove to the palate. In vain I looked from every height I reached for the longed-for sign, and wandered up hill and down, till the sun sank behind the distant blue mountains, and the first shadows of night spread over the land. I had passed over several hills in this manner, when I saw a valley before me in the twilight which I greeted with renewed hopes, but the darkness set in so rapidly, that I was unable to continue my journey. Feeling quite knocked up, I threw myself on the warm rocks, holding Czar by the rein, to wait for the rising moon. The sky behind me grew more and more red; the anxiously awaited light rose slowly about the hills, and looked down on the deadly silence that was spread over the whole landscape.

I had rested about an hour ere it grew light enough to continue my journey, and I soon reached the plain, where unfortunately the grass grew very high. I was obliged to mount my horse again, for it was impossible to walk through the grass; and though I was very sorry to do it, I urged the poor creature on, while he continually strove, by hanging his head and shaking his neck, to make me understand it was high time to go to rest. I had continued my journey for two hours without stopping, when the grass grew shorter, my horse every now and then stepped on stones, and I saw a tree or two again. I had probably passed the lowest part of the valley, and as I had found no water in it, there was no prospect of doing so at a greater elevation. I was awfully tired and sleepy, and my horse was quite as bad; I therefore unsaddled under an elm, fastened Czar to the tree by his long lasso, and in ten minutes I was dreaming of cool crystalline water; but for all that woke at daybreak exhausted and feverish, and to my horror missed my horse.

I sprang up, surveyed the wide plain, and who can describe my delight when I saw Czar's white coat shining a few hundred yards off over a small mimosa bush, behind which he was enjoying the fresh grass in a hollow. The knot of the lasso had come undone, and thus Czar had been able to look about for more agreeable fodder. I led him nearer my bivouac, and was just going to light my fire, when I saw smoke rising in the west, about three miles from me. I quickly pocketed my flint and steel, saddled, and rode toward the highest part of the ridge which divided the valley in half. When I had nearly reached the top I dismounted and crawled to the highest point, whence I surveyed the valley, and observed an Indian camp, round which some three hundred horses and mules were grazing. I saw through the grass that the various families were sitting at the fires in front of their leathern tents, with the exception of a few children that were playing about. The camp was on the other side of a stream which wound through the valley from the north. Though I longed so for water, I must avoid the neighbourhood of these savages, who might prove very dangerous to me in such an unknown and desolate country. I rode back through the valley in which I had spent the night, and into the mountains on its eastern side; for, if I had followed the valley to reach the river, I must have been noticed by the Indians on my white horse. The road was tiring, as I was frequently obliged to walk, and the heat on these barren hills soon rendered my thirst intolerable.

It was midday when I with a firm resolution to ride to the water, cost what it might, guided my horse down a ravine, and suddenly saw before me the fresh verdure of plants which only grow at very damp spots, under a heap of dry piled-up trees, among which a number of turkeys were running; I forgot the Indians and the risk, shot two old gobblers, and threw myself between the tall ferns, over the cold springs that welled up among them, in order to quench my fearful thirst. I lay for nearly half-an-hour, ate a bit of biscuit, and as I could not fully quench my thirst, continually applied to the spring. This was one of the most glorious meals I ever enjoyed, and I believe that I would sooner have defended myself against a whole tribe of Indians than leave this spot unsatisfied. The shade here was not sufficient, however, and hence I went a little lower down the stream with Czar and my two turkeys, where I found a cooler resting-place under a group of elms and oaks. After this hunger began to be felt, for, with the exception of a small slice of antelope and a little biscuit, I had eaten nothing since the preceding morning. I set to work on one of the turkeys, and spitted such a quantity of the meat, fat and lean, that I was obliged to laugh at myself. The exterior of the meat hardly began to get roasted ere I cut it away. In the meanwhile, the coffee was getting ready and I concluded my repast; after which I found great difficulty in keeping my eyes open. I fetched Czar, who had also enjoyed himself, and fastened him to a tree, took my rifle in my arms, and in a few minutes was fast asleep, forgetting all the dangers that surrounded me.

CHAPTER VIII
THE JOURNEY CONTINUED

At about five o'clock I was awakened by the sun, whose oblique beams were able to reach me through the trees. I felt refreshed and strong, made Czar get up, saddled, and followed the stream, which led me to the river I had seen in the morning. I approached the valley cautiously when I rode out of the mountain gorge, and carefully surveyed it with my glass, without finding a trace of the Indians anywhere. It was very important for me to know whether they had gone up or down the river; the latter was the more probable, because most of the buffalo herds I had seen lately were going southward, and the savages, as a rule, follow these animals. As the banks of the river were not high, I rode into it, watered my horse, and without any difficulty reached the other side, when I was soon on the path of the Indians, who had gone south, as I expected. I rode up this trail northwards, in order, if possible, to reach before sunset some stream coming from the mountains, as I would not pass the night where I was, for it appeared to be a pass greatly used by Indians, so that I ran greater danger here of meeting fresh hordes than I did among the hills. I rode very quickly, and at sunset turned into a narrow valley, bordered on either side by very lofty precipices. For about two miles I followed the torrent which wound through loose blocks of granite, and frequently could scarce get through the tall ferns and reedy plants which grew between the wildly scattered boulders. The gorge gradually became narrower and the granite walls steeper, and in the twilight I saw the end of it no great distance from me.

I had dismounted and was going with Czar round a block of granite, when a large stag dashed past me from the end of the gorge, hardly fifty yards off, and I distinctly saw another darker-coloured animal bounding after it through the tall grass. In an instant the flying stag, with its broad antlers thrown back, was twenty yards from me, and bounded over a rock close by, while at the same moment a panther of enormous size covered the track of the deer with its gigantic paws. It had scarce touched the ground, however, ere the bullet from my rifle crashed through its shoulder-blade, and the crack, echoing through the gorge, thundered in its ears. The panther ran its head into the grass, while its hind quarters flew up in the air, but at the next instant it rose furiously in the grass, showing its dazzlingly white teeth and stretching out its claws to leap on me. I held my rifle firmly to my shoulder, and as the animal rose, fired at the white stripe under the throat. The bullet passed through its breast, and rising on its hind legs it turned a somersault and died with a furious kick. It was very old, and had probably inhabited this tempting spot for many years, to surprise the game that came here to drink at the spring, and enjoy the fresh green pasturage. Eight feet long from the snout to the tail, the prince of the valley lay stretched out before me, and round it the bones of its victims were bleaching in the grass. I found above a dozen skulls of deer and antelopes, all of which had a hole an inch wide in the top. In addition to them, the skeletons of two buffaloes and an elk, and countless bones of other animals glistened in the grass. I went up to Czar who, probably recognising his foe, had run some hundred yards down the valley, and was looking after me with his head up. I led him up to the slain panther, but it needed much persuasion ere he would draw quite close to this arch foe of his race. After making Czar stand by the panther awhile, which I dragged about to remove his natural fear of the creature, I led him to the end of the ravine where the ground was covered with young tender grass, unsaddled him, and laid my traps under the evergreen oaks, in order to prepare my camp.

As the darkness had greatly increased I ran back to the panther, fastened the lasso round its neck, and dragged it to my camping-place, intending to skin it in the morning. I lit the fire, prepared supper, and lay down on my horse-rug, every now and then turning the spit or piling up the sticks round the coffee pot. The fire flared brightly, and produced a peculiarly beautiful illumination on the thick foliage of the oaks and the projecting shadow of the high reddish rocks, whose fissures and crevices appeared all the blacker in consequence. The russet moon was still low on the very dark sky, it peered into the ravine from the east, and did not spread sufficient light to overpower my fire.

While I was observing this pretty scene I noticed a light spot under the rock which was lit up by the fire. I took it at first for a buffalo skull, but drew a brand from the fire and crept under the low-branched oaks to make certain what it was. I held the brand over it, and saw a human skull grinning at me out of the damp dark background, and carried it to the fire. From its shape it was the skull of a Weico with a low forehead, and strong thick high back part: judging from the fine, slightly worn teeth it must have belonged to quite a young man, who probably fancied he had found a safe resting-place here, and carelessly yielding to sleep had fallen a victim to the panther, for the marks of teeth were quite distinct upon it. I kept up the fire during the whole night, which did not disturb my rest, as I had grown into the habit of waking up every hour to see all was right and going to sleep again. If it can be managed, as was the case here, the hunter chooses a large fallen tree, and makes his fire close against it with small wood, so that the trunk may catch. This smoulders during the whole of the night, and the fire can easily be made to blaze at any time by throwing on brushwood. The night passed without the slightest disturbance, and at dawn I skinned my panther, which had a great number of scars, principally arrow and lance wounds, as it seemed. After cleaning the skin from all fleshy particles, I spread it out to dry at the fire, while I bathed and swallowed my breakfast. I sought all round the bivouac for weapons or other articles belonging to the dead man, but found none, and as the sun was already high I set out on my wanderings again.

Just as I reached the entrance of the gorge I saw a herd of seven buffalo bulls grazing. In a second I leaped off Czar and ran from stone to stone, till I got within ten yards of the shaggy monsters, from which I was only separated by a large rock. I crept under this on the ground, till I had the buffaloes before me; the nearest one stood motionless, with its broad, hairy forehead turned toward me, and I aimed at the centre of it, although I had often tried in vain to kill a buffalo by a shot through the head. This time, however, the bullet did its work, and the other bulls fled round the rock toward the valley. As the fat buffalo would supply me with food for several days, I fetched my horse, took the axe hanging from the saddle, and set to work cutting out the sirloin, while Czar grazed by my side and now and then licked up the blood. It is very difficult for a novice to cut up a buffalo, for the hide is remarkably hard and elastic, and sits very close to the flesh, while any attempt to turn the carcase about is hopeless. We may fairly say that a novice in these countries, if what the practitioners call a "greenhorn," would starve with a dead buffalo, if he had not some one to show him how to cut pieces off it. I thrust my sharp bowie knife between the ribs close behind the shoulder blade, ran it up along the spine and down again to the chest, then in the same way separated the two last ribs from the spine, and made a cut under the belly to the end of the first cut. I then hacked the ribs with the axe, lifted the entire side up, which broke the hacked ribs, and thus opened the interior of the animal, like lifting a trap door. The entrails were removed without much difficulty, and the two enormous loins under the spine cut out. I removed a piece of the hide from the hump, in order to secure a part of the streaky meat; cut out the tongue between the jaws, as I could not think of opening the mouth, took two marrow bones, and left the remaining 1400 lbs. of meat for the wolves and buzzards. All these dainties were hung about my saddle, for the hotter the sun shines on them the less does the meat putrefy. With a parting glance at the ravine, I again struck the Indian trail, which I followed northwards up the river.

At 2 P.M. I crossed the river, as it trended to the west, and followed a beautiful valley, for some hours, to the north-east, where I did not notice a single trace of horses or Indians, while the path I had hitherto been following seemed to be exclusively made by nomadic savages. The valley I now traversed rose gradually with the stream, and seemed to form a plateau in the distance. It was covered with splendid mosquito grass, which is only the case with the richest soil. This grass never grows very high, but is very fine, and hangs in tresses like hair. Horses are excessively fond of it, and grow fat on it in a very short time. So far as I could see, the valley was covered with game of every description, among which I noticed several moose deer, the first I had seen on this tour. These animals are only found separately so far south, while they form herds farther north, especially in the southern Rocky Mountains. It is a deer of enormous size, reaching the weight of seven or eight hundred pounds, the antlers spread very wide, and often weigh as much as forty pounds. The flesh is not very toothsome, being hard and fibrous, and is not eaten by the hunter when he can get any better. The animal is not difficult to kill, for it is not very fast, and can be caught up by a good horse; the Indians throw a lasso over it, and then kill it with lances. For the time I was amply supplied with meat, and hence felt no great longing for these animals, but let them graze at peace. Like the other game here they were very familiar, and allowed me to ride within shot, which was a further proof that this valley was rarely visited by Indians. The country was well covered with stately elms, poplars, mosquito trees, and mimosas (I call the last tree thus to distinguish it from the mosquito tree, which is also a mimosa). Of course, such specimens as grew on the Leone were not to be found here. This valley will certainly in time be visited by settlers, for though poor in wood, no better ground can be desired by cattle breeders.

At about six in the morning I reached a spot where two streams joined, and I could not make sure of water further up the valley. Hence I followed the eastern arm, and reached at sunset the hills bordering the valley, between which I bivouacked, as I had everything I required. For several days I continued to follow a northern course. The character of the soil varied as before; the mountains had the same shape, were bare at top, and covered with loose stones, between which a few low cactuses, aloes, and torch weeds grew. I also rode over a good deal of tableland, but got away from it as soon as I could, for through the entire want of water the ground here grows very hot, and you are thoroughly roasted.

I found the grass on the prairie not very high, which made it easier going for my horse, but more difficult for me to approach the game, which appeared remarkably shy and restless. My stock of meat was exhausted, and I ate my biscuit and salt tongue as rarely as possible, so as to have food by me in case of need. I dared not ride down the buffalo, as my white horse could be easily distinguished from the uplands, and I must spare his strength. Nor did I care to go far from Czar afoot, as a single foot Indian might easily be hidden in the grass, and reach him more quickly than I could. Hence I deferred my chase till I reached the woods that rose ahead of me.

I rode over the rolling prairie till, on emerging from a hollow, I saw three very plump old deer grazing not far from me behind a few low mosquito bushes. I sprang off Czar, hobbled him, and crawled on my stomach through the grass towards the deer, dragging my rifle after me. Although I had got within shot, I wished to advance a few more yards in order to reach a hollow where I should be able to kneel and fire. On reaching it I pulled my rifle after me, and was just about to fire when a monstrous rattlesnake glided away from under my hand. I sprang up in terror, watched it darting through the grass with head erect, and away fled my deer over the prairie, and I had had all my trouble for nothing.

Though rattlesnakes are so numerous in these regions the sudden announcement of their vicinity through the movement of the rattles is a most unpleasant surprise, which never failed to produce a painful impression on my nerves. The whole south-west of America is troubled with these and other snakes, but accidents through their poisonous bite are rare. In spring and autumn, when the heat is not great, the bite of a rattlesnake rarely kills, and only in cases when a large artery is injured. If that be not the case, it only produces a soft swelling, which soon disappears again, only leaving a want of sensitiveness for a few days. In summer, however, when the heat attains its acmé, such a bite is more dangerous, and curatives cannot be employed too quickly. Cutting out to the seat of the wound without a moment's loss of time is the most certain remedy. Salammoniac, which has so often been recommended, is not of the slightest use; but sometimes a cure is effected by rubbing the wound with oil or lard, or by a poultice of the leaves of the large burr, which is so often entangled in the hair of domestic animals. The most infallible specific, however, is a bulb known to all the borderers by the name of "Seneca root." It has a leek-green leaf a foot long with a few brown spots. It is chewed into a pulp, which is laid on the wound and a small portion of the juice is swallowed; ere long the pain is reduced, the fever disappears, and the swelling ceases. This bulb may be carried about for years without losing its virtue. Moreover, all these snakes shun man, and it is only when they are startled by his sudden approach that they dart at the limb nearest to them. The rattlesnake rarely exceeds eight to ten feet in length, but the royal variety is somewhat larger, much more poisonous, and marked with the most brilliant colours. Other poisonous snakes found in our parts are the brown and black moccassin, which lives both on land and in the water, and the copperhead, a small but very venomous snake. When I settled on the Leone, these snakes were so numerous that after sunset I did not dare let my horse walk along a buffalo path, because they used to come out and cool themselves there. But as my swine increased in number, they gradually disappeared, for the former are exceedingly fond of eating them, and are not hurt by their bite.

I was very much annoyed: sent some strong language after the snake, and returned to my horse, who had been taking advantage of his rest in the long grass. I took off his hobble, and rode toward the forest, which seemed inviting me to enter its friendly shade. It was midday when I reached the wood, thirsting for a fresh drink. I hung my hat on the saddle, and greedily inhaled the cool breeze that blew through the majestic trees, and then followed on foot a buffalo path, which wound between the bushes. It led me to a clear stream, which poured over loose masses of stone, between rather high banks. I let Czar glide down, for the path was very steep; watered him, and made him leap up the other bank: then I filled my gourd, and quenched my thirst with the cold water.

I was just going to remount, when I heard the sound of a herd of peccaries or Mexican swine coming toward me, probably in search of water. As the undergrowth was not very dense on the side of the stream, I was able to see them coming for some distance. There were about twenty old pigs, with a lot of sucklings; they ran very slowly, and I had time to pick out a fat boar. I shot it; sprang on my horse at once, and, as I expected, found the whole herd dash furiously after me. I had room before me, and dashed through them into the forest. They did not follow me, and I granted them time to bid adieu to their fallen comrade, while I led Czar into the wild oats which grew luxuriantly here. In a quarter of an hour I rode back to my game. The herd had retired; and I at once cut away the musk gland which the boar had on its back, of the size of an egg: for if I had allowed it to grow cold it would have been impossible to eat the meat, owing to the powerful musky taste. The boar weighed about fifty pounds; I cut off the best joints, and took one of the tusks as a souvenir, on account of its remarkable length. The peccari is very frequently met in the western mountains of America, and often in herds of a hundred head. It has a handsome, silver-grey, long-haired skin, an enormous head for its size with tremendous tusks, and is remarkable for its extraordinary courage. If disturbed, it will attack a man as soon as a horse or a tiger, and is very dangerous through its agility, strength, and tusks five inches long. I have known a hunter to be attacked by a herd, and forced to take shelter up a tree, where he remained the whole night till the herd retired.

I rode for about two miles along the skirt of the next forest I came to without finding a buffalo path; and yet the forest was so densely overgrown with thorns and brambles that I could not enter it without a path. At length I found one, which had been probably trodden for centuries by millions of buffaloes. I followed it into the wood, and soon reached a small river, whose steep banks were about eight feet high. Here I refreshed my horse and myself, and followed the path on the opposite side, where the forest grew clearer, and I soon caught a glimpse of the prairie. The bushes and a few isolated trees ran for some distance out into the prairie. I dismounted and led my horse to the last bushes, in order to survey the plain ere I entrusted myself to it, and because I was undecided whether I would not bivouac here. I had advanced to the furthermost bushes, which were brightly illumined by the western sun, and I found the prairie was populated by a few deer and buffaloes, whose evident watchfulness and restlessness I could not ascribe to my appearance. I looked down the wood to the rocks, and to my terror, saw close under them on the prairie a war-party of about a hundred and fifty Indians, who were riding towards the forest one behind the other. I sprang in front of my horse, in order to cover its bright chest, and hurriedly raised my telescope. They were Lepans. I knew them by their plumed lances, gaily-decorated shields, and fine horses; for these Indians are the best mounted and most warlike on the western steppes. I stood as if petrified, for fear lest they might see a movement on my part, while I held Czar by the rein. They had not yet seen me, for they rode past, and drew close to the wood: a few yards farther and they would have been out of sight, and the danger momentarily passed. Suddenly, however, the whole party halted, and pointed toward me. I had been seen, there could be no doubt of the fact; for I noticed through my glass that they were holding their hands over their eyes to have a better look at me. There was not a mile between us; my horse had been travelling all day. The wood was very narrow, and the path leading through it very broad. I was aware of the courage of these Lepans, and saw no salvation save in the endurance of my horse. With one leap I was on his back; threw away the flesh and darted into the wood, with the whole band of savages after me like a whirlwind. The river made a number of bends, which I was compelled to follow. The Indians' horses were extremely swift; this was the first time I had ever known any horses keep up with mine. But I had not yet called on Czar: I now drove the spurs into him and let go the reins. I flew round the next corner, and then round the next, ere the Indians reached the first, which was a good mile behind. At this moment I saw that the river bank was covered for the next half mile with loose pebbles. I turned Czar round, and leapt him down the eight-foot bank into the river, whose bottom, composed, of soft sand and shallow water, he reached without injury. I then galloped up the stream in the direction I had just come, covered by the tall bank, and the wood between it and the prairie, calculating that the Indians would not miss my track among the loose stones, but would gallop through them to the next angle of the wood, which would give me a grand start. I remained at a gallop for about a hundred yards, so that the water met over my head, until I reached a deeper spot, where Czar was obliged to swim for a short distance. At this moment I heard the savage horde dash past, and the war yell of these unchained demons echoing through the forest! Probably the short extent of deep water saved me, for at this spot only a few thin bushes grew on the bank, and though the savages were some distance off, they would infallibly have noticed the water being dashed up by Czar. I again reached a firm bottom, and followed the stream as quickly as I could; while the yells of the Indians were audible a long way behind me.

I was beginning to feel more secure, when my progress was impeded by large masses of rock, between which the shallow water rippled. I leapt on one of these blocks, and gave Czar a gentle pull to follow me: he sprang up, clambered across, and reached without injury a good sandy bottom on the other side. I hurried down the stream—partly swimming, partly climbing— till I saw the lofty rocks on my right through the forest, and hence knew that I was below the spot where the Lepans had halted when they first sighted me. I still followed the stream, although the water came up to my horse's girths; but it suddenly made a curve, and ran close past the rocks, at a spot where they opened like a narrow gateway, leaving a passage for a rivulet that flowed from the interior. The entrance through the granite walls was not more than thirty feet wide, and the gorge about a hundred feet deep, beyond which was a beautiful little valley enclosed by the rocks, about a mile in length, through which the stream rippled.

I rode up the rivulet; on both sides of which the most exquisite flowers grew. Among them I specially noticed a sort of tiger lily, not only through the brilliancy of its hues, but the masses that covered the banks, so that the ravine seemed to be strewn with live coals. Sitting down on a rock at the entrance, I listened, but did not hear a sound of my pursuers. The rippling of the stream alone interrupted the silence, and only at intervals did the shrill cry of the white-headed eagle rise above it. That the Lepans had overridden my trail was certain; but it was equally certain that they would ride back when they noticed their error, and find my track; for my horse, in leaping into the stream, had left distinct marks on the bank, and its track might also be followed in the sandy bed. Moreover the banks were splashed with water, and that was sufficient to show an Indian the road I had followed. Hence it was certain that the savages could follow me, but doubtful whether they would do it, as they might be sure that I should get under cover, when my firearms would be very dangerous, and they would be unable to surprise me. Hence it was far more likely—supposing that they attached so much value to a white man's scalp or the possession of a fine horse, as to interrupt the war-trail for some days—that they would guard the prairies on both sides of the forest, as it was almost impossible for a horseman to ride through the latter.

While I was thus weighing my situation I inspected my firearms, which had got slightly wet; put on fresh caps, and was taking a look at my water-tight powder-flask, when a yell echoed through the wood from the east. I knew its meaning perfectly well: the Lepans had found my trail, and were assembling for a consultation. At this sound all prospect of an amicable arrangement departed, and I was determined, in the event of an attack, on defending myself here, as in case of need I could always escape down the stream.

All became silent again; evening spread her veil over the earth; the silver herons and flamingoes uttered their hoarse cry as they flew homewards; and the owl announced the setting in of night. The outlines of the trees and rocks continually grew more indistinct, and it was time to fetch up Czar, who was nibbling the tender grass along the stream. I secured him with the lasso to a very large stone behind the rock on which I was sitting, and threw before him an armful of grass and weeds, which I picked. In the event of an attack from the river, he was tolerably protected behind this rock, and he was close at hand if I wanted to mount in a hurry. Though I regretted having to leave him saddled through, the night, I only took the pistols out of the holsters and laid by them by my side.

Suddenly a loud, long, lasting yell was raised, which, however, seemed much farther off, and to come from the prairie on the south side of the forest. Probably, the Lepans had found my trail through the prairie, but it was a satisfactory sign to me that they had not attempted to follow me along the river bed. In all other directions my hiding-place was unassailable, unless there was a second entrance into the valley in my rear, as was probable. It had already grown so dark, that I could not distinguish my white horse from the rocks, although the stars shone brilliantly above me. Before it was quite dark I sat down by the side of Czar, to prevent him lying down. I grew very sleepy, but the yell of the Indians still sounded too loudly in my ears for me to indulge in repose. I tried to keep awake by smoking, which helped for a while; but smoking in perfect darkness is no enjoyment; hence I soon grew tired of it, and tried to keep awake by walking up and down. Czar, too, was tired of standing; he stamped impatiently with his fore-feet, and tried the strength of the lasso by tugging at it. At length, nature claimed her dues, and I could not possibly keep awake any longer: I took off Czar's load, laid it in the darkness against the stone to which he was secured, spread out my rug, and lay down on it with my rifle on my arm. Czar was not long in following my example, and tried as usual to have a roll before going to sleep, which might have injured me or the saddle in the darkness; hence I pressed his head to the ground, and we were both, ere long, as soundly asleep as the rocks around us.

Day was scarce breaking when I started up and looked around me with a disagreeable feeling of self-reproach: for how easily could an Indian have crept up and done to me while asleep what all the whole tribe could not effect while I was awake! Czar lay motionless, and I did not disturb him, for it might easily happen that his strength alone could bear me away in safety. I went out of the gorge and brought in some dry wood, lit a fire and made coffee, being obliged to breakfast on my biscuits and salt tongue, for the dainty lumps of pork I had cut yesterday had probably served a wolf for supper. While I was breakfasting, my faithful steed raised his head and rested it on my knee, that I might remove the bridle which I had left on during the night. I did so; hobbled him out in the grass, and then sat down again at my small fire, where I could see along the river and up the valley behind me, whose steep granite walls were just beginning to be illumined by the rising sun. In the valley itself the fog still lay like a white veil, and only a few tall trees raised their crowns above it. The stream by which I was sitting was all aglow with its tiger lilies, with which the dazzling white of my horse grazing among them formed a beautiful contrast. The mist in the valley was dissipated, and revealed the rich vegetation which grew there apart from the world. I remembered the fairy tales of childhood,— the enchanted Princes and sleeping Princesses, the Palace of Glass, and the Magic Valley,—and had they not been narrated before this continent was known to Europeans, I should have believed that the fables had their origin in this valley. I was very curious to learn whether there was another entrance besides the one I commanded; for if not, it was very possible that my hiding-place was unknown to the Indians, as the steep hills around did not reveal that they concealed such a fairylike kingdom in their interior.

It was about nine o'clock when, after washing and saddling Czar, I rode off to examine the secrets of the wonderful valley. I looked around at the lofty walls of granite, but could not notice any other connexion with the external world but the one through which I had come. The valley, about a mile in diameter, was covered with a most luxuriant crop of young grass and a number of clumps of trees and bushes, through which the rivulet wound. It struck me as curious that I saw no game on such rich pasturage, for, excepting a flock of turkeys, I had put up nothing, although I had reached the centre. The turkeys were very shy, and ran off when I dismounted to shoot one; but just as I was going to mount again, an old cock came running up, and my bullet put a speedy end to his existence. The report had hardly begun to echo through the rocks, ere a swarm of aquatic birds of all sizes rose right in front of me like flies in the sunshine; but, as I remained quietly seated on the grass, reloading my rifle, they soon settled down again. I walked through the bushes, and noticed a large pond with flat banks covered with all sorts of gaily plumaged birds, among which herons and flamingoes occupied a prominent place. The banks were literally covered with these birds, some of which were standing sentry on one leg, while others were up to their knees in the water and engaged in catching frogs. When I stepped out of the bushes all the birds rose again, a portion seated themselves with loud croaks on the nearest trees, while the rest rose in the air, and proceeded in various directions to less disturbed regions. It now appeared as if all the inhabitants of the valley had left it, and I was not sorry at having secured a good meal, for my stomach was beginning to complain about neglect. I hung the turkey on my saddle and rode to the pond, whose banks were so trampled by the birds that not a single blade of grass grew on them, but I noticed a great number of jaguar tracks, some old, others quite recent. The animals to which these tracks belonged must consequently live in the valley, as they would not climb over the rocks and had not passed my night quarters. It was now clear to me why this splendid pasture was so deserted and only visited by birds, while hundreds of buffaloes and deer would have found abundant food. I rode nearly round the valley, with a revolver in my hand, as I expected at any moment to meet the landlord; but I did not see him, and not a living creature remained in the valley but the few turkeys which had probably strayed thither. I rode back to my bivouac, as it was midday, and both myself and Czar felt hungry, and prepared a part of the turkey for dinner, while Czar had a hearty feed of grass. When we had finished our meal, I tied him up close to me under the overhanging rocks where the sun did not fall on us. I threw wood on the fire, and lay down to sleep to make up for the last night's lost rest. The sun was hardly illumining the tops of the eastern mountains of the valley when I awoke invigorated, and led my horse out into the grass again.

CHAPTER IX
HOMEWARD BOUND

I had already made up my mind to spend the night here, so I got about my supper at an early hour, and soon carried a good stock of wood to my camp with which to keep up my fire during the night. I slept undisturbed till daybreak, took a refreshing bath in the cold stream while my breakfast was getting ready; then rode Czar into a deep spot, washed him thoroughly, and was soon ready to leave this mysterious but so pleasant spot, with the resolution to visit it again sooner or later.

My road led into the river again, on whose rippled surface the night mist rolled along with the current. But on further reflection I saw how many obstacles now stood in my way. The current was very powerful, and the waves broke against my horse's strong chest; the bottom, covered with loose boulders, rendered its footsteps unsteady, and constantly put it in danger of falling. At length I reached the bed of rocks which blocked the entire breadth of the river, over which Czar had clambered with such agility: it now seemed to me purely impossible that a horse could achieve such a feat, although the marks of his shoes proved to me the contrary, I would not venture, however, to make my horse leap it again, but took my axe out of its sheath, entered the water, which was shallow here, and cut away the creepers and bushes hanging over the bank, and thus formed a much better path beneath them over a very few large but flat stones. I led Czar across, and then slowly walked on, constantly thrusting on one side the vines hanging with a length of fifty feet over the water, in order to force myself through them.

After great exertions I at length reached the buffalo path by which I had crossed the river on the previous day but one, and followed it again to the skirt of the wood, but this time with greater caution. I left Czar behind in the thick bushes and crept out alone to the edge of the prairie, and examined the latter carefully with my glass. The grassy expanse before me, far as I could see, was covered with countless buffaloes and numerous deer, which were grazing quietly and carelessly, and I recognised at a great distance a large troop of wild horses, which must consist of several hundred. These were the surest signs that no Indian had shown himself on this day upon the plain, so I returned to my horse, and pursued my journey northward through this prairie.

In about an hour I drew near the horses, which were giving vent to their playfulness by rearing, kicking, and galloping about. I rode along a hollow under the hill, in order to get as near them as I could, in which I perfectly succeeded as the wind was favourable. I rode to within a short distance of them under the hill on which they were standing, when Czar scented them, suddenly raised his head, and expressed his delight at the friendly meeting by a loud snort. In an instant the troop dashed up to greet the stranger. It was led by a coal black very powerful stallion, whose mane, some five feet in length, flew wildly round his broad neck. The thunder of their hoofs rolled along like a tempest toward me, till we faced each other at a distance of about twenty paces. The black stallion fell as if struck by lightning, and the nearest horses fell upon him in the wildest confusion, while Czar gave them to understand by a friendly whinny, that there was really no reason for such fear. It was a wondrously beautiful sight, when these noble powerful animals rose again and flew over the grassy sea, like smoke before the blast, the black with wildly flying mane, flashing eyes, and scarlet nostrils at their head. I looked after them for a long time, and regretted that I could not risk leading a captured horse home, as I could have easily thrown my lasso over the stallion. It is undoubtedly one of the most exquisite sights to watch closely a troop of perfectly wild horses in a state of excitement, especially on the western steppes, where every breed is represented. These horses are originally descended from those of the old Spaniards, who established a great number of military colonies in these parts, each consisting of several hundred men. These settlements, whose remains may still be found here and there, were established in the richest districts, and, when necessary, strongly fortified; maize was planted there, and silver, copper, and lead mines opened.

I found in this country numerous relics of the old Spanish times; more especially well-preserved dams in the rivers and water-courses, led through large plantations which are now overgrown with grass. These were employed to irrigate the country during a protracted drought, and thus always secure an abundant harvest, which was a matter of great importance to the settlers, as they were many hundred miles from civilized Mexico, and thus it was impossible to obtain provisions thence. The people were entirely left to themselves, produced their own food, had a great quantity of cattle, and bred many horses and mules. Even at that day, when these colonies were flourishing, it might now and then occur that some of their horses bolted, and lived and propagated in the glorious climate and on the rich prairies without the aid of man. At a later date, however, more warlike Indian hordes poured from the north over the south, which was inhabited by tribes held in subjection by the invaders, and destroyed these remote Spanish outposts whose garrisons they cut down and scalped. From this date, in all probability, came the numerous troops of wild horses, now spread over the whole of Western America; for the numerous horses of the military colonists were set at liberty, and even at the present day the old Spanish horse, with its long fine mane, small head, long neck, and hanging long tail can be recognised. Since, however, eastern civilization has been advancing toward the west, these troops have become crossed with all possible breeds and not of the worst sort, for the men who risked their lives on the border always spend their last farthing in taking a good horse with them, in whose speed and bottom they could trust when they came in contact with the savage Indian hordes.

From these border settlements, where the horses are necessarily turned out to graze on the prairie, some frequently escaped, as they are constantly surrounded by the wild horses. And every horse that has once got among such a troop, bids an eternal farewell to captivity. Hence we find among these animals the pure Arab blood, we recognise the clumsy English cart horse, the pony, the thorough-bred, and the racer. In short, there is such a display of every breed as no horse-fair in the world is able to show. I especially noticed an enormous number of greys, piebalds, and black horses among the troops; and that the differences of colour are far more frequent among them than with trained horses. They possess great speed for a short distance; for, on a lengthened race, owing to their grass feeding, they cannot keep up with a horse fed on corn, and hence they are often hunted down and captured by men mounted on the latter. For this purpose, the lasso is employed, whose noose is thrown over the horse's neck. So soon as the wild horse's neck is squeezed it falls quivering on the ground, and the captor finds time to place a halter or leathern thong round its neck. The noose is then slightly loosened, and a trial is made whether it will follow the rider by the halter. If it resists, the operation is repeated as often as is necessary to make the animal understand that it must yield to captivity. As a rule it follows soon; and can be easily tamed, especially when it is not too old. If these horses are fed on maize for awhile, they grow very strong and enduring. The fillies are the easiest to capture and tame. You need only chase a manada for some miles, and the fillies fall exhausted and do not rise again, and if they are raised on their legs after recovery, they will immediately follow the ridden horse, as their mares have disappeared with the troop.

These animals become as tame as dogs, and are of great value to the borderer, as it costs nothing to rear them, and they can be put to any work.

For all that the wild horse is greatly detested in the vicinity of a settlement, and many a noble brute has died there with a bullet in its heart. The borderer cannot shut up his horses and mules in stables. They must seek the food which nature offers them in such profusion, and hence they have the gate of liberty always open; but they do not fly, because they do not know what liberty is. But scarce do they see a troop of their wild comrades dash past, ere they dart off too, never again to bow their neck to the plough or the bit. They in such cases become the wildest of the troop, and can always be recognised at its head. My black stallion, whose wildly flowing mane I followed for a long distance over the prairie, had, however, never yet bent his neck beneath the yoke of man, for it displayed too fully the pride and strength which nature imparts to liberty alone on its black curly forehead: these animals had never seen the low roof, the simple palisade of a frontier house, and no fugitive thence had ever complained to them about the fate he had endured.

Czar was beside himself that he was not allowed to join in the race, and tried for a long time to check the speed of the fugitives by his snorts; he danced, threw his croupe from one side to the other, and furiously tore at the bit, but it was all of no use, and serfdom still lay on his broad neck, even though with rosy bonds.

The sun was rather low on the horizon when I found myself about five miles from what seemed to be a very large forest, behind which rose the mountains which I had noticed a few days previously in the azure distance when I took my first glance at this valley. I leapt from my horse, hobbled it, and crawled through the grass after two very old stags, one of which was quietly grazing behind a fallen mosquito tree, while the other, as if it had noticed something, thrust its thick neck over the stump in my direction. I had left my hat with Czar in order to attract less attention, and the sun shone hotly on my head; but what will not a hunter readily endure if it enables him to draw nearer the game? At length there were about one hundred yards between us, and I had reached a small patch of flowering jalap trees which covered me. I raised myself on one arm, and fired, aiming at the head. I saw that the deer was hit close to the heart: it ran about fifty paces with its comrade, and then fell dead.

After reloading, I rode up to the deer and laid in some days' supply of meat, hung it on the saddle, and continued my journey to the forest, which I entered about sunset by a very broad open buffalo path. I was sure that the forest was traversed by a stream, and resolved to seek the latter ere I selected my night quarters. I followed the path with my rifle on the saddle-bow, when suddenly my horse gave a start, and a very old bear entered the path hardly twenty yards ahead of me, stopped, and with its head turned from me, began nibbling at the roots of a few small bushes. It took scarce a moment to raise my rifle and pull the trigger, and in the next I pulled Czar round, and rode for the prairie. On looking round, however, I perceived that the bear had only sprung a few yards after me, and was now half sitting, half lying on the path and showing its savage teeth. When I slowly approached it, I noticed that its fury was heightened with every step I took, and only its inability to rise prevented it from attacking me. I, therefore, rode close up and sent a second bullet through its head. It was a very heavy fat bear, and I was really sorry that I could turn it to so little account.

Not very far from this spot I found the stream, and resolved to pass the night on its bank, as the forest on the other side seemed very extensive, and it was doubtful whether I should find there good provender for my horse. I watered Czar, filled my bottle, and rode back to the bear, from which I cut a paw, the tongue, and some ribs. I then camped in the forest at a spot where the most splendid wild oats awaited my horse. The paw was put to cook in the ashes for the next morning, but the ribs were to make their appearance on the supper table. A roasted bear's rib is indubitably one of the greatest dainties which the desert can offer the hunter, and I enjoyed it the more because I had been riding all day and had eaten nothing since my very early breakfast. A man soon grows used to this mode of life, which is necessary in the case of violent exertion in the hot sun, as it is very easy to bring on a fever by riding with a full stomach.

The night was dark and rendered the light which my fire cast upon the dark green roof above my head all the more attractive, while the giant brightly illumined trunks looked like pillars supporting it. I lay on my tiger skin and amused myself with counting the blood-red funnel-shaped flowers of the bignonia, which swung in long drooping festoons from one tree to the other, and, lit up by my fire, resembled so many red glass lamps. Around me a number of whip-poor-wills strove to outvie each other in uninterruptedly uttering their name, and frequently circled round my fire. At the same time fire-flies and huge glow-worms glistened and flashed in all the bushes, and the rustling of the adjoining stream supplied the music for this Italian night. My eyes gradually closed, the pictures of dreams became more and more blended with those of reality, until a calm sleep fell on me to strengthen and refresh me.

Day was breaking when I opened my eyes, and the scene which had so sweetly lulled me to sleep had faded away: the fire was out, and instead of the glow-worms a grey mist lay over the bushes, the grass around me was very damp and the bear's black hide was silvered over with dew. From all sides the loud chuckling of the turkeys reached me, and I felt a tickling in my forefinger to bend it upon one of these birds: but then I looked at the mountain of flesh which lay before me and rested my rifle again against the tree, and went to the fire to pull the paw out of the ashes. The fire soon burnt brightly, and dispersed the cold damp air around me; I put coffee on and a bear's rib before the fire, led Czar to the stream and refreshed myself and him. Then I returned to the fire, led my horse into the oats, and paid my respects to the bear's paw and rib. The sun was also darting his rays through the trees, when I was ready to start and rode through the stream towards the dense forest.

I rode for about three hours in this labyrinth, passing from one buffalo path to another, until the ground began to grow more uneven, and here and there large masses of rock rose between the trees. I dismounted, and was leading my horse up a narrow path by the side of a great boulder, when I suddenly saw, on raising my head, the entire forest literally covered with wild cattle. I returned to the rock, as a meeting with these most dangerous animals on an impracticable path like this was not desirable, and hanging the bridle over a branch, I again ascended the height in order to convince myself in what direction the cattle were going. The herd passed me bound westward, and I am certain I saw over 300 head pass. These denizens of the desert are the most savage and dangerous animals in Western America. Like the horses of the first Spanish settlements they are runaways, and have now entirely returned to a state of nature. You never see a spotted or black head among them: they are all chestnut with black extremities, and a yellow stripe down the back, and are more lightly and gracefully built than our cattle, and as rapid as deer. They shun man, but when startled or excited, they attack with the most frightful courage and obstinacy, and I would sooner defend myself on foot with a bowie knife against a black bear than with a rifle against a furious bull of this description. I remained for about an hour behind the rock before the last of the herd had disappeared between the trees, after which I rode across their deeply trampled path, and soon found myself on the edge of the forest.

From this point gradually rose a bald desolate mountain range that ran from east to west, and whose base was covered with bad grass and a few scattered granitic rocks. These mountains, the San Saba, are spurs of the Rocky Mountains, which I had already noticed from the elevation, where the granite follows on the limestone. I might calculate on wandering about there for weeks before again reaching watered valleys. Hence I resolved to alter my course and go farther east, until I reached the mountains which were the source of all the streams I had lately crossed, and return home along their base.

On this side of the forest the soil was too bad to produce good grass, hence I looked about for a buffalo path by which I could cross it again in a southern direction. These eternally wandering buffaloes, however, appeared to avoid the sterile mountains, and though here and there a lightly trodden path entered the forest, it was not open enough to be followed by a horseman. It was already noon, and I was still on the outside of the forest, when I noticed a tolerably beaten path in an angle where the forest jutted out farther into the mountains. I was very glad of it. Indescribable was the feeling of comfort when I reached the dense shade of the first trees: I threw my leathern jacket over the saddle, hung my hat by its side, and followed the path which ran between the rocks that rose among the trees and led deeper into the forest.

Suddenly a sound reached my ear resembling the fall of distant water, and the nearer I drew the more distinct it became. It was possible that the river here took a wide curve to the foot of the mountains, and I greeted it with delight. I soon saw that I was not mistaken, for on turning a large rock I stood close in front of a waterfall, which aroused my admiration both through the peculiarity of its shape and the refreshing coolness that it spread far and wide beneath the shady trees. A powerful mountain torrent, about thirty yards wide, fell over an immense rock twenty feet high, down upon another rock which had been hollowed to a depth of about three feet by the water, which had fallen on it for centuries and formed a basin, over whose front the agitated foaming stream dashed at a height of about forty feet over widely scattered masses of rocks and aged trees suspended between them, while on either side enormously lofty trees laid their thick crowns together over the roaring cataract and repulsed the inquisitive sunbeams. I soon stripped Czar, and hobbled him, lit a small fire, put the coffee-pot on it, and lay down on my blanket close to the fall in order to make a sketch of it.

When I was sufficiently rested, I went up to the basin, undressed and leapt into the foaming water. Never in my life have I found so glorious a bathing-place as this, which nature appeared to have made for the express purpose. The very cold waves dashed up to an immense height, and it was hardly possible to stand under the cataract, while behind it I was entirely shut off from the outer world as if I were in a palace of crystal. I remained till about five o'clock at this Diana's bath, as I christened it, and it is known by that name to all the hunters who have since visited it. It was too early, however, for me to camp; hence I mounted my horse and rode up once more to bid adieu to the cataract.

Far through the forest I was followed by the roaring of the fall, till the rustling of the river I was approaching overpowered it. At about one hour before sunset I reached the prairie at the southern end of the forest, and until nightfall followed its skirt in an easterly direction till I reached a spot where the stream emerged from it. I camped here quite concealed, and on the next day rode eastward towards the mountains. From this point I altered my course to the south, and rode there for several days. One afternoon, when greatly troubled by thirst, I reached a pleasant grass valley on which several mosquito trees grew; a fresh stream wound through the verdant bottom, and a few deer were grazing on either bank. I dismounted to refresh myself with the eagerly desired draught and grant my horse a little rest. A very large deer was standing over two hundred yards off, and staring intently at me. I was well stocked with meat, but the query whether I could hit it led me away as it had so often done, and while sitting on the bank I fired at it. The deer bled, ran a short distance in a circle, and then fell lifeless on the ground. After reloading I went up to it to fetch the fillet, and while engaged in fastening it to my saddle I noticed two foot Indians, one armed with a rifle, the other with bow and arrows, come out from behind some bushes and advance some twenty yards before they caught sight of me. I saw their terror and amazement, and that one of them crossed his arms on his breast, and laid his arms on his shoulders, which among them is a sign of friendship. I made them a signal to be off, and assured them of my friendly sentiments in the same way. Upon which they described a large circle round me, and escaped from sight a long way down the stream. I felt convinced that several of their tribe were hunting in the vicinity, as they must have heard my shot, and would assuredly not have emerged so carelessly from behind the bushes had they not believed it was fired by one of their comrades. I put Czar at a sharp amble, as the grass was not high, and hurried down into the valley, while carefully looking round in order to escape this menacing place.

About sunset I reached another small stream, where I halted, lit a fire, and prepared my supper, while Czar was enjoying his. Here I rested till night had set in; then saddled again, filled my gourd, and rode on for about five miles. Here I led my horse into a thicket which ran between two steep hillocks, and remained in it during the night. It was very probable that the Indians had informed their comrades of the presence of a paleface, and that they had followed me to my camp-fire, but had been unable to strike my trail in the darkness.

From this point my journey was for several days a most fatiguing and far from pleasant one. I constantly went up and down barren, stony hills, and found scarce grass enough to feed my horse; we also both suffered from the want of water, which was the more perceptible on the bare, heated rocks. I could only proceed short distances, as through the constant marching on very hard stones Czar's feet were beginning to swell, and though he was not lame, he put them down very gingerly. There was certainly no lack of game, as I always met turkeys and deer in the neighbourhood of water, and on such uneven ground it is very easy to stalk the game. Although it may offend the feelings of the true sportsman, I will confess that on this ride I shot several fawns for the sake of their tender flesh: I also killed a very large jaguar, which I attracted by imitating the cry of a complaining fawn. It leaped within twenty yards of me ere it noticed me, but then stopped, and looked round for its victim, swinging its long tail high up in the air. The bullet went through its head and laid it dead. The Indians make a sort of wooden pipe, which so admirably imitates the moan of a fawn, that every old animal within a distance of a mile round comes dashing up, and is startled neither by a horse nor its rider. I have seen instances where old animals continued to advance after being missed two, three or four times, till they lamentably fall victims to their maternal love. I always carried such an instrument about me, as all the larger beasts of prey can be easily attracted by it, such as bears, tigers, panthers, wolves, lynxes, &c., and the beautifully-striped leopard cats, which are very numerous about us, and are easily deceived by it.

I at length again reached the limestone region; but I must have been a great deal too far east; for the mountain chain was much lower than at the spot where I had crossed it. This view was soon confirmed when I went down into the valley and found all the streams I crossed small and insignificant. The country continually became more pleasant and rich, the valleys grew broader, and the vegetation was more luxuriant than in the desolate melancholy ravines I had been lately riding along. I daily expected to see well-known mountains, and looked about more especially for a very high point on a mountain chain which runs southward from Turkey Creek to the Rio Grande, on which the Indians have built a pyramid of large stones, either put up as a finger-post for the wandering tribes, or as a border mark between the different hunting-grounds.

One morning I had just left camp and was riding through an extensive prairie, when I fancied I could recognise this landmark, and convinced myself by the aid of my glass that I was not mistaken. I felt myself at home again, although this point was a good day's journey from my house: still, I knew in which direction my road lay, and eagerly went along it. About noon I reached one of those most troublesome cactus woods, which frequently run across the prairies. The present one ran like a wall for miles across my path. There is no chance of riding through these thickets, as the prickly plants grow closely together. Though they are most disagreeable to the hunter, their appearance is most attractive to the naturalist, through the brilliant colour of the cactus flowers, and the peculiar shape of the plants. This obstacle led me a long way from my route, as I was obliged to ride round it for several miles.

While I was riding close along this wall, still hoping to find a free passage, I suddenly noticed a deer, about twenty yards off, poking its head out of the prickles, and staring at me in surprise. I raised my rifle—Czar stopped instantly—and fired at the head, as I could not see any more of the deer. I could distinctly see through the smoke that the bullet smashed the right side of the deer's head, and heard it dash away a few yards, and then fall; but it was impossible to penetrate the prickly wall for this short distance, and reach the deer. The cactuses were here from sixteen to seventeen feet high, and so close together that I could not go a foot into them. Hence I was obliged to give up the deer, and was very glad on at length reaching a narrow glade which ran through the wood.

Late at night I rode along the bank of a river, which I took for one of the western arms of Turkey Creek, and was forced to halt and pass the night here by the numerous rocks that rose from the tall grass and ferns. The next morning I passed the spot where I crossed the river with the unfortunate Kreger by means of the trunk of the tree, and at noon reached the camp where the storm had treated us so ill. The revived memory of the unhappy man was very painful to me, and I hurried from the spot, in order to get rid of the blood-stained picture of the scalped naturalist. I now came again into my own hunting-grounds, where nearly every tree and shrub reminded me of a fine chase, and my desire for home and my faithful Trusty urged me on. I rode late into the night, till I reached at ten o'clock a camping-place, where I and Czar had often stopped before. It was evident that the sensible creature recognised his home, and again sought the same spot to rest where he had before stretched his beautiful limbs.

When day broke, I rose from my blanket with a feeling resembling that I felt on my birthday when a child: but soon wretched doubts forced themselves on me, whether I should find my little colony all right. Czar, on this day, was washed extra clean; all the beards of the turkeys I had shot on the tour were fastened on the bridle: the beautiful skin of the tiger shot on the mountains was laid over the panther skin to display it in the best way, and I then continued my ride toward the Fort, which I hoped to reach at noon, with a joyously beating heart. The grass, however, was so high and rendered going so fatiguing for my horse, that I advanced but slowly, and did not reach our first resting-place at the commencement of the tour till noon. Czar was very hot and tired, so I did not ride on, as I had intended, but unsaddled and boiled coffee, while the horse was reposing in the shady grass. When the greatest heat was passed, and I had washed Czar down in the stream, I started again homewards, and saw, as the sun was setting, my beloved virgin forest appear above the prairie, and the two immense poplars indicating the spot where the buffalo path that led to my settlement, entered the forest. It was about ten miles off, so that I could calculate on reaching home by nightfall without any great effort.

I had ridden through a small wood and had advanced into the prairie some hundred yards, when I noticed on my left at about a mile distance, five horse Indians emerge from a clump of oaks. Their horses were going at what is called a dog trot, although it seemed to be increased or diminished according to Czar's pace. I looked at them through my glass, and saw that only two of them had bows and the other three were unarmed. As their appearance did not cause me any apprehension, I quietly followed my road at a gentle walk. We constantly came nearer, and I soon saw that the Indians designed to meet me on the path. I therefore held my horse in so that they reached the path when I was about one hundred yards distant from them. They stopped, and when they saw that I did the same, one of the armed men turned his horse toward me and rode a few paces nearer. I made signs to them to go their way, and when I saw they had no result, I leapt from my horse and raised my rifle, again intimating to them to ride on. They now shouted to me, "Kitchi, Kitchi, Delaware, Delaware!" the names of friendly tribes, and at the same time made the signals of amity. I, however, signalled to them again, and raised my rifle to my shoulder, upon which they spoke together and went up the hill very slowly, one behind the other, till I lost sight of them.

The suspicions which I entertained of all Indians induced me also to ride up the hill to see what had become of them. To my great surprise I saw them a long distance ahead galloping across the prairie. This sudden haste could not be explained through fear of me. It must have another cause which I could only find in the fact that their camp was no great distance off, and that they wished to inform their tribe of my presence, so as to cut me off on the prairie, and lay wait for me in the woods on the Leone. From the direction they followed, if the tribe were encamped no great distance from the path that led into the wood, they could get there before me, whence I soon made up my mind and galloped off to another ford of the Leone, about twenty miles higher up. Czar galloped nearly the whole distance, and I reached the forest before sunset. I was now safe, for no one could pass through the wood on horseback, and the narrow buffalo path could be easily defended. I reached the Leone, welcomed it with heartfelt joy, and hurried down the opposite bank toward my home. About three miles from it I had to cross a hill, whence I could see my fort. I approached its crest with a loudly beating heart, because I must here obtain certainty as to the fate of my settlement.

I looked across the valley, and on the other side I saw the fort glistening through the gloom. A heavy load fell from my heart; I took my glass, everything was quiet, the smoke rose straight from the kitchen, and suddenly two of my dogs ran up from the river, and disappeared through the palisades into the interior of the fort. Czar, too, knew perfectly well that he was going home, for though I had ridden him unusually hard, he kept up his amble, while usually when he was tired he had a habit of stopping and biting the grass.

It had grown very dark when I rode up the last hill to my fort, and was received by the loud barking of my dogs which dashed through the holes in the palisades. But all their voices were overpowered by Trusty's bass from the interior of the building. The dogs soon recognised me, and springing up to Czar expressed their delight at my return by loud whining. I now raised my hunting cry, which was responded to by Trusty tugging furiously at his chain, and a hearty welcome from my garrison. The chain of the gate fell, and Trusty flew out and up at me, so that I was hardly able to keep my feet under his demonstrations of delight. My three comrades received me most heartily, and strove to show how much they were attached to me. My horses and mules raised their voices from the interior of the fort, and Czar answered them by his friendly whinnies.

When the first greeting was over, my three men asked almost simultaneously, "but where is Mr. Kreger?" I pointed to heaven and intimated by a short "by-and-bye," that I would tell them all about it presently. Czar was soon liberated from his burden, rolled himself heartily at his old place in the grass, and consoled himself with his long absent maize-leaves, while I doffed my travelling accoutrements indoors, and made myself comfortable by a wash and change of dress. We were soon seated round the old table at supper, at which I refreshed myself with a draught of fresh milk, and then I described the unhappy fate of my companion Kreger. An almost unanimous "did I not foretell it?" burst at the end of my narrative from the lips of my comrades, who all felt great sympathy in the unhappy man's fate.

In spite of my weariness it had grown rather late. Hence I rose, went out once more to Czar, who had heartily enjoyed his husked corn, and then proceeded indoors with my faithful Trusty, who resumed his old post on a thick bearskin with delight. But I felt so confined in my room that I was obliged to open all the doors and windows, and lie down on a buffalo hide on the floor, instead of resting in my bed. It is remarkable how soon a man forgets rooms when he has been living for any length of time in the open air, and how he feels like a fish out of water when he returns to them.

CHAPTER X
THE BEE HUNTER

I was the first to rise from my bed when day broke, and went forth to enjoy the cooling breeze. Czar was not yet awake, and merely raised his head a little from the ground, gazing at me with his glorious eyes as if he wished to say that it was too soon to rise, and then laid his head down on the ground again and accepted my patting without stirring. The cream-colour whinnied and turned about till it came up to me, when it took from my hand a piece of biscuit: the dogs leapt about me, but kept at a respectful distance, because Trusty was by my side and none dared venture near him. I aroused my garrison and then proceeded to the river, whence I could survey my maize field, which glistened like a dark pine forest, and in which a horseman would have been completely hidden; then I went into the garden, which I found in admirable order, and in which the most magnificent melons were ripening. When I returned to the fort the milch cows were leaving the enclosure, and shone in the morning sun as if they had been curry-combed. My favourite cock, Whip, called his numerous harem out to breakfast on the prairie; and two pigs hurried with their farrows towards the river, for the purpose of going to the wood.

After breakfast I saddled the cream-colour, for which the saddle girths had grown much too tight, and rode with one of my men and Trusty to the other side of the river, towards the old buffalo path that led to the prairie; we reached the skirt of the wood, and had not ridden far through it when Trusty, who was ahead, stopped and looked up at me. I dismounted and perceived a number of footsteps made by mocassins. A little farther on the grass was trampled down by a great number of horses' hoofs. My foreboding was then confirmed. The entire Indian tribe had laid wait for me in the woods, and I should certainly have fallen a victim to their treachery if my good star had not warned me of their design. I silently thanked my guardian angel, who had already led me through so many dangers, and rode back to the fort, which I reached shortly before noon, with a very fat deer I had shot on passing through the wood, and which hung across my comrade's saddle.

A few days' rest at home did me a wonderful deal of good; and I felt remarkably comfortable. In the afternoon I swung in a hammock in the verandah before my house, smoking a cigar; and in the evening I sat till a late hour in a rocking chair in my neatly furnished room, and sang to the guitar songs from the past days of youth and passion. My house consisted of but one large room, whose walls and ceiling were covered with the finest dark-haired buffalo hides, while a carpet of smooth summer deer hides enlivened the floor. Over my bed was the skin of a splendid spotted jaguar, and in front of it was spread a coal-black bear skin, on which Trusty slept. The walls were adorned with excellent oil-paintings; among them being a very fine specimen of Murillo; and from the ceiling hung a lamp, which, throwing its faint light on the dark walls, produced a weak but pleasant illumination. On the table in front of the glass stood two large orange-hued gourds filled with water, in which stood splendid bouquets of magnolias, which spread their vanilla perfume through the whole room; close by was a glass case containing my firearms; and on all the walls were displayed the most splendid antlers of our common deer, the giant deer, elks, moose, and antelopes. A collection of good engravings, a small library, and my drawing apparatus, completed the furniture of this asylum, to which I frequently retired when I returned home from a long tour, covered with dust and blood, and was beginning to grow tired of this rough, savage mode of life. At such times I looked out the clothes of civilization—the tail coat and polished boots; and Trusty in his amazement would not take his eyes off me, as if he were afraid that I should at last become quite another man. Although this metamorphosis may appear so ridiculous, it had something about it most soothing and pleasant for me. I then occupied myself for some days with reading, answering my letters, drawing, and music; after which I again donned my deer-hide suit, and threw myself into the arms of nature with my faithful companions.

I had been at home for about a week, had only hunted close to the fort, and in addition to domestic arrangements, occupied myself principally with fishing, for which purpose I fastened a strong cord across the stream, on which were a number of lines and hooks hanging baited in the water. A small bell in the middle of the cord informed us when a fish or turtle was tugging at it, and we fetched them ashore with the canoe. We only cared for large fish, and it was no rarity for us to pull up cat-fish and buffalo-fish weighing thirty pounds, trout of twelve, and turtles of forty pounds.

Early one morning I was engaged in shoeing Czar's forefeet, as I always kept a stock of shoes and nails by me, after which I returned to my room to write letters, as I intended to send one of my men in a few days with commissions to the nearest settlement. I had been writing about half an hour, with Trusty lying under the table in the middle of the room, when the door opened, and I of course expected it was one of my own people. Trusty, however, sprang up barking, from under the table, and pulled me down as I tried to hold him back by the tail. In an instant the furious animal leaped at the throat of a stranger dressed in leather, who came into the room with a long Kentucky rifle, pulled him down, and would certainly have killed him in a few minutes, if I had not thrust my hands between the dog's jaws and forced them open, though his teeth were buried deep in my fingers.

With all my strength I lay on the desperate dog, and my men dragged the stranger out of the door, while I was scarce able to hold back the animal, which leaped up madly at the closed door. I hurried out to the stranger, in whom I recognised a bee-hunter, who had paid me a visit about a year previously. He was seriously hurt, though not mortally, as it seemed. I at once took him into the house, continually applied cold bandages and nursed him as well as I could during the four days he remained with me. Then I discharged him, after stocking him amply with powder and ball, coffee and salt, needles, thread, and other articles, and begging him, when he next visited me, to knock at my door first. I was very anxious not to have these bee-hunters against me, as they might prove even more dangerous than savages. They are generally scape-gallows from the States, and live in the desert with their horse and rifle by hunting, and collecting honey and wax, the former of which they pack in fresh-sewn deer hides, and carry it with the wax and peltry to the Indian settlements for the purpose of selling or swapping. He left me perfectly contented, and with assurances of gratitude and friendship, and I was very glad to get rid of this unbidden guest.

One evening, as the sun was setting, I felt a necessity of hearing the crack of my rifle. Czar had fattened up again, and Trusty was anxiously awaiting the day when I should recover from my indolence. I rode down the river to a small pond on the prairie, which was filled with rain water in the winter and retained it till far into the summer. Strangely enough, all animals prefer this water to any other, and will go a long distance to drink it. I led Czar into the bushes, threw his bridle over a branch, and sat down on the edge of the forest upon the roots of an old oak, waiting for the game that might come to water.

It was growing dark when a herd of deer came across the prairie and posted themselves on a hill behind the pond. They were all rather large, but one of them had antlers far larger than the rest. After a short halt they advanced up to the water hole, with the big deer at their head. It had drunk, and was raising its head with the mighty antlers, when I pulled the trigger, and the bullet struck behind the shoulder blade. He ran away from the other deer to a broad, rather deep ravine, formed by the torrents, and which gradually grew narrower. I mounted Czar after reloading, and rode after the deer, which suddenly rose before me and leaped up the steep wall of the ravine. It was already very dark, and I was afraid of losing the deer, hence I called Trusty to follow it. Nothing could please him better; he ran after it up the wall, and pursued it into the prairie with loud barking. As the spot was too steep for me, I ran back, and when I reached the prairie lower down I saw the deer proceeding towards the woods, and two dogs instead of one following it. I gave Czar the reins, in order to cut the deer off; but Trusty caught it at the moment, and the supposed second dog, an enormous white wolf, attacked my dog. All three lay atop of each other, when I leaped from my horse within shot, and hurried to the scene of action. The wolf noticed me and tried to bolt, but Trusty held it tightly, and I ran within ten paces of them. The two animals were leaping up savagely at each other, when my bullet passed through the wolf's side, and Trusty settled it. The deer, which had thirty tines, had got up again, but soon fell on a leap from Trusty, and I killed it. I then rode home, fetched a two-wheeled cart drawn by a mule, drove out with one of my men, and brought back the deer and the wolf, whose skin, though not so fine as in winter, still made an excellent carpet under our dining-table.

There was nothing to do now in the fields, whence we seldom went there, and our visits were limited to one of us crossing the river at daybreak in a canoe hollowed out of a monstrous poplar, and walking round the field with a fowling piece, in order to put a check to the countless squirrels which sprang over the fence to reach the forest at daybreak, partly because they did great damage to the young maize, partly because they supplied an excellent dish for breakfast. Another animal which we killed in these walks was the racoon, which also injured the maize, and inhabited our forests in incredible numbers. We merely shot it because it injured the maize, for its flesh is uneatable. Its skin, though highly valued in Europe, fetches no price among us. It visits the fields at night, clambers up the maize stalks, nibbles a few seeds out of a cob, and then runs to another plant. The result is that the gnawed cobs rot and die.

I was taking this walk one morning round the field, when I saw on the railings at the hinder end several whole stalks hanging, and found one on the ground in the forest. I went into the field and found large spaces where all the stalks had been pulled up and carried off, but could not recognise a trail on the soil, which was thickly overgrown with weeds and grass. I followed the trail into the forest, and found at no great distance from the first maize stalk a footprint on the ground, which seemed made only with the heel, and which I took for a mocassin. The maize, however, was not ripe yet, and not even large enough for boiling, and hence it seemed to me improbable that Indians had carried off the plants. I sought farther, and soon found a quite distinct enormous bear's footprint, which indicated the thief more clearly. When evening came, I and one of my men seated ourselves in the maize with Trusty on a couple of chairs we carried there. I had my large double-barrel loaded with pistol bullets, and my comrade a double rifle. We sat for a long time, as the moon shone now and then; but at length we grew tired of waiting, and I got up to go home, but at the same moment fancied I could hear the crackling of drift wood. I fell back on my chair; at the same moment the railing in front of me grew dark, and almost immediately Bruin appeared with his broad chest, and peered about in all directions. Piff! paff! I let fly both barrels at him; he disappeared behind the railing, and we could hear him dashing through the wood. We went home, and on the next morning at daybreak we followed the trail along which Trusty led us to the dead bear, which had only run a mile. Its fat and meat fully compensated for the damage it had effected in the field.

It was the summer season, and the heat was growing very oppressive. Hence I carefully avoided hunting buffalo, for fear of tiring my horse too much, and restricted myself to supplying our wants with deer, turkeys, and antelopes in the vicinity; but our supply of salted and smoked meat was at an end, and I resolved to go after buffalo on a day which was not quite so hot. Trusty had run himself lame in following deer recently, as his feet had grown soft through doing nothing, so I left him at home and rode down the river on Czar early one morning.

About ten miles from home I saw from the wood whose skirt I was following, a small herd of about twenty buffalo bulls grazing on an elevation on the prairie. I hid my rifle in a bush that I might ride more easily, took a revolver from my belt, and went cautiously under the hill as near as I could to the animals. Suddenly they saw me, broke into a gallop, and tried to escape; I went after them, and though I had to ride over many stony broken places in the bottom on the other side, I soon caught them up, and fired a bullet behind the shoulder blade of a fat old bull; it at once went slower, remained behind the herd, and bled profusely from the mouth and nostrils, but still galloped on, as I did by its side a short distance off.

At a spot where a valley entered the prairie, I shot ahead, and, as I expected, it turned aside into the bottom. It was in a very bad state, and I awaited it to turn at bay any moment, when I would kill it with another shot; still it kept up its speed, and I, tired of the chase, rode up behind to kill it with a shot from a short distance. I had hardly risen in the right stirrup, however, and leant over to fire, when the bull turned with lightning speed, drove his horn under the stirrup, and hurled me such a height in the air, that, on looking down from above, I could see Czar dash off frantically and fall in the tall grass.

In an instant I sprang on my legs again, and three paces from me stood the monster with its head on the ground, braying furiously, and stamping its fore feet. It was nearly all over, but still I held my revolver pointed between the bull's little blood-red eyes, and waited like a statue for the moment when it charged, to send a bullet through its shaggy forehead. But it was in too bad a state, and hence turned away a few minutes after and went round me; the mortal spot was now exposed, I fired, and the bull fell dead; I then ran up the nearest hillock, through the tall grass, where I arrived greatly fatigued, and looked about for Czar, whom I saw in the distance flying over the prairie with his snow-white tail fluttering in the breeze.

I felt terribly frightened at this sight, for this region was rarely free from wild horses, and I was well aware that if Czar once got among them he would be eternally lost to me. I was looking after him in desperation, when I noticed in front of him a long black line apparently coming towards me; I looked through my telescope, and recognised a herd of buffalo which, aroused by some cause, were galloping towards my horse in a long line; Czar stopped, raising his head high in the air, then turned and came straight towards me with flying mane; I collected all my strength to reach one of the highest spots around that lay in the course of my terrified horse. He dashed through the last bottom over the trailing grass, dragging the tiger skin after him which hung down on one side of the saddle.

On hearing my cry he stopped and recognised me, ran to me, and stood trembling all over by my side, while timidly looking round at the pursuing column. With one bound I was on his back, and felt myself once more lord of the desert. The buffaloes halted on the nearest elevation, looked at me for some minutes, and then dashed into the bottom on the right. I then rode back to my buffalo, broke it up, hung its tongue and fillet on the saddle, and started home, fetching my rifle as I passed. I reached the fort at noon, saddled the cream-colour after we had drunk coffee, and then went out with the cart, to fetch the very fat meat of my vanquished foe. It was then cut into long thin strips, and packed into a cask with alternate layers of salt; after it had lain thus for a few days it was put up on long sticks, and hung over a very smoky fire in the burning sun, when in a few hours it became dry enough to be carried into the smoke-house, where it kept good for a very long time.

One morning my men were busily engaged in hanging up the dried meat in the smoke-house, when one of them came running up to me and informed me that a herd of buffaloes was coming up close to the garden on the river. I seized my rifle and darted out, shouting to my men to keep back the dogs, but to let them all loose when I waved my handkerchief. I ran out of the fort, and in a stooping posture along a prairie hollow, in order to get before the buffaloes, which were marching two and two in a long row up from the river to the prairie, and lay down in the long grass under an elevation for which they were steering. I had been lying there but a few minutes when the first bulls appeared on the heights, and I shot one of them, though without showing myself. The buffalo stopped, sank on its knees, and fell over, while the others gathered round it, looked at it for a long time, and then tried to make it get up by pushing it with their horns. If you do not show yourself, you can in this way kill a great number of these animals, as they are not frightened by the sound of a rifle.

After reloading I rose on one knee and shot a second, which I hit in the knee, however, instead of behind the shoulder. I saw that it had noticed me, for it turned round, and, with its head down, dashed upon me from the heights. I sprung up and waved my handkerchief, and then threw myself full length in a narrow gully, while the hunting cry of my people in the fort reached my ear, and I recognised Trusty's voice among my dogs.

I heard the thunder of the savage bull approaching me, as it made the ground shake under me, and I looked up, expecting every minute to see the monster leap over me; but when it was within about twenty yards of me it stopped with a terrible roar, as it had lost me, and now saw my dogs dashing up the valley like unchained furies. Prince Albert, one of my young bloodhounds, was the foremost, and behind him came Lady Elsler, his bitch, both equally fast and courageous. They dashed past me. I rose, and now came Trusty with his mouth wide open, furious that another dog should dare to assault the enemy before him. My hunting-cry echoed far over the prairie, where the two bloodhounds hung by the thick hide of the infuriated buffalo on its wounded side, while Trusty pinned its monstrous muzzle, in which he buried his fangs, which never loosed their hold.

The buffalo fell back a few paces, and then rose, with Trusty still hanging to its snout, on its colossal hind legs, snorting furiously. I could not shoot on account of the dog, and the raging brute dashed over the prairie, holding Trusty in the air, who only every now and then was able to touch the ground with his feet. Ere long, however, the whole pack had caught up the fugitives, and the brave dogs hung like leeches from the buffalo's shaggy coat. Still it dashed on with them toward the river, at a spot where the bank was forty feet high.

I looked after them with terror, for there was no doubt but that the buffalo would dash over, and in that case most of my dogs, and Trusty more especially, would be buried beneath it. A few more leaps, and they would have reached the precipice, but at this moment the monster rose in the air and turned over, covered by my dogs. It roared and raged, till the sound echoed through the forest, but was unable to get on its forelegs again, because Trusty kept its head pinned down to the ground. I could hardly breathe when I reached the buffalo: I held my rifle to its broad forehead, and sent a bullet through its hard skull. The fight was at an end, and Trusty came up to me, panting and wagging his tail, while he looked up to me as much as to say that it had been a tough job. He limped a little, and Leo, a very brave dog, had a considerable wound between the ribs, but none of the others were hurt.

We returned to the fort, and were preparing to fetch the meat in the cart, when we saw a horseman coming down the river, who soon dismounted at the gate, and walked up to me with a pleasant good morning, and shook my hand. He was indubitably the handsomest man I had ever seen, and the beauty of his form was heightened by his tight-fitting and neatly-made leathern dress. He was scarce twenty years of age, above six feet high, with a small head, long neck, broad retreating shoulders, a full chest, a very small waist, and muscular though handsomely-shaped legs, which were supported by very delicate ankles and feet, almost too small for his height. His lofty forehead was surrounded by black shining silky locks, and beneath his sharply-cut black eyebrows his blue eyes shone with a calmness and decision, but also with a kindliness, that it was impossible to offer him an unfavourable reception. His black silky beard passed under his straight nobly-formed nose round his smiling, partly-opened mouth, between whose cherry lips two rows of transparent white teeth were visible, and heightened the white complexion of his oval face and the fresh ruddiness of his cheeks. Thus this god of the desert stood before me with a grace and propriety such as are rarely met with in the gouty circles of high society; and I thought to myself that his appearance would attract attention and respect, in spite of the leathern garb, among the nobility of the Old World.

Without asking him who he was, I gave him the hearty welcome which his amiability claimed, led him to the dining-room, had his luggage brought into the fort, and his horse put in a stall and supplied with maize leaves. Then a breakfast was set before my guest, and after begging him, in the old Spanish fashion, to make my house his home, I apologized for being obliged to leave him a little while, as I had shot some buffaloes close by, which I wanted to get home.

"Will you allow me to assist you? I am a good hand at it," was his reply. He had soon finished his breakfast, and went with me out of the fort to the river bank where the buffalo lay. Although I had introduced Trusty to the stranger, the dog still pressed between him and me, which he noticed and remarked.

"You have a fine hound there, who has grown up in the desert. I have heard of him before. He is no friend of bee-hunters, and yet he does not seem savage with me."

I begged him not to touch Trusty, as he might misunderstand it, and we soon reached my quarry. The stranger, whose name was Warden, as he told me, laid aside his leathern jacket, which was tastily ornamented with fringe, turned up his shirt-sleeves, displaying thus his finely formed muscular and white arms, and drew a splendid hunting-knife from its sheath. We set to work together in skinning the buffalo, in which operation Warden displayed a remarkable skill, then broke it up, and while my people carried the meat to the fort we proceeded to the other buffalo higher up the prairie, and prepared it in the same way for removal.

While we were engaged in skinning this animal, Warden remarked he was surprised at my using rifles of so large a bore, as it was a settled fact that the long Kentucky rifles, one of which he carried, produced much greater effect with small bullets. I contradicted this assertion, and an argument ensued, as neither would give up his opinion. Warden offered a wager, and staked his rifle against one of mine, which I accepted. We cut off the buffalo's head with the skin attached to it, and had it carried to the fort with the meat, in order to try our rifles on it. It was noon when we got back. We cleaned ourselves and enjoyed our dinner, a buffalo fillet roasted on the spit, and some of the marrow-bones.

After drinking coffee and smoking a cigar, we carried the buffalo head outside the fort, put it in front of an oak, pressed a piece of white paper on the forehead, and then walked eighty paces back, I shot first, and my bullet passed through the paper into the head, and an inch deep into the oak. Warden fired next, and also sent his bullet into the piece of paper, but there was no trace of the bullet on the tree behind the head. We removed the skin from the skull and found Warden's bullet lodged under it, close to the hole which mine had made. Warden at once allowed the bet lost, but at the same time requested me to sell him a gun, as he could not exist without one. I naturally laughed, as my only object in the matter was conviction, and the bet had only been a joke. Warden, however, shot with surprising accuracy at one hundred yards with his rifle, which was four feet and a half long, the whole weight resting on the left hand in front; but his ball rarely passed through a deer, except when he was close to it.

After supper, while we were lying on the grass on the river bank, my guest told me that he was a native of Missouri, the son of a farmer, but had been compelled by unfortunate circumstances to quit home, and had been living for five years as a desert hunter. At first he remained on the frontiers of his own State, but the cold winters had continually driven him to the south, until he at last got so far down to a country whose climate agreed better with him. He remained a whole week with me, and made himself useful during the day through his skill in making all sorts of trifles; for instance, carvings in poplar and cypress wood, plaiting strong tight lines of different coloured horsehair, tanning skins, making neatly ornamental powder flasks out of buffalo horns, and charge measures of the fangs of bears and jaguars, while in the evening he described in a most lively manner the numerous dangers he had fortunately escaped, and the many fights he had had with the Redskins during the five years.

The unchanging calmness which usually covered his noble face often deserted him when describing these scenes; his eyes flashed like daggers in the moonlight, his brow contracted, and we could read on his forehead that he must be a terrible foe when aroused. But these outbursts of passion soon passed away, and the ordinary gentleness spread once more over his features. Among the feelings reflected on various occasions in his face, there was an unmistakeable melancholy, which must be produced by events of his life before the period when he bade farewell to human society, and this was proved by the fact that he spoke reluctantly about that time, and always became silent when the conversation was accidentally turned to it. Hence I carefully avoided alluding to the period, for if a heavy crime lay hid in his bosom, I was ready to excuse it; while if he was suffering undeservedly, I pitied him, and would not augment his sorrow by unnecessarily evoking his reminiscences.

I would have gladly kept him with me, as he was a pleasant, attractive companion in my solitude; but he would go, and it seemed to me as if the tranquillity he enjoyed at my house did not permanently satisfy him, and as if he wished to deaden memory by the wild, perilous life he led on his hunting expeditions. I equipped him as far as lay in my power with everything that could soothe his fatiguing life, and took a hearty leave of him in front of the fort. He parted regretfully, and was greatly excited when he shook my hand in farewell and mounted his powerful horse, which he had trained like a dog. He promised to pay me another visit soon, and galloped at such a pace over the prairie, as if he wished thus to dispel the thoughts which had mastered him. I watched him for a long distance, till he disappeared in a cloud of dust on the edge of the prairie.

Some time after I learned from the bee-hunter whom Trusty received so savagely the history of this amiable but unfortunate man, whom the former had known as a lad in Missouri. Warden's father was the son of one of the first families in Virginia; was educated at a first-rate school and studied medicine. He got into bad company, turned gambler and then highwayman, and was for some years the terror of post travellers in North Carolina and Virginia. About this time he fell in love with a very beautiful, fashionably educated young lady in Virginia, and ran away with her to Missouri, which was just beginning to be colonized. He altered his mode of life, was greatly respected by his fellow-citizens, and in a few years sent to Congress as deputy for Missouri. Thus he lived most creditably till his son was twelve years of age, and his daughter was married at the age of seventeen to a farmer. One day, however, he rode to the nearest town where a court was being held, and for the first time during many years tasted spirits. He had scarce done so, ere his old wicked foe seized on him again with all its might, and he rode daily, in spite of all the prayers and representations of his family, to the town, and returned at night in a most frightful state of intoxication.

On the next court day he was about to ride again to town, when his wife begged her son-in-law to accompany him. Warden had been drinking already, and said he had a feeling he should be killed during the day. He made his young son take a solemn oath to follow his murderer to the end of the world and take his life. Then he rode off to the town, soon became intoxicated, began quarrelling, at length began wrangling with his son-in-law, who tried to hold him back, and drew his knife on him; the latter defended himself, and Warden ran on his knife, and was carried home in a dying state. Warden once again reminded his son of the oath he had taken, and expired. The law was put in work against his son-in-law, who fled to Indiana and lived there in concealment. Warden's son grew up, and in his sixteenth year was the favourite of the whole countryside, but then he took his rifle and his horse, bade good-bye to his mother and sister, rode to Indiana, and shot his brother-in-law in his own house. He escaped from the police with great difficulty, and fled to the desert, where he had been living five years when he visited me.

CHAPTER XI
THE WILD HORSE

The departure of the unfortunate Warden, who had fallen a victim to passions which had not been held in restraint at an early age, was very painful to me, and the evenings, which I generally spent alone, grew very long, as I had before gossiped half the night away with him. Hence I went to bed early, and followed my old habit of rising before daybreak, I generally took my rifle, went with Trusty across the river to the forest and watched for game. At that hour the wood was most beautiful; the coming day drove the darkness before it through the mighty masses of foliage, the birds aroused one another from their sleep, owls, blinded by the morning light, darted like the last shadows of night into the densest thickets, and deer returned home from their nocturnal excursions through the dewy grass; the bear, startled by the rapidly-increasing light, trotted with hoarse growls towards its secret hiding-place, while the herons, bearing the first golden sunbeams on their silver plumage, rose from the tall trees and passed with flapping wing through the refreshing morning breeze.

I was cautiously walking one morning along this my favourite spot, and inhaling the thousand perfumes which had filled the recesses of the forest during the tranquil night, avoiding every dry branch for fear of startling its denizens, while Trusty followed at a short distance all my windings round the bushes and fallen trees. It had become tolerably light, when I fancied I heard a rustling at an open spot, in the centre of which stood several very large pecan-nut trees. I stood still for a moment and listened, holding my breath, for a repetition of the noise. I heard it again, like the breaking of twigs ahead of me, but in spite of my utmost efforts could not perceive that even a leaf was moving.

Once again the same breaking and rustling reached me, and on looking up accidentally I saw a thick black lump shining among the foliage of the pecan-trees. I soon distinguished a young bear busily engaged in drawing to it with its long paws the thin branches of the nut-tree, and putting the unripe nuts in its mouth, I quickly sprang under the tree, so as to make sure of the bear, which was about the size of a sheep; but I remembered its mamma, who might be in the neighbourhood, and easily come up to fetch her pet home. I stationed myself under the tree on which the cub was, and made Trusty lie down by my side, as he was beginning to growl, and pressing his nose against the tree.

The bear saw me, and became greatly alarmed; sprang from one branch to the other, and looked timidly down to me. I did not move, but listened carefully to every sound in the vicinity, while my neighbour came down to the first floor, above my head; and, sitting among the lowest branches, produced a cry like that of little children. It soon repeated its wail, and I heard far away in the forest a hob, hob, hob, hob, coming towards me. I sprang up, and placed myself behind the trees, after again forcing Trusty's head into the grass. I distinctly distinguished by the leaps that it was an old bear hastening to the help of her cub. I pointed my rifle in the direction whence it was coming, and suddenly it parted the foliage in front of me with its broad shoulders, whereupon I gave a loud "pst." In a second the bear sat up on its hind-quarters, and as the fire flashed from my barrel it made a couple of leaps towards me, but was rolled over by a second bullet through the head, while I shouted a "Down, sir!" to Trusty, who was on the point of springing up. I drew a revolver, ran up to the old bear, and sent a bullet through her brain, as she was still furiously hitting out with her terrible paws.

I next reloaded my rifle, and looked up at my neighbour, who had fled to the top of the tree, and was swinging with the branches. I called Trusty away from under the tree, bade him lie down in the grass behind me, and gave the cub something which brought it down like a ball, crashing through the foliage to the ground, when I put the other barrel to its forehead, and stopped its young bearish existence. After reloading, I broke it up, to give Trusty his share of the spoil—the kidneys, the only bear-meat he ever touched, unless he was very hungry. I then hastened home, and after breakfast I went back to the forest with one of my men and three mules, when we broke up the old bear, and carried the meat home on two of the animals, and the cub entire on the third.

Thus several weeks passed, during which I went little beyond the immediate vicinity of my house, in order to lay in our stock of meat either in the morning or evening, when the heat was less oppressive. During the day we were cutting steps in the perpendicular river-bank, out of which a very strong spring gushed about ten feet from the top, and in building a small dairy over it. We led the spring through wooden troughs, in which we kept the milk and butter sweet; while we hung up on the walls meat which remained fresh for several days. The dairy was on the north side, so that it was very slightly exposed to the sun, whose effects we also neutralized by a thick layer of overhanging reeds. This spot was most agreeable in the midday heat, at which time the atmosphere in the houses was most oppressive, while here it always remained cool and refreshing through the ice-cold water. The spring, however, was not so pleasant for drinking as the one I had on the side of the prairie near the garden, from which we fetched our drinking water.

After finishing my job, most of my stores were nearly expended, and I required a number of new tools. Hence I went myself to the nearest settlement, sold there my stock of hides, honey, wax, and tallow, and took home the articles I needed on my pack animals. While at the settlement I met, at the store-keeper's with whom I was bargaining, a Mexican lad, sixteen years of age, who had accompanied a brace of mules brought here from Mexico for sale, and had remained as waiter at the hotel. His name was Antonio, and he offered to go with me and stop. He was recommended to me by an acquaintance as a first-rate horseman and lassoer, and as he pleased me in other respects, I accepted his offer, and he rode with me home.

Antonio's skill in riding was extraordinary; it was all the same to him whether he had a bridle or not—whether he sat in a saddle or bare-backed; once on the animal's back, no rearing or kicking could throw him. I have often seen him go up to mules grazing on the prairie, and approach them quietly, lounging round them as if seeking something in the grass, till he was near enough to them, when with a spring he was on the back of one of them, and the terrified creature made all sorts of bounds and leaps to get rid of him. But it was all in vain. Antonio responded to the mule's efforts with his monstrous spurs, which he dug into its flanks at every volley, till he grew tired of riding, and sprang off again with the same lightness.

He also threw the lasso with a master hand. I have frequently seen him at full gallop catch a mule by the foot which I indicated. One day he lassoed by the fore leg a wild cow which had joined my milch kine on the prairie, hurled it to the ground, and so bound its four feet together that we dragged it along to the enclosure where my cows passed the night. Then we fastened it up to an old tree, and on the next morning Antonio leaped on its back, cut away the rope round its head, and galloped off into the prairie, where the cow leapt about as if mad. At last, after a lengthened contest, she threw herself on the ground; but Antonio stood by her side, gave her laughingly a cut with his whip, and the awfully terrified creature galloped away to the forest.

Between the fort and the mountain spring there were always a great number of wild horses, especially in the vicinity of a considerable elevation on the prairie, whose highest point was covered with a small very thick wood, where a white stallion resided with his harem. Owing to his beauty and noble blood, the Indians revered this animal with superstitious fear. The hunters had tried for years in vain to capture him, and the bards of America had raised him to immortality in their ballads and narrations. Very numerous are the wondrous tales which spread at that day about the noble animal over the continent of America, and even distant Europe. He was described in them as "the star of the prairie," as "the light of the steppe," or "the white spirit of the desert." While his titles varied so, the statements as to the position of his kingdom varied equally. But all these were merely traditions of the hunters of the Far West, the existence of the horse was still half fabulous, and I believe that I am the only man capable of saying anything on the subject from personal observation.

I have seen and admired this horse a countless number of times, as my hunts so frequently passed in his region, and quite as often I have yearned to possess, and revolved the means to get, him into my power. This was one of the reasons why I took Antonio into my service, as through him alone I had a prospect of attaining my wish. I have frequently crawled up to the animal for miles through the tall grass with the utmost exertions, and lain down on a small mound near him, with the resolution of creasing him, as the hunters call it—that is to say, sending a ball through the skin of a horse's neck, upon which it falls as if struck dead, and you have time to hobble it before it recovers. But when I raised the rifle on the noble creature, and had my finger on the trigger, it seemed to me to be murder, and I could never make up my mind to fire. I have often ridden up to him, and, so soon as he noticed me, he came toward me, proudly raising his graceful head in the air, with his white silky tail erect, and with a coat as white and tender as the finest alabaster or the plumage of the silver heron, with whose flight I have often seen him compete. He frequently came within fifty yards of me, looking round pretty often at his flying harem, then stopped and snorted through his dilated purple nostrils; then he trotted round me, and would fly like an arrow over the grass to his friends, at such a pace that no rider in the world would have made the attempt to catch him up.

In the past winter I went to his domain with the intention of capturing one of his children, and gave one of my men who accompanied me my rifle and revolver, in order to make myself as light as possible. I had got no great distance from the troop, ere the stallion noticed me, and when the others fled, he as usual trotted toward me. I gave Czar his head, and galloped towards him. The wild stallion reared, then turned, and dashed after his troop and past it, in order to assume the leadership. At the end of five miles I caught up the troop again, which consisted of about fifty head, and selected an iron-grey mare with black mane and tail, which appeared to be between a two and three-year old.

Had I possessed any great skill in using the lasso, I was near enough to the mare to noose her; but as it was I could only take advantage of my horse's greater endurance, and remained close behind the troop, up hill and down dale, while the stallion flew from one side to the other, as if encouraging his relatives to persevere, and this race was merely play to him. The animals became covered with foam, their breathing grew gradually shorter, and several left the ranks on either side, in order to seek safety in an altered direction.

At last only four old mares and the iron-grey followed the stallion, who as yet displayed no signs of fatigue; when suddenly the grey turned off into a hollow, fell into a walk, and at last stopped; so that I could ride up and throw the lasso over her head. She was so exhausted that she could hardly breathe, and stood motionless, while the perspiration ran down her in torrents. It was nearly a quarter of an hour ere she so far recovered as to be able to struggle against the fetters laid on her. The noose round her neck tightened; she fell to the ground, trembling all over; and I leapt from my horse to open the noose, before she was quite throttled. My companion now came up, hobbled his own horse and Czar, and helped me to convince the mare by repeated strangulation, that she must yield to her captivity: we made a halter out of a second lasso, while still keeping the noose round her neck, and I dragged her after my horse, while my companion urged her on. We thus reached home in the evening; and in a few weeks the mare was so tame that she could be treated precisely like my other horses: she was handsomely built, displayed all the signs of Arab blood, and became one of my best horses.

As I said, the possibility of capturing this stallion—the pride of the western deserts—was the reason of my engaging Antonio; and we at once set about our preparations to carry out the task. I owned a thorough-bred mare, Fancy, who belonged to the best blood that ever ran on American soil. Her sire was the renowned Waggoner, who was never beaten in speed either north or south, and for fourteen years won all the great stakes at American races. Her dam, Blossom, was an English thoroughbred, and had been imported to the United States from England: she won all the stakes she was entered for in the Southern States, and was purchased by one of the first breeders for a very large sum, that he might become owner of her noble progeny. Fancy, then, as regards breed, was as fine and noble as any horse that ever trod an American course, and defeated all her rivals until

I purchased her. I bought her as a four-year old when I bade farewell to civilization, and took her with me into the desert, where I frequently rode her, when I went out into the prairie with greyhounds to hunt deer or kill wolves. On my ordinary hunting trips, however, she could not take the place of Czar or the cream-colour, as she was not so attached to me by constant riding or so trained and familiar with a thousand dangers as they were.

The mare was now treated with very great attention, both as regards food, and cleanliness, and exercise; she had no more grass, and the corn given her was previously sifted. She was ridden every morning by Antonio, and the distance she had to gallop was daily increased. Then she was led about for half an hour, and when brought back to her stall rubbed down till she was quite dry and cool. Toward evening she was taken out again for half an hour's walk, and before she went to rest had a douche or a swim in the river. In a fortnight she hardly turned a hair after galloping several miles; she had grown thinner, but her flesh was firmer, and her golden-brown hair so fine that every vein could be traced under the skin. In the meanwhile, Antonio had been practising with the lasso, and had horribly tormented my mules with this disagreeable instrument.

The preparations lasted three weeks; after which, on a cool morning, we left the fort: Antonio riding a mule and leading Fancy, one of my colonists on the cream-colour, and I on Czar—in order to seek the stallion, and, if possible, deprive him of liberty. It was one of those days—not rare in our country—when the sky is covered with a thin stratum of clouds, which deprive it of its glorious azure, and which, though it does not conceal the sun, breaks the power of its beams. At the same time there was a breeze, so that the day was more like autumn than summer. We rode down the river, and soon saw the height emerge from the prairie, in whose vicinity the stallion usually had his head-quarters. Our horses were very active; Czar coquetted by the side of his lady friend, Fancy, in his most elegant prancing movements; shook his bit, and snorted through his moist nostrils; while turning his dark large eyes toward the lady, Fancy, conscious of her noble breed, walked delicately along, and carefully selected the footpaths.

While still some distance off, I noticed to the side of the wood on the knoll a dark patch, which I recognised through my glass as horses, but could not make certain whether it was our stallion's family. We approached slowly, and from every new height distinguished more clearly the shape of the animals. I had no doubt about it being the troop we were in search of, although I could not yet notice the stallion. A broad valley still lay between us, when we halted, and I saw through my glass the snow-white creature rise from the grass and look across at us, while many horses of the troop still lay on the ground around him. We rode down into the valley, the stallion stood motionless, and gazed at us; but when we reached the bottom, he suddenly trotted about among his troop. All the horses lying on the grass leapt up, looked at us, formed into a body, and dashed at a gallop over the heights.

Antonio now sprang into Fancy's saddle, gave his mule to our companion, took the lasso in his right hand, and only waited for my signal to give his horse her head. The stallion came toward us at a swinging trot, while we moved forward at a fast pace and bent low over our horses' necks. A finer picture could not be painted. He carried his small head high, long white locks floated over his broad forehead, and his long mane danced up and down at every step, while he raised his tail straight out, and its long curling milk-white hairs fluttered in the breeze. His broad back glistened as if carved out of Carrara marble, and his powerful shoulders and thighs were supported on graceful little feet.

I rode behind Antonio. The stallion was not fifty yards from us when I shouted to the Mexican "Forward!" and Fancy flew at such a pace toward the stallion that she came within five yards of him ere he recovered from his terror. The moment for his fate to be decided had arrived. He turned round and made an enormous leap ahead, that showed me the flat of his hind hoofs, while he held his head aside and looked back after his pursuer. The lasso flew through the air, the noose fell over the stallion's head, but it hung on one side of his muzzle, and the next instant the lasso was trailing on the ground behind Fancy. The stallion seemed to know that it was a fetter which had touched him, for he shot away from the man like lightning. Antonio coiled up the lasso again, and followed him over hill and vale, over grass and boulders, at full gallop, just as the tornado darts from the mountain into the plain. Czar was beside himself at the idea of being last, but I purposely held him back, partly not to excite the mare, partly to save his strength. There was still a hope that the stallion, living as he did on grass, would not keep his wind so long as our horses, and though he was now several hundred yards ahead, we might be able to catch him up. Up to this point, however, we had not gained an inch upon him, and our horses were covered with foam, though both still in good wind.

We had been following the stallion for about two hours, when he turned off to the mountains, and flew up them with undiminished speed. The ground now became very stony and unsafe, but he seemed to be as much at home on it as on the soft grass-land he had just left. He reached the summit between two steep mountains, and disappeared from our sight behind them. We dashed past the spot where we had seen him last, but the noble creature had reached the steep wall on the other side of the valley when we dashed down into it.

I saw plainly that he had a difficulty in keeping at a gallop on this steep incline. We gained a deal of ground down hill and through the grassy valley, and reached the wall before the stallion was at the top of it. Full of hope I could no longer remain in the background. Digging both spurs into Czar I flew on, past Fancy, and reached the summit to find the stallion trotting scarce fifty yards ahead of me. Fancy was close behind me, and I shouted to Antonio to follow me. But my cry seemed to have poured fresh strength through the brave fugitive's veins, for he dashed down into the valley, leaving behind the white foam with which he was covered at every bound he made on the rocky ground. Once again I drew nearer, and was only forty yards from him, when I saw ahead of us a yawning *cañon*, out of which the gigantic dry arms of dead cypresses emerged. Here the stallion must turn back and fall our prey while ascending the hill again.

But he went straight towards the abyss—it was not possible, he could not leap it. I remained behind him, and in my terror for the noble creature's life, held my breath. One more bound, and he reached the *cañon*, and with the strength of a lion, and that desperation which only the threatened loss of liberty can arouse, he drew himself together and leapt high in the air across the gap which was more than forty feet wide.

I turned Czar round toward the hill, and kept my eyes away from the fearful sight, so that I might not see the end of the tragedy; but Antonio uttered a cry, and I heard the word "over." I looked round and saw the stallion rising on his hind legs upon the opposite deeper bank, and after a glance at us he trotted off quite sound down the ravine, and disappeared behind the nearest rock.

We stopped, leapt from our horses, and looked at each other for a long time in silence; then I solemnly vowed never to make another attempt to deprive this princely animal of liberty. Our horses were in a very excited condition; the water poured down them in streams, and the play of their lungs was so violent that they tottered on their legs. We let them draw breath a little, and then led them slowly back to the mountain springs, where we intended to give them a rest ere we returned home. In the afternoon we reached the spot, excessively fatigued, and found there our comrade, who greeted us with a regretful—"that was a pity;" and had already spread our dinner on a horse-cloth.

We stopped here till the evening, and then started for the fort, which we reached late at night. For several days after this chase I could not shake off the excitement which had overpowered me, and even now I feel a cold shudder when I think of the chasm, and see the noble stallion, the pride of the prairie, hovering over it. I had now given up once for all all thoughts of capturing him, but I should have felt sorry had he at once left my dangerous neighbourhood, because his presence always caused me great pleasure, and I might have an opportunity of getting hold of some of his offspring. I sought him in vain during my hunting excursions the whole of the summer, and it was not till autumn, when the vegetation probably began to fail in the mountains, that he returned, to my great delight, to his old station; but whenever I approached him he did not trot towards me, but always took to flight as soon as he noticed my horse.

CHAPTER XII
THE PRAIRIE FIRE

The summer passed away amid sporting pleasures which, though they always consist of very monotonous events and results, still do not lose their charm for the man who feels a true passion for the chase. Otherwise how could a veteran sportsman, who in his time has shot so many thousand partridges, still feel a pleasure whenever he brings one down, and always find something new, something peculiar in the fact? How much greater and more permanent is this attraction in sports, where a thousand dangers offer themselves to the hunter, as is the case in hunting the larger animals of prey! I gratefully saluted every new day as the offerer of fresh joys: disregarding difficulties and fatigue, I constantly seized my good rifle again, and merrily followed the same routes.

The summer was at an end, and colder nights set in. On an autumn morning I was riding through the prairie about five miles from the fort; the grass was very high, and had been perfectly dried up by the burning summer sun, while the newly springing up grass grew splendidly in the shadow of the old. I had reached a bottom which was covered with a forest of sunflowers, which raised their golden disks high above my head, and whose long stems were girdled with bright varied creepers. I had not left this gleaming forest of flowers far behind when a very large deer got up from the grass just before me, arched its back, and then lay down again as if it had not seen me; while I noticed several old deer lying about in the grass.

Czar at once drooped his head as I raised the rifle to my shoulder. I shot the deer, but a little too far behind. It darted ahead, and Trusty looked up at me so imploringly, while showing the tip of his blood-red tongue, that I could not refuse him leave to follow the deer. I gave him a sign, and he shot through the grass along the blood-stained track. I loaded my rifle, while keeping my eye on the deer, which disappeared no great distance off in a small clump of low elms. I had just put on the cap when I heard Trusty's deep bass. I felt certain it was not the deer he was barking at, for he would have made but slight ceremony in that case, so I gave Czar his head, and in a few minutes reached the thicket.

I leapt down, ran in a stooping posture under the pendant elms, and saw Trusty lying on the ground defending himself with widely opened jaws against a tremendous panther, which was leaping over him, and every time it came down lacerated the dog's back with its tremendous hind claws. Trusty recognised the superiority of this savage foe, but defended himself as well as he could. But he hardly saw me arrive ere he leapt up with one bound, pinned the panther by the throat, and wrestled with it, while the latter dug its terrible fore claws into either side of his collar.

At the first moment I could not fire for fear of hitting the dog. The panther saw me, and tried to get away, but Trusty clung to it like a burr. The animal now turned, and my bullet passed through its heart and laid it lifeless. Trusty was terribly maltreated, and the wounds on his back were of the width of a finger, and I believe that his strong collar had alone saved his life. I sewed up his wounds, washed them with water, and then broke up the deer. Then I stripped the panther, and packed the game on both sides of my saddle, laid the skin over it, and placed Trusty on the top of all. I told him that he must lie quiet, and started homewards, leading Czar by the bridle. Trusty cut the most absurd face, but for all that did not stir, and after he had ridden a few hundred yards he helped me with his hind legs, when he slipped a little on one side, and I believe he would not have fallen off at a gallop. It was a week ere I could draw the threads out of the wound, and during that period Leo had to accompany me when hunting. At the end of a fortnight my faithful comrade had so far recovered that he was able to accompany me on short trips.

About this time I was riding, when the sun was rather low, up the river to the bank of a small stream, which joined the Leone a few miles above the fort, and slowly wound between its level banks through the prairie. It was here and there covered with bushes and groups of trees, while every now and then its bed widened and formed small pools. On this stream there were always a great many turkeys, and indeed the banks were visited by game of every description at all seasons. I rode down the quiet bright stream, and on coming out of a thicket on to a small clearing bordered at the other end by tall pecan-trees, I saw a flock of turkeys stealing away from me among the bushes on the bank. I ordered Trusty on, who had his nose already to the ground sniffing; he was among the fugitives like the wind; they ran, noisily and loudly pursued by Trusty, and settled on the trees. I rode close up to the wood, for so long as the turkeys see the dog springing about under them they are terrified, and look timidly at their pursuer, stretching out their long neck in all directions instead of flying away. I dismounted, shot an old cock on a tree growing close to the water, and saw it flutter down. I then turned with the other barrel to a second, which was standing on an oak farther in the thicket, and fetched it down also. I now looked round and missed Trusty. I had no reply to my shout, and the agitation in the pond aroused a fear that he had leapt in, and that an alligator, for such are always concealed in the deeper water of these streams, had seized and dragged him down.

I waited a good half-hour, it grew dark, and yet no sign of poor Trusty. Beside myself with grief at this irreparable loss I hung the turkey on the saddle, and mounted my horse, as longer waiting would be of no use. At this moment I suddenly saw Trusty at the head of the wood, lying down to rest by the side of the gigantic cock turkey. My delight knew no bounds. I galloped up the stream, dashed through it, and found my favourite on the other bank. I leapt from my horse and took him in my arms, whereon he gave vent to his joy by a widely echoing howl, and lashed his tail. I hung the turkey, which weighed over twenty pounds, and which he had carried Lord knows how far, to my saddle, and the faithful dog leaped up to my horse and barked in the utmost delight as we proceeded homeward.

We were busily engaged for a week in making some machinery on the river by which to employ the water power in turning a mill to grind the maize. A raft was fastened to the bank. A roller was placed on it, from one end of which a rather large wheel hung down into the water, while the mill was fastened to the other, whose hopper we enlarged so that we might not have to put in maize so frequently. It worked famously, and we all rejoiced at a successful operation which saved us a fatiguing job.

Owing to this I had not gone out much, and we were all longing for good fresh meat. As there were a good many buffaloes in the very neighbourhood, I resolved to hunt them on the morning after our mill was finished, as one of my men had seen large herds during the day on the prairie across the river. The morning arrived, but with it sprang up a very violent westerly wind, and a few light straggling clouds proved that it would not sink in such a hurry. In doubt whether to ride out or wait another day, my men persuaded me to the former course, as the chase would probably be soon over. Hence I rode off, but left Trusty at home, as on these prairies the dry grass was extraordinarily high and it would tire him too much to force his way through it, especially if we had to go quickly. I was soon across in the wood where, though the wind did not meet me, still it shook the tall trees so terribly that the dry wood constantly whizzed round my head. I reached the prairie on the other side of the forest, and saw several herds of buffalo in the distance.

Binding my hat firmly under my chin, I rode through the tall grass in a northern direction toward them. The storm grew more violent, and laid the grass so flat on the ground that I could not think of putting my horse beyond a walk in any other direction than with the wind, as, when the wind is blowing fiercely all game is usually more cautious than in calm weather, as it has to make up by the sight for what it loses in smell. The buffaloes noticed me and my horse, which was brilliantly illumined with the sun, a long distance off, and took to flight. I turned toward another herd, but with the same result, and saw at last that in this way I should not get within shot. After several hours of useless exertion I turned to the east, toward a spot on which some scattered oaks grew. Here I fancied it would be easier to approach the game.

The distance to the first tree-covered hill was about five miles, and I saw through my glass at the elevations behind a great number of buffaloes, which, however, seemed to be in a strange state of excitement. My horse found it hard walking owing to the dry grass, in which Czar was compelled to part the sharp tangled stalks at every step. I looked constantly toward the highland, and remarked, while the storm howled past my ears, that the sky was growing obscured and that the sunshine was not so bright as it had been a few moments previously. I looked around me, the heavens appeared to be veiled by a grey mist, and grew darker behind me, and on the edge of the prairie were perfectly black. I felt a cold shudder, for I knew the fearful element which had become allied with the storm, and would roar over the plain scattering ruin around. The prairie was on fire. It is true that I could not yet see the fire, but the black smoke clouds rose higher and higher on the horizon, and the storm soon bore them past me over the last blue patch of sky. Only one chance of escape remained. I must reach a knoll where the grass was shorter, and without reflecting I gave Czar the spurs and his head, and flew in rivalry of the storm-wind over the grassy plains before me.

I looked round; the whole black expanse behind me was gloomy and obscure as if night were setting in, and beneath the dark rising smoke-clouds the deep red glowing flames stretched out their long forks and cast their fearful light over the outlines of the cloudy columns of smoke. The whole plain seemed to grow alive. Far as eye could see, it was covered with flying herds of the denizens of the desert, whose black forms were surrounded by a fiery halo as they pressed over the plain. It was like the picture of the last judgment, which my fancy had frequently depicted.

Czar ran with long leaps through the tall grass, looking neither to the right nor left. With every moment it grew darker around me, and the reflection of the spreading sea of flame more and more tinged my horse's snow-white neck. It was not his ordinary strength that urged the horse to reach the knoll, but the force which desperation imparts to men and animals, but soon wears them out and ends in utter exhaustion. The sharp spurs and the thunder behind him urged my horse constantly on at a mad speed, but I felt his bound gradually lose its lightness and force.

I was not far from the hill in front of me; once more the spurs and my shrill hunting-cry, and I flew up the knoll, and hobbled my trembling, snorting horse on the bare table-land, which was covered with pebbles and thin patches of grass. I ran back to the tall grass with a lucifer in my hand, lit it, and in an instant the flames rose, struggling wildly against the storm, and darted round my hill, till they joined on its eastern side, and dashed along like an avalanche with the howling storm. I now looked back for the first time, holding my brave horse by the bridle, at the fearfully animated plain, and watched the dark living forms hurrying past on either side of the knoll. The whole animal world seemed assembled here, and to be exerting their last strength in escaping a death by fire. On both sides beneath me thundered past in wild confusion herd after herd—buffaloes, horses, deer, and antelopes were pressed together, and between them rushed bears, tigers, panthers, and wolves, one after the other, with their faces averted from the glow, which the storm blew with a thick black cloud of ashes over the land. Dark, black night now encompassed me; only a pale reddish glare gleamed through the dense ashes; while the hurricane developed its highest fury, and blended its howling with the hollow, earth-shaking thunder of the flying masses of animals below me.

The sea of fire was scarce half a mile from me, when the ashes passed over my head, and granted me a full look at it. The flames right and left, far as eye could see, lay obliquely over the ground and stretched out their quivering tongues for at least fifty feet over the grass. They darted forward with frightful rapidity, and caught up countless animals flying before them, whose wearied limbs could no longer carry them along quickly enough. Three old buffaloes collected their last strength to reach my knoll, but at the foot of it the flames closed over them, I saw them rear, fall back, and disappear. The heat was stifling; I and my horse,—who, trembling all over, yielded to his fate—turned our backs to it, and the stream of fire passed us on both sides, crackling and hissing.

Gradually daylight returned, and the sky became blue over my head. Thousands of large and small predaceous birds followed the flames, and fell now and then in them. On all sides lay the black carcases of the countless victims which this prairie fire had destroyed, and many animals struggling with death were rolling in their agony on the plain. Czar and I were completely covered with ashes. I now mounted my horse to get away as quickly as possible from this scene of destruction and death, and reach the green forests of the Leone by the straightest line. I rode down to the three buffaloes, two of which were not dead and strove to rise, but fell back powerless on the earth. It was a fearful sight offered by these burned monsters, and their frightened snapping for air and blind rolling of their heads induced me to put an end to the pain of the poor tortured creatures. I put a bullet through each of their flat foreheads, and after reloading, I rode in a southern direction towards the Leone.

I saw many animals still wrestling with death on both sides of the road, and might have expended the whole of my ammunition in trying to help them out of their agony. Most of the burnt animals were buffaloes and deer, but I also saw a bear and a horse and a number of wolves lying lifeless on the ground.

My road over the black, bare, burnt fields of desolation was tiring, and my horse was so worn out that I frequently dismounted and led him: although the wind was no longer so violent, it brought with it a quantity of fine ashes, and rendered both seeing and breathing difficult. I frequently came across birds of prey, whose wings only displayed the bare quills, the feathers being burnt off: they sate helpless and wretched on the ground, and tried in vain to rise into the air when I approached them. These birds regularly follow the prairie fires in large numbers, in order to eat its countless small four-footed denizens, after the fire has passed over them, and either rendered them helpless or killed them. They looked at me in terror with their large rolling eyes, spread out the quills of their wings, and uttered a complaining cry. I went past them as I could not help them.

About a mile from the wood on the Leone I saw, to my great surprise, on my right hand a very large deer and a horse walking together across the plain to the wood. They tottered along slowly side by side, and seemed not to notice me at all. I rode up to them: I fancied they had been blinded by the fire, but it was not so; for they now stopped and gazed at me with their bright eyes, as if imploring me not to prevent them from reaching the wood. Both were slightly scorched, though the horse had lost mane and tail: they appeared to have suffered more from excessive exertion, and to be yearning for the water of the Leone. I could easily have killed the deer, but I pitied the creature, and besides did not care to eat its hunted flesh or put a further load on Czar. Hence I quitted the poor creatures, and reached the wood, which is not very broad here; and soon after the river, where Czar refreshed himself for a long time in the cool waters.

Annually nearly all the western prairies are burnt by the Indians, towards spring: when they leave the south and go north to hunt they fire the old grass, so that when they return in autumn they may find on these extensive plains fresh food for their large troops of horses and mules. They have, however, I fancy, another motive. If these plains were not singed with fire, a perfectly different vegetation would arise on them within a few years. Trees and bushes would rapidly grow up and convert the prairies into an impenetrable chapparal or forest, which would be very troublesome to the horse Indians, in their hunts and journeyings. In this way, however, fire destroys every growth but that of grass. If a sapling springs up in spring from seed borne thither by the wind or by animals, it is burnt down in autumn. Prairie fires are generally dangerous neither to men nor beasts, as the fire, with an ordinary wind, advances very slowly, and over a limited region. If you arrive at very tall grass where the fire would kill, you have always time to get away from it; and when the grass is not unusually high, you can always find a spot to leap over the flames. If the storm is accompanied by rain the grass does not burn at all, hence, only a hurricane with a clear sky, as is not rare among us in autumn, produces in alliance with the fire such destruction among the occupants of the steppe.

It was evening when I reached home, tired and without booty. My people had seen, by the smoke which covered the sky over them, that the prairie was on fire, and they were very anxious about me on account of the violent storm. I soon sought my bed, and slept till the sun rose. Czar would not get up when I went into his stall; while my other horses and mules, with the exception of Fancy and the cream-colour, who stood in the large enclosure round the fort, had been grazing for some time outside, fastened to their long lassos. I made Czar rise, led him down to the river, where I gave him a good swim, and then led him back to the rich grass, where, however, he soon lay down again in the shade of an elm.

The day was fine and perfectly calm, and as we had no fresh meat, I determined to procure some, without tiring myself excessively. The prairie hens had already collected in large coveys, and I had lately seen very many of these pretty birds in the neighbourhood of the fort. Hence I resolved to try my fortune with them; saddled the cream-colour, took my shot gun, and rode out with Tony, a spaniel.

These hens are very like our heath-powts in size, shape, and manner of life, save that they have golden red plumage, and the cocks are ornamented with a yellow and black collar, like the golden pheasant. They are extraordinarily shy, and fly off in a straight line when approached. If you follow them they sit closer, and after being put up a few times, they settle down separately in the tall grass, where they hide themselves till the dog puts them up with its nose.

I had not ridden very far when a covey of about fifty got up before my dog, and settled again about half a mile farther on the prairie. I rode up to them, leapt from my horse, followed the dog, and again the covey got up at a long distance. I fired both barrels among them, but was too far off to hurt them much with my rather small shot; they flew some distance, and I saw them settle on a mosquito-tree, so I reloaded and rode slowly towards it, when the dog stood; I leapt off, went up to it, and ordered it on: the hens rose, and I brought down seven of them with my two barrels, while I looked after the rest, and saw them settle separately not far from me. I now hobbled my horse and sought the hens concealed in the grass, and in half an hour shot some twenty of them.

This sport affords much pleasure through the ease with which it is performed, and the very delicate game most amply rewards the sportsman for the slight trouble. I was home again by noon, when we had some of the birds for dinner; a number of the others were hung up in the dairy to keep fresh, while the rest were cut in pieces, boiled in water with laurel leaves, spice, and isinglass, vinegar poured over them, and the whole set to cool in a large earthenware pot, in which the liquid soon becomes a jelly. Game preserved in this way remains for several weeks good and tasty.

CHAPTER XIII
THE DELAWARE INDIAN

One day after dinner, when we had drunk coffee, my sentry shouted that a party of Indians were coming up the river, and I perceived through my telescope that they must belong to one of the civilized tribes, as they were not armed with lances, and bows and arrows, but with firearms, and wore clothes, if we may call them such, consisting of leathern breeches and jackets, and a coloured handkerchief wound round the head like a turban. There were ten Indians, who halted at the great gate of the palisade which enclosed my fort, in a large semicircle, with both its ends joining the river. They shouted "Captain," and then gave me to understand that they wished to speak with me. I went out, accompanied by Trusty, with my large gun loaded with slugs on my arm, and found that the men belonged to a tribe of friendly Delaware Indians, whose chief I knew, and who had several times camped in the very neighbourhood and paid me a visit.

They told me they had encamped several miles down the river, where they had arrived on the last evening; their chief had sent them to tell me that the prairie fire on the previous morning had been caused by the negligence of his men, but that it had spread against their will, and had not been purposely caused. Then they asked whether the chief would be allowed to visit me, and rode back to camp after I had appointed his visit for the morrow.

The next morning at about seven o'clock the chief of the Delawares duly rode up with three of his men. They bound their horses by lassos to pickets which they drove into the ground, carried their baggage into the fort, and accepted my invitation to enter the house, where our parlour and kitchen were. Delawares have always been on the most friendly terms with the United States Government, fought on their side against England in the War of Liberation, and have assumed a number of customs from the whites. They have, as their property, a district of land on the Kansas, where their villages are situated, and their squaws, children, and old people carry on agriculture and cattle breeding, while the men, with some of the squaws, hunt in the desert for nine months of the year.

The Delawares are generally good-looking; the men tall and well-built, with expressive, marked features, aquiline noses, large dark eyes, long black hair, and not a very reddish-brown complexion. The women are small, but neat and pretty, and in spite of their darker hue, produce a pleasing impression through their regular sharply-cut features, dark curly hair, and brilliant coal-black eyes. They dress themselves with some degree of taste. Their clothes consist of gaily-painted deer-hide, ornamented with beads, and the gayest calicoes, which they obtain from the Government trading posts by bartering peltry for them.

After our guests had taken their places, I lit a pipe, and handed it to the chief, who, after taking some twenty pulls at it, passed it to his next man, and so it went from hand to hand, or rather, from mouth to mouth, till it returned to me. During this ceremony of the pipe of peace not a word was spoken, but the chief now broke the silence. After puffing out a portion of the swallowed smoke in a dense cloud from his lips and nostrils, he told me they were the best friends of the white men, and would remain so, and intended to stay for some weeks in the neighbourhood for the purpose of hunting. I assured them that we entertained the same feelings toward them, and that I intended to pay them a return visit at their camp.

After this dinner was served up, which they greatly enjoyed. They behaved with great propriety at it, were acquainted with the use of knives and forks, and it could be seen by their conduct that they frequently came into contact with white men. After dinner the chief imparted to me, that his people wished to have a deal with me, and swap tanned deer and antelope skins for powder, lead, and flints. I told him I should be delighted, and should expect them in the afternoon. One of them, who called himself "Black Tiger," pleased me remarkably. He was a young, good-looking man, of about eighteen, tall, thin, with an open, kindly face, and displayed great animation and conversational powers for an Indian. He spoke English very well, and seemed much attached to me, which he repeatedly told me, and at last displayed more fully by expressing a wish to remain with me. I took it for a joke, laughed, and told him that in that case I would build him a house for himself and give him everything he wished to have.

They then rode away, after indicating the position of the sun when they intended to return in the afternoon for the purpose of making the barter. At about 4 P.M., some twenty Delawares dismounted in front of the fort, and displayed their wares on the prairie. No tribe prepares hides so finely as this one, and I was very glad to obtain a number of them for use by myself and my men, as we made our clothes out of them, and were unable to prepare them so handsomely ourselves. The exchange was soon arranged to mutual satisfaction, although I had given but little powder, lead, flints, and pressed tobacco in proportion. The chief was presented with a small portion of the above articles, as is the custom on such occasions, and then the whole party followed me into the fort, where I regaled them with coffee and bread.

When they prepared to depart, the chief told me that one of his men, Black Tiger, would stop with me, as I had offered to build him a house and give him everything he required. He would in return be a very good friend to me, and he (the chief) would hear on his return in the following year whether he remained a Delaware. I saw now that it was no jest, and replied that I would be a good friend to him as to all the Delawares. On parting I gave him the assurance that I would visit them next morning at their camp. Black Tiger remained behind in great delight, carried his saddle and pack into the fort, placed his long rifle and hunting pouch in the parlour, and then came to me begging I would build him the promised house. I intimated to him that this would take some time, but in the meanwhile I would give him a handsome tent. I fetched a very large white and red striped marquee and asked him where I should put it up for him. He pointed out a spot at the eastern end of the fence under an elm-tree on the slope over the river, and when I told him that I locked the fort gate at night, he laughed, and replied that in that case he would shut up his house too.

He was quite beside himself with joy when the handsome tent was up, and the long red, white, and blue American pennant floated over it. He now refused to have another house, as this one was much finer than mine. A trench was dug round the tent to carry off the rain water, and the ground inside was covered with some buffalo hides, after which Tiger carried in his baggage and weapons, quite delighted with his house. In order to delight him even more, I hung upon the tent-post a looking-glass, put in a chair, and gave my young friend a gay coloured silk handkerchief, with which he bound his fine black hair on the right side of his head, and let the end hang over his shoulder. After supper my new guest went to his tent, and when we closed the fort, a merry fire was still blazing before it, behind which he sat on his stool and smoked a short pipe which I had also given him.

The next morning, almost before sunrise, I went to Tiger and saw him turning some spits at the fire, on which he had placed the breast of a turkey, while by his side lay another young cock which, as he said, he had fetched for me. He had been hunting on the other side of the river, to which he had crossed in my canoe. An hour after he came to breakfast with me, and enjoyed it heartily, especially the milk and bread. Then he went to his tent, and slept till I called him to ride with me to the camp of his tribe.

I had mounted Czar, and one of my men the cream-colour, when my young Tiger rode up to us in full costume. The lower part of his face, from the corners of his mouth to the ear-tips, was painted pure red with vermilion; from this a black stripe ran to the eyes, while the edges of the eyelids were again thickly daubed with vermilion. His hair, fastened with the silk handkerchief, hung over his shoulders, and in front of his chest he had hung from a leathern thong the looking-glass from his tent, which completely covered it. He glowed with pride and joy, and was of opinion that his brothers in camp would stare when they saw him with these splendid things.

Tiger was mounted on a magnificent piebald, with an enormous black mane and tail. The saddle was of wood, and home manufacture, and from it hung two large wooden stirrups by leathern straps. Over the saddle lay a shaggy buffalo hide, under which the tomahawk, fastened to the saddle bow, and a rolled-up lasso peeped out. The bridle was composed of leathern straps fastened under the horse's jaw with a slipknot, and vermilion dyed strips of deerhide were plaited in the mane. The long single rifle hung downwards over Tiger's left shoulder, while he laid his powerful forearm on the stock. A small medicine bag of beaver skin hung on his right side, and on the strap passing over his right shoulder a number of strips of shaggy buffalo hide were fastened as a rest for the rifle. The young rider's dress consisted of leathern breeches adorned on the sides with a delicate fringe of the same material, and fastened at top by a strap to the short leathern petticoat that was gathered round his hips, and decorated with very long fringe. On his feet he had deerhide mocassins, round his neck was a collar of very large white beads, very finely cut out of shells, and round his arms was a number of polished brass rings. He sat his horse nobly, and turned his flashing black eyes in all directions.

We soon reached the Delaware camp, hobbled our horses in the grass close by, and went up to the chief, who was lying at his fire, in front of his great buffalo hide tent, and being served with food by his two young squaws. Without rising, he invited us to sit down by his side and smoke the pipe of peace with him, while he silently gazed in admiration at Black Tiger. The camp consisted of some forty tents, of white buffalo hides, erected under clumps of trees on the river bank, and before which an equal number of fires was burning. From the trees around hung a number of skins of every description, stretched out to dry in the sun, while men, women, and children lay round the fire and were eating their dinner. A heap of dogs were running about the camp, while some hundred horses and mules were grazing around. We sat down on a buffalo hide by the chief's fire, and he at once told us about his journey which he had made in spring in the Rocky Mountains; he wished to remain during the winter in the south, and next spring pay a visit to his home on the Kansas. He described in a very animated way the hunts he had made there, and the bloody fights with hostile tribes; gave me a very attractive description of the mountains, rivers, and valleys of those parts, and remarked, with a slightly jealous look, that I occupied the best land. I answered him that this land was free as before to friendly Indians like the Delawares: the latter could sleep the more tranquilly, because I only pursued the foes of my Indian friends, and had cast my bullets solely for them. This speech produced a very good effect upon my red friend, and with a cordial laugh, he took my hand in his two and shook it with an expression of the most hearty and sincere friendliness. Soon after he said a few words to one of his squaws, and one of his little ones, about four years of age, came out of the tent soon after, dragging an enormous tanned, exquisitely painted buffalo hide, which he presented to me, while his father nodded kindly.

While we were sitting thus cosily together, several of the Indians in the other tents prepared to go hunting, mounted their horses, called their dogs, and rode off; while others got their fishing tackle ready, or sported with the girls at the fire. Two young squaws went out in front of the camp followed by several youths, and stood side by side to try their speed in running. They were sixteen or seventeen years of age, gracefully built and really pretty; they only wore their leathern fringed petticoat, a couple of long red strips of leather round their hanging black hair, with beads on their neck and brass rings round their pretty arms. With their brilliant fiery eyes they waited, dancing on their little feet, laughing and teasing each other, for the signal to start, and the two goddesses of the desert glided like lightning through the short grass, scarce touching the ground with the tip of their feet, while their long hair, with the red streamers, flew out behind them. Far away on the prairie stood the tree, which they touched almost simultaneously, and they darted back with a laugh that displayed their pearly teeth. I involuntarily rose at the sight of these pretty creatures, and was surprised at myself, for years had elapsed since a female glance had melted the ice of my heart. I looked for a long time at these graceful little savages, as they teased each other and bounded about with the most pleasing movements; then I once more assured the chief of my friendship, and rode back to the fort.

The young Indian was already quite at home and always in good spirits. I was thoroughly acquainted with the character of these men, who had grown up in a state of independence, and knew that my only way of keeping him was by gradually accustoming him to the minor pleasures of civilized life, while at the same time avoiding everything that might lessen his liberty, such as he enjoyed in the nomadic life of his tribe. Eating played a great part in this—coffee, milk, bread, eggs, cheese, and butter were delicacies which he heartily enjoyed, and he soon grew accustomed to them. Whenever his hunting permitted it, he was rarely absent from meals. At times he disappeared, struck his tent, and we saw nothing of him for several days; at others, he stopped at home, and hardly crossed the river to shoot a turkey or deer. It was an incalculable advantage to have a trustworthy Indian with me, as any hostilities against me affected him and consequently his tribe, and would be avenged by the latter. The Delawares are the most respected among the savage western hordes, as they have better weapons and more weight with the United States Government than all the rest. Hence, I regarded this chance enlistment as very fortunate, and was resolved to make every effort to retain my guest as long as I could. Among other amusements, which I strove to procure him, was chessplaying, which he soon learnt and passionately loved. He became so excited that he would spring up and dance about as if mad, and would frequently play far into the night.

If by chance any of my horses or mules got loose and bolted, Tiger was soon galloping after them, and drove them home; it was the same with my milch kine when they did not come to be milked at the regular hour. In smoking meat, plaiting lassos, tanning hides, &c., he was very useful to me, and he very often accompanied me on my hunting excursions, when he proved a pleasant companion and famous adjunct. Shooting with shot guns was something new to Tiger, and afforded him great amusement; and as the clouds of passenger pigeons had arrived to devour our abundant mast crop, we frequently went across to the forest in the evening when the birds were settling, sent our shot among them, and brought down hundreds.

It is incredible in what countless numbers these pigeons fly, I remember on several occasions watching from the fort their flight over the forest, when they flew in a line from one end of the horizon to the other, almost uninterruptedly for two hours. In the woods where they settle to devour the mast, in a few weeks not an acorn is literally to be found, and at the spots where they rest at night many trees do not retain a single leaf on their branches, because the latter are broken by the birds settling on them in masses. In those parts of America where pig breeding is carried on extensively, these birds are regarded as a plague, as they entirely eat up the mast in a very short time. The pigeons are very good eating, but we who had such an abundance of large game only followed these smaller varieties for fun, and it is a rarity to find a shot gun on the border.

Our horses had enjoyed a rather long rest, when I one morning rode across the river with Tiger to the northern prairies for the purpose of procuring fresh meat. We had been an hour under way when we reached a stream, which winds through the prairie to the Leone and is densely overgrown on both banks with birch bushes. The stream through its windings forms here almost an island, as it flows past again only a few yards from its own bed. I saw from a distance a remarkably fat buffalo in the young fresh grass of this island, and on the other side in the prairie a herd of about four hundred of these animals. I dismounted behind the birches, and left Tiger with the horses; then I sprang through the stream, and crawled on my stomach through the grass toward the buffalo, Trusty following me exactly in the same way. The buffalo continued to graze, and did not seem to notice me at all. The sun burnt fiercely, although the breeze was very fresh, and I became frightfully hot on this march. The buffalo was one of the largest bulls in the herd, and seemed to have selected this luxuriant spot for itself; it frequently looked across to its friends, and drove away with its huge fat tail and horns the flies which on this day were most troublesome. Not far from it grew an old mosquito-tree, the only one on this round, rather large meadow, and a very long, strong, but withered branch grew horizontally out of its trunk about four feet from the ground.

I was near enough to shoot with certainty, but the buffalo was turned from me, and I was obliged to wait till it moved before I could kill it. I lay for a long time motionless with Trusty behind me, whose head I pressed down to the ground. At last the bull started round, as the flies had probably given it too fierce a sting, and exposed its whole enormous side to me. I aimed just behind the shoulder-blade, and as soon as I had fired laid myself flat on the ground. The buffalo darted round several times looking for its enemy, but then tottered against the tree, where it leant against the withered branch to keep itself from falling, while it burst into a fearful roar and rolled its enormous head. I gave Trusty a nod, and with a few leaps he was in front of the buffalo and pinned it by the nose. I had just reloaded when the bushes parted on the other side of the meadow at a hundred points, the whole herd of buffaloes dashed through and galloped towards me. They had heard the complaints of their lord and Trusty's furious barking, and hurried up to help their comrade. I stood quite exposed, and expected that on seeing me they would take to flight, but they dashed on straight towards me. The foremost of the herd were only thirty paces from me when I took out my white pocket-handkerchief and waved it in the air. The ranks now broke, and the terrified animals dashed past me on the right and left; upon which I sent two bullets after them, which certainly went home, but were carried away by the wounded. Tiger at this moment came through the bushes with the horses, and said to me, laughingly, that if I had not had the handkerchief the herd would certainly have run over me. We went up to the shot buffalo, while our horses grazed near us, paunched it, and then put up a number of

white rags we had brought for the purpose, and fastened to sticks, an a white cloth over it to keep off the carrion crows. Then we mounte horses for the purpose of riding home and fetching the meat in the r cart.

We were in our saddles when a herd of about 400 buffaloes appeared a rise in the prairie, halted in a long point, and stared at us in amazemer The distance was scarce 300 yards. Tiger looked at me with a smile, an cried "Alligator Creek," while pointing to the herd. I made him a sign to ride on, and we were soon galloping behind the flying buffaloes, which pressed close together and thundered on ahead of us in a cloud of dust. Tiger's clear hunting yell urged the terrified monsters to a more rapid flight, and in ten minutes we approached a swampy stream which crossed the prairie obliquely, and which we had christened "Alligator Creek," from the number of those animals in it. The banks were very steep and above twelve feet high, the water almost dried up, and the deep bed only contained black thick mud.

The dense mass hastened before us towards the banks of the river bed, and rushed down into the swampy bottom with deafening roars and grunts. Buffalo after buffalo fell into the ravine till we pulled up on the bank above them and laughed at their confusion and the efforts with which they ascended the other bank all coated with mud. I fancied that at least one half must break their necks, but not one of them remained in the mud. They forced their way to the other bank atop of each other, and sprang, apparently at least, quite unhurt up it. I had dismounted and shot a fat cow, which had borne a calf this year and hence was very plump. The cows only drop one calf every two years, and for this reason it is the more inexplicable that the number of these animals is not more rapidly reduced by the great destruction that takes place among them. The cow followed the herd but a short distance, and then fell dead on the prairie. We were obliged to go a long way up the bank before we could find a low path by which to cross, but soon reached the cow, put up rags round it, but left the paunching to my people, as we did not care to dirty ourselves with the mud that covered it.

We now rode the shortest way to the forest on the Leone, and again crossed the stream on which I had shot the bull about three miles below the spot where it lay. We passed through the thick bushes out into the prairie, but Trusty did not follow us. He trotted down the stream, stopped every now and then, looked up to me and gave his deep bark. I looked at him curiously, for I knew that he was on some track, when all at once he disappeared in the bushes and stopped. I gave Czar, whom the well-known voice had rendered impatient, his head, and soon reached the bushes among which Trusty was

baying, with a revolver in my hand. I turned Czar into a gap between the bushes, when suddenly the shaggy head of a furious buffalo rose above the bank within a yard of me. My startled horse swerved, and cleared the bushes by a tremendous leap, while the monster dashed past me with a roar and galloped across the prairie. I soon got out of the bush, however, and went after it, while Tiger came to meet me. I was close behind the bull, when Tiger flew past it and gave it a bullet from his long rifle near the neck. The buffalo followed the piebald with terrible fury, dyeing the prairie with its blood, when I darted past it and gave it a bullet from my revolver behind the shoulder-blade, which lamed its left fore leg. Trusty now attacked it in the flank, and it stood at bay, holding its head close to the ground, with its nose between its fore feet, and holding one of its short sharp horns against the dog. The buffalo stood motionless with its tail erect, while Trusty sprang barking before it, waiting for the moment when it should raise its head. But its hour had arrived. I rode within twenty yards, and shot it through the heart: it fell lifeless.

It was one of the bulls I had wounded in the morning, when they hurried to the assistance of their comrade: feeling bad it had gone to the water to cool itself, and Trusty had followed its trail to the spot. We put up rags round this one too, and rode sharply to the fort, whence I sent off two of my men with the cart and two mules, accompanied by Tiger. They returned late at night, and brought a heavy load of meat home, which we cut up and salted the next morning. Of the three hides, they only brought the one shot first, which was employed in making a very long lasso.

Hunting occupied us pleasantly through the autumn, and Tiger grew more and more used to our mode of life: it became rare for him to remain away several days without our knowing what had become of him; he also took greater pleasure in domestic jobs, and applied himself to them more frequently than at the first period of his stay with us. He learned to milk the cows, and readily helped in it as he was so fond of milk, as well as in making vinegar, which he also liked much, and which is made of the large wild grapes with which the prairie thickets are covered. For this purpose I had two large empty whisky casks fetched from the settlement, and this year our vinegar turned out first-rate. Previously we had made it in smaller quantities of mulberries, plums, or honey, which was not half so agreeable as that made of grapes.

Tiger was able to make butter and cheese, and at a pinch cook. Our table was now always well covered, as we had a superabundance of the finest vegetables. The potato crop had turned out very well, and we had more especially an extraordinary quantity of sweet potatoes, as they are

called. This is a tuber like the potato; the plant itself consists of tendrils, which spread flat and thick over the soil, and can be easily multiplied in spring. The shoot bears in autumn an extraordinary number of tubers, which are employed precisely like potatoes, except that they have a much more agreeable flavour, resembling the chestnut. A small, most prolific bean, which we plant between the maize, and which spreads over the whole field, had produced us a large stock, while the less hardy vegetables, such as lettuce, spinach, and cabbage, covered the garden all the winter through.

The winter in this region is very mild, and may fairly be termed the pleasantest season of the year. We have no lasting rainy season, although rain falls more frequently then than in the summer months, but it rarely lasts longer than a day, and then the cloudless blue sky gleams pleasantly over us again. Frost is rare and trifling; but sometimes it sets in towards morning, and will last a whole day if accompanied by a wind blowing down from the northern Rocky Mountains. These Northers are usually called something terrible in the whole of the United States, but in reality they do not at all merit this reputation. Certainly the cold is felt much more among us than elsewhere; because, as men accustomed to warm weather, we rarely lay in a stock of winter clothes. The houses, too, are not calculated for cold, as they are built very airily and lightly, and have no stoves—only fireplaces. When the Northers blow the people fly to these fires, while the cattle seek bottoms and dense thickets, where they conceal themselves.

I remember on a splendidly warm forenoon the sky becoming overcast from the north, and it began to blow and rain, which caused the whole country to be covered with ice in a short time. If such a storm assails a traveller in his light summer dress, he is certainly in an unpleasant position, and if he is a stranger it easily happens that he tells a terrible story about it when he gets home. These disagreeable storms from the north, however, are infrequent; we have perhaps six or eight in a winter, and they rarely last longer than four-and-twenty hours, and are then driven away by very bright warm days. The winter proper—which may bring cold weather—does not begin till January, frequently later; hence we have a very long delicious autumn. The days are no longer oppressively hot, and the nights become so cool that we are glad to snuggle under a buffalo robe or a woollen blanket. This is the season when we recover from the exhausting continuous summer heat, and the body regains its energy.

CHAPTER XIV
IN THE MOUNTAINS

It was on a bright healthy morning in November that I, accompanied by Tiger and Trusty, left the fort, and rode down the river toward the Rio Grande Mountains. I had never made any excursions far beyond that river, and even when hunting had rarely reached its banks, as it is enclosed on both sides by savage rocky mountains, which neither man nor brute can easily traverse. Tiger had formerly been several times on the other side of the Rio Grande, and told me there was more game, and more especially more bears there, while rich valleys ran between the mountains. Hence I resolved to spend some weeks in those regions, and provided myself for this tour with provisions, some buffalo robes, and a small tent, which articles were carried by Jack, a most excellent mule. The animal followed my horse without being led, and I may say that it could not be kept away from it except by force. We had no trouble with it but to saddle and load it in the morning, and take off its burden again at night. It would certainly stop now and then at a fresh patch of grass and snatch a few mouthfuls, but then it galloped after us again and followed at our heels.

We rested at noon at the mountain springs, which I had not visited for some time, and we were forced to cut an entrance into the little thicket, as it was completely overgrown. They rewarded us on our arrival with some fat turkeys, which were never absent there, and whose delicate meat we enjoyed, while our horses rested from their hot march over the open prairies. About 3 P.M. we started again, and rode in a northern direction toward the foot of the mountains, as Tiger told me that higher up a river ran towards the Rio Grande, with a rather broad valley on either side, and I believed that this stream must be Turkey Creek. We crossed the Leone toward evening at a shallow spot well known to me. This spot, at which I had often rested, surprises the traveller coming from the open prairie with a very pleasant scene. Bordered on both sides by the grandest vegetation, magnolias, plane-trees, and enormous oaks covered with the most splendid creepers, the foaming silvery stream dashes between scattered masses of rock, with such a roar that visitors can hardly understand each other. The atmosphere beneath these dense masses of foliage is cool and constantly fanned by the breeze produced by the violent motion of the current as it breaks on the rocks, and falls over them in countless small cascades.

When we arrived the scene was enlivened by silver herons and flamingos, some soaring high in air, others standing on the dry rocks jutting out of the water, and forming a striking contrast with their white and green plumage against the dark green background. We cautiously guided our horses between the rocks, while Jack followed close behind, and the birds raised a hoarse croak of surprise over our heads. The primeval forest on the other side of the stream is broad, and day had yielded the supremacy to night, as we moved along the buffalo path which was only at intervals illumined by the moon. I knew here nearly every step, and we reached the prairie all right, when we remounted, and half an hour later reached the equally familiar sources of a stream which falls into the Leone a little lower down.

It was a favourite spot of mine, where we took the load off our animals. A cheerful fire soon blazed and threw its light upon them, while they lay in the young grass around us. The moon had not set when we had finished supper and fell into a refreshing sleep. The eastern sky was already tinged with red, when I woke and saw several spits with meat already put before the fire. The horses were grazing round our camp, but I missed Tiger, whose weapons lay on his buffalo hide. I went a little way round the bushes, and saw him on the open prairie on his knees with folded hands and uplifted face, awaiting the appearance of the sun, in order to offer his adoration to it. I heard him speaking softly to himself as it sent its first beams towards us, and he continued his prayer till it had fully risen above the horizon; then he rose, and with a pleasant smile came back to his seat at the fire. He then produced his small mirror and box of vermilion, laid the former on his crossed knees and painted his face, as he supposed, very grandly; then he arranged his splendid hair with a comb I had given him, rubbed it with bear's grease and tied it up with strips of red leather.

During breakfast Tiger told me about his last tour in the Rocky Mountains; of the mountains covered with eternal snow; the beautiful valleys containing famous pasturage; his fight with a desperate grizzly bear, which he killed, &c., and accompanied his words with the most animated gestures. It is a peculiarity of Indians to enliven their remarks with signs and gestures which render it easy to understand what they say; and Tiger, in spite of his knowledge of English, had retained the sign language, which had grown habitual to him. I remarked that I felt a great inclination to take a trip there in the next spring, and he was delighted at the prospect of being allowed to accompany me.

It was late when we started, and continued our journey in a northern direction. The prairies here grew narrower; the woods closer connected, and the country more uneven. Although we kept as far as we could from the mountains on our left, we crossed small streams, which either came down from the mountains and went to form the larger streams, with which they flowed through the hills to the Rio Grande, or which had their sources in the eastern plateaus, and pursued the same course. The country was picturesque; the small prairies, beset by clusters of bushes and clumps of trees of the most varying shapes, were covered with juicy fresh grass and a quite new flora; here and there huge blocks rose out of it, in whose crevices grew large yuccas and mimosas of different sorts, cactuses and aloes, which represented the southern world of plants; on the left the hills rose over each other in terraces, and indicated the course of the large river.

We had ridden the whole morning and not fired a shot at game, although we had seen a good deal. Our fresh meat was quite finished, and I was just saying to Tiger that it would soon be time to shoot something as the dinner hour was at hand, when I saw turkeys running in a small scrubby patch ahead of us, and made Trusty a sign to follow them. In an instant he put them up, but as a dense forest rose just before us, they all but one entered its impenetrable foliage. The latter, an old cock, rose straight in the air, and settled on the top of a very tall cypress which grew on the skirt of the forest, and whose roots were washed by a small spring. It waved backwards and forwards on the thin branch, as if challenging the hunter who would dare to fire at it, while Trusty leapt up at it and barked loudly. Tiger looked at me laughingly, pointed upwards, and asked, "What do you think?" I gave him a nod to try his luck. He sprang from the piebald, took a long aim, fired, and the cock did not stir, but continued to oscillate and look down at Trusty. I felt an itch to try my skill. I sprang from my horse, raised my rifle, and with the detonation the haughty bird opened its wings for the last time, fell like a ball and smote the ground heavily. Tiger laughed, and said that he would have brought it down too, if it had not swung so on the bough. It is a curious fact that the Indians armed with rifles, and even the Americans, never think of firing when the object is moving at all quickly, although they have so many opportunities of practising it. The chief motive may lie in the very long and heavy guns they carry, which cannot be moved so rapidly and lightly as our rifles.

We could not have chosen a better spot than this for our mid-day rest, as our horses found the best grass, the clearest spring water flowed close past us, and the virgin forest offered us its cool shade. We therefore quickly unsaddled, hobbled our horses, and set to work cooking the turkey. We unwillingly left this pleasant spot a few hours later, and were obliged to ride a couple of miles up the forest before we found a buffalo path wide enough for us to pass through. For about an hour we rode through the leafy labyrinth, ere we reached the open plain again on the other side. Here Tiger rode up to me again, and talking and jesting, we kept our horses at a brisk amble, while Jack trotted after us.

Suddenly I heard a "hugh!" from Tiger's lips, and pointing to the ground before us he stopped and said that the buffalo dung on the path was quite fresh and the animals must be in the vicinity. He galloped on and we soon reached a narrow wood, which ran through the prairie in nearly the same direction we were following, and through whose centre ran a small stream. We had scarcely reached this wood ere Tiger leapt from his horse, pointed to the ground before us, then pointed to his ears, and made a motion with his hands as if breaking a stick. He sprang away with the lightness of an antelope, scarce touching the ground with his toes, and never treading on a branch, which might produce a sound; then he suddenly stopped, lowered his head slightly and listened for some minutes. After which he shot ahead again at such a pace that I could hardly keep up with him. He presently lay down on the ground and made me a sign with his hand that the buffaloes were entering the water just under us, and were going across to the prairie. In a few minutes he leapt up again, signed to me to follow him, and flew down the wood, through the stream, and up the other bank, where we arrived behind the last bush on the prairie, just as the buffaloes had only gone a few yards along it, and two of them were standing on the other side of the bush and staring intently at us.

We both had our rifles raised and I gave Tiger a nod to fire first. I kept the sight between the eyes of the buffalo, standing on the right, and as the flame poured from Tiger's gun, I fired and ran round the bush to be able to use the other barrel; but it was unnecessary, for the two gigantic animals were rolling on the ground at the last gasp. Tiger's buffalo was shot through the heart, and the bullet had smashed the skull of mine. We hurried to our horses and packed the best bits of our ample booty on faithful Jack's back.

The sun was not very high above the mountains, but it was too early to spend the night here. Our cattle had rested a little, and so we merely allowed them to drink, filled our own bottles, and rode merrily on in a northern course. Tiger was remarkably colloquial on this evening, and the time slipped away and we scarce noticed that the night had spread its dark wings over the road, which now wound between conical barren hills. I remarked to my comrade that we should have a hard camp, which he denied, and moving his hand across a long chain of hills in front of us, he said that we should sleep softly on the other side of it. While saying this he laid his cheek on his hand and closed his eyes.

It was late when we reached this chain of hills. The mountain side was very steep; although we selected the lowest spot to cross, we were obliged to dismount and lead our horses. Our foothold grew more and more uncertain on the loose pebbles, and our horses, too, were obliged to exert themselves in clambering over the many large stones with which the ravine was covered.

While we were clambering on in this way, Trusty suddenly growled, trotted a few yards past us with bristling hair, and then barked into the depths behind us. Tiger said a jaguar was following us, and put his rifle under his arm. We at length reached the top, where we let our animals breathe, and looked back for a long time at the valley behind us, but could see nothing of our pursuer, although Trusty continued to growl. We marched along the top, which soon sloped down and allowed us a glance at the valley on the other side. The slope was not so steep as the one by which we ascended. The valley before us looked gloomy with its black shadows, and its depths were covered with a white strip of fog, while the opposite mountain side, illumined by the moon, glistened with indistinct bluish tones.

We descended the hill, and in an hour reached the grassy damp bottom, where we remounted and shortly after pulled up on the bank of a large river whose other side was bordered by a thick wood. Here we unloaded our cattle and soon sank into the most tranquil sleep, leaving to faithful Trusty the care of our safety. His powerful voice soon awoke us, however, and made us clutch our rifles. We called him back, stirred up our fire, and as we could see nothing of a foe, we fell asleep again. The faithful dog awoke us again several times, but when morning broke, he lay rolled up by the fire, and was fetching up the rest he had lost in the night.

We were up at an early hour, and Tiger found in the dewy grass not far from our camp the trail of a very large jaguar, which had prowled round it during the night and disquieted Trusty. We bathed in the deep clear river, then breakfasted and set out again. The river flowed westward through a rather wide vale, bounded on the north by a wood, on our side by rich prairies, while a range of bald conical shaped lime hills ran along either side. Judging from its distance from the Leone, this river could only be Turkey Creek, on whose banks I had spent that stormy night with the unhappy botanist. We followed its windings westward for several hours, crossing a number of small streams which came down from the ravines. The valley was here considerably broader than at the spot where we passed the night, but in front of us the hills approached each other again; then the river turned a little westward and afforded a prospect between the rocks of the western cedar-grown banks of the Rio Grande.

The prairie over which we rode led us to the banks of this large river, which runs at a depth of at least fifty feet between the widest masses of rock. At this time it contained very little water, as it does not begin to swell to any extent till January, and we at once made preparations to cross it. We selected from the quantity of dry driftwood, with which the steep bank was covered, pieces of light cedar-wood, bound them together as a small raft, and anchored it to a great tree trunk on the bank. We laid our provisions, saddle-bags, and clothes upon it, and Tiger leapt in the very rapid stream, holding the loose end of the lasso between his teeth, and swam to an island covered with willows, which lay about fifty yards from our bank. When he had swam so far as to haul the lasso taut, I thrust the raft off, and it rapidly followed the current behind Tiger, who, however, guided it to this island and landed about two hundred yards lower down. Then he went to the end of the island, dragging the raft after him, and pulled it into the calmer water on the other side. Then he threw the lasso over his shoulders, and easily pulled the raft to the other bank, where he fastened it to some heavy driftwood. He was soon back by my side. I hung my holsters over my shoulders, took rifle in hand, and we flew on our horses down the stream obliquely till we reached the island, which we soon crossed and guided our horses into the quieter water on the other side. We landed on the western bank of the river at the moment when Jack, who had reached the island, uttered a frightful bray of delight, while looking over at the horses: then he cautiously entered the river again, and soon trotted up to his comrades, who enjoyed the scanty grass that grew on the bank while we were dressing.

As it was noon, and high time to eat something, we lit a fire a little higher up the hills under a leafy plane, and prepared our meal, while I reclined on my buffalo robe and gazed in delight at the wildly romantic scene that was expanded before me. The very deep river bed, cut in limestone strata, is very wide higher up, so that the river, when swollen in spring by the mountain torrents, quite fills it up, and attains a width of half a mile. On both sides of the bed rise grey masses of rock in the wildest shapes, leaving yawning ravines between them, through which the torrents flow to the river. The mountains on the eastern side are generally bare, and bushes only grow in these narrow valleys, out of which a solitary cypress here and there raises its crown to heaven: the western heights, on the contrary, are covered with dense cedar woods, whose dark lustreless foliage, added to the grey steep precipices, imparts a saddening and gloomy aspect to the scenery. In face of us, however, opened between a lofty rock gate the pleasant valley of Turkey Creek, through which we had come. Foaming and roaring, it leaps over gigantic strata of stone into the deep bed of the Rio Grande; while on its south side, far up the valley, the prairie glistens with its fresh verdure, and on the north the dark shadows of a colossal virgin forest run along the mountain range.

We took leave of these banks for a short period, and marched up a steep ravine to the dark shade of the cedar woods, which soon offered us their agreeable coolness. The mountains here were of a conical shape, and so closely overgrown with not very tall cedars, that we were compelled to dismount on our buffalo path—although it had been used by the Indians on their expeditions for centuries—in order to get along at all. Never in my life did I grow so tired of a road; it seemed as if we rode round every hill, and after we had ridden for an hour and had a prospect eastward for a second, the wild rocky valley of the Rio Grande lay at our feet just as if we had but just left it. But a perfectly new and beautiful flora rewarded me for the monotonous, slow ride; in these shadows grew a number of exquisite plants, whose seeds I collected to transfer them to my home.

We had been marching for three hours through these woods, when the country became clearer, the mountains formed into large masses, and the valleys between grew wider. It was twilight, and we had, as I thought, surmounted the last short but steep rise, when Czar suddenly darted back, and a jaguar appeared about thirty yards ahead, gazed at me for a moment, lay down flat on the grass, and drew up its hind legs for a spring. This did not take an instant; and I had pointed my rifle over the neck of my rearing steed at my enemy, when it made its first leap. At this moment I fired, but heard simultaneously the crack of another rifle behind me. Czar turned round at my shot, and almost leapt on Tiger, who was standing behind me on foot, and then darted down the hill. I shouted to him to stop my horse, and saw the jaguar appear on the top of the steep. I sent my second bullet through its chest, and it rolled down toward me in the most awful fury. I called Trusty to me, and fired a couple of revolver shots into the gigantic body of my foe, which ere long gave up the ghost with savage convulsions. My first bullet had passed through its left side; but Tiger's had seriously hurt the spine behind the left shoulder. Tiger's shot had certainly gained the victory, as it robbed the brute of its springing power, and it caused him great delight when I acknowledged his victory, and surrendered to him the fine large skin, which I bought of him on the same evening for a number of trifles to be delivered when we returned home.

It was rather dark when I lit a large fire, and we set to work stripping off the fine spotted skin of the royal beast. As it was very uncertain whether we should find water, we unsaddled, hobbled the cattle, and put on the coffee water to boil. We soon had the jaguar's huge skin off, and hung it

stretched on young cedar branches, on a tree close to the fire to dry. Then we prepared supper, drank coffee, and ere long were asleep near our horses, while Trusty patrolled round camp.

A splendid morning awoke us from our dreams and displayed to us the wild but beautiful scenery we had noticed on the previous evening. We had camped at the entrance of a plateau, bordered on the east by the cedar-clad hills sloping down to the Rio Grande, while on the west a chain of large mountains ran northward. The plateau was abundantly covered with grass, but its surface did not display the same monotony as those lying to the east of the Rio Grande; it was covered with patches of wood, and here and there huge masses of rock arose. We marched northward, and as the mountains to the west appeared to us too difficult, we soon crossed a splendid small stream where we watered our horses and filled our flasks. For three days we followed its course through this park; at times over fresh green prairies, at others through thick woods or *cañons*. We met a great many antelopes and deer, but only saw a few buffaloes at a great distance. Among others Tiger pointed out to me a buffalo on the western mountain side, and said it was lying on the ground. After repeated search I managed to discover a small black dot in the direction indicated, and when I called my glass to my help I really saw an old solitary buffalo lying there among the rocks, and was astonished at the extraordinary sight of my young Indian friend.

CHAPTER XV
THE WEICOS

On the third evening we approached the western mountain chain, which bordered the northern end of the plain we were crossing. Our road slowly rose, while we steered toward a gap in the mountains, where we hoped to find an available path. For an hour our path was steep and vegetation had nearly entirely disappeared, only a few reeds were visible in the crevices between the rocks. Deep yawning gorges and *cañons* opened between the overhanging limestone strata, round which we had to make fatiguing circuits, while frequently we had hardly room to lead our horses along the precipices over deep abysses. The sun was setting, and the lofty mountain sides cast their broad shadows over the rocky depths. It soon became dark, but we pushed on, still hoping to find a suitable spot for camping. We had almost reached the highest point, when we saw gigantic red granite walls rising in front of us like a fortress. They hung a long way over us and the deep abyss, from which wildly scattered colossal blocks, illumined by the parting sunbeams, rose, while on the other side of the gorge the mountains were heaped up against the dark purple evening sky. Our path was very narrow and strewn with small pebbles, so that we were obliged to lead our horses with a short rein.

All at once Tiger shouted to me to halt, and immediately after I heard him utter "Pah," in his Indian language. It was water he wished to indicate, and he told me he could hear the rustling of a stream. Our path grew rather broader, and ran into the granite masses on our left, while on our right the slope was not so steep, and sank into the ravine between a few large blocks of stone. We had scarce gone one hundred yards when the road before us proved to be blocked by scattered masses of stone, between which stunted oaks and bushes grew, while I found myself in short grass, which Czar greedily attacked. I shouted to Tiger that I could go no farther, and he led his piebald up to my side, who with the never-failing Jack also went at the grass. Tiger was of opinion that it was a famous spot, as the water was close at hand below us, and disappeared among the rocks. He soon returned, dragging after him several dry branches, while we broke up and lit a fire, which soon lit up the immediate neighbourhood. The rocks on our left were deeply excavated, and hung in large strata with broad cracks, covering a large tract of ground, which bore at various points traces of fires which must have been lit by Indians, who had camped here like ourselves. We prepared our supper, but had great difficulty in putting the spits up before the fire, as Tiger had not lit it on the grass, but under the rocks. While we were thus employed the moon rose slowly behind the mountains, and threw her first pale rays into our wild valley. Gradually her light became more brilliant, and the dark masses around us emerged in their various shapes. Tiger now leapt up, placed one of my revolvers in his belt, took a cedar brand, and went down a narrow path between the rocks, carrying our two large gourds by a strap over his shoulders. I watched the ruddy dancing light of the torch which lit up at one moment the rocks, at another the dark green foliage of the oaks; it continually grew smaller, till it appeared in the depths below like a bright point. It soon returned, however, and Tiger appeared between the rocks with our bottles full of spring water, so cold and clear that my lips had not tasted anything to equal it for a long time. He told me that below was a small pool, into which the springs ran; buffaloes must have been standing there a little while before, and he therefore believed that we should be able to lead our cattle down to water by daylight. I gave Czar a share of the refreshing draught.

We seemed to have entered the kingdom of owls, for their hoot was audible on all sides. Tiger listened for awhile very attentively to these sounds, but then lay down tranquillized on his buffalo hide, saying that one of the sounds resembled the voice of a Weico; but he had not signalled again, or he (Tiger) was mistaken. The fire was supplied with large logs, and we then wrapped ourselves in our skins and slept till daybreak. We blew up our fires, put on our horses' bridles, and led them down the hill side to water, along a path on which we now distinctly noticed fresh buffalo signs. It was a tiring road by which we at length reached the bottom, where a small basin filled the entire breadth of the gorge, into which a clear stream noisily poured. The basin was washed out of the stony ground, and we led our horses into it after a number of mocassin and rattlesnakes had taken to flight with a menacing hiss. We then turned back to reach our camp again. Tiger led his piebald in front, but stopped and said he felt much inclined to climb up the opposite wall of the gorge, as it was full of crevices in which doubtless bears were hybernating. He also said he had heard from his people that the Delawares always shot a great number of bears at this spot, though he had never visited it before himself. I hence took his horse's bridle, and called Czar to follow me, while Jack completed the party, and Trusty trotted on ahead.

After a fatiguing climb I again reached our camp, where I hobbled the cattle in the grass and sat down to the fire to get breakfast ready. I had just finished and lit a pipe, when the crack of a rifle reached me from the opposite wall, and I supposed that Tiger had shot a bear, when a few moments later a second shot was fired, and the frightfully shrill sound of the Indian war-whoop echoed through the gorge. There was no doubt but that Tiger had come into collision with hostile Indians. The yell rolled down the valley, and ere long two shots were fired in rapid succession. I quickly threw our saddles and baggage behind large rocks, and led the piebald some way down the slope, while Czar and Jack followed me; then I fastened the cattle up to trees a little off the path, and sent my hunting cry across the gorge at the full pitch of my lungs. Tiger at once answered me. I ran down to the pond and up the opposite wall, continually uttering my cry and receiving an answer. Trusty went a little ahead to clear the way, and then I climbed on from rock to rock, until another shot was fired, and I heard Tiger's yell higher up the mountain. I carefully noticed the direction whence the yell came, and calling Trusty to me, I ran forward rapidly, though cautiously, between the scattered boulders.

I was standing before a small grass-covered mound when Trusty growled and sniffed; I went up in a stooping posture, and hardly had reached the top when I saw Tiger with his back turned to me, holding in one hand his rifle, in the other the bleeding scalp of his murdered foe, and gazing at the latter, who lay outstretched in the grass: without turning, he told me that the Weico had almost sent him to his fathers, but his heart trembled, and hence he aimed badly. Tiger had seen his enemy first, and fired soonest, but missed, and the other had not hit him either, as he ran. Tiger pursued him, and both reloaded while running, till the Weico reached the spot where he now lay, and the Delaware sprang on the grass plot a little higher up. The Weico fired and missed again, and Tiger in response sent a bullet through his loins, though without being aware that he had hit him. The Weico disappeared in the grass, and Tiger too, as he fancied the other was reloading; but when he had performed the same operation himself and saw nothing of his foe, he crept to an adjacent rock which he mounted, and saw the other in the grass reloading, upon which he sent a bullet through his heart and speedily scalped him. Tiger now took his conquered foe's gun, medicine-bag, beads, and armlets, and made me a sign to return to the horses, while he sprang from rock to rock with the lightness of a deer.

We saddled, and soon left our camp, as Tiger said there were several Weicos in the neighbourhood, for on the previous evening they had made each other signs with the owl hoot. Our road ran from here close to the precipice, and for some few hundred yards was very difficult. We were obliged to lead the horses, and make them leap over several granite blocks, while the grass grew to a man's height between the loose stones, and we could not see where we stepped. Here, however, the road became better and led us in a pretty valley through which a stream wound, while on both sides granite walls begirt it to a height of at least three hundred feet. Trusty was some distance ahead all the time, and was trotting along the birch-covered bank, when he suddenly barked, and I saw something leaping through the grass on his left. The piebald darted past me at the same moment, and Tiger shouted "a panther." I had no inclination, however, to join in the hunt, but merely cantered on, saw the piebald leap several times through the bushes, and a little later heard Tiger's rifle crack. But when I joined him he laughed, and said that the panther had too many feet, and pointed to a thicket on the right-hand hills, in which it had disappeared.

The valley here became very broad, and we saw, a long distance off, three buffaloes grazing under some mosquito-trees, and, when we drew nearer, Tiger proposed to chase them, as, in the fresh close grass, there was no other way of getting within shot of them. Suddenly the buffaloes noticed us and fled, but Tiger set his horse in a gallop, and stormed after them down the valley. I was just able to see that he had caught them up, when a small blue cloud of smoke rose before him, and I shortly after heard the crack of his rifle. He disappeared with the flying buffaloes on the prairie, and I followed him at a quick amble. At the spot where I last saw my comrade, thick bushes ran along both sides of the stream. I went into them, but was obliged to dismount in order to pass through the thicket. Crossing the wood, I gave my hunting-cry, which was answered close by, and, a short distance farther on, Tiger came to meet me, and said that it was no go with the buffaloes either; he had hit one of them clumsily, and not killed it. The piebald was in a frightful perspiration, so Tiger turned him round and we reached the skirt of the wood, where we sat down in the cool shade of the lofty trees, while our cattle, freed from their loads, grazed around us.

The stream wound out of the forest close by. I had gone to it to fill my bottle, when I noticed a number of bees on the bank, which, however, did not fly into the wood, but into the prairie before us. I called up Tiger, who seated himself by my side, and we accurately observed their course by the compass, and saw that they all flew to an old plane-tree which grew in the grass about a thousand yards from us. We went up to the tree, and found that the bees went to a very large bough, which had an opening at the top. We fetched our weapons and axes, and brought out our cattle under the plane, where I also ordered Trusty to lie down. Then we went up to the tree, whose stem was at least eight feet in diameter, threw a lasso over the lowest branch, clambered up it, and went to the branch containing the bees. It was at least a foot and a-half in thickness, and we had to work with our small axes for nearly an hour before it gave way, and fell with a crash to the ground, whereon the startled bees rose like a pillar of smoke, and swarmed off toward the forest. We soon went down the lasso, and began eating the clear honey which flowed out of the broken branch. We ate, and took pieces of the largest combs to our camp, where we laid them in the shade.

Europeans will be surprised, and ask how it is possible to take the honey from the irritated bees without being stung to death. The bees in this country, however, are not so spiteful as in the Old World: it is only when you are near a filled bee-tree, and strike at the bees with a branch or a cloth, that you are attacked and pursued by them; but if you go quickly up to the honey, and are careful not to touch any bees, you are never stung. The honey of these wild bees is far sweeter and more toothsome than that in England: it is very spicy, but at times so impregnated with pepper, that much of it cannot be eaten. I have often felled bee-trees whose honey was so clear that it could not be distinguished from a glass of water put by its side. If you are near home when you cut down a bee-tree, you drive the creatures, which have collected close by in a swarm round their queen, into a bag, take them home, and shake them out into a hollowed tree, nail a board at top and bottom, cut a hole in the lower board, and place it above-ground at a spot protected from the north wind. The bees at once set to work, continuing it winter and summer, and in a short time the hive is filled with honey and wax. We only regretted that we had no vessel in which we could take a supply of this exquisite honey with us.

We had eaten heartily of it when we set out about 3 P.M. and continued our journey down the stream. The sun was sinking behind the mountains on our left, when we again struck the stream which we had left in pursuing a northern course, and resolved to pass the night here. The valley was narrow to the west and to the east; the prairie rose towards the mountains, and some old oaks grew on it. We had unsaddled, hobbled our horses, and lit a fire, when Tiger took his rifle and went towards the western hills to see whether he could procure any fresh game, as our stock was entirely exhausted. The sun had set, the time hung heavy at the fire, so I rose, took my rifle, and walked slowly down the stream, while Trusty ran ahead in the scrub. I had hardly gone a hundred yards when I noticed that the stream turned to the west a little lower down, and its banks were covered with rocks. Suddenly there was a crash in the scrub ahead of me, and I heard a loud wail which filled me with terror, for I knew the sound but too well—it was the wail of a jaguar cub, which Trusty held in his teeth. I ran up and saw him shaking one, while another was escaping in the bushes. As I knew exactly what would happen, I looked around, with my cocked rifle in my hand, and saw the mother coming down with terrible bounds from the oak clumps higher up. There was not a tree near, and I must await it in the open. Trusty placed himself close to my side, and with every hair bristling he uttered his most savage bass notes through his gnashing teeth. The only thing now was to hit, or else Trusty at least was lost, and myself too very probably. Forty paces from me the infuriated brute crouched, displaying its fangs and lashing its sides with its long spotted tail. When I shot, the beast turned over, but then flew towards me with a fresh spring. I shot again, and it rolled on the ground. The ball had broken its spine, and, unable to move its hind-quarters, the raging brute rolled and roared, and dug its mighty claws into the grass, which it dyed with its blood. It was now harmless, and I regretted that I had not my sketch-book with me to draw it in its paroxysm of fury. It was a majestic animal, and the splendid golden yellow of its coat, with its black and white spots, was heightened by the dark red of the blood which streamed from its back and chest. Lying on the ground with its hind-quarters, it stood erect on its mighty fore-legs, and with its thick round neck slightly bent down, it raised its savage open jaws towards me, while the large, yellow, catlike eyes flashed. At the same time the brute made the valley ring with the most fearful roars uttered at intervals. So soon as I approached it it sprang towards me, and dragged its hind-quarters along on the grass, while showing its terrible claws. I went up close to it, and fired a revolver bullet through its head, whereon it fell lifeless.

After reloading, I went back to camp to wait for Tiger, whom I had also heard firing. It was dark when I heard him coming, and saw his brown elastic form coming through the bushes. Over his right shoulder hung two deer legs, and the stripped-off meat of the back was thrown across the barrel of his long rifle, which rested on his left shoulder. He threw down his load, lay on his stomach on the river bank, and quenched his thirst. Then he returned to the fire, and said that I had been shooting too, and intimated by three fingers the number of shots I had fired. I answered him that my deer was lying down the stream, but we would sup first and then fetch it.

We now attacked the excellent venison and enjoyed a hearty supper, when I gave Tiger a sign to follow me. I led him to the jaguar, and he uttered a loud cry when he saw it lying on the grass with the cub by its side. The moon lit us while we stripped off its splendid skin, which was larger than the one we had obtained a few days previously. We took the cub to camp, as Tiger told me its flesh was a great dainty; then he stripped and paunched it, and hung it up to a tree. We then stretched out the large hide, put it in front of the fire, and slept quietly and undisturbed till morning.

I was very curious about the new dish which I was to taste for breakfast. The very white meat of the young jaguar, which was about the size of an ordinary shepherd's colley, looked very tempting, and I put some pieces of it before the fire, while Tiger made his breakfast entirely of it. I tasted it when it browned, and it was very nice, though it had a musky flavour which prevented me from eating much of it. Hence I applied once more to the deer meat, which I liked better, and concluded my meal with the rest of the honeycomb which I had carried on Jack, wrapped in large magnolia leaves and a piece of deer hide. Tiger revelled in his meat, and on saddling packed up the rest for supper.

On this day we followed the stream, which flowed for about five miles westward, but then suddenly turned round a tall hill to the east, and probably fell into the Rio Grande. Here we left it, however, and rode up a small stream which joined it and came from the west. We followed the narrow valley through which it ran and found there a rather broad, though at times stony road. It was bordered on both sides by granitic hills, and ran rather steeply up to the heights, where it expanded into a table-land. This plateau lay on the top of the mountains which we had seen to the west when riding up, and I resolved to follow it in that direction, so as if possible to reach the declivity on the other side before night surprised us, as the barrenness of these lofty plateaus recalled unpleasant reminiscences. This plateau was about fifteen miles in breadth, and in the afternoon we reached its western side, where an endless plain stretched out at our feet, bounded in the remote distance by very lofty mountains, a few spurs of which ran out into the valley. The valley was thickly covered with grass, and, as it seemed to me, well watered and wooded. From our stand-point it must be at least one hundred and fifty miles broad, and to the south we could not see its termination. The plain, as far as we could survey it, was covered with herds of buffalo, while nearer to us deer and wild horses were grazing. How many thousands of men could easily find a living here, while in old Europe law-suits are carried on for years about an acre of land, and yet I was the only white man whose eye had rested on the inexhaustible treasures which nature had stored up here. Still the time will come when the plough will cross this beautiful plain in all directions; the smoke will rise from the hearths of prosperous planters; the church bells will summon the neighbours to church, and "hell in harness" (as the Americans call the locomotive) will snort and whistle through their valley.

Our road down to the plain, though not very steep, was fatiguing and wearisome, as the hill-side was here and there cut up by broad *cañons*, which we were compelled to ride round. As we were going down one of these ravines, one of the beautiful leopard-cats, so frequent in these mountains, sprang out of the loose stones not far from us. I sent Trusty after it down the ravine, and ere long he began barking. We hurried on as quickly as we could, and on looking down I saw the beautifully-spotted creature crouching on an isolated rock, while Trusty was leaping round it and barking. It was too far to fire with a certainty of killing, for though Trusty was quite as strong, he might easily be so injured as to be unfitted for the fatigue of our tour. Hence I dismounted, and crept near the stone on which the leopard-cat lay. I went up high enough to see it, and sent a bullet through its head. The rock was too high for me to climb up it and fetch the beast down, so I was obliged to wait till Trusty arrived. I raised him on to the rock, and he pulled the creature down. Then I returned to our cattle, while Tiger stripped the cat and brought me the skin.

These handsomely-marked animals are most dangerous to game: they kill, even when quite full, merely for the sake of the blood, and never miss an opportunity to capture their quarry. They creep with incredible skill and certainty, as well as indefatigable patience, up to the game, on which they leap with lightning speed, and do not let it go till it has given them its blood. When wounded or beset, they attack their pursuer with great fury and determination, and many an Indian, under such circumstances, has been severely injured by them. They generally live and hunt in couples, and prefer rocky regions to the plains, but also come down to the woods, where they leap down from the trees on the game, and bite it to death in the neck. Tiger shot two more of these animals before we reached the plain, which took place in the afternoon, and we camped on a stream at an early hour.

CHAPTER XVI
THE BEAR HOLE

For about a week we traversed this extensive plain, first northward, following the base of the hills we had crossed, and then westward, towards the more western ranges. Everywhere we found the richest soil, and water in abundance, as well as game of every description, and many wild horses. We lived like fighting cocks, always had the best buffalo meat, as many deer as we wanted, and also killed several antelopes. In a narrow patch of wood Trusty aroused a one-year-old bear from its winter sleep, which it was enjoying under some old fallen trees, and drove it out into the prairie. We followed it, and Trusty pinned it to the spot by a few bites in its breeches. I was just going to fire when Tiger cried to me not to do so, sprang from his horse, and ran towards the bear, laughing and leaping, with his long knife drawn. Trusty leaped, barking, in front of the irritated animal, which showed its teeth savagely, and kept him off with its forepaws, while Tiger crept behind it, and—worthy of his name—leapt past the bear, digging his knife into its side. The bear made a blow at him, but too late; and Trusty attacked it on the other flank. Tiger soon passed again behind the bear, and buried his knife between its ribs; and thus the two fought till the bear fell breathless, and Tiger stabbed it to the heart. He was not a little proud of his grand exploit, laughed, and said that he had killed an old bear in the same way once, but had unfortunately lost his good dog. I was obliged to promise him a son of Trusty, to whom he henceforth especially gave his friendship. The bear weighed some hundred pounds, and supplied us with excellent meat, in addition to its skin. We packed a good lot of it on honest Jack, and improved our meal with it that evening at the foot of the Rio Grande mountains.

Here the limestone rocks ran down to the plain, and on the distant heights we could again notice dark masses of cedar forests which had so impeded our progress. From this point our road became fatiguing and at times dangerous, as the whole country consisted of rent limestone mountains, through whose gorges and crevices we had to wind our way. In the fear of being possibly obliged to camp without water, we followed a rivulet up stream into these mountains: though we frequently had to leave it, we still kept as close to it as we could; about noon we reached a plateau which was entirely covered with petrified wood, of which thick branches and even trunks lay scattered about. It was apparently cedar wood, and I took several fine specimens of it as souvenirs. In the evening we again reached our stream, and though it was still early, and the grass not particularly good, we unsaddled, and arranged our camp. While I was thus occupied, Tiger took his rifle and soon disappeared among the rocks, which were scattered about in enormous blocks on our left, while on the right they were several hundred feet high, and displayed numerous rifts, out of which a tree here and there grew. Tiger soon returned and told me he knew where a very old bear was asleep. We would go and fetch it next morning; it was lying in a rock crevice, and judging from its track it must be a sturdy fellow.

Day had scarce broken ere we quickly finished our breakfast, and in a short time came to a spot where good grass grew; here we unsaddled, fastened our horses to a tree, and then ascended the hill-side, which became steeper the farther we got. Quite at the top, between the highest peaks, Tiger went to an overhanging rock, and stopped before an opening only a few feet wide, which ran downwards. Here he plucked a quantity of long dry grass from between the stones, rolled it rapidly into a long, thick, loose band, and then made me a sign to stand near the hole; he next lit the torch and crawled on all fours with his rifle into the rocks. I could hear only for a few minutes the sound he produced by crawling farther into the cave, and then there was a silence again. I stood with Trusty for some time without hearing the slightest sound; when suddenly a stifled echo, resembling a powerful gust of wind, came out of the crevice, and directly after, a scratching and rustling were audible, advancing towards the orifice, till all at once a heavy black bear appeared with a bleeding face.

I was standing only a few yards from the cave, and for the sake of Tiger wished to let it come out entirely ere I fired, as I felt convinced that the brute was wounded, and by firing prematurely I might turn it back on my comrade. I pressed close to the rock, and the bear had made some forward bounds, when I sent both bullets through it, although without checking its pace. The bear disappeared behind the nearest rock, and at the same moment Tiger came out of the cave all right, and ran off as quickly as a deer after the bear. I followed, and was compelled to use every exertion to keep Tiger in sight, when I noticed that in running he reloaded, and suddenly sinking on one knee, fired. But he at once sprang up again, and while reloading, sprang from stone to stone, till he knelt once more and fired. I kept as close as I could behind him, and was running up a rather steep incline, over large masses of stones, when I heard Tiger's rifle crack for the third time. In a few minutes I got round a large rock table and saw him carelessly sitting on a stone and re-loading. When I went up to him he raised his left arm and pointed to a heap of piled-up rocks, where to my surprise I saw the bear peeping over one of them like a preacher in his pulpit. It had flown there, mortally wounded, to defend itself, and showed us its bleeding terrible range of teeth.

I quickly loaded and shot it through the head, upon which it rolled down from its elevation. I took out my pocket-book and made a sketch of the rocks, while Tiger skinned and broke up the bear. I did not notice the latter retire; but when I missed him I rose and looked about for him. On going a few paces round the rock, I saw him on his knees among the bushes praying, while before him smoke curled up from a fire of leaves. I quietly walked nearer, and heard him muttering to himself, while a piece of the bear hung before him on the bush over the smoke. He soon rose, came up to me, and when I asked him what he had been about, he laughed cunningly, and answered that this meal of meat out of the bear's chest was for the god of hunting; other Indians were not acquainted with this, and hence the Delawares alone shot fat bears, while the others had lean ones. I asked him how it was the bear had not choked him in the cave. He said, laughingly, "Bear no love fire," and told me that he had crept a long way into the rocks, till the cave became very spacious; then holding his torch aloft he looked about him, and saw the bear's eyes glittering a long way in the background. He fired at it, but his bullet hit the beast on the cheek. The bear sprang up and rushed at him, but he placed himself close to the rock and held out his torch, while the bear rushed past him.

We hurried back to our horses, which took us nearly half an hour, although we went for the most part down hill. They whinnied as we approached, and waited impatiently to be noticed. Tiger mounted his piebald and rode back to the bear to fetch the skin, claws, and some of the meat, and was back in camp by noon. We merely drank coffee, packed our animals, and laid the bear's enormous ragged skin, with the fleshy side upwards, over Jack, who looked terrible in consequence.

We still followed the rocky valley up till about evening, when we reached a capital spot for our cattle, and I had dismounted to pass the night here; but Tiger pointed to the north, where the sky was slightly overcast, and then up the hill, where brushwood was hanging about the loose stones, and said, "We must go higher up the stream, or else we should sleep in the water." He now showed me that this brushwood had been lodged among the stones by the swollen stream, and we consequently camped higher up. For the first time during this tour our tent was put up, and our baggage placed under it. Then we dug a deep trench round it, and laid in an ample stock of firewood. We lit the fire under a large rock, so that it was protected from the north wind and drove strong pickets into the ground in order to fasten up our cattle close to the tent. We consequently let them graze by the water side till it grew dark, and then led them up to the camp, where we secured them. We sat till a late hour over the fire, while all nature seemed to have gone to rest. There was not a breath of air, and only the crackling of our fire interrupted the silence, and lit up the great masses of rock around us.

As we were both sleepy, I went into the tent and lay down on my buffalo robe, but Tiger lay by the fire, and we were both in the deepest sleep, when a frightful crash startled me, and a flash of lightning illumined my tent. I leaped up and found Tiger busied in blowing the fire. A pitchy darkness surrounded us, so that I could not see the horses, which were but a few yards off. Suddenly the lightning shot down the rocks, accompanied by a deafening peal of thunder, which was quickly followed by other peals. The storm soon rolled over the hills, and the rain fell in torrents. Although we had blown our fire into an enormous flame, it was put out by the rain. The flashes darted here and there, and an uninterrupted thunder rolled along the valley, while the rustling and plashing of a rapid stream became audible, and we soon saw beneath us the white foamy crests of a terrible stream pouring over the banks of the rivulet, where our horses had been peacefully grazing a few hours previously.

We stood by our horses with our buffalo robes over our heads, turning our back to the wind, and waited longingly for the moment when the storm would break. It lasted, however, till shortly before daylight.

"How are we to light a fire now?" I said to Tiger, for our wood was wet, and no hollow trees grew between the rocks around us, in which we could look for dry wood. He laughed, however, ran a short distance, returned with an armful of dry twigs which he had hidden there on the previous evening under a rock, and said, "Indian more cautious than white men." Our fire soon burnt up again, and produced a tremendous glow, before which we hung up our buffalo robes and tent to dry. The bearskin of the previous day not being dry yet either, we also hung it up to the fire, and then prepared a breakfast, a meal our cattle were obliged to go without, as the grass was completely flooded.

So soon as the wet things were dry, we started for the higher mountains in order to find a spot where our cattle could satisfy their hunger; as the road was very bad we progressed slowly, crossing a great number of morning trails of panthers, leopards, and ocelots, which were deeply trodden into the soft lime soil, and reached about noon a grassy plateau which extended to the dark cedar woods. Here we hobbled the cattle while we lit a fire against a withered mosquito-tree, and enjoyed the delicate bear meat. The air was cool, and the conical mountain peaks covered with cedars were smoking.

In the afternoon we rode toward the gloomy forests to try and find a path through them. We certainly found a number of small tracks, but not one old and used enough for us to trust it, so we went southward on the plain till darkness stopped our march. We stopped for the night at a hollow filled with rain water, and on the next morning continued our journey along the woods till, to our great joy, we found a much trampled buffalo track, by which we entered them. It led us down between two high hills, and hence I was afraid lest it might be a path which, made by animals grazing on the hill down to a stream, would terminate there. In half-an-hour we reached some large springs which gushed out of a rock and flowed in a south-eastern direction through a very narrow gorge covered with bushes, dry wood, and overarching cedars. The path, however, ran hence, to our great joy, eastward, and we dismounted, as the cedar branches hung too near over the path.

We had almost reached the top, where only a few cedars stood before us. Suddenly I fancied I could hear a tremendous rustling some distance off. I cautiously ascended to the top of the hill, and saw here, about forty yards ahead of me, three enormous condors, one of which was standing on the ground with expanded wings, while the other two were springing round it, and rising each time some feet from the ground. I sank on one knee, and sent a bullet into the broad chest of the first, while the other two fluttered their wings with a frightful yell, and soon rose high in air above me. Just as I was going to fire the second barrel, Tiger's rifle cracked behind me, and the eagle I was aiming at turned over in the air and fluttered down. I turned round to the third, and fired at it as it was soaring over the depths near us. I saw the bullet enter the soft feathers under the belly, and it shot like a dart with outstretched wings between the hills, where it disappeared among the dark cedars.

Tiger had cut off his eagle's head by the time I ran up to mine, and found under it an antelope, which the brave bird had just killed, and which had only lost its eyes and tongue. Its body was but slightly ripped up, but the whole back was covered with blood, which flowed from countless small holes produced by the eight-inch long claws of these rulers of the air. Tiger was beside himself for delight, for the wing and tail-feathers of these birds are the greatest ornaments an Indian knows, and he will readily give his best horse for them. He wears them on the band which confines his hair, and the claws, sewn on a strap, form a necklace. I told him I intended to skin mine, and take it home to stuff; but he was of opinion that he must fetch the feathers of the third condor, which had fallen into the valley, and he at once disappeared. I did not consider it possible to get down there, and utterly so to find the eagle, for I had watched it fly at least a mile. I at once set to work skinning my bird, and had not finished when Trusty growled, and Tiger really soon ran up with the spoils of the other bird.

These condors rarely come down into the lower hills; they live exclusively on the highest points of the Andes, which no human foot treads, and from the lower lands can only be seen as black dots on the blue sky. The last night's storm must have surprised these wanderers in their eyrie, and carried them before it, till they sought shelter in these mountains. Starving from their involuntary journey, they wished to taste the delicate game of these countries, which are not situated so near the clouds, when our bullets cut off their return home. The condor I first shot was by far the largest, and probably the mother of the other two, which she was training to plunder; while, on the division of the spoil, she reserved the right of taking her share first. The outstretched wings of this bird measured from end to end very nearly fifteen feet.

It was noon when we mounted our horses and rode down the stony incline. We moved along around the hills again, and seemed hardly to leave the spot, for we frequently rode for half an hour, and then suddenly found ourselves again in front of an old withered tree, or a rock emerging from the cedars which we had seen before. We rode without interruption until the sun hid itself behind the highest peaks, and cast long shadows over the hills glistening in the evening light. The sunny spots on the mountains constantly grew smaller, until at length only a single cone stood up as if gilt above the dark country. We had not yet seen a trace of the Rio Grande, and we must still be a good distance from it, for from the highest points we crossed we could see nothing as far as the horizon, except the same conical hills covered with gloomy foliage.

We halted in one of the countless hollows of these stony mountains where rain-water had collected, and decent grass grew on a small open space, took the burdens off our very wearied horses, and soon lay on our skins near the fire. A very large dry cedar trunk rose with its upper half out of the coppice. We lit our fire against its side, so that it soon began to smoulder and gave out a great heat. During the night we scarce needed to look at it, and in the morning found small flames still playing round the half-burnt tree. A strong breeze was blowing when we crawled out from under our buffalo robes. We threw plenty of wood on the burning trunk, and felt very comfortable in the warmth. While our cattle were eating their scanty breakfast, we roasted bear and antelope meat, and drank in coffee the health of the condors that had supplied us with the game. Ere long, however, we mounted, in order to bid farewell the sooner to these inhospitable forests, and see once more the frontiers of my home—the Rio Grande.

We pressed on, uphill and downhill, at one moment riding, at another leading our horses, and frequently impeded by wide torrents and broad ravines. About noon we had a prospect of a deep rocky valley, on whose sides no cedars were to be seen, and greeted it as the bed of the long-looked-for river. The mountains sank, our path ran in a straighter line towards the valley, and in little more than an hour we were riding in a long broad gully through the rocks which bordered it. The familiar river lay before us, a little deeper than we swam through it a little while previously; but, to our sorrow, the rocks on the opposite side, as far as we could see, were so steep that it was impossible for our cattle to climb up them. Nor was it possible to ride down the river, owing to the boulders and masses of drift-wood which covered the whole bank, and hence nothing remained but to ride back and seek a passage to the south among the mountains. Our cattle certainly shook their heads when we turned them back into the gully, but Tiger laughed and said that we should still sleep this night across the river. On reaching the summit we at once selected the nearest hollow, and turned to the south, following the river. It was a fatiguing journey through loose stones, fallen trees, and at times dense cedar woods, but for all that we progressed better than I had feared, and at the end of an hour we saw at an angle of the river that another large stream flowing from the eastward, fell into it, which seemed to me to be the Leone. We were obliged to go higher up the hills here on account of numerous obstacles, and lost sight of the river for awhile; still the sun had a good hour before setting when we entered a broad buffalo path which led down in a straight line to the river. I soon recognised on this road objects I had seen before, and was now certain that the eastern river was the river of my home.

So we found it to be when we rode down the Rio Grande, and unsaddled our horses there. We consulted in what way we should get across, and agreed to make a raft again. We soon had a couple of cedar logs fastened together, a heap of brushwood laid on them and our baggage on the top, and lastly we covered it all with the large bearskin, and secured it all round with straps. Tiger left his rifle behind and rode into the stream, which was not very deep here. He held the end of the lasso fastened to the raft in his right hand, and thus dragged it along. When he had gone across about a third of the river his horse was obliged to swim. The current pulled him down stream, and he was compelled to follow with his horse. He was now in the strongest current, and I noticed that he had great difficulty in keeping on his horse, when he suddenly fell off it, but kept the line between his teeth and worked his way into dead water. He soon reached the other bank and gave a loud yell, while his faithless piebald had turned back in the middle of the river and trotted up to me, shaking himself. Tiger secured the raft, ran a little way up the bank, and swam across to me with incredible speed. We now mounted our horses and swam across, Jack saluting his native land with a song of joy.

The sun was setting as we trotted up the Leone in order to reach a camping place in the hills, where I had rested many a night undisturbed, and to which I knew the road perfectly. It soon became dark, but the stars were shining. We could see enough not to lose our way, and hurried forward wrapped in our buffalo robes, for the wind blew hard, and we had become chilly in crossing the river.

When near our destination, we were riding slowly up the last ascent, when Tiger uttered his familiar expression of surprise, "Hugh," and turning round pointed behind him, to the Rio Grande. I looked back and saw a column of flame rising on the hills on the opposite side, which rapidly spread southward. The flames covered the whole hill, and the brilliantly illumined smoke clouds rolled away over them. The fiery waves poured savagely and uninterruptedly from hill to hill, checked their speed but for a short time in the deep valleys, and then darted with heightened fury up the next hill, devouring everything that came in their way. The cedar woods were on fire, and probably our last night's camp fire was the cause of it. The violent wind had doubtless blown the ashes of the burning trunk into the coppice and assailed the surrounding cedars; ere long the whole southern horizon was a sea of fire, out of which here and there isolated hills, spared by the flames, rose like black islands. We lay till late at night by our small camp fire, and watched the terribly-beautiful scene, regretting our incautiousness or neglect, which had entailed such fearful destruction. How many thousand animals had found a martyr's death on that night, and how probable it was that Indians resting there had been devoured by the flames! After lying silently for a long time looking across, Tiger uttered the words, "Poor Indians, sleep warm," accompanied by a deep sigh.

It was not till morning that fatigue overpowered us, and we fell back on our saddles. We awoke when the sun was pouring its golden light over the world, and brilliantly illumined the gloomy scene of desolation. The bare, black burned lime hills rose there above each other, wrapped themselves in black smoke-clouds, and seemed to accuse us to awakening nature as the cause of the disaster. It was really a disagreeable reproach cast at me by those hills, and we soon set out, in order to escape the sad sight, and refresh our eyes as soon as possible by a view of our cheerful home.

We crossed the Leone about noon, at the same pretty spot as when we began our journey, and soon saw the pleasant mountain springs on our right. Our cattle also knew that we were going home, and increased their pace. At length we reached the hill where the first view of the fort could be obtained, and joyfully greeted its grey wooden walls. It was still early when we rode up to my settlement from the adjoining valley, and two shots of rejoicing welcomed us from the western turret of the fort, to which we responded by firing our rifles. Everything was in the old state, the garrison healthy, and the cattle in excellent condition; the only change that had occurred was, that one of my mares had enriched me with a young Czar, that several calves had been dropped, and some dozen little pigs more were running about the fort.

CHAPTER XVII
THE COMANCHE CHIEF

I felt very comfortable in my pretty house, and Tiger informed me with great satisfaction that no one had been in his tent during our absence, in accordance with a promise I gave him when we set out. For some days we hardly left the fort, but enjoyed a rest. Tiger tanned the skins we had brought home. I stuffed my condor, at which my young friend was greatly amazed, and firmly declared that I restored the bird to life. After this we rolled cigars, made new clothes, repaired our saddles and bridles, and employed ourselves with the thousand domestic jobs which gather even during a short absence. But after we had attended to the chief matters, several wants became visible which we could only satisfy on the prairie. Thus, among others, our substitute for sugar, honey, was expended, and at the supper table we resolved on going out on this hunt the next morning, if it was fine.

The morning dawned bright and calm, and both conditions are required for a winter bee hunt, as at this season the bees only work in warm weather, and their course cannot be watched when the wind is blowing hard. We got ready immediately after breakfast, Tiger and I, armed as usual, but Antonio and one of my colonists provided with heavy sharp axes and buckets, while Jack carried two empty casks, a copper kettle, large wooden spoons, and a tin funnel. Thus we trotted over the spangled prairie across to Mustang Creek, crossed it and its thick wood by a broad buffalo path, and then rode down the prairie to a fork formed by the forest on an affluent of the Mustang, joining that on the latter river.

Here we halted, stuck a long pole, on which a small tin frying-pan was fastened, into the ground, lit dry touchwood in it, and laid on the top a piece of comb in which some honey remained. Not far from this we put up another pole with a paper smeared with honey upon it. The smoke of the boiling wax and honey serves the bees cruising over the prairie as a guide to the paper, and soon the busy gatherers arrive from all the bee-trees in the neighbourhood, load themselves as heavily as they can, and then go straight home in a direct line. The hunter now observes in which direction the greatest number of the insects swarm, because this leads him to expect a richer tree as well as a shorter distance to go. When he has decided on his route, he follows the swarm with his bait as far as he can see it, then puts up the pole again and waits till they settle, or the honey ones move and then fly home. Thus he follows the industrious insects, till by their restless activity they show him the spot where their treasures, collected during many years, are concealed, and he then disturbs the colony with cruel hand, robs it of its laboriously gathered stores, kills thousands of the colonists, and drives the rest away homeless.

We, for our part, behaved no better, except that we had brought sacks in which to carry the shelterless bees home, and give them an abode. A very large swarm went toward the Leone and another to the affluent on the left. We decided for the former, however, and in less than half an hour found ourselves in front of a gigantic maple that grew on the skirt of the forest, in whose long trunk, between the lowest branches, the orifice of the tree was completely covered with the insects. We hobbled our horses some distance from the tree, lit a fire near it, and two of us set to work with the axes to cut it down. Tiger and I had the first turn, and when we were tired the two others took our place, till we thus working in turn made the proud tree fall with its whole weight on the grass, where its splinters flew a long way around.

Each of us seized a firebrand and ran with buckets, spoons, and knives to the cracked part of the trunk, where the honey was exposed while the bees circled high above us in the air in a dense swarm. The firebrands were laid on the ground near the honey, old damp wood was laid on them to increase the smoke, and we hurriedly cut out the comb, and poured the liquid honey into a bucket which we emptied into the kettle which was slightly warmed by the fire. Honey runs from the cells with a gentle heat, and when it is liquid enough, the latter are pressed between two boards, till all the honey runs out, after which it is strained through a coarse sieve into the cask.

By the time we had secured our booty it was noon, and we recovered from our fatigue over a cup of coffee and maize cake, then we went back to the spot we had started from and followed the swarm to the small affluent, where we found the bees in another old plane close to the prairie. We also robbed this tree; it was even richer than the first, and contained layers of honey probably fifteen years old, the oldest of which were nearly black. When we had finished this job our two casks were full, and the bucket loaded with quite fresh comb.

Evening had arrived, and the bees had collected in a dense mass on a branch of the felled tree. We held an open sack under them, shook them in, and then rode back to the first tree, whose colony we also took. We returned home with our sweet stores, emptied our sacks into two hollow trees, and placed them on a scaffolding near the fort. The honey was conveyed to the storeroom, and the wax melted and laid by when cold in plates. The Indians keep their honey and bear lard in fresh deer hides, which they slit as little as possible in skinning; they cut off the neck and legs, sew the openings up very tightly with sinews, fill the skin, and close the last opening in the same way, into which they thrust a reed and squeeze the honey as they want it through the latter. The honey keeps in this way very well, and is easier to carry on horseback than in hand vessels. We employed the honey in every way sugar is used in the civilized world. We sweetened our coffee and tea with, it, employed it in cooking various dishes, in preserving fruit, such as grapes, plums, mulberries, &c. In a word, it fully took the place of that expensive and hardly procurable product of civilization, and could always be obtained in such quantities that we never ran short of it. When hunting in the neighbourhood we very often found bee trees, which we marked in order to plunder them as we wanted.

Our table was now enriched by a fresh delicacy which we enjoyed during the winter months: it consisted of wild ducks and geese. These birds visited our river at this season in great numbers, and spread in flocks over the water. The very lofty banks, the numerous sharp turns, and the insignificant breadth of the stream rendered it extraordinarily easy to kill heaps of these birds in a short time. I usually took with me two guns and a man with a pack horse, who followed at some distance and placed the dead birds on the saddle. I followed the steep river bank, every now and then creeping down to the incline, and could then see from one bend to the other where the birds were resting on the water. I generally contrived to creep through the wood exactly over this spot, without the birds perceiving me. I then whistled, while holding the muzzle of my very large gun over the bank, and the birds in their fright drew closer together. Then I sent a charge of shot among them, and fired the other right among the rising flock. Then I took the other gun and sent the contents of both barrels after the flying ducks or geese. I frequently shot in this way twenty in one flock. The remainder generally joined the next flock farther down the stream. Trusty and some spaniels accompanied me on this chase and fetched the shot birds.

Most of the ducks and geese that visited us were very like the European, though rather larger; both are very fat and well tasted, which is probably caused by the splendid acorns they find among us. We generally carried a whole load home, from which we merely cut the breasts, legs, and livers, and boiled them into a jelly.

One afternoon, when Tiger had ridden off at an early hour in pursuit of game, I took my gun to go after geese down the river, which I heard croaking from the fort: I went out without calling a dog, and ran down to the water;

I passed the garden and the ford, where the river winds to the north in the wood, and went into the bushes in order to approach the geese, which I had seen about a hundred yards farther on. All at once I heard something like the footfall of a horse echo through the forest on the opposite side. I listened, and convinced myself that I was not mistaken. Tiger had gone southward in the morning to Mustang Creek, and I could not imagine how he was now returning from the north. I lay down among the bushes, so as to keep an eye on the ford: the noise drew nearer, till a mounted Indian appeared on a path on the opposite side, who stopped there and looked cautiously around.

After a while the Redskin crossed the ford, ascended the opposite bank, and taking his long rifle in his right hand, he led his horse into a thick bush about forty paces ahead of me. There he fastened it up, laid his rifle across his left arm, and shook fresh powder into the pan from his horn. What could the Indian intend, and to what tribe did he belong? These questions occurred to me simultaneously with the suspicion that he might probably have hostile designs. My gun was loaded with not very heavy shot, but it carried as far as the Indian's rifle, though it did not kill so certainly. I had, however, some slugs in my hunting pouch, and while he was repriming, I, as I lay flat on the ground, pulled out two of the largest bullets that fitted my gun. I thrust them both into the barrels, and then slowly drew the ramrod, pressed two paper wads on the bullets, and returned the ramrod to its place.

During this the Indian had returned his powder-horn to its place, taken his tomahawk from the saddle and thrust it through his belt, woven several large leafy branches of evergreen myrtle and rhododendron under his saddle, so that they concealed the colour of his light horse, and then, leaving the path, went in a stooping posture through the wood toward my garden. I cautiously followed him at a distance of about one hundred yards, bending down close to the ground, continually keeping behind the bushes and disappearing in the grass when he stopped or made a movement as if to look round. He seemed, however, only to keep his eye on the garden, and bent lower the nearer he got to it. Suddenly he fell into the tall grass between the evergreen bushes, and disappeared from my sight. Had he heard me or seen me fall down? The point now was which of us should see the other first. The grass in which I lay was not very high, but green bushes hung down to the ground in front of me, too close to be seen through by my foe, but still leaving me sufficient gaps through which to peep, while the bushes round him were scrubby and the grass alone concealed him. If he had seen me he would certainly not remain lying, as he would have the worst of it.

I had raised myself sufficiently to survey his place, and after a while noticed the grass waving a little to the left of the spot where I had last seen him. Everything became still and motionless again, and we lay thus for nearly a quarter of an hour, when I saw the Indian raise his head out of the grass and look about him; he had not noticed me yet, or else he would not have exposed himself so recklessly to my fire. He rose slowly and glided towards the garden; he got close to the fence, which was made of ten logs placed in a zigzag over each other, and on the outerside were heaped up the branches of the trees from which the wood for the palisades had been cut. I had put this up to prevent the buffaloes and deer from forcing their way into the garden.

The Indian now stepped close to the wall of dry branches, while I lay in the bushes about a hundred yards behind him. He stopped, looked into the garden for a long time, and then round the wood; he then stooped and crept under the brushwood up to the fence, seated himself crosslegged close to the latter, and laid his rifle across one of the logs. While he was working his way through the branches and brushwood, I crept on all-fours nearer to him and remained behind an oak about forty yards from him. Just as I reached the tree, I broke a thin dry branch with my hand, and the very slight sound scarce reached the savage's ear, ere he started round and gazed intently in my direction. I did not stir, but held my gun firmly, with the determination that he should not leave the spot alive.

He looked towards me for nearly a quarter of an hour, still trusting to the sharpness of his ears, when suddenly one of my men, who was coming down from the fort with two buckets to fill at the spring, could be heard whistling on the other side of the garden. The Indian started round, thrust his rifle through the fence, pointed at the spring, and knelt down behind its long barrel. At the same instant I sprang out from behind the oak, raised my gun, and sent the charge of the right-hand barrel between the savage's shoulders; he leapt up, and while doing so, I gave him the second charge, after which he fell backwards into the brushwood. I shouted to my man who, in his alarm, was running back to the fort, and rushed to the Indian, who was writhing in his blood and striking around with hands and feet. My comrade hurried through the garden, and clambering over the fence, gazed down at the shot man in horror. I explained to him in a few words how accident had preserved his life, as the savage had been lying in wait for him and had his rifle pointed at him, and I then buried my knife in the heart of the quivering savage. We took his rifle and medicine bag, fetched his horse after I had reloaded, and took it up to the fort, where we fastened it inside the enclosure.

I impatiently waited for Tiger to obtain an explanation from him, as I feared lest the shot man might be a Delaware. The evening came and Tiger was not back yet. A thousand suppositions, a thousand suspicions involuntarily crossed my mind. Could Tiger be a traitor? could the

Delawares have broken their long-tried friendship with the white men? We drove our cattle in earlier than usual, rode them down to water, laid our weapons ready to hand, and prepared to oppose any possible attack. I went to the eastern turret and gazed over the wide prairie, when I suddenly noticed far on the horizon a black point that seemed strange to me. I looked through my glass, and to my great delight recognised the large white spots of Tiger's piebald.

I now felt lighter at heart, ran down and waited for him at the gate. At length he rode up to me from the last hollow, loaded with deer and bear meat, and the hide of a small bear, leapt from his horse and heartily shook my hand. I told him what had happened, and he listened most attentively. His eyebrows were contracted and his usually pleasant eyes flashed savagely. He said nothing but "kitchi kattuh," made me a sign to enter the fort, and when we reached the dining-room where the dead man's hunting-bag lay, he cried, "Kitchi," placed two fingers of his right hand before his mouth, so that they seemed to be emerging from it, and repeated "Kitchi," *i.e.* two tongues. He then led me out of the fort, when he stopped, and said to me that the false kitchi had laid watch for him in the garden and intended to take his life, so that the Delawares might fancy we had killed him and take their revenge on us. It had indeed gradually grown a custom in the fort that Tiger, when he was at home, fetched fresh water from the spring before supper, and his supposition appeared to be well founded; still the unexpected appearance of one of my men seemed to have turned the kitchi from his original purpose, because he was on the point of sending the bullet intended for Tiger through the chest of the latter.

We now helped to hang up the meat brought in by Tiger, and sat down to supper, when the occurrence naturally became the sole subject of conversation, and was regarded from every side. We agreed to bury the Indian, and I went, accompanied by Antonio and Tiger, with a spade and a cedar-wood torch, through the garden to the dead man. Tiger drew him out of the brushwood, took off his beads, armlets, and leathern breech clout, and then dragged him with Antonio's help nearer the river, where we dug a deep hole and buried the corpse.

We soon forgot this incident, and went on with our winter avocations as before. We slightly enlarged our field, which was a fatiguing job, as it lay in the wood, and the bushes grew very close together there. These and the smaller trees were cut down and piled up round the larger ones, after the latter had been out into the wood. After they had dried for a week, they were kindled, which dried the bark of the large trunks, and thus killed the tree. We then set to work with a heavy plough to turn up the ground: this operation is always performed twice or thrice through the winter, before the seed is put in the ground in spring. It may be asked why we did not lay out our field in the prairie, as we should thus have saved this labour? The reason is that the prairie soil is remarkably difficult to plough, because it consists of a black hard earth, in which the delicate young plants have unusually large roots, as hard as glass. I afterwards cultivated land of this sort, and at the first breaking up had six or eight draught cattle fastened to the plough. Then again, this land, owing to its hardness, produces scarce no crop in the first year, in the second a very poor one, in third a moderate one, and not till the fourth a full crop. It is always much more difficult to cultivate than the forest land, as the heavy rains in the winter season always more or less restore its firmness, while the forest soil bears prolifically in the first year.

In the garden we had plenty of work too; the potatoes were laid in beds, in order to grow the tap roots, which are cut off in spring and planted out in the field. Then the tobacco beds were put in order, from which the young plants were transplanted in February. The same plant produces among us three or even four crops, as we always leave a young shoot to grow, when the leaves are ripe enough to cut. Then there were vegetables to sow, vines to prune, fruit-trees to graft; in short, we had our hands full, and I only went with Tiger away from the fort to hunt bears, whose fat we were obliged to collect at this time, as it is not nearly so abundant at other seasons.

One morning I resolved to go to Mustang Creek, and choose a suitable spot where I could build a carriage bridge across it, as I frequently had meat to fetch from the prairies on the other side, and I also intended to make, by degrees, a passable road to the settlements. I rode away at an early hour, accompanied by Trusty, but at some distance from home I noticed that Milo, an old bear-finder, was running after me, which was a bore, as the good old dog, if he by chance hit on a fresh trail, would be sure to follow it, and I had not intended to hunt bears on this day. The dog was much too slow and deaf, and I only gave him food for the many faithful services he had rendered me: I did not care to ride back, and hence called him closer up to my horse, and continued my journey.

I soon reached the river and was busy examining the banks, when suddenly old Milo gave tongue, and had run too far into the bushes for me to check him. I was sorry, for if the old fellow had a row with a bear by himself, it would be all over with him. I heard his bark going farther and farther, and though I felt grieved, I was obliged to leave him to his fate. After a while I fancied that I heard him continually barking at the same spot. I listened, and it seemed more than probable that he had attacked a bear. I must hurry to his assistance, so I rode as far as I could into the bushes, tied up my horse, and forced my way through the thicket.

The Backwoodsman | 147

I soon leaped through the last bushes, and to my surprise saw Milo sitting in front of an old cypress and barking up at it. I examined the gigantic trunk, and clearly saw on its bark the traces of a bear which had climbed up it. In the first fork the tree was hollow from top to bottom, and I did not doubt for a moment but that Bruin was having his winter sleep in it. To cut down the tree was a heavy task, as it was above eight feet in diameter, and then, too, it stood among a number of other giants, against which it might easily lean in falling, when we should not be able to get at its occupant. I tapped round the tree to see whether it was hollow far down, but I could not settle the point satisfactorily, as I had no axe with which to hit hard enough.

I quickly formed my resolution, caught up Milo, carried him away from the trail, and hastened to my horse, which speedily bore me home. Tiger was at the river washing deer hides, when I arrived on the bank and informed him of my discovery: he quickly packed up his skins, ran to his tent, and hurried to the prairie to fetch the piebald. In less than half an hour we were *en route* for the bear, accompanied by Antonio and one of the colonists armed with axes, while Jack followed us with a large pack saddle, and Trusty leaped ahead of us. We soon reached the river, led our horses some distance down it, and tied them up in the thicket; then we went to the cypress in which our sleeper was. We examined it and found it quite sound for over eight feet from the ground, but from that point hollow, and more so on the western side.

We soon raised a framework of thin branches round the tree, on which one of us was raised by turns, and cut an opening in the trunk at the spot where the hollow began. While one was engaged in this way, the others brought up dry wood, which we piled up against the opening like a bonfire. We then lit it, and ere long the flames crept up the stem, and the dried bark fell off with a cracking sound into the fire. We arranged ourselves round the tree at some distance in such a way that we could cover it pretty well from all sides, and expected every moment to see the bear quit its winter quarters. We had been standing there, however, for above an hour, and the gentleman did not make his appearance, though the smoke was rising from the hollow. The bear probably lay below the hole, and the smoke passed over it without annoying it.

All at once I saw sparks flying out of the tree, which proved that it was beginning to catch fire inside. I shouted to the others to look out, and just after I heard a crash, and with it appeared the black form of a very old bear between the first branches. The fright and embarrassment of my gentleman were extraordinary, when he looked down into the fire under him, and moved backwards and forwards undecided what path to choose. I had told my men not to fire so long as the bear was over the fire, but to let it advance on the long branches far enough not to fall into the flames, which would have deprived us of its splendid skin.

Master Bear had by this time selected a very stout branch and crept cautiously along it, looking down first on this side and then on that at the flames, and was on the point of making itself into a ball to have a drop, when I fired at it, and in falling it clutched the branch with its claws in order to drag itself up again. At the same moment, however, four more bullets flew through it, and it came down with an enormous blow. I ran up with a revolver, and shot it through the head, whereupon it became quiet. It was one of the finest bears we had killed during this year, and gave us a large quantity of fat and a splendid skin. We broke it up, packed on Jack as much as he could carry, and distributed the rest among our horses. We then went home heavily laden, and sat till late in the kitchen, busied in melting down the grease, after enjoying some roast bear ribs for supper.

At times there were slight domestic annoyances. A pig or a calf was torn by the wolves, a few hen's nests plundered by the racoons, a dog killed by the snakes, or a horse ran a thorn into its foot. However, up to the present we had preserved our health, we knew naught of sorrow, and the thousand passions which civilized life entails, and which become the source of endless suffering, were entirely lulled to sleep among us. On the other hand we were deprived of many enjoyments which social life affords, but at the same time had countless pleasures, which must be given up there. The hardest thing to me was that I could not obtain books without great trouble and expense, while events in the civilized world were more or less unknown to me. At times I received a packet of old newspapers, whose fragments, however, only helped to render my confusion worse confounded. To tell the truth, I was beginning to yearn for a nearer connexion with the world and a little more society.

One morning the dogs barked in an unusual manner, and one of my men ran up to me and told me that one of my buffalo calves, which I had captured in the last summer, and of which I possessed eight, had leapt into the river, because the dogs were tormenting it. I ran down to the river, and after considerable exertions we succeeded in getting the animal out, uninjured, but very fatigued. These calves were remarkably tame, more so than those of our cows, and never went far from the fort. In spite of their terrible appearance they were very comical; all had names to which they answered, and caused us much fun. I intended to train them for working, and to breed a mixed race with my cattle, which, however, only offers an advantage in meat and size, as the buffaloes yield much less and worse milk than our domestic kind. It is not possible to produce a breed between our tame cow and the buffalo, as the cow cannot give birth to the calf owing to the hump on the shoulders, and almost always is killed by it; but the opposite breed flourishes and is capable of further procreation. Buffalo oxen are excellent for work, as they grow very tame and possess enormous strength; the only fault is that when they are thirsty, no power on earth can restrain them from satisfying their thirst. I knew a planter on the Rio Grande, who employed a couple of these animals, that ran away once with a heavy cart to the river, and dashed over its steep bank to satisfy their thirst, but he got them out again all right.

Just as we were taking the saved buffalo up to the fort, the sentry came to me and announced that five white men were riding down the river, upon which I went to the turret and saw that the new arrivals were three white men, a negro and a mulatto. About half an hour later the strangers rode up to the fort and dismounted at the gate, while the coloured men took their horses and unsaddled them. A fine looking man of nearly sixty years of age advanced to me, shook my hand and introduced himself to me as a Mr. Lasar, from Alabama, one of his young companions as his son John, and the other as his cousin Henry, of the same name. The old gentleman had something most elegant and attractive about his appearance, which evidenced lengthened intercourse with the higher social circles; over his high bronzed forehead shone his still thick though silvery hair, while long black eyebrows overshadowed his light blue eyes, and his fresh complexion seemed to protest against his white hair. Though fully six feet high he carried himself with the strength of a man of thirty, and his bright merry eyes proved that his mind was still youthful. He was an old Spaniard, had settled when a young man in Alabama, and though the blue eyes contradicted his origin, it was manifested in all the rest of his countenance. His son John was shorter and lighter built, with black curling hair and very dark, but pleasant eyes, a nice looking youth of seventeen, and cousin Henry a young man of twenty odd, of middle height and narrow between the shoulders, showed by his auburn hair and grey eyes, that his blood was mixed.

I conducted the strangers to the parlour and set before them a breakfast, among the dishes being one of duck's breast in jelly. The old gentleman was greatly surprised, and said that he had not expected to find anything at my house beyond very good game and roasted marrow bones. When I treated them to French wine and cigars, and they surveyed the ornaments of my room, they expressed the utmost surprise at the amount of comfort they found, and John said that I had everything precisely as his father intended to have it when he settled here. The old gentleman now informed me of his intention to come into my neighbourhood and requested my advice and aid. He had a cotton plantation in Alabama, but the number of his negroes had increased so considerably that he could not employ them all on his estate, and must hire out the majority at very low wages; land was too high in price there, so he preferred taking up Government land here and submitting to the privations and dangers of a life on the border. He now proposed to inspect the land, then return and send on John with fifty negroes, so as to get a maize crop ready, while he would follow in autumn with his family and five hundred slaves. I was very glad to have such neighbours, so I gladly offered him my services in showing him as much fine land as he wanted close to mine.

My guests rested for a few days and amused themselves with inspecting my farm and arrangements, and making small hunting trips in the vicinity, in which old Mr. Lasar eagerly joined. It is true that he shot deer and turkeys with his large fowling-piece loaded with swan shot, through which many a head escaped him, and I reproached him for doing so, as I considered this shameful butchery. He allowed his fault, but said that no other weapon was employed in shooting where he came from, but when he came out to join me, he would also introduce the rifle.

After my guests had rested sufficiently, I rode with them over to the Mustang river, passed through its woods and followed its course southward to its junction with the Rio Grande. Here we turned back up the stream, and rode along the forest to our morning track, so that the strangers had ample opportunity for examining the land on both sides of the river. Mr. Lasar was much pleased, and at once decided on this land, as it fully satisfied all his wishes. We reached home at a late hour, and Lasar was so perfectly contented that he proposed returning home at once; but I urged him to look at other land to the north of me, for which tour we made our necessary preparations on the next day. On the third morning we rode up the Leone to the spot where my border line crossed it two miles from the fort. From this point to the source of the river lay very fine land too, although the woods were not so extensive as lower down it.

We spent the night at the wellhead, and then rode northwards to Turkey Creek, in which tour we found a great deal of land well adapted for ploughing, although the smaller quantity would have rendered it better suited for small settlers. Still the country here aroused Mr. Lasar's admiration, and he declared that before two years had passed it should be all occupied by friends of his from Alabama. I reminded him of the human skulls and bones, which I had shown him at the sources of the Leone, belonging to settlers murdered by the Indians, who had come from Georgia, and only enjoyed the pleasures of a border life for a few months. He said, however, that so many families must arrive simultaneously as would hold the Indians within bounds. For his own part he decided on Mustang River, and on reaching the fort again, he rested two more days with me, which we employed in talking over and settling everything. On this occasion I proposed to hire of him twelve negroes whom he could send with his son, for I wanted to begin cotton planting. He agreed most willingly, as, when he settled, he would require a good many things of me, such as maize, pigs, cows, fowls, tallow, bear's grease, &c., and we could deduct their value from the rent. On the third morning I accompanied my guests some distance and then rode home with the brightest prospects for the future.

A most unexpected event brightened my hopes for the future even more. A few days after Lasar's departure a party of seven Comanche Indians came riding up the river, armed with unstrung bows, and no lances. They rode up to the fence, and one of them shouted—"Captain, good friend," and I went out to them and asked what they wanted. One of them spoke English very well, and appeared to me a Mexican, who had probably been stolen by them in childhood and had since lived among them. He said that the chief of all the Comanches, Pahajuka (the man in love) had sent them to ask me whether he might come and make a friendship with me? He had heard that I was a good friend to other Indians, and wished me to become his friend as well. The message greatly surprised me, as hitherto, when I had come in contact with men of this nation, we had used our weapons. My first feeling was a suspicion that they wished to effect by treachery what they had not been able to do by arms: still I would not entirely repulse them, and said that if they were speaking to me with one tongue, and desired my friendship, I would readily give it to them; but if they were double-tongued I would become still more their enemy, and in that case they would not be able to sleep peacefully in these parts.

I told them at the same time that I should expect their chief on the next morning, on which their speaker intimated that their tribe were encamped a long way off, and Pahajuka had sent them down from there, but when the sun rose for the tenth time he would be here. I promised to wait for him on the appointed morning, and then the savages rode away and soon disappeared behind the last hill on the prairie. Whatever might be the results of the impending conference, I was resolved to make every effort to produce, if possible, more pleasant relations between myself and the Comanches, as by far the greater number of Indians who visited our country belonged to this nation, and the incessant hostilities with them became the more annoying to me in proportion as my cattle and property became augmented.

It was now winter, and in addition to our domestic tasks, we principally employed our time in hunting bears, as I greatly needed their grease on the arrival of the expected new settlers and could sell it very profitably. For the sake of fun we also went out singly at night to shoot deer by the system of pan-hunting, so usual in the Eastern States, but which I rarely employed, although it is remarkably productive. This hunt is effected on horseback: the sportsman carries over his left shoulder a stout stick about six feet in length, to the upper end of which a frying-pan with a high rim is fastened. In this pan he lays some small-cut pieces of pine-wood, which, when kindled, burn for a long time with a very bright flame, and allow him distinctly to see every object for a long distance, while himself seeing nothing of the fire behind his back.

Deer, antelopes, and other animals when they see the moving fire, hurry up to it in order to satisfy their curiosity. The hunter can see the animal's eyes glistening at a distance of eighty yards, while he is scarce visible himself. He rides nearer up to distinguish the body more clearly, but generally contents himself with the eyes, which he takes as his mark, and discharges his rifle at them. Owing to the light which falls from behind on the barrel and the back of the sight, a most careful aim can be taken, and as a rule you can ride up to within thirty or forty yards of the animal. Even after the shot I have seen the unhit animals only run a few yards and then stop curiously, so that I have been able to give them a second barrel. Over the horse's hind-quarters a large wet blanket or hide is laid to protect it from the sparks or coals that might fall out of the pan. It is the easiest way of killing game, and in places not thickly covered with wood this mode of hunting promises an extraordinary charm, through the wondrous illumination which the fire produces on the green, flower-clad foliage. A whole forest may be depopulated in this way, and hence I regard it as quite unworthy of a true sportsman.

For all that, we now and then went pan-hunting for the sake of the fun, but never shot till we could plainly distinguish the animal, which prevented any butchery. In the old States, where people only care about killing the game, this mode of hunting is almost exclusively employed, and in those regions where game still exists, you rarely enter a planter's house without seeing a pan behind the door. Very frequently, though, in those inhabited districts, the nightly sportsman is disagreeably undeceived by the yell of agony from his own steer, mule or horse, which he has attracted from its pasture by its fire, for the flashing eyes do not tell the nature of the animal. I remember going one night on foot, with the pan on my shoulder, round my field to check the deer, which were doing great damage to my beans. Suddenly I saw a pair of large eyes gleaming before me which slowly approached and constantly became larger and more fiery. They came slowly along the fence to me, and seemed such a height from the ground that I could not imagine to what fabulously large animal they belonged. They stopped, but I did not know whether at a distance of twenty or fifty yards. I fired, heard something dash across the field, and the eyes disappeared. The next morning I went with Trusty to the spot where I had fired, and we soon found a dead lynx, which had come toward me in the darkness walking on the fence. In those parts, where the cattle graze at liberty, this sport is consequently most dangerous, as you run as much chance of killing your best horse as a deer or tiger-cat.

We also had great fun this winter in destroying the wolves, which we pursued in every possible way, as they were very dangerous to my cattle. The easiest way of killing them is poisoning with strychnine, but I did not employ it near my house through fear of hurting my dogs. For this object we always rode some miles away, threw a fresh deer-paunch on the ground, and trailed it after us by a long rope. Thus we rode past the wood out into the prairie, where we pulled up the paunch at a spot which displayed little grass, and then scattered the little lumps of poisoned meat. This was always done in the evening, and on the next morning we rode back to the spot, where we found the dead wolves lying about, which rarely went a hundred yards from the spot where they devoured the meat.

It caused us greater pleasure, however, to capture them in traps, a quantity of which we always had set round the fort. They were made in the following way:—Four stout posts were driven into the ground, forming a square of about four feet, and inside of them other longer posts were laid till they formed walls about three feet in height: we then drove four more posts into the angles of the walls, and fastened them securely to those outside. In these chests we placed a flooring, so that the captured animal could not escape by scratching up the ground, and on the top of the cage a cover, weighed down in front by large stones. The other end of the cover was fastened to the trap with very strong withes, and the forepart was raised, a prop was placed under it, which fell at a slight touch, and caused the cover to shut. At night we trailed a fresh deer-paunch from a long distance to the trap, threw meat in, then dragged it to the next trap, and so on till all were baited. We caught a great many wolves in this way, which we often took home alive and let the dogs hunt them to death on the prairie. In order to take them alive out of the trap we used an iron fork, which we struck into the ground over the wolf's neck, and then pressed its head down till we had fastened its feet. It is remarkable what an innate dislike dogs entertain for these animals. Frequently when I had killed one of them, whose skin was not worth taking home, I merely cut off its nose and threw it on the ground near the fort, upon which all my dogs gathered round and kept up the most fearful barking for hours.

At length the day arrived on which the chief of the Comanches had appointed his visit, and at about 7 A.M. three of these savages came up to the fort to inform me that their leader was encamped half-an-hour's distance off in the woods of the Leone, and expected me there. I asked Tiger's advice, and he advised me to ride out, as the Comanches meant honestly. I therefore saddled and rode, accompanied by Tiger, one of my colonists, and Trusty, out to the Indians, and told them they could ride on and I would follow. We soon reached the spot where Pahajuka was encamped, and I noticed to my satisfaction that only a squaw and a single man were seated at his fire.

I dismounted, left my man with the horses, and walked up to the chief, who now rose and folded me in his arms twice. Then his squaw came to me and evidenced her friendship in the same way. Pahajuka was a man of about sixty years of age, of middle height, plump, and possessing a very pleasant, kindly appearance. He was entirely dressed in deer-hide, had very fine beads round his neck, and in his raven black hair he had fastened a tail of plaited buffalo hair five feet in length, on which a dozen round silver plates, four inches in width, were fastened. He wore this tail hanging over his right arm, and it seemed to me as if this ornament was only worn on solemn occasions, as I never saw it again, though I met this savage frequently. The squaw was a powerful, stout, extremely pleasant matron, who appeared to take a great interest in establishing friendly relations between us. She was very talkative, and the interpreter could scarce keep pace with her tongue.

After the first explanations why they desired my friendship, the squaw fetched several sorts of dried meat in leathern bags, spread them on a buffalo hide, and begged me to take the meal of friendship with them. Tiger, too, sat down, and my other companion was obliged to do the same. It tasted very poor to us, whose tongues were spoiled by the culinary art; still we did our best, and the same with the pipe, which Pahajuka sent round afterwards. When these forms had been gone through, the old squaw packed up her traps again on her mule, and mounted it, while the chief seated himself on a similar animal, which was of very rare beauty.

We now rode, followed by the Indians, to the fort, where the latter camped outside, while Pahajuka and his squaw sat down in our parlour. I had coffee and pastry served up to them, both of which it seemed they had taken before, and they disposed of them heartily. Then I gave them both a pipe and tobacco, and then the conversation began, in which the interpreter's services were greatly called upon. They told me that before I came into these parts, the Comanches had always been able to sleep here quietly, and their children and cattle had grown fat; but since I had been here, their hearts had always beaten with terror, and they were unable to sleep at their fire at night. They now wished to make peace with me, and when they came to me, carry their weapons into my house, and fold their arms, so that their cattle might graze in peace, and their children grow fat.

After this affair had been long discussed, and all possible assurances of friendship given on both sides, I turned the conversation to my guests, and heard that Pahajuka was supreme chief of the whole Comanche nation, and his wife a person of importance in all consultations. The old lady was very sensible and really amiable. She moved with a great deal of gracefulness, and was constantly in the merriest temper. She laughed and joked with her husband as if she were a young girl, and if he reproached her for it by a serious look, she turned laughingly to me, and asked me if she looked so old as not to be allowed a joke? At dinner the two old people behaved very properly, although they could not quite manage to eat with a knife and fork, and frequently helped with their fingers. They enjoyed everything excessively, and said they would take with them a bit from each dish. I was curious whether they would sleep in the fort or prefer the camp of their people. The evening came, and after we had supped, and food had been given the Indians outside, I prepared a bed for the old couple in the parlour, put up two tallow candles for them, and told them when one was burnt out to light the other, as candles delighted them uncommonly. Then I intimated to them that I always closed the fort at night, as they must tell their Indians. They were quite satisfied and lay down on the unusual bed, laughing and jesting.

I chained up all the dogs during the night to prevent any disturbance of the peace, and was awakened at a very early hour by my new friends rapping at my door. They had both slept famously, and assured me that ere long all the chiefs of their nation would come to make friendship with me, and wherever Comanches lived, I could now ride and lie down to sleep in safety. The old people had something so honest in their manner, that I no longer doubted the truth of the sentiments they expressed; and though I never carelessly trusted to the honesty of isolated Indians of this tribe, the assurance of the couple was confirmed, and I was never again engaged in hostilities with these people.

My guests remained three days with me, after which I dismissed them with numerous trifling presents, consisting of articles of clothing, coloured handkerchiefs, tobacco, a couple of blankets, small hand-glasses, &c. I accompanied them on their first day's journey, slept with them that night, and then took leave with promises of a speedy meeting. Afterwards they visited me regularly several times a year, and as they had predicted, all the tribes of their nation came in turn to make peace with me, and their example was followed by others, such as the Mescaleros, Kioways, Shawnees, &c.

CHAPTER XVIII
THE NEW COLONISTS

A few months had passed since my Alabama friends left me, and I had heard nothing more of them, when one morning the watchman told me, with great joy, that a long train of men, draught cattle, and carts was coming down the river. I soon recognised through my glass young Lasar and his cousin Henry, surrounded by a large number of negroes. The train moved very slowly onwards, and did not stop before the fort for some hours, when I greeted the new-comers most heartily. John had sixty odd strong negroes with him, twelve of whom were intended for me; and brought stores and tools with him on five large waggons, each drawn by six oxen. He had made the journey by steamer, *viâ* New Orleans, and partly on the Rio Grande. When they landed he bought the draught cattle, and had reached me without any accident. I kept them a few days with me to let them rest, and then proceeded with them across to Mustang River, where they camped on the ground selected by Mr. Lasar.

They chose for their maize-field a spot in the advance woods, where the soil was rich and loose, and the trouble of blazing the trees and ploughing round them was saved. The negroes advanced in their job with almost incredible rapidity, and in a short time a field of some hundred acres was cleared, ploughed, and fenced. Up to that time, the negroes lay at nights under tents or in their carts, but now they built blockhouses and put up fences, in which the mules and horses rested at night. John rode over to me regularly to spend the night with me, and on Sunday we hunted in the neighbourhood. He was a good shot, laid aside the shot-gun for the rifle and pistols, and soon learned to use these weapons excellently.

My life from this time underwent a change. I had twelve negroes at my disposal, and must so employ them as not only to get their hire out of them, but also attain the object for which I had hired them, namely, making a profit. With this the careless, happy life which had surrounded me for years, far from humanity, was at an end, and the god of gold, with his thousand sufferings, hatefulnesses, and sorrows, began to establish his despotic rule even here. I now made a second extensive field which was sown with maize, by the side of my old one, while in the latter I planted cotton, as this plant does not flourish in new ground. I took young oxen from the pasturage and forced them into the strange yoke. My mules, which had hitherto only fetched at rare intervals our few wants from the settlements, were now attached to the plough at daybreak, and forced with the whip to toil till sunset. My colonists had so much to do all day that they went to bed at an early hour, and we no longer sat, as of yore, cozily round the table, talking and jesting about the unimportant events which had occurred during the day. In a word, the whole colony felt the change. Peace had departed and made room for the restless activity of civilization. Tiger did not like the change, although I carefully avoided everything which might render his residence among us less agreeable. He was now obliged to ride out hunting alone, while we required far more meat than before. Still I frequently tore myself away and went with him for three or four days into the desert, in order to recall past times, if only temporarily. Summer arrived with a rich harvest, and with it again fresh, uninterrupted toil. My neighbours had also been rewarded for their exertions by an immense maize crop, and employed the late summer in building larger houses for the reception of Lasar and his family. Strangers came to prospect the land in our neighbourhood, and all went away contented with an assurance that they would soon settle here. Among them were many unpleasant characters, but I consoled myself with the thought that they would not become near neighbours of mine, for I possessed all the forest land down the river, so far as it was suitable for cultivation, and up stream Lasar had purchased a large district adjoining my frontier. They could not settle on the open prairie without water or wood, and hence they must proceed to the streams farther north, where I was tolerably out of their reach.

In autumn, Mr. Lasar arrived with his wife, two daughters, and a younger son, and brought with him about five hundred negroes, a number of fine horses and splendid cattle. Our social circumstances thus advanced a stage. This highly educated and amiable family offered me pleasures which appeared to me quite new and attractive, and I did not reflect that I had bidden farewell to them some few years back through sheer weariness. The deer-hide dress was now frequently changed for the costume of former days, the razors looked up, an old negress hired who knew how to wash and iron, and imperceptibly many long-forgotten follies and considerations crept into our simple, natural life. Civilization, however, had set its foot in our paradise once for all, and nothing was able to oppose its rapid advance.

The winter brought several large planters to Mustang River, above Lasar's estate, and the land toward the northern rivers was occupied by others, while to the south of us the settlements of the Rio Grande also increased. All these new-comers were persons who occupied large districts, by which the disagreeable small neighbourhood was avoided. Still a few squatters had already settled here and there on the less valuable small lots between our estates, and among them were some most unsatisfactory persons.

One Sunday morning I was riding several miles above the fort through the woods in the direction of the Leone. I had thrown the reins on Czar's neck and was no great distance from the river bank, when Trusty stopped and looked round to me with a growl. I called him back and rode slowly up the small elevation whence I could look down at the river. To my surprise, I saw there a pretty young woman, with a man's arm round her waist, sitting on the bank, where they had made coffee over a small fire, and were now comfortably drinking it. Not far from them a powerful horse was grazing, and close by stood a two-wheeled cart, which contained some household articles and provisions. The long single rifle lay by the man's side, and a couple of deer legs and a turkey were hanging on the tree behind him. "Hilloh, sir, you are on Indian territory!" I shouted to the stranger, and he hurriedly leaped up rifle in hand, but I rode up to him with a smile, and blamed his recklessness, remarking that if I had been an Indian he would no longer be among the living.

I was surprised at the beauty of the female, whose raven shining hair formed an admirable contrast with the deep carmine of her cheeks and lips, and the transparent alabaster of her delicate skin. She also rose and looked at me with her large blue eyes, from under her long lashes. A loose, light dress was fastened round her waist by a red silk handkerchief, and advantageously displayed her tall graceful figure, and little feet thrust into light shoes of deer-hide. I asked whither they were going, and if they were acquainted with the country? The stranger said that he intended to settle in the neighbourhood: he had followed the wagon trail of the planter who had settled on the Mustang, and was told by him that no more land was to be had here; hence he resolved to go farther north and look for a farm. The restless, shy look of the man displeased me, and hence I did not invite him to rest with me and lay in fresh provisions, but wished him luck in his undertaking and continued my journey. I heard afterwards that he was living twenty miles to the north of me; that the woman he had with him was the wife of a prosperous planter in Kentucky, whom he had murdered: they fled together and reached the desert, where human justice could not follow them. Some years later I saw him again near his small log hut, wretched and wasted, and shortly after he died of an arrow wound in the chest, which an Indian dealt him. Such persons unfortunately are always among the first pioneers of civilization, and disturb the social relations of the borderers.

Although our changed mode of life offered many pleasant and interesting hours, still I was unable to drive from my heart the yearning for the old utter independence, which had almost grown a second nature. Frequently, when I rode at an early hour through the dark woods, the sounds of my neighbour's axe aroused me from my dreams; or, when I rode over the wide prairies, where I was accustomed to see the endless expanse covered with grazing herds of buffalo, I now only noticed here and there small bands of these animals passing hurriedly and timidly as if frightened at having strayed among the settlements. The antelope, that ornament of the prairies, could only be seen on the most remote heights; the deer had remained more constant to their grazing-grounds, but they too had grown more restless and attentive to the heightened danger.

The other side of the Rio Grande was less changed, and game will be protected there for many years to come, by the insurmountable mountains that surround the valleys; but it required a much greater outlay of time to seek the game there which formerly animated the immediate vicinity of my residence. Tiger was beginning to grow impatient, and often said to me that the game in our vicinity had now got too many eyes and feet, and he would go northwards to the great mountains before spring arrived. For a long time past I had been desirous of passing through the Rocky Mountains, but never was the yearning greater to throw myself once more into the arms of virgin nature than at this moment, when civilization drew me back by force into its sphere. In spite of the repeated representations which reason and my material interests urged against such an undertaking, I resolved to start in February for these unknown countries. One of my men was an excellent farmer, and in every way deserving of my entire confidence, so that I could with safety place the management of my settlement in his hands; while one of the other two, of the name of Königstein, insisted on accompanying me, to which I readily assented, as he had given me a thousand proofs of his fidelity and devotedness. With these qualities, so valuable for me, he united a determination and courage which nothing could daunt, and I have often seen him in the most desperate circumstances laughingly defy the danger. John Lasar was enthusiastic when I told him of my intention; he earnestly desired to accompany me, and begged me to procure his father's consent. The enterprise appeared to the old gentleman rather daring, and he made all possible objections, but he at last yielded to our entreaties, and equipped his son with a brace of splendid revolvers, while I supplied him with one of my double-barrelled guns. Königstein was armed with a double rifle, but also carried in a leathern sheath fastened to his saddle a four-barrelled gun, two pistols in his belt, and two in his holsters.

While we were engaged in making our preparations for the great journey, several of Lasar's friends arrived from Alabama, among them being two young men, a Mr. MacDonald and a Mr. Clifton, who came to me with John, and earnestly asked my leave to form the party. I was glad to have them, as their exterior was very pleasing, and our number was still small for a journey in which thousands of dangers and fatigues awaited us. We worked hard at getting ready, in which John's elder sister materially assisted us. New suits of deer-hide were made, two small tents prepared, and a large sheet varnished to make it water-tight and thus protect our baggage from the rain. Then biscuits were baked, coffee, salt, pepper and sugar stamped into bladders, a small cask filled with cognac, cartridges made, and our saddlery inspected; in short, there were a thousand matters to attend to, and thus the last days of January found us with all hands full of work for our expedition, while we had appointed February 1 for the start.

On the last day of January there was a grand review in front of the fort, where we appeared fully equipped for a start in order to inspect everything and discover anything that might still be wanting. An invention of mine caused us great amusement. It was a transportable boat to convey our traps across large rivers, consisting of a large round very firmly sewn piece of linen, resembling an open umbrella put on its point. The edge was covered by a very broad leather, in which was a drawing cord. The linen was thickly covered with linseed varnish and hence quite waterproof. When in use, eight stout sticks were laid crossways, with the ends thrust into the edge of the linen, so that they expanded it and drew the running cord tight. We expanded it, carried it to the Leone, placed Antonio in it, and Tiger swam through the river on his piebald and dragged the vessel after him to the other bank and back again, while Antonio was not touched by a single drop of wet. After the sticks had been taken out the linen was rolled up, and formed a small bale, which was packed with other articles on the mule. I had seen something similar among the Indians, who take for this purpose a fresh buffalo hide and stretch out in a similar way with staves. Our equipment was hence as perfect as it could be for a journey on which the traps can only be carried on mules, and the second of February was appointed for the start, while we would take leave of the Lasars on the first.

Pleased and full of enthusiasm about our enterprise we spent the day, and on saying good-bye in the evening Lasar promised to accompany us with his family and spend the first night of our camp life with us. The next morning found us busied at an early hour in arranging our baggage and dividing it among our cattle. Czar displayed his full beauty and strength, and expressed by loud neighing his delight at starting this time with so large a party. Königstein saddled the cream-colour for himself, who also looked the picture of strength, and proudly raised his long black tail over his croup. Tiger's piebald impatiently stamped with his forefeet, and responded with a neigh to every mark of joy from Czar and the cream-colour. Antonio saddled for himself the iron-grey mare, and decorated its bridle and saddle with gay ribbons and strips of leather. Honest Jack was loaded with provisions and other effects, which were placed in two baskets, while our tent was laid atop, and the whole covered with the waterproof linen. Trusty was still chained up and attentively watched our movements, but knew already that he was going to accompany me, as I frequently spoke to him and had put him on his new broad collar.

We had almost completed our preparations when we saw a long train of riders coming from Mustang River over the prairie, led by a gentleman on a powerful dapple-grey, and a lady on a black horse. They were our friends from the Mustang; at their head rode old Mr. Lasar on a fine Virginian thoroughbred, and by his side pranced a coal-black stallion, who did honour to his pure Andulasian descent from his muzzle to the tip of his flying tail, and proud of the load he carried on his back, bowed his strength before the delicate hand, which guided him by a dazzlingly white bridle. Julia, Lasar's eldest daughter, was the mistress of this splendid animal. Her tall graceful form, her brilliant black locks falling under her tall hat, her dark eyes overshadowed by long lashes, and the long white feather which waved in her hat, reminded me of her noble ancestry in the days of Ferdinand and Isabella. Behind them rode John Lasar by his mother's side on a chestnut mare of pure Arab blood, then came the youngest daughter and the youngest son, MacDonnell and Clifton, several neighbours from the Mustang, and lastly loaded pack-horses with a number of mules. The caravan came over the last height to the Fort, and was joyfully welcomed by us. A cup carved out of a buffalo horn, filled with Sauterne, was handed to the guests on horseback, and then also emptied by us to the toast of a pleasant journey and fortunate return, and we at once took leave of home for an indefinite period.

The end of our journey, as we had temporarily arranged, was the highest yet known point on the Rocky Mountains, the Bighorn, which is situated in the 42° of latitude, and to which we had a distance of about eight hundred miles to ride. Our road ran eastward from the mountains and did not ascend the Rio Grande, along whose bank is the road through the several old Spanish forts, which begins at El Paso del Norté and passes through Santa Fé to Taos. If it is borne in mind that the entire distance had hardly ever been trodden by white men, and that consequently no settlement existed there; that no other roads led through the Rocky Mountains and almost impenetrable forests except buffalo paths; that our journey would be made through the hunting-grounds of the most savage and hostile cannibal hordes—it will be felt that the moment of parting was an earnest one. The charm, however, which dangers, privations, and difficulties possess for man—the thought that entirely new scenes of nature, a whole new world was about to be presented to us, rendered the leave-taking light. And so we turned our horses away from home toward these unknown regions.

Tiger led the file, and at once commenced his duties as guide. I followed by the side of Julia Lasar, whose proud steed appeared to be jealous of Czar, then came the other friends in pairs, till our pack-horses completed the train. Trusty bounded before us and expressed by barking his delight at the large party, which was a novelty to him. A little way below the Fort we crossed the river, where each watered his horse, and then proceeded towards the wood on the opposite side along a narrow buffalo path. I cut away the creepers and vines hanging over the path, in which Tiger helped me, for this was the first time it had been ridden by white ladies. On reaching the prairie on the other side of the wood, where the grass was still very short and offered no impediment to our horses, we rode in frequently varying groups, galloped from one to the other, tried the speed of our horses, and shortened the length of the road by jokes and laughter.

We had chosen Turkey Creek as our halting-place, and rode at a quick pace in order to reach our camping-ground by daylight. At noon we made a short halt at an affluent of the Leone, to give our ladies time to dine, and at the same time allow our horses to graze. During this short delay the buffalo-horn, filled with wine, was passed round, and was accompanied by singing and merriment. No one appeared to reflect that the next morning would bring a parting more or less hard for us all, but all yielded to their gay humour without a check. At about one o'clock we held the ladies' stirrups—helped them on their horses again, and ere long the whole party were moving northward. The short rest had done the cattle good, and they hastened in a quick amble across the prairie, which was already beginning to be adorned with its spring beauty. The breeze was fresh, the sky clear and diaphanous, and everything around seemed to be powerfully cheered by the splendid weather. Snorting and neighing, our horses pranced after Tiger's flying piebald, and right and left amazed deer, and at a greater distance rapid antelopes leaped up.

While riding through a narrow coppice, we suddenly saw before us, at no great distance, a herd of grazing buffaloes, who for a moment gazed at us in astonishment, and did not appear to have formed a decision as to whether they should bolt or stand an attack. A loud hunting shout ran along our ranks, and I saw on all sides pistols and revolvers being torn from the belts. In vain did I strive to master the enthusiasm of my comrades, and hold them back by the observation that we were heavily loaded, were not hunting, but commencing a long journey, in which we must spare the strength of our horses. Away the cavalry flew after the piebald. I could hardly hold back my impetuous steed by the side of Miss Julia's black, whom the very sharp bit alone prevented from bolting, till the lady uttered a wish to follow the chase, as these were the first buffaloes she had seen. Her younger sister joined her, and thus only Lasar and his wife, the negroes and pack animals, remained behind.

On flew the noble black stallion, guided by the steady hand of his young mistress, from whose hat the white feather floated, while the ends of the long red scarf tied round her riding habit fluttered behind her. I held Czar in a little, so as not to excite the black horse too much, while Julia's sister's pony followed us at some distance, and behind it honest heavily-loaded Jack came panting, whom the negroes had been unable to keep in the ranks of the pack cattle. We were soon close to the flying herd, whose thundering hoofs drowned the sound of my comrades' pistols. We dashed past an enormous buffalo, which had sunk seriously wounded with its hind quarters on the ground, and standing on its huge fore-legs was holding its broad shaggy head towards us. Immediately after we saw another quit the ranks in front of us, and dash after John, who was flying before it on his fast mare. I shouted to Julia to check her horse, in which she succeeded after some efforts, and we now rode up to the wounded buffalo, which, with head down, was preparing for action. We stopped about fifty yards from it, when John, who saw that I had raised my rifle, shouted to me not to fire, as he wished to kill the animal himself. He fired, and the buffalo rolled over in a crashing fall. Our comrades also collected in the distance round one of the animals, which, being wounded, stood at bay, and was soon killed. Then they rode back with shouts of triumph, and stopped with us till Mr. and Mrs. Lasar came up. The ladies were delighted with the savage, though splendid scene, and confessed that hunting possessed an attraction which might easily render a man passionately fond of it. We left the negroes behind with a few pack animals, to take the hides and best meat from the killed buffaloes, then ordered them to follow our trail, and rode on to the camping-ground on Turkey Creek, which we reached at sunset.

Lasar's spacious marquee was quickly put up, and the long pennants hoisted over it: in front of this tent a large fire was lit, and buffalo hides spread round it, on which the ladies reclined. We attended to the horses, carried our baggage to other fires at which we intended to spend the night, and then gradually collected in front of Lasar's tent, where the coffee was already boiling and various kettles for supper were standing in the ashes. The negroes too soon rode up with heavily-loaded cattle, and each of us put some of the meat on a spit in front of the fire, or laid a marrow-bone to roast. The night was magnificent, not a breath of air stirred the dark leaves of the primæval evergreen live oaks, which spread out their long horizontal branches over our heads. Between them the moon, in its first quarter, spread its silvery light over us, and the sky was covered with twinkling stars. In the dark distance we could hear the notes of nocturnal birds of passage, which proved to us, by their northward flight, that the winter there could no longer be very severe; till these notes were lost in the rustling of the adjacent stream, which filled up every pause in our animated conversation.

We sat for a long time round the brightly-burning fire, till the ladies retired inside the tent, and we proceeded to our several fires and wrapped ourselves in our buffalo robes. Trusty alone still sat with his nose in the air when my eyes closed, and it was his voice woke me, when one of Lasar's negroes rose. I also leaped up, led Czar—though he felt no particular inclination to rise—into the grass; took my rifle, and went to the river, where I could hear the gobbling of the turkeys. It was still too dark to shoot with certainty, when I got under the lofty pecan-nut trees which stood on its banks. On their highest branches the birds were sitting and saluting the dawn. I listened to them for a long time ere I raised my rifle, and sent a bullet through one of them. It fell from branch to branch, and startled the others, which flew off noisily, while the hundreds standing on the trees around, timidly thrust out their long necks, but would not leave their night quarters.

· The cock had fallen into the river, and was flapping its wings violently in the quiet waters, so I cut a stick with a hook in order to pull it in. I had scarce secured it, ere a platoon fire burst forth all round me from my comrades' rifles, whom my shot had aroused from sleep, and now ran up to take part in the morning's sport. They produced a terrible slaughter among the poor foolish birds, and each of them carried at least two to camp. I went down the river a little way, however, to have a bathe. When I returned all were busy and seeking by occupation to avoid beginning a conversation which must necessarily hinge on the approaching leave-taking. The ladies helped in getting breakfast ready, the young men packed up their traps, the negroes struck the tent and rolled it up, and old Mr. Lasar went from one to the other offering his advice. At length nothing more was left but to eat breakfast, saddle the horses, and say good-bye. We silently collected round the large fire; coffee was swallowed, and with it many a tear, which involuntarily ran from the eyes. No one ate properly. Even Tiger thoughtfully scraped a bone with his knife, solely by this employment to make the heavy time pass more quickly. At last feelings could no longer be overpowered—hearts found a vent in tears, words, and sobs; and without further delay we exchanged assurances and signs of affection and friendship. When all were mounted, we turned our horses toward the river, waving a farewell to our friends as long as we could see them.

We soon passed through the wood on to the prairie, which ran along its north side, and halted to have a last inspection of our small corps. I, who had been elected captain, now assumed my duties, as from this moment our journey really began. I examined how the goods were divided among the mules, of which animals two others accompanied us besides Jack, Sam and Lizzy, whom John Lasar had supplied; for it is important on such a journey to take the greatest care that the animals are not galled by the saddles or baggage. The best protection against this is a thick blanket of woven horsehair, which is laid on the animal's back under the saddle; the hair, through its elasticity, always offers a passage for the air, and hence avoids the great amount of heat produced by woollen cloths.

When I had convinced myself that everything was in order, I called my party's attention to the fact that strict obedience to my regulations was indispensably necessary for our common safety. Tiger was entrusted with the guidance, and always rode about a hundred yards ahead, while one of us formed the rear-guard by the mules. I had with Tiger a long consultation as to the route we should follow, and while I proposed to keep more to the north-west, he insisted on a due north direction. I was of opinion that the lowest passage to the north would be found at the spot where the Rio Grande mountains sloped down to the east and joined the San Saba mountains; while, on the other hand, Tiger asserted that the mountain chain could be passed most easily due north, near the sources of the Rio Colorado. It is remarkable with what certainty the Indians know the nature and course of mountains and rivers, as well as the climatic circumstances of the country, and judge distances. The sense of locality is marvellously developed among the savages. Without being able to explain why it is so, the savage will indicate in an instant—without any examination of trees, rocks, &c.—the exact direction of the point he wishes to reach. Animals, and especially horses and mules, obey the same instinct. Frequently, when I have been hunting buffaloes in all directions over the prairie, and evening warned me about returning home, I have been in doubt as to the direction in which the Fort lay. I certainly knew that, for instance, I was on the north side of the Leone, and hence must ride southwards; but I could not determine whether I ought to proceed farther east or west, and an incorrect course might easily bring me to the river miles above or below the Fort. The horizon was bounded by the sky, as if I were at sea, and not a hill or forest reminded me of any familiar point. In such cases I laid the bridle on my horse's neck, let him graze for awhile, and then told him to go on, though without touching the bridle. The horse, missing the usual guidance, looked around him for a few minutes with upraised head, and then went in a straight line homewards. Remembering this, I followed Tiger's advice and went due north.

The weather was glorious, and the sun poured down its cheering beams upon us from a clear sky. With jokes and anecdotes, our hearts filled with expectation of the marvels that lay before us, we trotted after the quick-footed piebald, who appeared as pleased as his master to leave the civilization of the pale faces behind him. It is true that the grassy plains over which we rode were not spangled with flower-beds of every hue as in spring or autumn; but for all that the illimitable bright-green expanse did our sight good, while we were greeted by a few budding flowers. Even though the coppices, rising every now and then from the prairie, were not clothed in the luxuriant dark foliage of other seasons, still they did not display that picture of utter death, which the traveller finds during winter in the forests of northern climes. The soil of the forests is at this season covered with wild oats, growing to a height of four feet. The scrub consists principally of evergreen bushes; above it rise many varieties of trees of moderate height, which never entirely lose their glistening leaves, and these again are crowned by the different families of the magnolia, which do not lose their ornament either. Evergreen creepers climb to the highest branches, and hang down from the airy height in long streamers, which serve as a plaything to the slightest breath of air.

Four fine days we passed over these extensive plains, from whose lap higher and steeper hills gradually rise, until the latter form into a chain and impart to the landscape the character of mountainous scenery. We were among the spurs of the San Saba mountains, which do not run so far south here as they do farther west, and everywhere found water for ourselves and provender for our cattle. But now the stone-covered hills gradually became higher and the valleys narrower; we frequently crossed large ranges of table-land, on which the mosquito grass grows scantily; and as this is the only sort that remains green in winter, we could not let any opportunity slip to feed our cattle when we came across good pasturage. We need not be so anxious about water, as nearly all the valleys between these mountains are supplied with it in winter.

CHAPTER XVIX
A BOLD TOUR

We had been going for several days through the mountains with considerable difficulty, when one afternoon we reached a splendid pasturage, where we resolved to let our cattle rest. It was at the same time warm. We had doffed our leathern jackets and felt very comfortable when we found thick cedar wood on the western side of this meadow and were able to rest in its shade. We had scarce lit our fire to prepare dinner, when Tiger sprang up, pointed to the north, where several small clouds were rising, and then laid his ear on the ground. "A hurricane (a fearful storm frequent in the Rocky Mountains) is coming up. We must place our cattle in safety," he said, as he leapt up; and we all set to work dragging our traps to the other side of the meadow, where a low rock hung over and covered a considerable space.

After carrying across our traps, partly on our animals, partly in our arms, we hastened to collect as large a supply of dry wood as we could, in which an old trunk lying near the rock was of great service to us. This was cut into several pieces, which were rolled under the stone roof, and a fire was lit against one of them, while our horses were quietly grazing. We had scarce completed these preparations when the sky grew dark, and we heard a roaring and hissing, which quickly increased with the growing obscurity. We brought our cattle under the rock and fastened them to pickets we drove into the ground.

The cloud grew heavier and darker with each moment and rolled over the mountain crests in a southerly direction. With the roar of the wind was blended dull thunder, and an icy cold spread over the ground. These were merely the announcers of the frightful hurricane, which now dashed down from the Rocky Mountains and announced its approach with a crash that shook the earth. The thunder was so deafening that we could not hear each other speak, and standing silently by our trembling horses we watched the storm drive the clouds of icy rain in almost horizontal direction over our heads, and level the cedar-trees so that the roots stood up instead of the crowns. The cold increased every moment, and ere long everything was covered with a thick crust of ice, while the rain was frozen and hurtled round us in heavy hail. The ground shook under us, and the peals of thunder were repeated by a thousand echoes on the sides of the mountain. Under these circumstances we could consider our situation a fortunate one; for if we had been surprised by this storm, we might easily have fallen victims to it, or at least we must have lost our animals, which no human strength could have mastered in the icy rain. Though pressed closely round the fire and wrapped in our buffalo robes, we shivered from cold. The storm howled till late in the evening, at which time, though dense rain fell, the wind had sunk, and by nine o'clock the clouds broke too. A dead, frozen landscape surrounded us; the moon's bright light shone down into our frozen gully as into a palace of glass, and wherever we looked we saw transparent masses of ice, while the reflection of our fire glittered in brilliant colours on the crystals of ice near us. Not a breath of air stirred, and had it not been for the numbing cold and the glistening ice around to prove the reality of this fearful scene, we might easily have been tempted to regard it as a dream.

Our cattle, too, felt the cold greatly and trembled all over. We covered them with all the blankets we could spare, and I took special care of Czar, whom I fastened up as near the fire as I could. We made a tremendous blaze in order to render the cold to some extent endurable. One of us was obliged in turn to watch at the fire during the night, while the others lay round it and stretched out their feet to it. Morning arrived, and with it we welcomed the sun which appeared over the mountains in the blue sky. Everything glittered and shone around, as if the world were covered with a sheet of glass and brilliants; the grass plot was hidden by a layer of transparent pieces of ice, which brilliantly reflected the sunbeams; every bush, every shrub glittered with the hues of the rainbow, and the ice almost blinded our eyes. The sunbeams gradually rendered the cold more endurable. We crept out from under our rock and tried to warm ourselves by jumping. We were compelled to leave our horses tied up, as the grass was covered with ice, even where there was no drift. We could not go up to the spring which bubbled up in a gorge below the destroyed cedar-wood, because the path leading down to it was too smooth and slippery; hence we filled our pots with hailstones and thus procured water for our breakfast. The ice disappeared again as quickly as it had fallen on the unusual ground; it was only where the hail had drifted in large layers that the masses of ice lay for a longer period.

We resolved to remain here till the next day, because both our horses and ourselves required rest. My comrades wished to obtain permission to go out hunting, as Tiger had already done so without asking my leave, for he paid little heed to our laws. John Lasar and Mac, as we called MacDonnell for the sake of shortness, went off in different directions. The former followed the spring which joined a stream about a mile from us, whose banks were covered with a dense undergrowth, while Mac went north into the hills. The rest of us remained in camp. Shortly before sunset Mac returned, told us he had shot a large deer and two turkeys close at hand, put a pack-saddle on Sam, and went with Antonio to fetch the game. He had scarce left ere Tiger came in and triumphantly informed us that he had killed a big bear in its lair, and we must go and fetch it in the morning, for it was dark when Mac and Antonio returned with the game, and John had not turned up yet, which rendered us rather anxious. Still I had heard him fire several times, so he could not be far off; but I was afraid that an accident had happened to him, as it was now getting on for nine o'clock. We repeatedly fired our guns, and though it was so late, Tiger went down the stream and raised his hunting yell, but received no reply. At night it was impossible to follow his trail, so we lay down to sleep; but at daybreak we swallowed our breakfast and prepared to go in search of John. I took Tiger and Mac with me, and told Antonio to follow us on Jack. Trusty trotted ahead, and we had not gone many hundred yards from camp when John came riding down between the hills. We were very anxious to learn what had caused him to spend the night away, and he now told us that he had got among a herd of peccaris in the wood, and after shooting one of these animals, was compelled to seek shelter in a tree which they invested. Although he shot several of them, they did not retreat, and hence he was obliged to wait for daybreak. Of course, he had passed the night in the cold, shelterless, and was now very anxious for rest. He rolled himself in his buffalo robe, while I, with Tiger, Antonio, and Mac, left camp in order to fetch the bear. We took Jack and Lizzy with us to carry ropes and an axe.

We ascended the hills on the east for about half an hour, till Tiger went round a lofty rock and showed us a small round opening about six feet above the spot where we were standing. Tiger crept into the hole with a lasso to noose the bear's throat. He soon came out again, and we all three tried, but in vain, to drag it out with the rope. We harnessed Jack in front and Tiger crept in again to the bear to push: now matters went better, and the black monster soon appeared in the opening, and rolled down the little slope to us. Jack and Lizzy, startled at the sudden apparition, leapt on one side, but were soon pacified, and we began skinning and breaking up the animal. I was anxious to have a look at the interior of its abode, and crawled into the entrance, which was at first very narrow, but then widened, and at length became two walls leaning together at the top, but about eight feet apart at the bottom. The floor of the cave was covered with cedar branches, on which the bear reposed. I lighted a wax-taper, and was thus enabled to examine the cave narrowly. Tiger had crept up to the bear with a lighted wisp of grass in his hand, shot it in the left eye, and killed it on the spot.

We packed the best of the meat and fat, as well as the skin, on our mules, and returned to camp, where we arrived at about ten o'clock. We packed up, and were under way again by two P.M., following Tiger, who led us through the mountain passes, which here became much steeper. We rode nearly the whole day up hill, and only at intervals came to small table-lands, on which our cattle rested for a while. Trees grew rarer; here and there a small clump of cedars rose from a gorge, or an isolated group of prickly yuccas decorated the rocks, and at times a mimosa hung over our path from a crevice. A plant, whose three feet long narrow leaves grew out of the rock in tufts, and are used by the Indians for plaiting baskets and mats, was very common here: in the spring it has a whitish yellow flower, which grows on a stalk nearly six feet high, and through its graceful form is a real ornament to the landscape.

After a tiring ride the sun began to decline and illumined the red bare granite mountains that now rose before us, and which we could still have reached; but, as we found grass and water here, and our cattle longed for rest, we halted and made our camp. We were all hungry and tired, and hence enjoyed the capital bear meat, and stretched ourselves before the fire in our buffalo robes, where we awaited the morning without any disturbance. Refreshed, and strengthened, we gazed down from our elevation at the dense clouds which filled the valleys below us, while the dark sky in the east over the mountains continually became redder, until all at once the sun appeared like a burning ball over the distant misty blue range of hills. It shot a few golden red beams over the awakening earth, and quickly rising poured its fiery stream of light over the world. From the sea of mist beneath us the sharp howling of the jaguars reached us, and we saw a long train of rapid antelopes, probably flying before these beasts of prey, darting over a hill that emerged from it. We had soon finished breakfast, and the mist in the valleys had not entirely dispersed, when we guided our horses up the hill of granite before us. The air was so cool that we buttoned up our jackets, and pulled over our laps the part of our saddle-cloths hanging over the holsters.

Before us the mountains illumined by the morning sun rose ever higher and higher, while the valleys between them were wooded and seemed to contain a great many evergreen oaks. Our path ran at a rather great height along precipices, and it was not till noon that we crossed a ridge, where a valley ran across before us, and we were compelled to go down to it. This valley, which was not more than three miles broad, surprised us by its peculiarly beautiful appearance: it was literally covered with rocks of the most gigantic size, which lay near and on each other, as if rained down from the sky. In some places these were so piled up that at a distance they resembled castles with their turrets and keeps. Between these red masses of stone groups of live oaks emerged, and here and there small ponds could be seen glistening.

We had for a long time been enjoying this strange scene, and were on the point of going down to the rocky valley, when a loud yelling and barking was heard on our right beneath us, which rang through the valley, as if raised by a thousand animals. It rapidly drew nearer, and on looking in the direction of the sound we saw, at the foot of the precipice on which we were standing, a foam-covered old buffalo dash past with a pack of about fifty white wolves at its heels. The old fellow seemed very tired, and with flying mane raised its weary feet in its gallop, spurred on by the yells of its bloodthirsty pursuers. It soon disappeared with its tormentors round the rock, and far into the valley we heard the wild chase; but certainly the hunted brute eventually fell a prey to the furious band. It is only at this season that the white wolves collect in large packs, when they make very daring attacks on the largest animals, and even man, and many a western hunter has before this fallen their victim.

We rode down into the valley, following a very deeply-trodden buffalo path, which ran between the blocks of granite, some of which were as tall as a house, and at noon reached a small stream in its centre, which ran westward. Its water was clear, like all the small streams in the west, and was thronged with fish and turtle. Mac and Clifton soon threw their lines in and fetched out the fish as quickly as the hook fell. They had pulled out several cat and buffalo fish weighing twenty pounds apiece, when Mac hooked a very large turtle, and was afraid lest it might break his line. John, who was known as a good fisherman, ran to his help, took the rod from Mac, but slipped, as the turtle gave a sharp tug, down the steep bank, and sank up to his head in the clear waters. He was an excellent swimmer, like all Americans, at once came up and darted after the rod, which was hurriedly following the stream; we threw him a lasso and pulled him and it out. Then we let down a lasso, which Antonio managed to put over the turtle, and we dragged it ashore. It weighed some thirty pounds, and afforded us a first-rate dinner with the fish.

Our horses had here excellent grazing grounds, which are much larger than they had appeared to us from the mountains, and as we did not wish to hasten our journey and reach the north too soon, where the vegetation was still dead, we resolved to rest here for a few days. Still, as the stream might perhaps swell rapidly, we thought it better to pass it and camp higher up. It was about fifty yards wide, and rather rapid, and the buffalo path on which we were went down into it at such a pitch that it was difficult to convey our traps across. Tiger and I consequently went up the stream in search of a spot easier of access. We had hardly gone a mile between the rocks, when we saw four large elks grazing on a meadow, which did not notice us. We were obliged to make a lengthened ascent to get to windward, and after a fatiguing clamber up and round the stones, we at length reached a large rock about eighty yards from them. We marked the animals we would fire at, and pulled triggers almost simultaneously. Tiger's elk fell dead, but mine got up and went off with my second bullet which I gave it, though it was in a very bad case. I sent Trusty after it, and heard him bark once, and then become silent. The distance at which I had heard him was too far for me to run the risk of seeking him, and hence I sounded a couple of notes on my hunting horn to recall Trusty. While we broke up the elk the faithful dog came in, bearing the signs of victory on his blood-stained coat; we followed him to the elk, which he had captured, and found it dead with its throat torn out.

We broke this one up too, and then returned to the river to find a convenient passage. About a mile farther on we came to a buffalo path, so deeply trodden in the bank that it led with a lower pitch to the water, while on the other side the bank was low and the stream shallow; we therefore hurried back to camp, and marched up the river with our baggage. Tiger, Königstein, and Antonio rode off with two mules to fetch the game, and rejoin us at the indicated spot on the river. On reaching the latter we at once prepared to cross, and on this occasion our boat was used for the first time. We unpacked it, laid it on the grass and expanded it, after which we carried it to the river, and secured it with a lasso to the bank. It floated splendidly, and was packed with those articles which must not get wet. Ere long our comrades came in with the game, of which they had only taken the best joints. Antonio laid down his weapons and saddle-bags, and rode into the river with the cord in his hand, which was fastened to the coracle. He got across all right, but the water was too shallow to bring the boat close to bank, and he had nothing to which he could fasten it in the stream, but Tiger soon helped by jumping into the river, swimming across, and carrying the articles severally on land; then he brought back the coracle to us, as there were several more articles which must be protected from the wet, and because he also wanted to cross the river with a cargo.

We packed our boat again, and Tiger laid his long rifle on the top, though we dissuaded him from doing so. He swam off, and had reached the middle of the river, when the rifle lost its balance through a pull at the lasso, and sank in the river before Tiger could catch it. He seemed, however, to care but little about the accident, for he laughed heartily and swam quietly across to Antonio, who held the boat while the Indian carried its contents on land. When it was unloaded, it lay light as a feather on the water, and was pulled up and fastened to the bank. The young savage now leaped into the river again, dived like a stone at the middle of it, and came up a few seconds later with his rifle in his right hand, while he swam with the left. He mounted his piebald, and we all followed him into the stream, holding our weapons above our heads, and reached the other bank all right. When in camp on an elevation a short distance from the bank, Tiger lit a fire, and laid his rifle barrel in the ashes until the damp powder in it exploded and drove out the bullet, after which he ran down with it to the river, and cooled it in the water.

For three days we rested our horses here, and amused ourselves with fishing and hunting, for which the valley afforded every opportunity, as all sorts of game swarmed and the covered ground enabled the hunter to approach it. At night the whole valley seemed at times to be alive; the tramping of flying buffaloes rang on our ears, which were close to the ground, and the yells of hunting wolves could be distinctly heard: now and then the terrible roar of the jaguar rang through the damp moonlit night, and often so close to camp, that we leaped up and seized our rifles, while Trusty replied with furious barking. The couguar or maneless American lion (panther), which is very frequent here, often raised its plaintive cry; while the hoarse, dull growl of the bear echoed through the rocks. Countless owls floated spectrally, with lengthened flapping of their wings, over this nocturnal landscape, or glided like a breath over our camp. Although we were frequently roused from sleep by this night life of the animal world, it never disturbed us for long, for so soon as we convinced ourselves that there was no danger for us, we fell asleep again. During our stay we killed a great quantity of game, of which we only used the tidbits, and thus behaved no better than all these four-footed beasts of prey, whose behaviour is after all far more chivalrous than ours.

On the morning we had appointed for our departure I was awakened by the yell of a jaguar. I sprang up, and heard it again at no great distance from our camp. Our fire was rather low, and hence it had ventured rather nearer to us, and our cattle had probably aroused its appetite for blood. I made Tiger a sign to go with me, took my rifle and crawled with Trusty at my heels in the direction whence I had heard the jaguar. The grass was very damp, so that we could creep on without making the slightest noise. We stopped and listened. I fancied I had heard the puffing sound I had previously noticed with these animals, and which, I believe, is produced by their blowing out the dew which impedes their organs of scent. I heard it again, and not very far off, when suddenly the sharp snapping yelp was raised close before us, I hurried up some rocks, and saw the huge creature standing on a small clearing about thirty yards from me. The grass on which it was standing was still rather dark, and only the highest haulms displayed heavy drops of dew, while the breaking dawn was reflected in the brute's smooth yellow-black spotted body. I had fallen on one knee on the grass, when the royal brute again raised its half-open throat and uttered its murderous cry, accompanied by a blast of its hot breath, which rose like a strip of mist in the cold breeze. It stood motionless. I rested my arm that held the rifle on my knee, and everything was so still that I could distinctly hear my heart beat. I now fired, and with an awful roar the brute first rose straight in the air, then turned over and writhed in the grass. I had shot it near the heart, and in a few minutes it was quite dead. Tiger was greatly delighted with the splendid skin, which he stripped off the brute with extraordinary skill, and left the huge claws on it.

At about ten o'clock we were ready to start, and rode through a narrow gorge toward the hill ahead of us, which soon brought us to a wide plateau, on which we and our horses were greatly troubled by the sun, as the breeze was very slight. For several days we proceeded without any great difficulty through the mountains, which constantly surprised us both on the heights and in the valleys with the most beautiful landscapes, the wildest rocks, cascades, uprooted trees piled on each other; and then again the pleasantest and most peaceful valleys, in which we every moment expected to see the smoking chimneys of a settlement or a slowly turning mill-wheel. The mountains now grew much more impracticable, their sides steeper and the valleys narrower; our paths frequently led us from our course, wound round the precipices, and at times trended due south; so that during a day's ride we only advanced a few miles to the north. We reached a small river, which wound through the rocks from the north-east, and which Tiger told us was the Rio Colorado, which flowed in a great curve through these mountains and Texas to the Gulf of Mexico. We had great difficulty in passing its steep banks, and spent half a day ere we found a spot where we could ride through it. On its banks we found enormous cypresses and live oaks, and a generally rich vegetation for these regions, and above all, musquito grass, which was of incalculable advantage for our cattle.

We had hardly scaled the heights on the opposite side and were riding through a narrow path between two not very steep slopes, when we heard the barking of a hunting dog rapidly advancing towards us. I leaped from my horse and at the same moment there appeared on the left-hand precipice a flying antelope and at some distance behind it a black and white spotted dog, which only barked faintly at intervals. The buck was very fast and took enormous leaps over the loose boulders, and when it passed within a hundred yards of us a shower of bullets was sent after it. It turned a somersault and rolled down the precipice to our feet, when we cut it up and divided the game among our mules. The dog, however, halted on the rock with hanging tail, and looked at us for a while thoughtfully, then turned and slowly made back tracks. Tiger said it was an Indian's dog, but not thoroughbred, as the latter never bark (I do not know whether they cannot, but I never heard them bark). As we rode along we looked for the dog's master, but did not catch sight of him.

The farther we went from the river the less steep the mountains' sides became, and the valleys widened again. On the following day we crossed two other rivers, which were also arms of the Colorado, and went down toward the northern spurs of the San Saba mountains. The mountain chains here ran severally over larger surfaces, on which a great many hills rose, but they had nearly all already donned the garb of the prairies; they were covered with a red grass that is rather hard, but does not die in winter, while in the lowlands grew the fine hair-like musquito grass. Numerous patches of postoak crossed this country, and here and there the hills were covered with thick leaf wood. The streams, begirt by fine forests, all ran eastward, and were all full of fish, and the crystalline water which so greatly distinguishes Western America from all other countries. We found here again large troops of wild horses, though we had seen none on the mountains, and enormous quantities of game of all sorts. The prairie more especially was covered with buffaloes as far as we could see. We were constantly supplied with the finest meat which we shot in passing, without stopping any length of time or tiring our horses.

One afternoon, however, we noticed among a herd of buffaloes two white ones which excited our cupidity, and we resolved to hunt them. We left Antonio and Königstein behind with the mules, laid aside our superfluous baggage and slowly approached the buffaloes. They were standing on a knoll on the prairie, and allowed us to ride rather close up ere they took to flight. We galloped after them and were soon in their ranks, which gave way as we pressed in, and spread on both sides with such roaring and snorting as deafened the thundering noise of their hoofs. The two white animals, an old bull and a cow, were right in the front. In spite of the choking cloud of dust in which we were enfolded we kept them in sight and at last got up to them. Tiger was some paces ahead and first up to the buffaloes, but at the moment when he raised his long rifle to fire the bull turned on him and the piebald gave a tremendous start: Tiger lost his balance and would assuredly have fallen, had he not caught hold of the mane and sprung from his rearing horse. At the same instant the buffalo received our bullets, and dashed furiously first after one then after the other, while being continually wounded afresh, until it at last sank on its knee exhausted and received the death shot from Tiger's rifle. I now rode back to those in the rear and brought them to the dead bull, while the others skinned it. The hide was splendid, very long haired, and shaggy, and snowy white without spots. A white buffalo is a rarity. The savage Indians regard it with superstitious awe, and make a sacrifice of sumach leaves ere they attack and kill it. They set an extraordinarily high value on the hide of such an animal, and either use it as a valuable present or sell it for a large sum. After the bull was killed, I had the greatest difficulty in keeping Tiger from following the herd which was out of sight in order to take the hide of the white cow, and it was not till I assured him that the hide of the dead one belonged to him and that I would purchase it of him, that he remained with us. An hour later the bargain was concluded, and my Indian perfectly contented. White deer, antelopes, and bears are more common, but for all that are regarded as rarities.

CHAPTER XX
THE ROCKY MOUNTAINS

We now reached open plains, where only here and there an isolated musquito tree or a thickly foliaged elm offers a little shade on the boundless glowing surface, and the sky forms the horizon all around. To these single shady trees the deer and antelopes fly in the midday heat, and lie down close together, so that you may be always certain to find game under these trees, so long as their leaves are standing. At the same season the grass is high also, and it is easy for the hunter to creep unseen within shot, and shoot the fattest deer through the head. Even at the time of our visit, when the leaves had fallen, these animals frequently reposed under the scattered trees and rose as we passed, forty or fifty in number, gazing anxiously at us. The buffalo, on the other hand, always remains in the sunshine, and seems able to endure the greatest heat, but also the greatest cold before all other quadrupeds. It marks its endless marches from north to south and from south to north by its skeletons, which bleach for many a year in the sun. Now, when the grass was short, the whole surface in the distance had a whitish tinge, which is produced by these bones, out of which the skulls rise like shining dots. For about a week we rode through such land, only here and there interrupted by small elevations, and frequently suffered with our animals from drought. During this period we were often obliged to quench our thirst with standing water, with which the heavy showers fill great hollows in the prairies, and which remains in them even at the driest season. As the inhabitants of these plains, and especially the buffaloes, must also quench their thirst in them, and also wallow there, we frequently found the water as thick and warm as chocolate, and were obliged to strain it through a cloth to get rid of the hairs before we could drink it.

After a very hot day, on which we had suffered greatly from thirst, we suddenly saw from a knoll a large expanse of water before us, and greeted it at the first moment with great delight. We hurried on in order to reach this oasis as soon as possible, but surprised to see no bushes or trees on its banks, and even more when on drawing nearer we found far around only thin, dark grass, between which the ground shone quite white. Tiger shouted to me that it was salt water, and neither we nor our horses could drink it. This affected us the more deeply as we had indulged in the hope of a hearty drink, and we silently turned again to the west, in order to ride round the lake. Tiger laughed and said that we should have good water, as several large streams flowed into it from the west. This proved to be the case; for after riding about five miles along the bank of the lake, we reached a perfectly clear, sweet-water stream. We halted in order to refresh ourselves and our cattle, but we were obliged, as was the case nearly the whole week, to kindle a fire of *bois de vache*, to prepare our supper. At times, when in passing over these prairies we found a dry musquito tree, we fastened a few logs to our saddle, so as to have firing for the evening; but this was too tiring, and we always hoped to come across wood, whence this precaution was generally neglected. In such regions there were no objects to which we could bind our horses; but this is easily managed by cutting a long, sharp wedge out of the very firm soil, thrusting the knot of the lasso in as far as possible and stamping in the wedge again with the foot. As the bound animal pulls almost horizontally at the very long lasso, while its end goes down nearly perpendicularly into the ground, the rope offers such a resistance that it will sooner break than be pulled out of the ground.

Gradually we saw more hills, and among them forests, while a few distant chains of mountains ran from west to east. One afternoon I was riding with Tiger about a mile ahead of our party, in order to have a better chance of approaching game, when we heard two shots behind us. We looked round and saw our friends gathered in a knot on a small knoll, and a swarm of about fifty Indians galloping round them. We gave our horses the spurs and flew back to them, while Tiger raised a hideous yell, in which I supported him to the best of my strength. Our friends now fired a general salvo at the assailants, which knocked over two horses, but their riders were immediately picked up by their comrades. On seeing us the savages took to flight with gruesome yells. We rode up to our companions, who had placed all the animals in the centre to protect them. Königstein had luckily seen some horses' heads over the crest of the next hill which aroused his suspicions, and had employed the time in assuming a posture of defence, or else we should probably have lost our mules. Tiger saw, from the saddles of the shot horses, that they belonged to the Mescaleros, who are considered the most savage tribe in the west, and would certainly not have given up their attack so soon had they not recognised Tiger's war-whoop as that of the Delawares. The number of Mescaleros is not large, and they are constantly at war with many other tribes, so that they do not care to make fresh enemies among their red brothers. This little danger, which we escaped without loss, was not unpleasing to me, as our precautions, which had nearly been forgotten, were aroused once more by it.

For about a week we marched through a very pleasant country, and arrived at a rather large river, which Tiger stated to be the Brazos, and which falls into the gulf to the eastward of the Colorado. I had seen it before at San Felipe, and would not have recognised it, for there it moves sluggishly through a thick-wooded bed of heavy clay, and has a dirty red colour, while here it rolls merrily over rocks, and its crystal surface is covered with a snow-white foam. From this point we proceeded to the north-west, as Tiger noticed that we had gone a little too far east, and would have much greater difficulty in crossing the rivers than farther west, where, though the country is mountainous, the streams nearer their sources are smaller and more frequent. The mountains were composed of limestone, and contained exquisite little valleys, where the vegetation was already bursting into new life. All the softer-wooded trees were budding, and the flowers were springing up all over the prairies. We seemed to keep equal pace with the reawakening of the vegetable world northwards, and even to go faster than it.

On a warm day we had been riding without a halt over desolate, stony hills, and were quite exhausted. When our tired and thirsty horses clambered up a barren height, we suddenly looked down into a lovely valley covered with fresh verdure, through which a broad stream wound. The view soon enlivened horse and rider, and we merrily hurried down to the bank of the stream. We had hardly reached it and ridden our horses in to let them quench their thirst, when a long train of Indians appeared on the opposite height bordering the valley and came straight toward us. Tiger looked at them for a moment, and told us to wait here while he rode across to see who they were. We dismounted, led our horses together, and got our weapons in readiness. Tiger galloped through the valley to the hill side down which the Indians were coming, and checked his piebald at its foot. We saw him making signs from a distance to the approaching horsemen, which were answered in the same way, and ere long the whole party pulled up around him. They held a long consultation and then rode toward us with Tiger at their head. They were Kickapoos out on a hunting expedition, and had recently left their villages on the Platte, where they have settlements like the Delawares, and their squaws and old men grow crops and breed cattle.

I had a long conversation with the chief, in which Tiger played the interpreter, told him the purpose of our journey, invited him to visit me on the Leone next winter, and asked him how far it was to the next water. He assured me that we should come to good water and grass before the sun sank behind the mountains, and so we parted, very glad to get away from the fellows, whose appearance was anything but satisfactory. The party consisted of about eighty men, twenty squaws, and a number of small children. The first were dressed in deer-hide breech-clouts, and had round the body a leathern belt, through which a very long and broad strip of coarse red cloth was passed, whose two ends were pulled through between the legs and fastened into the belt behind. In addition, several of them had deerskin coats, others calico coats, but the majority merely wore a buffalo robe over their bare shoulders, and nearly all were armed with rifles. The squaws wore a short leathern petticoat round their loins, and a buffalo robe on their shoulders, while those who had infants carried them fastened to a board upon their backs. They had already unpacked their horses and prepared their camp to halt here, as we rode away from them over the hills, and Tiger came up to me, saying, "Kickapoo no good—two tongues." I had heard before that these Indians were false, spiteful, and hostile to white men, and only the advantage they derive from being on friendly terms with the United States induces them not to appear publicly as their enemies.

We quickly advanced, and reached at a rather early hour a valley in which we found grass and water, and chose our camp at a spot where the stream ran close under a precipice, while on this side was a small copse in which we could fasten our cattle at night. It was an almost circular kettle enclosed by steep limestone walls, which had an opening only on one side, through which the bright stream flowed. The sun was sinking behind the lofty gray rocks and dyeing the dark blue sky with a glowing tint which no artist would venture to reproduce on his canvas. About midnight Trusty aroused us by his loud savage bark: he was at the opening of the valley and would not lie down again, but we could not discover his motive, as it was quite dark. Tiger fancied, however, that the Kickapoos were trying to steal some of our horses. When day broke and cast its first faint light over the gray walls of the valley, I awoke and saw at the entrance a herd of deer apparently browsing down the stream. As it was still rather dark I hoped to be able to approach them behind the few leafless bushes that grew on the bank, as crawling through the dewy grass was too fatiguing a job to be rewarded by a deer, especially as we still had a supply of game.

I crept down the stream, and had got within shot, when I made a forward leap in order to reach a rather thick bush, from which I could fire more conveniently. At the same instant the deer started apart in terror, and I saw that an ocelot had leaped on the back of one of them, which laid back its broad antlers and galloped down the stream, while a second cat followed it with long high bounds. Two of the terrified deer darted past me, but I did not fire, as I felt an interest in watching the hunt of the two beasts of prey, which I followed as quickly as I could out of the valley. The deer ran about a mile down the stream, then reared and fell over backwards, when the second cat also sprang on it, and hung on its neck.

The deer collected its last strength and tried to rise on its hind legs, but sank exhausted and sent its plaintive cries echoing through the mountains. I crept, unseen by the beasts of prey, within thirty yards of the scene of battle, and shot the first, while I missed the second, as it bolted, but sent Trusty after it, and soon heard him at bay lower down the stream. I soon reloaded and hurried after Trusty, who was barking round a small oak in which the ocelot had sought shelter. I shot it down and dragged it up to the other, which was lying by the dead deer. All were up in our camp, as they had heard my shots, and John and Königstein hurried toward me to see what I had killed. My clothes were as wet as if I had been in the river, and I turned myself before our fire while the others went out with Jack to bring in the game. Higher north I did not come across these small leopards, while farther south they are very frequent.

For several days longer our road ran through mountains, which were bordered by savage precipices and crossed by grassy valleys; then we rode for some days across open, boundless prairies, and again reached low ranges of hills, between which we crossed the southern arm of Red River, which divides Texas from Arkansas and falls into the Mississippi in Arkansas, after flowing a distance of nearly one thousand miles. There it is of a dirty red, and muddy, and moves sluggishly between lofty poplars and planes which overshadow its flat banks, while the long gray grass hangs down from thence to the surface of the water and literally covers the trees. This moss hangs from every branch in creepers twenty feet long, and conceals the swampy soil in which those fearful monsters, the alligators, lie by thousands and await in their pestiferous lair the unhappy victims whom accident leads to them. Here and there a half-decayed blockhouse peeps out from under these weeping banners, and as everything there offers the picture of rapid desolation, you see in this house, where so many families have died out one after the other, the pale, yellow wasted faces of the new-comers peering out, like candidates for death, till it becomes too late to escape from this pestilential abode.

How perfectly different, however, the river appears here! Clear as crystal to the bottom, it dances from rock to rock; refreshes as it darts past the luxuriant ferns and the thousand-hued flowers with its waves, and displays to the visitor its living wealth, as well as the vegetable world on its bed, in the most brilliant hues. The purest, lightest breeze sports over its high banks and drives the diseases, which are the curse of South-Eastern America, out of the paradise which lies beneath the haughty cypresses, pecan nut-trees, planes, maples, and colossal oak-trees that border it. How is it possible that men can be terrified by the dangers of the West, and patiently expose themselves to a certain, slow, awful decay in those poisoned forests, where Death inexorably swings his scythe all the year round?

The Rocky Mountains now rose in the west, and glistened with their snowy peaks, while around us the plants announced spring by their bursting buds. We drew nearer to them, although in this way our route became far more fatiguing than farther eastward, where the wide prairies extend to the north. But Tiger employed this precaution in order to get out of the way of the great Indian hordes pursuing the buffalo, who do not find in these mountains sufficient food for their troops of horses and mules, and cannot hunt the buffaloes there so well as on the prairie. Hence our journey was continued more slowly; but at this season we could reckon on water, and the small valleys offered our few cattle abundance of food. The mountains constantly afforded us more game than we needed for our support, and we could approach it with greater ease than on the prairies.

We had been winding for some days through wildly romantic mountain gorges, and our eyes were involuntarily fixed on the distant reddish mountains which rose in the north toward the transparent sky. We had left many a charming valley, turbulent current, and precipice behind, when at about noon one day we were stopped by a deep ravine, through which noisily dashed one of those mountain torrents which escape from the snows of the Andes and make their long course through the valleys to the Gulf of Mexico. Here we could not think of riding through, for the precipices on either side were at least fifty feet deep, while the width of the cavern was several hundred paces. We rode up the ravine and got among such rocks and loose stones that we were forced to dismount, and with the greatest difficulty reached a plateau where the banks of the stream were not so tall and steep, and we were able to remount. A few flat rocks were scattered over the bank where we were, while the opposite one rose steeply, and was covered with thick scrub and low wood.

I was riding with Tiger ahead of our party when, on turning a rock, we saw a very plump bear leap from the bank through the shallow but foaming stream, and disappear in a coppice opposite. It was too quick to enable us to fire, and when we reached the spot where we first saw it, we found a large elk lying behind some thick prickly bushes, which was still warm, and hence must have been recently killed. One leg was torn up, but the rest was in good condition, and we halted to await our friends and put the game on the mules. When I was about to dismount, Tiger remarked that the bear would return to the elk in the evening, and as we should soon be obliged to camp, owing to the growing darkness, we could hunt it.

The Backwoodsman | 183

Our friends came up and we marched about a mile farther, where we found excellent grass in a gorge on the left of the river. We unsaddled, hobbled our cattle, and prepared supper, although it was rather early. The question then was who of us should go after the bear, and as all wished to do so we agreed that the dice should decide. The lot fell on myself, Clifton, and Königstein, and without delay we took our weapons and walked down the stream to the spot where the elk lay. We advanced cautiously, as the bear might already be at its quarry, and as we noticed nothing of it we selected our posts no great distance from the elk. I was at the centre, behind a large rock, Königstein lay on my right near the stream in the dry grass behind some bushes, and Clifton was on my left, covered by a fallen dead tree.

We had a good wind, and if the bear returned we should have it under our guns, and it would hardly be able to escape. We sat without moving: the sun sank behind the mountains and scarce illumined the heights, while around us the gloom was already gathering; there was not a breath of air, and only the buzzing and chirruping of insects and the rustling of the stream disturbed the silence. Trusty, who had hitherto been lying at my feet, raised his head, looked at the thicket opposite and then up to me. I shook my finger at him not to growl, which he quite understood, and thrust his head down on the ground. Directly after I heard a cracking in the thicket, which soon became more distinct. At length the bear burst out of the scrub and came down a small path to the stream. We had agreed not to fire until it reached the elk on this side. It stopped for a few minutes in the water to drink, then leapt from stone to stone up the bank, and walked slowly toward the elk. The bear had scarce reached the prickly bush ere we fired simultaneously, and it rolled over, but got up again and leapt into the water. Clifton and Königstein sent two bullets after it, which, however, did not seem to hurt it much, for it dashed ahead to the other bank. Königstein at once leapt, revolver in hand, into the stream after the bear, and was standing between it and me, when he put a bullet into its leg at a short distance. The bear, noticing its pursuer, turned and went toward him with a hoarse roar, while Königstein, still standing in the water, put a second bullet into its chest. I ran up and fired my rifle bullet into the left breast of the furious animal, while Clifton gave it another in the belly from his long pistol. The bear fell into the water but a few yards from Königstein, who, seeing it rise on its fore paws, shot it through the head with his revolver. Though the water was shallow, it was so rapid that it would have carried the bear away, so we both threw away our weapons, leapt into the stream to Königstein, and dragged the beast on land. Here we let it lie, reloaded, and returned to camp, where our comrades were, greatly pleased at the lucky result of our hunt. We waited till the moon had risen, then took two mules, and I proceeded with Tiger and John to our quarry, in order to fetch its skin and the best meat.

It was late when we got back to camp, still our appetite had been excited again, and instead of going to sleep, we sat joking round the fire, each with some spitted bear-meat before him. The coffee-pot also went the round, and the steaming pipe accompanied us to our buffalo hides, on which we lay conversing for some time. Clifton insisted that he ought to be rewarded handsomely by Königstein for saving his life by the pistol-shot, while the latter tried to prove to him that he had aimed too low to hit the bear's heart, and hence, as a punishment, ought to have its paw stuck on his hat. The answers, however, gradually became rarer, and we soon were all fast asleep. Excellent health, and a consciousness of strength, of which the polished world is ignorant, are the blessed companions of such a natural life; and no awful nightmare, no frightful dreams, such as visit the silken beds of civilization, venture to approach the hard couch of our Western hunters.

I was awakened by the cold about an hour before daylight; sprang up, poked the fire, which was nearly burnt out, wrapped myself in my buffalo robe, and fell asleep again soundly, till my comrades shouted to me that the coffee was ready. The whole neighbourhood was covered with a thick white rime, and though the frost was not heavy, we felt it severely. Our large fire, however, soon dispelled the cold, and we lay very cozily round it eating our breakfast. We soon mounted, crossed the stream without difficulty, and followed a buffalo-path up the hills. Our journey during the last day had been fatiguing for the horses, and, in spite of the long distance we had ridden, we had advanced but little northwards, so we gladly followed an easterly course, which brought us nearer the great prairies. From here we also noticed that the highest mountain peaks were a little farther to the west, and consequently off our track.

The sky became overcast, and in the afternoon it began raining, so that we were obliged to put our buffalo robes over us, and at night pitched our small tents to protect us from the heavy, incessant rain. Tiger, though, refused to crawl into the tent, but collected a great heap of brushwood near the fire, laid his saddle-cloth on it, sat down a-top, with his knees drawn up to his chin, and pulled his buffalo-hide with the hairy side out over him, tucking it under him, so that he looked like a huge hairy ball. During the night we were frequently obliged to feed the fire to keep it burning, and in the morning we saw no sign that the clouds were about to break. We could hardly distinguish the nearest peaks, and round our camp rivulets had formed that conveyed the rain to the valley. We could not think of starting, as all our traps were wet through. Hence we grinned and bore it; killed time with eating and smoking, and looked at our cattle, which, with hanging head and tail, let the rain pour off them.

Thus the whole day and the next night passed, and it was not till ten the next morning that we saw a patch of blue sky. This lasting heavy rain proved to me clearly that we were already in a more northern region, as in our country the showers are much heavier for the time, but never last longer than a day. We lay up for this day too to let the ground dry a little, and a strong cold wind which had sprung up helped to effect this. Our cattle had good grass, we were amply supplied with firewood, and had abundance of the best game, so that we wanted for nothing. John and Mac went out shooting together, and killed some turkeys and a deer, which they brought into camp on Sam. Tiger went out alone, and returned in the evening with two deer legs and a beaver, having surprised the latter on land while nibbling off the branches of a fallen tree. Our supper-table was hence splendidly covered again, and we greatly enjoyed the beaver tail, which is one of the best dishes the West offers.

Our various skins, tents, blankets, &c., were now tolerably dry, and the next morning we left camp and travelled northwards, towards the sides of the mountains, and the spurs they shoot out, into the great prairies. The sky was still covered with a few clouds, between which the sun shone warmly and pleasantly. Two days later we altered our course again to the west, in order not to leave the mountains, which here enclosed large patches of grass-land. Crossing these low mountain spurs, we passed through many extensive valleys with excellent soil, firewood, especially oak, and abundant water, which assuredly ere long will be sought by civilization advancing from the East. In the West the mountains now rose higher, and raised their white peaks far above the clouds. They were probably a hundred miles from us, and the horizon was enclosed by mountain ranges like an amphitheatre. The mountains rose higher and higher above each other in the strangest forms and colours, terminating in peaks on which the heavens seemed to be supported. Tiger called them the Sacramento mountains, which run southward nearly to Santa Fé.

One evening we reached a stream, which came down from these mountains through a rather wide valley, which Tiger told us was an arm of the Canadian river that falls into the Arkansas, between which and the

Kansas the territory of the Delawares is situated. When a boy, Tiger added, he had often been hunting up this river and in these mountains with his father, and in a few days we should reach another arm of this river, on which his father's brother was torn to death by a grizzly bear. On that river there was a very large iron stone, which had fallen from heaven, and with which the god of hunting killed a Weico, who was hunting here improperly. When we reached the river bank, we found its water very turbid, and so swollen that we could not ride through, owing to the furious current. Hence we unloaded, though it was still rather early, and found ourselves on a steep bank, where the stream could not hurt us, even if it rose higher. Tiger was of opinion that the water would have run off by the next day, and enable us to continue our journey, as these torrents rarely last longer than a day. John and Mac went down the river to hunt, and Tiger went up it, while we looked after the cattle and prepared the camp. The first two came back early with an antelope, while Tiger was not in camp when night had settled on the mountains. I had heard him fire twice, and we were beginning to fear that an accident had happened to him, when he came out of the gloom into the bright firelight with his light, scarcely-audible step, but without any game, which was a rarity. He had fired thrice at a black bear, followed it a long distance, but had been obliged to leave it owing to the darkness, especially as he had hit it awkwardly, and it was strong enough to run a long distance. The night passed undisturbed, morning displayed a bright cloudless sky, and promised us a beautiful day; but the river had not fallen so much as we expected, and we preferred awaiting its fall here to going higher up and seeking a shallower spot.

The sun had scarce risen over the low hills in the east when I took my rifle and went down the river with Trusty to try my luck in hunting. I soon reached a low thin skirt of bushes, which covered the valley, and through which many small rivulets wound to the river. I had not gone far into it, when I noticed a great number of turkeys running about among the leafless bushes. I ran up to them, frequently crossing the brook, till I at last got within shot of an old cock, and toppled him over. I hung the bird on a tree, close to the brook which I fancied was one of those that came down the valley no great distance from our camp, and had scarce gone a hundred yards beyond the brook when I saw some head of game, which were too large for our ordinary deer and too dark-coloured, and yet did not resemble elks.

I crept nearer and convinced myself they were giant deer, which are not uncommon in the Andes. I shot at a very large stag, which had already shed its antlers, and it rushed upon me, but soon turned away, and I gave it the second bullet. It went some hundred yards bleeding profusely, so that I expected every moment to see it fall, then stopped, and I employed the time to reload and get within eighty yards of it. I was on the point of firing, when it dashed away and got out of sight. I put Trusty on the trail, and followed him, crossing the brook several times up the valley toward our camp, as I fancied. At length I saw the stag standing under an old oak, and I succeeded in getting within shot. I fired, and saw the bullet go home; but for all that the deer ran up a hill on the left and disappeared. My eagerness in following the animal was more and more aroused; I reloaded and went with Trusty after the bleeding trail over the hill and down the other side, then through a thicket in the valley and over another hill to a stream, where I at last found the stag dead. It was a splendid giant deer, distinguished from our royal harts by its size, blackish-brown coat, and proportionately higher forelegs. I broke it up, gave Trusty his share, and it was not till I was ready to start that I thought of my road to camp.

CHAPTER XXI
LOST IN THE MOUNTAINS

It was near noon, and I had generally walked fast. I looked around me, and tried to recollect the numerous windings I had made, but soon saw it was impossible to recall them, as I had paid no attention to them during the chase. I now looked at my compass; I knew that the stream on which we were camping ran down the valley from west to east, and that hence I was on its southern side to the eastward of our camp. I must therefore go due north to reach the stream, and then follow it in order to reach camp. The calculation was correct, and could not fail to bring me home soon. I therefore walked on quietly, and every now and then blazed a tree, or laid a bush upon a rock, to be able to find the stag when we went to fetch it. The first hour passed: at one time I walked through thinly-wooded, narrow valleys, then over stony hills, or crossed small streams and grassy meadows, but saw no sign of the river.

The second hour, during which I doubled my pace, passed in the same manner, and yet I saw nothing of the river. I looked repeatedly at the compass on my rifle stock and the one I carried in my pocket. My calculation was correct, of that there could be no doubt; but how was it that I had not yet reached the river? It might possibly make a small bend northwards here; but I must strike it, as it belonged to Canadian river, and all the waters from these mountains flow to the east. I was certain of my matter, and laughed at myself for imagining for a moment that I had lost my way. I marched cheerily on, especially up the hills, as I fancied I should see the looked-for river from each of them, and did not notice that I was exerting myself excessively. A certain anxiety crept over me involuntarily. I hurried on the faster the deeper the sun got behind the mountains; I ran down the hills and hurried up them, dripping with perspiration, with a strength which only the feeling of impending danger can arouse. My energy and presence of mind still mastered my growing anxiety, as I hoped, felt almost convinced, that I should soon reach the river which had disappeared in so extraordinary a way, until at last the sun sank behind the highest peaks of the Cordilleras, and the gloom of night spread its mantle over the earth. Exhaustion followed long unnatural exertion so suddenly, that I sank down on the last hill I ascended, and my strength of mind and body gave way utterly. In a few minutes I fell into a deep sleep, and must have lain there for five hours, as when I woke I felt on my watch that it was midnight. I remembered everything I had hitherto done, and the last thought which had accompanied me up to my unconsciousness startled me out of it—the thought that I had lost my way.

When I got up, my faithful Trusty nestled up to me and licked my hands, as if wishing to remind me that he was still with me, and I was not quite deserted. I threw my arm round his strong neck, and pressed him firmly to me, for at this moment he was an unspeakable comfort, and restored my resolution and strength of will. I soon reverted to my old rule, which I had kept for years, of always assuming the worst in disagreeable situations, and making myself familiar with it; then a man has nothing more to fear. I had lost myself, and must seek my road to camp in some direction alone. I felt strong enough to do so, but must reflect on the mode of doing it. I had sufficient powder and bullets for my weapons; this was a precaution which I had constantly urged on my comrades since our start, never to go out with half-filled powder-horn or a few bullets for the sake of convenience.

My box was full of lucifers, and I had also flint, steel, and punk. I carried bandages and a housewife, as well as a little bottle of old brandy in my knapsack, and a rather large gourd at my side, I was fully equipped to make this tour, which, honestly speaking, was now beginning to appear interesting to me, and I laughingly thought of the friend of my childhood's years, "Robinson Crusoe," who at that day sowed the first seed of my later irresistible desire for such a life. I was soon decided, and regained my entire calmness. I sprang up, and went cautiously down hill to reach the valley, in which on the previous evening I had looked in vain for the river. The darkness and the rocky sloping route made my walk very difficult; but still I reached my destination at the end of an hour, and entered a very narrow valley, in which I soon found enough dry wood under the trees to light a fire. I had turned cold, and the warmth it spread around me did me good. Close by I found a fallen tree, to which I carried the burning logs, in order to produce a longer lasting fire to throw out more heat; then I piled up a heap of bushes and brushwood, laid myself on it, with my bag under my head, and after drinking some brandy and water, fell asleep as soundly as if I had been in my bed on the Leone.

The sun was high in the heavens when I awoke, I felt as strong as usual, and lit a fire for breakfast, drank some more water from my gourd, and went northwards in good spirits. I thought of the possibility that this river might not be the one named by Tiger, and might lose itself in a subterranean bed; but, extraordinary to tell, I did not for a moment reflect that it could run due north parallel with mine; my only idea was, that it perhaps made a great bend. I had been walking near an hour, and had crossed several stony hills, when I looked down into a narrow gorge, in which alders and poplars grew, leading to the supposition of water, and on going down I noticed an old animal quietly grazing. I crawled very cautiously nearer to it, for now I seriously needed some meat, and on looking up from a deep ditch excavated by the rain, I saw a small deer by the side of the old one, which was staring at me over the bushes, I fired and saw the deer dart among the bushes, but knew that it bore death in its heart. The old animal dashed close past me, but I did not fire as I was certain of securing the deer and did not care to waste a bullet unnecessarily.

I reloaded, went back to the bloody trail, and found the deer dead about thirty yards ahead. I broke it up, skinned it, and placed the rump and bits of the liver before the fire which I lit, while Trusty had the kidneys and then amused himself with the shoulder blades. I stretched the skin out before the fire, as I intended to take it with me to sleep on. I enjoyed my breakfast, to which I ate but little of the salt I carried in my bag in a bladder in case of need. Trusty had also eaten heartily and pacified his hunger. I cut some good lumps off the deer's back, filled my flask with fresh water, and set out once more, still hoping to reach the river. I walked up hill and down, having on my left the lofty mountain ranges, and in front of me a sea of rocks whose end I could not see. I was accustomed to such scenes of solitude, still I now greatly felt what a difference there is in looking down from the back of a stout horse on the desert and having to cross the enormous tracks on foot. The only anxiety that oppressed me was the agony my comrades must be feeling about me, as they would naturally suppose that some accident had happened to me. I knew they would not quit these mountains till they were certain of my fate, and I listened continually for signal shots. I dared not fire them for fear of expending my ammunition, and it would have been unnecessary, as they would certainly not neglect this method of showing me the road to them.

The day passed without my hearing the echo of a shot, and the sun was rather low when I reached a small stream whose banks were both rather thickly covered with wood. I resolved to spend the night here, as I had wood and water, and was protected from the weather, which had got up rather fiercely since the afternoon, I looked for a suitable spot, carried wood to a fallen tree, and was about to light my fire, when I looked up at the hill before me and felt a desire to take a look from it at the valley beyond to see whether the long looked-for river was there. It was still early, the sun had not yet set, and though I was tolerably tired I set out. I walked up a steep gorge into which several narrow passes opened on both sides; it was covered with several large masses of rock and loose stones, and the nearer I got to the top the narrower it grew, and the steeper were the precipices enclosing it.

I had just passed one of these narrow gorges on my right and was approaching a second, when I noticed an opposite pass on my left. I cautiously crept along the rock to be able to have a peep into this pass, and see whether there was any game in it, and was only a few yards from the angle of the wall, when suddenly a small bear, which I took for a one-year-old black bear, though it looked different, sprang from the pass on my right and hastened up the opposite one. As I said, it appeared to me rather smaller than a one-year-old black bear, but there was no time for reflection, and its skin might be of great service to me. I raised my rifle, fired, and saw the bear roll over the stones like a ball, uttering plaintive cries like those of a child; at the same instant the hasty bounds of a heavy animal reached my ears simultaneously with an awful roar. It became dark at the angle of the precipice before me, and the upright gigantic form of a grizzly bear appeared only a few paces from me. I fell back a step in horror, involuntarily stretched out my rifle to keep the bear off, and at the same moment saw Trusty fly past me under its belly. The rifle exploded—a fearful blow hurled me back several yards against the precipice—my eyes flashed fire—I lost my senses and fell.

I must have lain here about half an hour, and on opening my eyes again felt that my forehead was wet and cold. I saw that Trusty was standing over me with his honest face and licking me. I got up and sprang on one side in horror, for close to me lay the shaggy body of the bear, with widely opened throat, from which a stream of black, curdled blood ran under me. It was a she bear whose three months' old cub I had shot, and she had wished to avenge its death. My guardian angel had saved me, for my bullet, which entered its throat and passed through the skull, had killed the bear on the spot. In its fall it had torn the rifle from my hand, and forced me back so violently that I had struck my head against the rock, and the pain deprived me of consciousness. As on so many previous occasions, an invisible hand had again saved me from a terrible danger, whose extent I could appreciate now that I saw the monster lying before me. I stood motionless reflecting on my position, when the hoot of a passing owl reminded me that night had set in. While reloading, I remembered that this was the pairing time of the bears, and that very possibly male bears would be following the female, and hence this was the most dangerous spot I could select. I went up to the cub, threw it on my back, and hurried down the gorge to my camping place, where I at once made a blaze, the safest and only way of protecting oneself against the four-footed denizens of these regions. I now saw for the first time that brave Trusty was covered with blood, and had three severe wounds on his back, dealt him by the bear. Two of them I at once sewed up and washed them repeatedly with the clear cold water by which I was camped. I then skinned the cub, put a sufficient quantity of its tender fat meat to roast at the fire, made a bed of brushwood, and after supper I rolled myself in the shaggy, fresh bear-hide upon my deer-skin, and fell into my usual sound sleep.

I had not been sleeping long when Trusty barked sharply several times, and I sat up and seized my rifle. A frightful howling of wolves rang from the heights through the valleys, and between it a hollow roar resembling that which the bear raised when she attacked me. The night was very dark, and the fire, which had burnt down, solely lit up the nearest spots, while I could only distinguish the outlines of some evergreen holly-trees around me standing out against the clear star-lit sky. I quickly threw some small wood in front of the glowing trunk and blew up the flame. At this moment I heard something dash away close by, and directly after, at the foot of the ravine, renewed howls and roars, while Trusty stood close by my side growling. I carried some heavy logs to the fire, rolled myself again in my warm skin, and fell asleep, though I only allowed one ear to sleep, as Tiger said. The howling lasted the whole night. I looked after my fire every now and then, and was waked by the dawn without having had my sleep any further disturbed. After breakfast, I hung the two skins on my back, and followed the valley for about three miles ere I crossed the heights to the north, as I wished to avoid the spot where the bear lay, upon which the wolves and bears had held a grand feast during the past night. On reaching the saddle of the mountain, the idea occurred to me for the first time that the lost river must necessarily flow to the north, and I was amazed at myself for not thinking of this sooner. Hence I marched due west, and saw about noon a chain of hills whose direction lay northward, which animated me with fresh hope of finding my comrades again. At the foot of these hills, from which spurs stretched out eastward like ribs, the valleys were thickly wooded, and displayed generally a richer vegetation than the small gulleys in which I had hitherto been marching. With much difficulty and toil I reached the mountain chain in a few hours, exhausted and starving; but the longing to learn whether I should find at its top a pleasanter change in my prospects did not let me rest. I selected the least steep spot, and climbed up over loose boulders which constantly rolled away under me and brought me down. I had only one hand at my service to hold on to the few mimosa bushes or to pull myself up, for I carried my rifle in the other, and would sooner have injured myself than it.

At last I climbed the last patch, bathed in perspiration and red-hot, and words fail to describe the joyous surprise which befel me, on seeing before me the wooded vale and river, which I had been seeking so long in vain. In the first joy of my heart I forgot that it was still very uncertain whether I should find my comrades there, and that my existence might depend on a charge more or less in my possession. I fired my rifle and listened attentively to its echo as it rolled away along the mountains. I halted for a long time awaiting an answer, but to no effect. I looked long up the river with my excellent telescope to try and discover smoke, but also without success. Far and wide the rocky landscape lay before me, with no other sign of life than that of the buzzards circling round the heights. I had been resting for about half an hour and cooling myself in the fresh breeze, when I seized my rifle and proceeded down to the valley, which I reached in a much shorter time. I went up it to the foot of the hills, where I had fewer obstacles to contend with than in the wood that covered the river banks, till the declining sun as well as hunger and fatigue warned me to select my camp.

I had gone a considerable distance when the sun stood over the distant hills, for I had walked on without resting, and had no rocks to scale. I turned off to a spring in the wood, and threw off my skins on the first bushes I came to, as they fatigued me too much, though their weight was not great. My fire was soon lighted at the roots of a stump, a stock of wood collected, my meal made, and supper eaten, which consisted of the remainder of the bear meat. Before I entered the wood, I had looked up to the hills above me, and reflected whether at nightfall I should light a fire there, which would certainly be seen a long way down the river. I might possibly give my friends a hint of my whereabouts, but equally well betray my halting-place to hostile Indians, who, if any were in the neighbourhood, would see something unusual in it. But then again it was an easy matter to hide myself from them, and as I was without a horse, seek a refuge which could easily be defended. I resolved to carry out my design, took my weapons and went up the hills, whose summit I reached at nightfall. I then collected fallen branches and brushwood round an old stone piled them up to a great height, and the fire quickly darted up crackling and roaring. I carried up a great number of logs from the trees lying around and threw them on the fire, which reminded me of the bonfires we used to light at home when I was a boy. When I thought the pile of wood large enough to last at least an hour I left the hill and went to the nearest knoll, where I sat down near some rocks and lit a pipe, which enjoyment I only allowed myself morning and night in order to make my tobacco last as long as possible, as the leaves of the sumach, which are a good substitute for tobacco, were not to be had. I had been sitting there for about half an hour when Trusty got up, uttered an almost inaudible growl, and gazed at the slope under my feet. I pressed his head to the ground, laying myself on the top of him, and distinctly heard beneath me light human voices and some footsteps, which went under the precipice to the hill on whose top my fire was burning. What had I better do? Should I call out? They might be my friends, but if they were strange Indians, I should expose myself to unnecessary danger; if they were my friends, on reaching the fire, they would certainly make themselves known by their voices or by firing. I remained perfectly quiet and gazed steadfastly at my fire. After a while I saw a dark object moving before it, then another and another, and I was soon able to see clearly through my telescope that the men moving round it wore no hats. They were consequently Indians, and I was very glad I had not betrayed myself.

All at once I saw a long way off to the south-west a light which rapidly grew larger, and in spite of the great distance so increased that I could distinctly perceive the smoke through my glass. I greeted it with a loudly beating heart as the answer of my friends, for no one in these dangerous regions lights a widely gleaming fire save under such circumstances, and I was now certain I should join them again next day, for they were safe to keep up the fire, so as to show me my course by its smoke. I remained quietly seated under the rocks, and did not think of sleep though I was very tired, for I did not dare return to my camp, as the fire was certainly still burning there, and the Indians would have seized my skins, whose absence I now severely felt. I was beginning to chill, and as I could not await daylight on these bare heights, I resolved to march during the night as well as I could. I crept in a stooping posture from my seat to the nearest hollow which ran down from the hills to the valley, and on reaching the foot of them, I walked slowly on through the darkness.

I had been walking for about an hour, and had fallen several times, though without hurting myself, when I heard a shot right ahead of me. It was doubtless fired by my friends, who were seeking me in spite of the darkness: my fatigue disappeared, and I walked with greater certainty over the bare sloping ground. I soon heard another shot, and now could no longer refrain from answering it. I fired, and soon after heard two shots responding to me. It was a terribly tiring walk, for though it was bright starlight I could not distinguish the boulders and small hollows sufficiently to avoid them. I also got several times among prickly scrub and swamps between the hill sides.

I was just forcing my way out of such a damp spot overgrown with thorns, when the crack of a rifle rang from the hill side in front of me, and I at the same time heard Tiger's hunting yell, though a long way off. I fired again, and was again answered by two shots. I breathed freely and hurried over the slippery rocks, and just as I came under a hill slope I heard Tiger's shrill yell over me; I answered with all my might, and ere long this faithful friend and the equally worthy Königstein welcomed me. Their joy, their delight were indescribable. Trusty sprang round us as if mad in order to display his sympathy, and I was obliged to call to him repeatedly and order him to be quiet, ere he mastered his delight. It was a strange meeting among these wild mountains, whose dark forms we could now distinguish against the starlit sky, while the deepest night lay around us. Tiger proposed to light a fire; but when I told him that Indians had passed me and gone to the fire, he said it was better for us to keep moving. I was too tired, however, and must rest first, so we lay down under some large rocks where the wind did not reach us. I took Trusty in my arms and pressed him to me to keep him warm.

In order not to fall asleep, I now told my comrades how I had fared, and heard that Tiger had explained my disappearance to my friends precisely in this way. At length the first gleam of coming day showed itself, and was saluted in the valley by the voices of numerous turkeys. We leapt up, went down to the wood, where these early birds were standing on the trees, and brought two of them down. A fire blazed, and the breasts of the turkeys twirled before it while we warmed ourselves at it. Königstein had a tin pot and coffee with him, which improved our meal, and when the sun was beginning to shine warmly we started for the camp, from which we were about five miles distant, and where news of me was anxiously awaited.

The joy at meeting again was great. From a distance we were welcomed with shots: all ran to meet us, and each wanted to be the first to shake my hand and express his joy at my rescue, as they all except Tiger had given me up for lost. Czar raised his head and the forefoot buckled to it, and neighed in delight at seeing me, while Trusty ran up to him and leapt on his back. All were in the most cheerful temper, and a thousand questions and answers flew round our camp fire.

My friends had gone in search of me on the evening when I did not return to camp, and Tiger had found the turkey shot by me, and followed my trail to the first stony knoll over which I pursued the wounded stag; but from this point he had been unable to find my track, and returned to camp when darkness set in. The next morning at daybreak he returned to the same spot, and had gone ahead of my trail in a wide curve, in order if possible to recognise it in crossing. Toward evening he had really succeeded in finding first Trusty's trail and then mine in the valley where I shot the deer on the first morning, and reached the spot where I made my breakfast off its meat. But from this point every sign disappeared, and any further search would be useless as night had set in. Afterwards they lit a large fire on the nearest height, and kept it up all night, though I had not noticed it. On the next morning Tiger left camp at an early hour with Königstein, and told the others that they would be back in eight days if they did not find me before. They looked for me during the whole day, and had just collected wood on a knoll over the river to light a signal fire, when they saw mine flashing against the dark sky, and hurried toward me.

After all the events of the last restless days had been sufficiently discussed, I longed for rest. I made my bed in the shade of a live oak, covered myself with a buffalo robe, and giving my comrades directions not to wake me under any pretext, I slept undisturbed till the sun withdrew its last beams from the valley, and sank behind the glittering peaks of the Andes. I felt strengthened, and after dipping my head in the river to refresh me, I sat down with my friends and ate a hearty supper composed of all the dainties of hunters' fare.

The next morning found us mounted at an early hour to scale the heights on the other side of the river, whence we followed its course in the next valley. Toward noon, however, the road became fatiguing, as we had to climb rather large hills that jutted out from the mountain chain on our right, and we were soon so wedged in among steep precipices that we saw no prospect of advancing. After many attempts nothing was left us but to turn back and recross the saddle we had last surmounted, after which we followed the valley to the north-west. Here, too, our road was rendered very tiring and dangerous by huge scattered masses of rock, as we often had to lead our horses over them, and they might easily have been injured by slipping upon them. We wound our way through, however, without any accident, and were riding towards evening over grassy meadows under a steep precipice, when we noticed on the top of it a herd of about twenty buffaloes, following a path that ran over a plateau several hundred feet above our heads. It was remarkable with what certainty these apparently clumsy creatures followed the path which was at times hardly a foot in breadth, close to an abyss on which a man might have hesitated to venture.

I dismounted and aimed at an old bull which led the file, while I shouted to my comrades to fire at the fifth head in the herd, which was a cow that would not bear a calf this year, and hence must be very plump, which can be easily seen by the dark glistening hair. We shot nearly together. My buffalo made a spring forward, rose on its hind legs, and fell over the abyss, falling on projecting rocks till it came down to us in the valley regularly smashed. The cow, hit by many bullets, fell on its knees, and, as if foreseeing its fate, remained in this position for some minutes, till its strength deserting it, it lost its balance and fell head-foremost from rock to rock down to us. Both animals were frightfully smashed, their ribs and bones protruded from their torn hides, and large pieces of rock had been forced into their monstrous carcases. The other buffaloes trotted along the path till they disappeared from sight behind a knoll. The smashed animals were perfectly suited for our use, as we only took the best bits, and especially the loins from the spine, cut the tongues out of the broken jaws, and removed the marrow-bones, leaving the rest to the vultures and buzzards which soon circled over our heads.

Towards evening we reached a small stream which wound through the mountains to Canadian River, and offered us a very pleasant camping-place through the fine grass on its flat banks, as well as an abundance of dry wood.

We were lying in the twilight round our fire, when we heard a long way up the valley the hoot of an owl, and at the same time saw a large very white bird flying along the dark precipice. We all seized our rifles to bring it down, when it settled on a projecting rock opposite to us. None of us had ever seen a bird like it before. Several of my comrades ran up nearer to it, and fired simultaneously; it swung itself in the air, however, with a loud flapping of wings, and circled round our camp, flying no great distance above me. I had more luck than my friends, for I tumbled it over with a broken wing. It was a snow white owl of extraordinary size, and with such beautiful plumage that I kept its skin to stuff. I therefore killed it, hung it up, and on the next morning skinned it, and prepared the skin for carriage.

CHAPTER XXII
BEAVER HUNTERS

We left our camp at a rather early hour, and soon found below it numerous signs of beaver trees, a foot and a half in diameter, lay with a great number of smaller ones along the banks of the stream, and farther in the wood we saw trees glistening whose bark had been peeled off several feet above the ground. Any one unacquainted with these animals and their habits would surely have believed that new settlers had been busy here, and cut down wood for their block houses. The splinters lay in heaps round the bitten-through trees, as if we had been in a carpenter's shop, and many of the felled trees had been stripped of their branches. These most interesting animals generally settle on the smaller streams and brooks, and their families at first consist of but few members. On such a stream they cautiously select a spot where several tall soft-wooded trees, such as poplars, aspens, ashes, maples, &c. stand on both sides of it, then proceed together to one of the trunks, stand on their hind legs, and follow each other slowly round it, tearing out of the tree at each bite great bits of wood, as if they had been hewn out with an axe. They cut away more wood on the side of the tree turned to the river than on the opposite side, so that it becomes overbalanced and falls over into the water. Thus they fell one tree after the other across the stream, nibble off the branches, and carry other bits of wood between and under these trunks down to the river bed, while they fill up the interstices with twigs. After this is finished, they fetch on their broad flat tails mud and earth from the bank, and plaster the wooden dam, till it becomes so tight that the water rises before it, and overflows on both sides frequently for miles.

In this lake, produced by their art, the beavers build their houses, which are generally of three storeys, though at times of four. They are round and pointed like a sugar-loaf, are about twenty feet in diameter at the bottom of the water; the floors are about two feet high, and separated by a flooring, in the centre of which is a round hole, by means of which they go up and down the house. The only entrance is at the bottom of the water, and generally only the highest floor emerges from the water, so that the latter is always dry. The creatures build their house of branches three feet in length, which they bind together with twigs and earth, and make the walls nearly a foot thick.

They thus build one floor over the other, each higher one being smaller, till the highest one terminates in a point. They line the interior with grass and moss, so that it affords them and their young a dry, warm abode in winter.

The females give birth at the end of May, or beginning of June, to from two to six young, which are brought up in the colony and remain there; on the other hand, they never admit a strange beaver, and fight sanguinary battles with it, if it tries to force its way into their settlement. In proportion as the family increases, more houses are built, and I have often seen lodges in which a dozen houses peeped out of the water. The beavers, however, do not fell the trees solely to build their houses, but also to procure food from the tender bark of the thinner branches. They convey these branches in autumn, cut in lengths, to their houses, and pile up a large supply in the lower rooms, on which they live in winter. They go on land at this season, too, and for this purpose keep holes open, in the ice on the banks of their ponds, and I have also found their track in the snow; but as a rule, they remain at home at that season. If the family grow too numerous for the space and the food to be found in the vicinity, several members of it emigrate and establish a new lodge close by: frequently an old beaver colony will contain a hundred. The beaver is one of the most cautious and timid animals in creation, and it is very difficult to get at it on land and kill it with firearms; on the other hand, it is wonderfully easy to capture in traps, and in this way an entire colony can be extirpated to the last one in a very short period.

The male beaver carries in two bladders the *castoreum officinale*, a very powerfully-scented, oily fluid, which the hunter collects in a bottle and mixes with spirits, partly to keep it from putrefying, but principally to impart to it another odour, by which the beaver is induced to believe that it emanates from a stranger. In this bottle the hunter thrusts a twig, the point of which he moistens with its contents, then thrusts the other end of it into the bank of the beaver pond, so that the point projects over the water at a spot where it is not very deep. Exactly under this twig he places in the water his heavy iron trap, to which he fastens, by a long thong, a very large bush, which he throws on the bank. So soon as a beaver raises its nose on the surface of the pond, it smells the castoreum on the twig, swims up to convince itself whether it emanates from a stranger, and while going on land steps on the trap, which closes and catches its forefeet. It darts away with the trap into deep water, and wrestles furiously with the torturing iron, for which reason a beaver thus captured is never found to have sound teeth—till, quite exhausted, it tries to rise to the surface to breathe. The trap, however, keeps it down, and the prisoner is drowned in its own element. The next morning the hunter sees the bush floating over the spot where the beaver is lying, and pulls it up with the trap. The beaver hunters who visit these western deserts often take some dozens of traps with them, so that when they arrive at a colony, it is speedily destroyed, on which occasion they also capture in the same way the otters living there.

Usually these hunters go quite alone into the desert with a horse that carries the traps, some buffalo hides, salt, gunpowder, and bullets, and lead thus, several hundred of miles away from civilization, a most dangerous and fatiguing life for two or three years. At night they set their traps, and in the morning take out the captured animals, whose skins they dry before the fire, while their flesh serves them as food. When they have cleared out the spot, they pack up the skins, conceal them in caves, under rocks, and in hollow trees, and go farther with their traps. In winter, when the hunt is not very productive, they build huts of skins, or seek a cave in the rocks, in which they find a shelter from the harsh climate, and hunt other varieties of game, while they keep their horse alive on a stock of dried grass, collected in autumn, weeds, or poplar bark. At the end of some years, during which such a hunter has collected a large stock of skins, he proceeds to the nearest settlement, fetches pack animals thence, takes a sufficient number of men into his service, and proceeds to his hunting-grounds, in order to carry to market the produce of his lengthened labour. It is often the case that such a hunter receives from three to four thousand pounds for the skins collected during this period, but still more frequently he pays for his daring with his scalp and his life. The Indians themselves do not kill beavers, but regard the trappers as the pioneers of the white men, who eventually advance farther into their hunting-grounds, and take from them one piece of land after the other, by which they are daily driven farther back, and come into hostile collision with one another. Hence the trappers are hated by all the Indians, and pursued by them whenever they are seen. Only the great concealment and difficult approach to the regions where they hunt, and the great caution with which they manage to hide their abode from the eyes of the Indians, render it possible for them to lead this life for years, and constantly deceive the savages, when they accidentally acquire a knowledge of their presence. It is incredible what acuteness and skill such iron characters develope, and we must feel surprised that a single one of these adventurers ever sees his home again, I have lain for whole nights at the little fires of these people, and listened to their stories—how they became familiar with this life in their earliest youth, and returned to it when grey-haired, although able to live comfortably on their savings in the civilized world. As the seafarer dies on the water, the desert becomes the element of this hunter; and he rarely closes his eyes elsewhere—with the rifle on his arm.

The sign of beaver lodges which we saw was so fresh and numerous that probably no one had as yet appeared here with traps: the stream spread far over its bank and formed a very large pool, from whose surface a number of houses peeped out; but we could see nothing of the mysterious denizens of the settlement. We were compelled to ride close under the precipice on our right, where our cattle were up to their knees in water, in order to cross the inundation, while below the dams the stream remained in its narrow bed.

We reached Canadian River, which, however, here trended so to the east that we took the first opportunity of crossing the hills that bordered it and pursuing our course toward the north. On the other side of them, which we reached about noon, we came to another small stream, on whose banks we saw a number of peeled trees, and also found here a beaver lodge. We rode through the stream, and had left it about a mile behind us, when we suddenly heard a shout in our rear, and saw a man, who had stationed himself on an isolated rock, and was making signs to us. Tiger told me he was a beaver trapper. We rode back to bid this son of the desert good day and hear whether we could be of any service to him. When we drew nearer, the tall dark form disappeared from the rocks, and a man stepped from the thicket on our left, with a long rifle in his hand, and came up to us with the question—"Where from, strangers?" He was above six feet high, thin, but muscular, with extraordinarily broad shoulders, a dark bronzed face and neck, a long grey beard, and a haughty demeanour; his small, light-blue eyes flashed with great resolution under his thick black brows, while a pleasant smile softened the impression which his glance might have produced on a stranger. His exterior revealed at the first glance that he had endured a good deal in his time, that he had often defied fate, and that nothing could easily happen to him which would throw him out of gear and make his resolution totter. Deer-hide tight trowsers, shoes of the same material, and a jacket of the same composed his dress, and a scarlet woollen shirt, unbuttoned, allowed his bronzed chest to be seen. A beaver-skin cap proved that it was made by the wearer, and the same was the case with the hunting-bag he carried over his shoulder.

I rode up to the stranger and replied—"From the Leone on the Rio Grande," and offered him my hand, which he shook heartily. "Are you a trapper? and where from?" I asked him. "From Missouri; my name—Ben Armstrong—has been known for the last forty years in the Rocky Mountains, and I have now been back for a year from the old State." He invited us to go to his camp and spend the night with him, as he longed to hear something about events in the old States. We accepted his invitation, and followed him along a narrow path through the bushes and rocks to a spot some hundred yards above the pond, where we dismounted in front of some thick scrub, and passed through it with our host. We stepped on to a cleared spot, from which the axe had removed the bushes, at whose northern end heavy masses of rock rose above each other, and hanging over at a height of thirty feet, covered a large space. Over the whole place a number of dried beaver skins was suspended from the branches, as well as the hide of a grizzly, and many others of deer and antelopes. Under the rocks lay several bundles of beaver skins, while one of them drawn up near the fire seemed to have served our host as a seat.

Antonio and Königstein went down to the pond with our horses, where there was excellent grass, and watched over them in turn with my other comrades. I saw a track of a horse leading to our host's abode, and asked him whose it was, to which he replied that on this trip, for the first time in his life, he had taken a partner, a young Kentuckian of the name of Gray, who was at present out hunting on horseback, to get some venison, as they were sick of beaver meat. The next day, he said, they intended to leave their camp, as they had trapped all the beavers round, otherwise he would not have been so incautious as to lead so many horses to his hiding-place and thus betray it to passing Indians. He always led his own horse through the scrub up the stream, and let it graze on the opposite side, so that its track might not lead to his camp.

Our host now filled a cup from a small cask of whisky three of which lay under the rocks, and, as he told us, constituted his sole luxury. He loaded an extra mule with them when he started, but it had been killed some months previously by a couguar, as it had got loose at night. He readily offered us his favourite liquid and a cup of fresh spring water, and after taking a hearty pull himself he put six beaver tails in front of the fire, and we put all our coffeepots with them, and unpacked our small stock of biscuit, while we set the remaining marrow-bones from yesterday to roast.

The sun had not set when our friendly host's partner arrived with his horse, loaded with deer meat. He was greatly surprised at finding so large a party, and very pleased to have an opportunity of hearing news from the States, even though it was not of the freshest. He was young and tall, with a healthy, merry face, brown eyes, pleasant mouth, a commencing beard, and long, dark brown curls hanging over his shoulders. His tight-fitting leathern dress was made with more coquettishness than Armstrong's, and displayed his handsome person, while a broad-brimmed black beaver hat slightly pulled over one ear, imparted to his whole appearance something resolute and determined.

Our cattle were now brought up and fastened to the withered trees in the open space—then we lay down on our skins round the fire and enjoyed the beaver tails, while our hosts paid special attention to our biscuits and coffee, which were a rarity for them. After supper Armstrong sent the whisky-cup round again, then pipes were lighted, and we first answered the thousand questions asked us about the state of affairs at home, and which principally referred to politics. When this subject was exhausted, Armstrong spoke and told us the principal events of his life since he last bade farewell to civilization, his various bloodthirsty fights with the Indians, the dangers they had often escaped with difficulty, and the fatigues and unpleasantnesses they endured, among which he mentioned the hailstorm, which had also annoyed us. He told us of successful hunts with the traps, and promised to show us the next morning the last beaver to be found in these parts.

Then he told us how the ex-owner of the monstrous bearskin, which hung behind us on a tree, had paid a visit one evening to their camp, and how they killed it. For fear of the Indians they dared not light a large fire, and the few coals had not frightened the bear, which advanced within a few yards of them, when both fired their rifles at its head, and laid it dead on the ground. While telling this story, Armstrong pulled off his shirt and showed us on his sides and back a regular mass of scars which he had received from the embraces of dying grizzlies. He narrated so picturesquely that the matter was fully brought before the listener: his powerful deep voice, which kept pace with the fire of his narrative, the passionate gestures by which he accompanied his narrative, as well as his coarse form, illumined by the fire and the surrounding scenery, produced a remarkable and permanent impression on me. We listened to the stories till a late hour, when fatigue at length closed our eyes.

At the first beam of dawn we led our cattle into the grass, got breakfast ready, and then went with Armstrong about half a mile down the stream, where he had traps still set. We pulled up three beavers with the bushes floating on the water, and our host remarked that now there was only one old fellow left, who had escaped his traps several times and would not go near them again in a hurry. On returning to camp, we packed our animals and took leave of our kind hosts, to whom, to their great joy, we gave a portion of our stock of coffee. We then described to them accurately the district where we had seen the numerous beaver lodges, and wishing them all possible luck, rode again up the mountain's side where we had heard Armstrong shout.

For several days we followed our course without any particular difficulties, while the country retained much the same character. The Sacramento mountains seemed to run farther to the west, and attained their greatest height here. We soon got among higher mountains, and found we should have done better by going more to the east into the prairies, for we were obliged to turn and ride a long way back, as we could not pass through the mountains. At length, however, we reached a river of some size, which flowed to the north-east, and resolved to follow it until we reached lower and more accessible regions where we could pursue our course again. We spent the night on the north side of the river, and found, after riding a few miles down its bank, that the valley through which it flowed constantly grew narrower and the precipices on its sides steeper. It was still early, and the sun had been unable to overpower the thick fog which had gathered in the valleys during the night. It appeared, indeed, still uncertain whether it would rise or fall, as it hung about the rocks in long, narrow strips. It was as cold as on a damp autumn morning; the grass and bushes were as wet as after a heavy shower, and heavy dewdrops hung on the old spider's webs between them. We had put on our buffalo robes and guided our horses between the many loose blocks of stone and step-like strata, while the river constantly displayed larger and smaller cascades, some of which were twenty feet high, and its bed continually became deeper.

We had just reached one of these falls when we noticed on the other bank two very large grizzly bears, one of which squatted on its hind-quarters and stared over at us. They could not hurt us, as the stream above the fall was too rapid for them to swim across without being carried so far that they would go over the fall, and below the latter the banks were at least fifty feet high, and so steep that it was impossible to climb them. Tiger, for all that, advised us not to fire at them, as he was of opinion that they might find a spot where they could cross to us, and then they would give us a good deal of trouble. We therefore rode past without disturbing them, and only watched them as they licked their paws and passed them over their clumsy heads, while sniffing at us from time to time, and even following us a few yards along the bank.

The gorge down which the river dashed grew deeper and our route the more dangerous, until we suddenly came to a ravine which ran across our road into the river bed. Our farther progress was here checked, and we were obliged to try and make a path up it, which was effected with great difficulty, as the stones lay wildly about. We soon reached an old very practicable path, which, as it appeared to us, was used not only by buffaloes, but also by Indians, and which ran north-west. Tiger was of opinion that this was the road through these mountains to Santa Fé which the foot Indians employed, as they avoid the prairies in order to get out of the way of the mounted tribes, and because travelling in the tall grass is too fatiguing for a pedestrian.

We gladly followed it, for the road through the rocks was more impassable than ever; it ran up hill rather sharply toward the highest mountain saddles. The nearer we advanced to them the better and more passable the path became, and our horses scaled these high hills at a good pace, and at times had an opportunity of drawing breath on small plateaus. The sky was perfectly cloudless and the sun warm, so that we welcomed the light north wind. Eastward the low hills lay at our feet in the extreme distance, between which we could watch the various mountain torrents for a long way, while here and there the rich green of the fresh turf peeped out between the red masses. On our left, the mountains were piled on each other in the strangest forms until their glistening ice-peaks rose into the azure sky. Our path frequently wound along the precipices, where it could be seen for a long distance like a white stripe, and it did not seem possible to pass along it; but when we reached the spot our horses stepped lightly over it, and we found that it looked worse than it really was.

Thus, toward evening, when the sun was sinking behind the mountains, we saw our path suddenly disappear behind an abrupt precipice, and expected a dangerous bit. When we arrived there we considered it really better to dismount and lead our horses. The path constantly grew narrower under the precipice, and the abyss beneath us steeper and deeper at every step. We advanced as it was no longer possible to turn back, and with each foot our situation became more serious. We wound round the face of the rock and looked down into a dizzy ravine, whose bottom was already hidden by the gloom. The path was only a few feet wide, and at many places washed away by the rain. Tiger, with his piebald, was ahead of me, and was leading his horse by a long bridle; all at once he cried to me, "Take care," and I saw his horse step down and then spring up again. The rain had excavated the path here to some depth, and by its side the rocks went down sheer. Without hesitation, I seized the end of the bridle, quickly crossed the dangerous spot, and Czar did the same gallantly. Königstein followed me, and then one after the other till the mules at length came up. Jack was ahead; he went cautiously up and down, and I saw the basket on his left side graze the precipice; still he got across safely. Lizzy followed at his heels; but Sam swerved when he arrived at the spot, made a leap to get across, struck his basket against the precipice, and was hurled out into the abyss, down which he fell with all four feet in the air. A general "Ah!" was the sole sound that passed our lips, for we were not yet out of danger ourselves. Ere long, however, the path grew broader, and ran over a grassy plateau, whence we could look back at the dangerous point and into the dark abyss. Had we arrived from this side, not one of us would have dared to lead his horse over it, and we should have been obliged to ride round a long way.

The loss of Sam was serious to us, for he carried our coffee, spirits, several buffalo robes and articles of clothing. A little coffee was still packed on Jack, as we had opened a fresh bladder that very morning, and that animal carried all the articles for daily consumption. Still the matter could not be helped, and we regarded the loss as a very fortunate one, as we might just as easily have lost one of our horses, which would have been far more serious. We unpacked, as the sun had set and we did not know what roads we might still find. We had grass for our hungry cattle, and water for ourselves we carried with us. We made a small fire of bois de vache, to which Tiger presently brought a few twigs of mimosa, so that we were able to cook our supper; then we supplied our friends whose bedding had fallen into the abyss with such blankets and hides as we could spare. The night was very cold, and we missed a good wood fire terribly. We rolled ourselves tighter in our blankets and skins, but could not keep warm, and were glad when daylight came and we could make our blood circulate by moving about. All of us, except Antonio, hurried off to look for firewood, in search of which we had to go some distance; still the movement did us good, and each brought an armful of wood back, so that we soon had a good fire at which to warm our benumbed hands.

It was very early when we rode off with our buffalo robes over our shoulders: we pulled the large woollen blankets that hung over the saddle across our lap, so as to keep our knees warm, and throwing the bridle on the horse's neck, we put our hands in our jacket-pockets. The whole landscape looked as if sugared, the grass and bushes sparkled in the sunbeams with their coating of hoar frost, and the rocks completed the wintry scene by the cold blue tinge they had in the shade. This picture, however, passed away very rapidly, and in an hour the rime was hardly to be seen even at the shadiest spots. Our path continually ran upwards, and went up and down from one mountain saddle to another. We saw several bears climbing up the rocks, for in these remote regions they are not very particular as to the mode of going home, and came across a herd of antelopes, some of which we shot. About noon we reached a hollow between two ranges of hills, where we found fresh grass and a stream whose banks were covered with low bushes.

We noticed about a mile to our left at the spot where the stream ran out of a precipitous and very narrow gorge, eight buffaloes quietly grazing, and resolved to hunt them. We left our cattle under Antonio's charge and crept toward the animals. Here my comrades hid themselves in a dry bush overgrown with raspberry creepers that stood nearly at the centre of the opening, and Tiger and I crept up to the buffaloes, which were standing at the highest point of the ravine: we reached some bushes not more than ten yards from the animals without their perceiving us, and lay down on the ground in the midst of them. We had each selected a buffalo, when they stared into our bush with tails erect, as they had probably scented us; we fired together, and at the same moment there was a trampling over us as if a cavalry regiment were charging. I jumped up and fired again at the flying monsters, which now had to run the gauntlet of my comrades' guns. One dropped close to them and a second fell a little farther on, while the rest galloped down the stream. Tiger sprang up too and cut off a buffalo near our bush, which he said was the one I had shot: his had fled with the others. For my part, I had not seen it, for the powder smoke still hung over my rifle, when the brutes charged over us, and we might consider ourselves fortunate that they had not trampled us with their huge feet. We skinned one of them in order to use the skin as a substitute for the one we had lost, although an untanned buffalo hide is a very clumsy thing to carry on pack-animals.

We laid in a stock of the best meat, took all the marrow-bones and tongues, and then followed a very decent path, which here left the main road and went down the stream eastward. After a little while the path trended more to the northern hills, where we saw the smoke of numerous fires rising farther to the north. Tiger said it was lucky we had chosen this road, as on the other we should have ridden right into an Indian camp.

For two days we followed our path and crossed various streams which flowed more to the south, till the low hills became more scattered and the glens between them wider. The vegetation was springing up here, and the good pasturage induced us to grant our cattle some days' rest, as they had been on short commons lately. We selected a very pretty camping-place, where a small stream ran under a precipice and was covered on one side with scrub and a few leafy trees, while on the north and east a rich prairie opened out, and to the west the forest became thicker. We had abundance of game of every description, and many a head bled to death around us, merely for the sake of the fascination which hunting exerts. All had left camp in turn to hunt except Clifton and myself, and the latter asked leave on the second morning to try his luck. It was a fine day and I proposed to accompany him, but stipulated that we should ride. Clifton was delighted, and quickly saddled his iron-grey, a horse of remarkable value, who up to the present had been the least fatigued of all our cattle by the journey.

We rode away from camp and received from our laughing comrades a seasonable hint to take care and not lose ourselves. We rode up the stream, from which a thick wood soon separated us, on whose skirt we had followed the prairie. We had ridden for about an hour, when we noticed a little distance off some wild cattle proceeding toward the wood. Clifton was very eager to kill one of these animals, but I warned him to be most cautious, and reminded him that this was a most dangerous hunt. We rode slowly to the skirt of the wood and reached the spot where the herd had entered it, when Clifton pulled up under a young oak, wound his horse's bridle round a branch, and ran off with his rifle and knelt behind a large plane tree. He had done this almost before I knew what he was about. I rode a few paces farther and saw a large bull grazing with its head turned towards us, but at the same moment Clifton fired. The bullet was hardly out of the rifle ere the bull rushed at him with lowered head, and Clifton, throwing away his gun, took to flight. He reached a young tree and swarmed up it, while the savage brute dashed under his swinging legs and charged the iron-grey, which attempted in vain to tear away its bridle from the branch. In an instant the bull drove its head under the poor horse, and with its monstrous horns tore its entrails out. The horse fell to the ground with a fearful piercing cry, and at the same moment I sent a bullet through the bull's shoulder; it turned and followed me furiously into the prairie, where I fled before it in a wide circle. It became exhausted, stopped, and uttered a furious roar, while hurling up the turf with his horns and stamping on the ground with its feet. I turned Czar a little to the right, kept Trusty back, and sent my second bullet between the bull's shoulders, upon which it sank on one knee and soon rolled over.

I now hurried to Clifton, who was standing with tears in his eyes over his dead horse and repenting his want of caution, but too late. Mourning over this sad loss, we went back to camp on foot and there aroused great sorrow by describing our misfortune. We consulted as to what was now to be done, and there was no choice left but for Clifton to ride the mule, Lizzy, while we divided her load between Jack and Antonio's mare. We sent to the scene of the accident to fetch Clifton's saddle and some meat from the bull, and remained all day in camp in sorrowful mood.

CHAPTER XXIII
THE GRIZZLY BEARS

The next morning we followed the river for some hours, and then entered a path which ran northward through a lateral valley. We had done a good day's march, and were busy preparing supper in a small wood at a spring, when Trusty began barking, and we heard the sound of horses. We all ran to our horses and brought them together, while we got our weapons in readiness, when Tiger leapt out of the bushes and shouted some words we did not understand, to which no answer was given, though the sound of the horses' hoofs ceased. Tiger hurried back, shouted to us to fasten up our horses in the thicket, which was effected in a moment, and then post ourselves round it behind the trees, as he believed that they were hostile Indians. All at once a single voice was heard not far from us, whose language was equally incomprehensible to us, but which Tiger at once replied to; and springing up behind his tree, he uttered his hunting yell. He ran in the direction where we had heard the voice, and shouted to me they were friends, Delawares. Our joy was great, for our position would not have been a favourable one if we had been attacked here by a superior force: it was dark, and our thicket was commanded by thick scrub and trees, so that our cattle at any rate would have been exposed to bullets or arrows from a close distance. Tiger now came up to our fire with an Indian, whom we soon joined, and he introduced to us his friend, the Chief of a Delaware tribe, whom he called Young Bear. Several of his men soon joined us, most of whom spoke English, and all were very friendly to us. They seemed all to have known for a long time that Tiger was living with us. Every one questioned him and appeared satisfied with his answers. The chief remained at our fire, while his people went to camp close at hand. He told us they had just left their settlement, and were going to the Southern prairies, where the most buffaloes were, but intended to march down the mountains to kill bears and lay in a stock of grease and skins. Farther east there were a great many Indians on the prairie, and we should do better in not leaving the hills entirely, although no tribe would venture openly to attack us so long as Tiger remained with us. He stopped to supper, and then returned to his camp.

The next morning we visited the Delawares, and were pleased at the cordiality with which they welcomed us. There were about forty warriors, about half as many squaws, and a heap of children. They had at least a hundred horses and mules with them, some of which were remarkably handsome. Clifton requested me to ask Young Bear whether he could supply him with a good horse, as his people appeared to have more than they required. The chief spoke to them on the subject, and ere long several came up with horses, which I advised Clifton, however, to decline, as they were not good; for I was aware they would produce their worst horses first. After we had inspected and declined a number of horses, a young Indian came up with a black horse, which was really handsome. It was a powerful, finely-proportioned animal, and showed in all points its noble breed. The price he asked was two hundred dollars, upon which I offered him thirty, and after a long chaffering we agreed on fifty, which Clifton paid. He was delighted with his purchase, and had long reason to be satisfied, for the horse turned out most useful and excellent in every respect.

We breakfasted, Young Bear sharing the meal with us, and were busily preparing for a start, when the chief came to me and said that one of his men was inclined to go with us, and it would be better for us to have him with us; he had often been on the Rocky Mountains, and was acquainted with the tribes living there, while Tiger was only a young man. I was very pleased at the offer, which seemed to me to be made chiefly on Tiger's account. I told the chief I should be very glad, and we would pay the man for his services; he had better ask him what he expected. The Indian, a powerful man, between thirty and forty years of age, now came forward, and we agreed that we should pay him five dollars for every month he spent with us, till we returned home. He was very pleased, fetched his horse, and joined our party. We stopped at the camp of our friends, bade them a hearty farewell, and marched northward, animated by fresh courage.

Our new comrade, whose name was White Owl, was a very quiet, good-tempered, and sensible man, who in a short time gained the goodwill of all; he helped us in everything, and appeared anxious to supplant Tiger in our favour by his activity and valuable services. He was at the same time a first-rate hunter and good shot. So that he rarely returned to camp from hunting without game.

In a few days we reached open prairies; the mountains to the west seemed here much farther off, and resembled blue clouds. These were the mountain chains in which Santa Fé lies, and whence annually enormous sums of silver are sent to Mexico; on the eastern side they are bordered by rich boundless prairies, while their western slopes are washed by the Rio Grande. On these plains we found vegetation more advanced, and though the fresh grass was not enamelled by such a varied flora as the prairies on the Leone at this season, still we saw around us several pretty flowers, which offered an agreeable variety to the eye. Small knolls and bushes, as well as clumps of trees, frequently broke the dead level and saved the eye from resting on an indistinct horizon. At the same time these plains were enlivened by an extraordinary number of buffaloes, large herds of wild horses, antelopes, and deer; so that at every moment the hunter's straying eye rested on something to interest him. We marched for eight days due north, during which time we crossed many rivers flowing to the east, and came across hunting-Indian tribes repeatedly. One night we camped with a party of Shawnees, whose chief was called Greengrass, and who behaved in the most friendly manner to us. He promised to visit us next winter, and made us a present of several beautifully dressed deer-skins, as he thought we should soon want them. In addition we met Osages, Creeks, Choctaws, and a small tribe of Pawnees: the latter displayed unfriendly intentions, but as we treated them sternly and resolutely, they soon quitted us. Tiger shouted to them on parting that we could see their scalps at night as well, and so they had better keep away from us. The Pawnees are the most warlike tribe among the Northern Indians, are splendid riders, have first-rate horses, and live between the Platte and Missouri rivers; in proportion to the other northern tribes, they are armed with but few firearms, but use the lance and lasso with remarkable skill.

At the sources of the northern arm of Canadian River we crossed the path, which runs from Santa Fé to Fort Bent, on the Arkansas, and thence to Fort Leavenworth, on the Missouri, and a few days after crossed another road, running from Independence, on the Missouri, _viâ_ Taos in New Mexico, to St. Francisco and Saint Fé. The country here became very hilly; the vegetation had scarce sprouted, and the nights were cold. Our cattle were badly off here, for grass was scanty, the roads very stony and covered with loose boulders of red granite, which hurt their bare feet, and they also suffered severely at night from the cold. We now began to feel the loss of our coffee, which lay buried between the mountains with Sam, and we equally missed on these cold nights the brandy which had shared the same fate. In a few days, however, we shook off these habits, and our meals did not taste the worse without these articles of luxury.

We proceeded west-north-west, in order to enter the real Rocky Mountains, and see the Spanish peaks, the highest in this range, which lie to the south of the Arkansas, from which river we were now no great distance. The weather favoured us; it was warm in the day, and the young grass was sprouting in the valleys. During these days we generally ascended and crossed a number of small streams that flowed from these mountains to the

Arkansas, and always found good provender for our cattle on their banks. The mountains in the west continually rose, and the snow-clad Spanish peaks, of which three were much higher than the rest, stood out more and more distinctly against the blue sky. We reached a mountain saddle, and on its plateau, a rather frequented path, which appeared to have been originally made by buffaloes, though we noticed old horse-tracks upon it. As it trended to the north, we followed it, as it must certainly lead to the banks of the Arkansas. The path became very fatiguing for our cattle, as it was covered with flinty boulders, some of which had very sharp edges, and injured the hoofs. At the same time we found but little food for them on this bleak elevation, and noticed with sorrow that they were losing both flesh and strength.

We had been following this path for four days, when we were compelled to lead our horses and expose our own feet to the sharp pebbles, for all were more or less lame and unable to carry us any farther. Jack was the only one that underwent no change, though he placed his little feet very cautiously on the ground. We marched from sunrise to dusk, without meeting with grass or a drop of water. Our feet were painful, too, and we eagerly scaled every elevation in the hope of finding consolation on the opposite side. The sun had set, and night would long before have put an end to our journey, had not the moon lighted us. Tiger, who had gone on ahead, awaited us on a knoll with the cheering news that there was excellent pasturage here for our cattle, and water probably no great distance off. We passed through a rock-gate into a glen, where we soon stood in high grass, and our animals greedily bit at it, while we hobbled them, and Tiger went off with Owl to look for water. The latter soon returned, and told us that a stream ran along the valley on the right, after which he informed Tiger of his discovery by several shrill yells, and we now rose from the stones among the grass, on which we had sunk greatly fatigued, to reach the desired water. Tiger soon found us, and he and Owl led us between huge masses of scattered rock down to the stream, where we refreshed our cattle. A crackling fire of brushwood soon illumined the surrounding scenery, as we found plenty of wood to keep it up. Late at night we lay round it, and watched our cattle enjoying the sweet grass, for we felt a reluctance to fetch them in and tie them up. At last, however, weariness compelled us to place them in our vicinity under Trusty's charge, so that we might rest after our exertions.

Morning showed us that we had camped in a small glen, which, being watered by numerous springs, displayed a rich vegetation for its elevated situation. The grass was fresh, and mingled with many juicy plants, which our cattle seemed to be very fond of. The stream on which we had camped had a good deal of bush on its banks, out of which grew a few stunted trees, which by their growth, and the moss covering their bark, clearly showed that they did not feel at home in this region. We were very pleased to have reached this oasis, and resolved to let our cattle rest here for at least a week, not only to enable them to regain their strength, but also to give vegetation more time to sprout.

We made many hunting excursions, but always on foot, as we wished to grant our cattle perfect rest, and we could get through the mountains better in this way. We did not find the common deer here, but the elk, whose dry flesh soon became repulsive to us. Now and then we killed an antelope, and Tiger brought in one evening a mountain sheep, an animal exactly like the ibex, which lives in large flocks in these mountains. Its meat is agreeable and tender, and its skin produces first-rate leather for clothes.

Our stock of game was again reduced to the dry flesh of an elk, when at daybreak I cooked a bit of it for breakfast, and, after eating it, seized my weapons and left the camp with Trusty to go in search of better game. I followed the stream some distance, and soon reached the bare slopes which ran down to the Arkansas: here I turned to the stream which ran through the valley about six miles under me, and its banks were covered with green meadows and numerous bushes. Down to it ran bare, smooth strata of rock, between which countless gorges opened on to the stream, which had been hollowed out by the mountain torrents in their furious course. Between them lay, on the steep slopes, patches of large and small rocks, often piled up on each other as if human hands had arranged them. Little vegetation was to be seen here. A few bushes rose from among the stones, while here and there the broken, withered stems of torch weeds, which plant seemed the most common here, stood in groups. Not a tree or bush offered a relief or variety to the eye gazing over this solitude: right and left, as well as across to the mountains on the other side, so far as I could distinguish objects, nature seemed to be utterly dead. I looked again at the narrow, green strip which ran like a long snake along the glistening stream, and tried to discover the game grazing on it through my glass.

I noticed several elks, as well as a single buffalo, and had walked about half an hour along the rocky strata, when I reached a group of stones which attracted my attention by their remarkable and picturesque arrangement. The lower layer consisted of three enormous rock-plates, at least five feet thick, on which again smaller ones rested, and several stones rose in this way, so that the edifice resembled from a distance a pyramid, which could be seen through at several spots. I had walked to the base of this mass of stone, and was examining its strange form, when, on looking back to the river, I noticed three dark forms, which were moving sideways toward me up the steep, and were scarce half a mile from me. At the first glance

I recognised in them three grizzly bears, rapidly advancing at a sling-trot behind one another. I knew the danger of meeting these savage brutes, and quickly measured the distance back to camp. But I was on foot, and felt as if I had lead boots on which bound me to the spot. It was hopeless to think of escaping; the animals were following a course as if they wished to pass above the rocks near which I was standing, when they must cross the recent track of myself and Trusty, which they would indubitably follow at once.

It was pairing time, at which season all beasts of prey are more savage and active, and hunt more from the pleasure of killing than to pacify their hunger. The grizzly is so fast that it can catch up a buffalo or a horse going at full speed, and its gigantic strength renders it more enduring than any other animal. Only one chance of escape is left the man it pursues, and that is, a tree, for this bear cannot climb. But then there was not a tree anywhere around, and besides I could not take Trusty up one with me, and he must be saved. I had no time for reflection, as the peril rapidly approached. I laid my rifle on the first layer of rock, seized Trusty round the body, hoisted him on my shoulders, and helped him on the rock, up which he scrambled: with one bound I was by his side, then aided him up the second and third layers, and laid myself close to him on the uppermost blocks, where I placed my weapons and ammunition ready to hand.

If the bears passed under my fortalice I would let them go in peace, for in that case it was probable they would not find my track; but if they passed above it, I must throw away no opportunity to render them harmless as soon as possible. I peeped over the rock with my rifle, when the three monsters were scarce fifty yards from me, proceeding to cross my trail above me. An old she-bear slouched carelessly along in front. Close behind her followed a gigantic, very old he-bear, and a short distance in the rear came a rather smaller male. The old one drew up to the she-bear and laid his right paw on her leg, but she was greatly offended by this caress, and dealt my lord such blows with her enormous paws that the hair flew out of him. He sprang back; she sat up, showing her frightful teeth, and with her side turned to me, I pressed my barrel firmly against the rock, and pointed it at the heart of the she-bear. I fired; she crossed her paws over her face, and sank lifeless in a second. The old bear ran up to her and laid his paws over her, but his rival came up, and a fearful struggle began between the two monsters, in which they rolled over and over, and tore out each other's greyish brown wool in great masses. The old bear had the best of it, however, and sat up, uttering frightful growls at the smaller bear. By this moment I had reloaded and sent a bullet into the brute near the heart. With one bound it leapt on its foe, which tried to escape it, but the old bear held it tight in its fore-claws, and dug its monstrous teeth into the other's back. The other bear defended itself desperately, and soon found that the old brute's strength was giving way: it sprang on it and buried its tusks in its chest, and standing over it tore it up with its two hind-paws.

I was certain of the victory, and was so careless as not to reload my rifle, but fired my second barrel at the younger bear without concealing myself properly behind the rock. I hit it well, but it scarce felt my bullet ere it turned its savage head toward me, and galloped toward the rock with an awful roar. In an instant it reached the base of my fortress, and sprang with its fore-legs on the first layer, while it opened, its blood-stained throat, and, with smoking breath, uttered the most fearful sounds. At the moment when it raised itself on the rock I held my revolver as near as I could, and fired between its small glowing eyes: it fell back, but at once got up again, and tried still more furiously to scale the rock, by springing with all four feet at once upon the first stage, and raised its blood-dripping face just under me. I had pulled out my second revolver, and held it cocked in my left hand. I pointed both barrels at the monster's head and fired them together: it turned over, and rolled motionless on to the ground. I looked at the two others which still lay quiet side by side, and could scarce believe my eyes as they gazed down on the victory which I had gained over these three terrors of the desert. I quickly reloaded, and looked around carefully from my fort, especially in the direction from whence the brutes had come, for other male bears might easily follow their track. I could see nothing to alarm me, and now sprang down from the rock with Trusty, went cautiously up to the bears, and found them all lifeless. They were three monstrous brutes: the old bear must have weighed at least fifteen hundred pounds, the she-bear one thousand, and the smaller bear eight hundred.

These beasts are often found on the Rocky Mountains, where they are very numerous, as the hunters do not care to pursue them. Everybody is glad to get out of their way, and only uses weapons against them when he is attacked, or can fire at them from a place of safety, such as a boat on a river, when the bears are on land, or from a stout tree. The Indians also only fight them in self-defence, and hence their claws are considered the greatest mark of honour with which they can adorn themselves. The value of a grizzly stands in no proportion to the danger the hunter incurs in pursuing it, for its hide is too heavy, and its hair not so fine as that of the black bear: it never becomes so fat as the latter, and its flesh is not so delicate. Hence people are glad to avoid it, and the hunter willingly surrenders his booty to it, when on following the bloody track of a head of game he runs a risk of being caught up by the grizzly. This animal does not know what fear is, and once irritated it will fight and hit as long as it is able. I know instances in which a grizzly had some thirty bullets in its body ere it was killed; but if hit at the right spot, it falls as easily as any other animal. The she-bear gives birth, from November to January, to two or four cubs, which soon follow it on its forays, and are trained to hunt, which speedily develops the savage, cruel qualities of the young monsters. It hunts both in the mountains and on the prairies: in the former it lays in wait for the game, and darts down from the rocks on its unhappy victim, while on the latter it will chase its terrified quarry for miles, and mercilessly rend it when captured; for instance, it seizes buffaloes, horses, wild cattle, &c., at full gallop by the hocks, tears out the sinews, and in a second renders them incapable of flying farther. When caught quite young and trained, these animals become very tame, but they must never be trusted, as any negligence may cost one's life, and I knew several instances on the frontier of men being torn by such tamed bears, or at least losing an arm or a leg.

I had had enough sport for to-day, and fled from the battle-field, as I was fearful of the advance of other foes. I went straight to camp, and was saluted by a hurrah! as my early return indicated a successful hunt. I had the two mules got ready, and invited the Indians and John to go with me. They all wanted to know what I had killed, but I merely told them that I had killed a heap of game, as they would soon see. We made a hurried dinner, and then started with the mules. We soon reached the slope, and rode quickly down to the river, during which I constantly saw my rock fort, but it was too far to notice my quarry. My comrades believed that the game lay on the river, and kept their eyes turned towards the latter, while I led them a little to the west of my rock, to keep them from seeing the bears as long as I could. When we were in a right line with them, I turned aside, and we suddenly caught sight of them. The amazement and surprise of the Indians were very great, and were expressed by the most extraordinary outbreaks. They danced as if stung by a tarantula, swinging their rifles over their heads, round the dead bears, and imitated their roar in a remarkable manner. At one moment they crept close to the ground up to the animals, then ran past them with fierce yells, or leapt over them, swinging their guns with wild shouts of delight. After they had finished this dance of triumph, they sat down on the old bear, sharpened their knives on small stones they took out of their medicine-bag, and wished to cut off its claws. I told them, however, that I wished to keep this skin with the claws on, but the two others were at their disposal; with which they were perfectly satisfied. We skinned the largest bear, and cut out the best meat and the fat, which we intended to take with us. We took the paws and fat of the other two, after the Indians had appropriated the claws. I pulled all the tusks out of the three heads, and we now packed the mules to convey our booty to camp. As we intended to remain a few days here, I asked the Indians if they would dress the large skin for me, to which they readily assented; for this purpose they split the head with an axe, and took out the brains.

We rejoined our comrades before sunset, who were also very pleased at my success. We at once took some of the bears'-grease we had brought, and fastened it with strips of hide round the hoofs of our cattle, as this fat refreshes the horn, and deprives it of the brittleness which is the principal cause of its breaking when marching over stony ground. My bearskin was staked out on the grass, and we all set to work with our knives scraping off the flesh and fat, after which the brains were rubbed in and the skin rolled up. We then laid heavy stones on it and hurried to supper, which we greatly enjoyed after our powerful exercise during the day.

We repeatedly changed our camping ground, partly to get fresh grass for our cattle, partly to have a new stock of dry wood at hand; and thus went farther down the stream. We stopped here nearly a fortnight, by which time our horses were quite restored, my large skin dressed, and we bade good-bye to the glen which had given us such a kind reception. We followed the path again which had brought us here, and in a few hours reached the Arkansas, on which we found excellent pasture. In the afternoon we crossed it and rode up its northern bank, till evening put an end to our march, and we camped in a wood, which was already adorned with young foliage. The next morning we discovered close by, to our great delight, a bee tree, out of which the warm morning sun had already drawn the busy artisans. It was an old plane several feet in diameter. We soon attacked it with our axes, and ere an hour had passed it crashed to the ground, and the hollow burst open filled with most delicious honey. We had a glorious feed, and a man must, like us, have been for awhile put on simple fare in order to appreciate the pleasure which such a variation produces. Unluckily we had no vessels in which to carry off much of it; still we packed a large stock of comb in deer-skins, and carried it with us for some days, but the comb soon ran and dirtied our baggage, so that we were obliged to leave it behind.

We had ridden up the river for two days, when we reached an arm of it coming from the north, up which we proceeded for a day, and met with no special difficulties. One path ran through a pretty glen, on the right side of which the mountains gradually rose, and stretched out their peaks far in the distance, while on our left the river-bank was overhung by colossal precipices, over which the mountain chain rose steeply with its snow-covered pinnacles. On the fourth morning, however, our bank became very rocky, and we rapidly ascended toward the mountains. We spent several nights without fire or water, and even during the day the latter, as well as grass, was very scarce. My large bear-skin, which Owl had made very soft, was of great service to me with its long close hair, as it was large enough to wrap three of us in, for the nights were chilly, and my comrades complained greatly of cold. We here crossed the highest point we had yet reached, and the snow peaks did not appear to be very far from us; still we found sufficient grass for our cattle in the gullies between the mountains.

We halted for a day at one of these grassy spots, and I went with Tiger early from camp to procure meat, when a flock of mountain sheep drew us farther into the mountains. We had fired several bullets at them to no effect, and followed them in growing excitement from one rock to another until, some hours later, we reached a plateau which was shrouded in fog. Our sheep flew over this and disappeared in the mist. We stood amazed at this phenomenon, whose cause we could not explain, for it was a clear, bright morning, and the hills around shone in the brightest sunshine. We went up to the plain, and found to our surprise that the mist covering it came from hot springs, which rose to the surface in immense numbers, the highest with a jet of about three feet. The plateau, which was about a mile in diameter, was quite covered with these springs, which produced a great calcareous deposit. This lime formed a rim round each spring, over which the water poured and collected into a rivulet, which ran down the eastern slope under a thick cloud of steam. We could drink the hot water, though we could not hold our finger in it for a minute. We walked between these hot springs, on which the sun produced the most brilliant rainbows, to the eastern side, where the water flowed away, and reached it bathed in perspiration, for the steam was very hot, and we were constantly enfolded in it. We could watch the course of the stream far through the mountains, for steam continually rose above it. The water had a slightly saline taste, and was very like weak chicken-broth. There is no doubt but that these springs are mineral water, which probably in a hundred years, or a shorter period, will prove most valuable to suffering humanity. At the spot to which a flock of mountain sheep led me and an Indian there will then rise palaces, and gaily dressed ladies and gentlemen will drive out, and the time when only naked savages and a few adventurers admired these beauties of nature will be forgotten. But whether it will be so beautiful there then is questionable; for it is this very untouched nature which is so charming, with its mosses and weeds on the bare rock, its bushes growing out of the crevices, its clumps of trees, and its solitary gigantic pines, behind which are the distant blue ranges. All these pictures will be altered by human hands, but as a rule not improved. Before we proceeded after the game, I carved my name and the date of the year in a large upright rock, and we looked back frequently from the mountains at this strange scene.

We soon found sheep again, but they fled on our approach to the most inaccessible rocks, where they leaped with wondrous strength and certainty from one pinnacle to another, and sometimes after a desperate leap reached a peak on which they had scarce room for their four feet. In such cases they looked round for a few minutes in their airy position, and then flew with equal strength across to the nearest precipice, frequently over dizzy abysses whose bottom was concealed by mist. After a long, tiring, and unsuccessful stalking we scaled a height, and saw below us a flock of these animals standing on a slope over which they could not leap. We had cut off their retreat, and did not consider it possible that they could find their way across the scattered peaks to a lateral valley, which was about twenty feet broad and about fifty long. We would not fire at them where they stood, as they would have fallen over the precipice, and we could not have got at them; hence we showed ourselves and shouted, on the supposition that they would dash up hill and pass us. But they no sooner saw us than an old ram leaped with an enormous bound on to a projecting stone, and thence to a second, till he reached the gorge on our right, and darted up it. We ran up to the gorge, and I toppled the ram over with a bullet. The other animals followed it leap by leap, and all reached the other side of the gorge, excepting one ram, which jumped short and fell backwards into it. We looked after it, and I felt certain that it would be killed and become our prey; but it fell on the monstrous horns which nature has given these animals as a protection in such dangers, turned over, and leaped with the lightest bounds up the gorge, where both Tiger and I missed it. We reached the dead ram by a long circuit, paunched it, loaded ourselves with the best meat and the handsome skin, and returned to camp. About a mile farther on we shot down another large sheep from a rock, and sent Owl out to bring it in.

The mountain sheep, as I said, bears a great likeness to the ibex. The ram has enormous curved horns, with the points turned slightly outwards, as thick as one's arm close to the head, and surrounded with rings. Its hair is more like that of a goat than a sheep, of a brownish gray colour, and with a dense coat of underwool. The female has also horns, but they are smaller, and not turned outwards at the point. They bear two lambs, which, while still very small, follow them on their dangerous paths in the mountains. At night the mountain sheep descend to the lowlands, and are there easily killed by the hunters who lay in wait for them, while following them day by day in the mountains is most fatiguing, dangerous, and generally unsuccessful. The skins of these animals are greatly sought by the Indians to make clothes of, as they furnish a handsome, soft leather; their meat is fat and agreeable. They live in large flocks, and may be seen by day in the Rocky Mountains standing about the highest peaks, at spots which it appears impossible for a quadruped to reach.

We had no lack of game, but saw to our great regret our supply of salt running out, for the greater part of it was lost with unlucky Sam. Our clothes, too, were beginning to get defective, especially our linen, as we had lost our changes on the same occasion. We mended our shirts as well as we could, and cut off from the tails to repair the damage higher up; but for all that they were speedily wearing out. Our stock of tobacco was all but expended, but this article was the easiest to supply, as the leaves of the wild sumach represent it very well. We were provided with the essentials, however, especially powder and ball, as these were distributed among the animals, and we had enough to last us a year. A great privation was impended over us when our salt was consumed, and we so restricted its use that it would last for some months, in the hopes of obtaining a fresh supply at one of the forts of the fur companies, which are in the vicinity of the Rocky Mountains. Our good spirits did not desert us, however, but enabled us to endure all the fatigues of this mountain tour. We passed two nights on fields of snow, where we could hardly find sufficient firing to prepare our supper.

At length our route descended to lower hills, and we reached at their base a plain, which, as it seemed was enclosed by even loftier mountains, whose saddles still bore the signs of winter, while on the streams in this elevated valley, which our Indians called Salade Park, May was flaunting in her spring garb. Although the vegetation that surrounded us here could not be called luxuriant, it did our cattle a deal of good. For a long time past we saw for the first time herds of wandering buffaloes, among which we produced great destruction, as we had long been yearning for their marrow-bones and tongues.

One morning we approached a herd which was grazing among large scattered rocks, and we all crept up to them under cover of the latter, with the exception of Antonio, whom we left with the horses. We lay in a long line in the grass and behind stones, and had shot five of the animals without being noticed, when Mac fired and got up after doing so. He had hit the old bull he fired at badly, and the latter, slightly wounded, charged furiously at him. At this moment Clifton jumped up not far from Mac, fired his two bullets at the infuriated animal, and then bolted with Mac. The buffalo dashed furiously after them, while the two fugitives, running at full speed, threw away their rifles and lost their hats. Fright carried them over the grass as if they had wings, between the numerous rocks, and they had contrived by making a long detour to get within hail of us again, when Trusty, whom I had laid on, caught up the bull, and attacked it in the flank. A kick from its hind leg, however, threw the dog on his back, and without stopping the savage brute dashed after our comrades, and was only a few yards from them when Mac slipped and fell among the rocks just as we discharged all our rifles at his pursuer. The buffalo flew over him, followed Clifton but a short distance, and then turned with a fearful roar on Mac, who was trying to get up. It sprang with lowered head toward the fallen man, when a second shower of bullets was sent at it; but it would certainly have impaled Mac had not Trusty come up and pinned it by the snout. Our shouts encouraged the brave dog; the buffalo rose with him on its hind legs and fell backwards on the ground, while we ran up and honeycombed it with pistol bullets. We now helped Mac up, who had not, as we feared, been trampled by the buffalo, but had sprained his leg, and complained of great pain; hence we put him on his horse, rode with him back to the stream we had crossed shortly before, where he bathed his foot, while we returned to the dead buffalo, and cut out the best meat, the marrowbones, and tongues. The result of this chase afforded us great dainties, on which we revelled for some days, as the meat kept good for a long time in the cold temperature.

CHAPTER XXIV
ASCENT OF THE BIGHORN

In a week we crossed the valley by short stages and again reached the loftier mountains. One afternoon we arrived at a stream where we resolved to pass the night, as we did not know whether we should find water farther on. Tiger at once hastened off to look for game, and as my comrades preferred a rest, I set out to try my luck too. I told Antonio to follow me on Lizzy, that I might not have to carry the game myself, and had got about a mile from camp when I noticed from a clump of oaks a herd of deer on a grassy spot ahead of me, which looked like the ordinary Virginia deer, but were darker-coloured. I took up a deer-call to draw them toward me, as the spot where I was standing was too barren for me to be able to stalk them. I posted myself near an oak, and Antonio sat on Lizzy behind me. The herd advanced toward me on hearing my call, and were near enough when Antonio cried to me, "Here! here!" I fancied he was alluding to the approaching deer, and whispered that I could see them; but he repeated his "here!" and presently added, "Look to your right!" I turned and saw an enormous snow-white bear forty yards from me, I tried to fire, but the bear got behind a large oak, and then behind another, and so was a good distance off ere I could despatch a bullet after it, which I heard enter a tree. It escaped me, as I had left Trusty in camp, for his feet were sore from running over sharp stones lately. The bear heard the call and hurried up, believing that there was booty for it. It was only a variety of the common black bear. I would gladly have secured its beautiful skin, as it is a rarity, but it was out of my reach, and hence I returned to the deer, which after my shot had disappeared in a distant wood. I went after them, and found them grazing again: when I emerged from the bushes I shot a large deer, and found to my surprise that it belonged to a genus I had never seen before. It was of a very dark, almost black, colour, much larger than a Virginia deer, and more lightly built, with a longer black scut. It had cast its antlers, and the new ones had already grown to some size. We packed the entire animal on Lizzy, and carried it to camp, where Owl called it a mule-stag or black-tail deer, a variety not uncommon in the lower regions of the Rocky Mountains.

Our road rapidly ascended from here to the higher mountains, and became daily steeper and poorer in vegetation; still the path we followed was very fair, so that we rather rapidly surmounted the heights, on whose small plateaus our cattle were able to rest again. We left behind us in a few days many mountain chains with their narrow valleys, when suddenly the mountains before us became covered with snow, and we were soon in the wintry landscape again. We suffered terribly from the cold, as our clothes were not at all suited for such a temperature; and though we wrapped ourselves in our skins we could not keep warm. I was the best protected, as I hung my large bearskin over me, and, sitting upon it, wrapped myself up from head to foot; but for all that I did not get warm during the ride, and we were very glad when we reached a hollow in the evening, where we found but little snow and a clump of fir-trees, in which we camped, and warmed the atmosphere around us with an enormous fire.

On the following day our road ran principally over snow-covered rocks, but we came now and then to spots where the sun had melted it, while all around us rose mountains which even at midsummer do not doff their winter garment. At last, early one morning, after spending the night at a very poor fire, we ascended a saddle, whence we looked down into a plain, whose end in the blue misty distance was bordered by high mountains, while on the west and east it was begirt by immense ranges, whose lower chains ran down sharply on both sides in the most remarkable shapes. The steepest rocks here rose precipitously over the valley, and the white stone formed long pinnacles, round domes, globes resting on their pillars, in a word, the strangest shapes, so that our wondering eyes were tempted to see in them towers, castles, and monuments, while farther on the mountain masses rose above each other with a reddish-blue tinge, and touched the clouds with a few isolated peaks. The valley itself, if it may be called so at this elevation, was well watered, and from south to north glistened at the base of the western mountains the surface of a large river, while on the right-hand side signs of water were also visible. Except the forest of pines on the sides of the mountains, vegetation seemed to be restricted to the vicinity of this water, where we noticed a good deal of bush and some rather lofty trees of the aspen and poplar kind. The greater portion of this extensive undulating plain only displayed desolate tracts of stone and rocky knolls. Our Indians call this mountain glen Old Park, and the river before us the sources of the Rio Colorado, which flows through New Mexico and California to the distant Pacific, where it falls into the Gulf of California.

We hastened to the lower regions, and on the third day reached the river, whose course we followed. A few days after we were surprised by two men, as we were letting our horses graze at noon. They were beaver trappers who had been hunting for some years in these mountains, and paid us a visit in the hope of procuring provisions from us. We showed them, however, that in this respect we were almost as badly off as themselves, and that with the best will we could not meet their wishes. They were both Canadians, of French origin, and had led this life in the desert for many years. They were men of very slight education, with repellant manners, and a disagreeable, very coarse appearance, so that we were not sorry when they took their rifles and went away with a hurried farewell.

We marched for about a week near this river, till we reached a bend, when it suddenly trended to the west, and thence pursued its uninterrupted course through the enormous plains. We crossed here an arm of the river which came from the east, and followed another up stream to the north-east. We constantly drew nearer to the mountains on the east, and ere long the highest peak, clad in eternal snow, rose distinctly against the blue sky before us. The Indians called this the Bighorn, which agreed with the statement of the two trappers, of whom we had inquired. I had been determined from the commencement of the journey to get as high as I could up this peak, and hence steered toward it.

On the second evening we reached the outer hills, and resolved to take our cattle as far as was safe regarding food for them, and then continue our journey afoot. It was the second half of June, the weather splendid, and the heat at times oppressive by day, while the nights remained extraordinarily cold. The farther we advanced in the mountains the scantier food became for our cattle, but on that account they were all the safer during our absence from an attack of hostile Indians, who rarely venture so far into the mountains. On the third day, after crossing a considerable chain of mountains, we reached a small glen, which, on the east side, was enclosed by precipices, and on the south-west offered an open view of the mountains of Old Park. It was covered with good grass, amply supplied with pine-wood, and watered by a beautiful stream, which forced its way through the ravine by which we had entered. This spot exactly satisfied our purpose, as it was remote from regular paths, protected against possible storms, and could be easily defended. Hence we formed our camp here, conveyed our traps under overarching rocks, where they were protected against storm and rain, and hunted for some days in the neighbourhood, in order to provide those who remained behind with food for some time. I had selected Tiger to accompany me, and wished only to take one other of my comrades with me, while the other four remained in camp, I proposed that John, Mac, and Clifton should draw lots as to who should accompany me; but the two latter gave way in favour of John, who gratefully accepted.

On the morning of our departure I rolled up my large bearskin and sewed straps to it, in order to be able to carry it on my back; John and Tiger did the same with buffalo hides, and ere long all our preparations for a start were completed. We urged on our comrades the greatest caution, and then said good-bye in the hope of finding them all right on our return.

We walked bravely up the mountains, from one chain to the other, Tiger being ahead and Trusty behind. Sometimes we came to paths along which we went pleasantly; at others, we crept on hands and feet up the steep granitic strata, and with every hour we had a more extensive view to the west. On the first day we covered a considerable distance, at least five-and-twenty miles. We saw an incredible number of mountain sheep, which, at our appearance, flew up the precipices and gazed down at us in amazement. Tiger shot a large ram, and we each took a lump of the flesh with us, while we left the rest to Trusty. Toward evening we came to a stream, and though it was still early we halted, as we found plenty of scrub in the vicinity with which to light a fire and roast our meat. It was an exquisite spot where we camped; beneath our feet we recognised quite distinctly the white rock towers which border Old Park, and between which our friends were encamped. We gazed at the immense mountain valley below us and the windings of the stream through it; we noticed on its western side the mountain chains that ran up to it, and saw clearly where the water forced its way through them, taking a south-western course. Still these mountains formed the border line of our view, as we were not yet high enough to be able to see over them. The air was pure and clear, but it soon became very cold, and so soon as the sun sank behind the mountains we rolled ourselves up in our hides. We had collected a large stock of wood in order to be able to make a blaze quickly, but determined to keep it up all night; but we had forgotten our fatigue, which soon made us fall asleep, and we did not wake till daybreak.

Dawn aroused us, and animated the extensive landscape around us, whose glens were covered by a thick damp fog, while a fresh breeze blew round the heights. We soon finished breakfast, and when the sun shone on the first peaks of the western mountains we were again ascending the mountain in the direction of our object. After filling our gourd-bottles afresh, we went the whole day indefatigably up the steeps, through desolate rock strata, almost entirely denuded of vegetation, between which, with the exception of a few clumps of fir, only grasses, reeds, and torch-weeds sprang up. We very frequently came to water, which indubitably had its source in the snow melting on the peaks. Toward evening we reached a plateau, which seemed to separate the higher regions from the lower, and extended up and down the mountains, with but slight breaks, as far as we could see. It was at least three miles in breadth, and offered us a free prospect of the mountain saddle and its isolated peaks, of which the Bighorn rose far above the others. All these peaks were covered with a bluish coat of ice, and shone and glistened so in the sun, that it hurt the eyes to look at them for any length of time, while the hollows displayed the pure white of the snow. A number of snowy peaks stood in a large circle around us, among which two enormous domes rose to the sky, the northernmost being the highest, and bearing the name of the Bighorn. On its northern side it is a perfect precipice, while on the south it forms several steep terraces, while the lower peak bears to some degree a resemblance to a truncated cone.

We soon recognised the impossibility of reaching these icy heights, still it appeared to us feasible to scale the back of the mountain farther to the north, as we noticed there in a deep gap which ran almost to the summit isolated spots free from snow.

The sun was now approaching the distant mountains in the west, the sky gradually turned red and at last stretched out over them like a stream of fire, from which their ice-clad peaks stood out like gleaming flames, the whole boundless landscape around us was suffused with a warm red light, and the peaks in the east had changed their brilliant white into a dark transparent carmine. We stood in silent admiration and saw the last beams of the glowing sun disappear behind the mountains; ere long the gloom of nightfall spread over the earth. The eastern sky was covered with the nocturnal dark purple blue, and the still illumined snow peaks alone looked down on us, like the last gleam of departing day. An icy cold wind reminded us that it was time to look for a resting-place, and without long consideration we went toward the mountains and reached a group of scattered rocks, between which we found a species of moss and dry hard grass, which offered us a softer couch than the bare stones.

We were not quite asleep, when the fearfully plaintive tone of some animal which was probably bidding farewell to life in the claws of a grizzly bear rang through the mountains; still this did not prevent us from falling into the soundest sleep, and trusting our safety to the faithful dog. The rising sun saw us again *en route* over very difficult ground. The ravines which we always followed in order to skirt the precipices, were at times so full of large blocks that we could not jump from one to the other without danger, while the rock strata we were compelled to climb were often too high for us to lift ourselves upon them. Hence we were obliged to make numerous circuits and could not advance so rapidly as the distance would have allowed. About noon we were scaling a height when suddenly a mighty condor spread out its enormous wings with a loud yell, and rose from a rock with a great effort, and we saw a mountain sheep hanging in its claws. It swung itself on to the nearest peak and sat down there, looking over at us with extended wings and croaking hoarsely. We raised our rifles almost simultaneously and the eagle sank lifeless on its quarry. Tiger climbed up and threw both down to us. The sheep was a one year old ewe and welcome to us as delicate food: while Tiger appropriated the eagle's feathers and claws, we cut the flesh from the sheep and rubbed salt into it, after giving it a hearty beating, for thus when our stock of roast meat was expended, we should be able to fall back on raw meat, as we had no fire materials.

We continued our journey and soon reached snow, which only remained, however, on the north side. The air became very cold, which rendered breathing difficult, and we could not walk fast. Evening surprised us completely surrounded by snow, and we had to go a long distance ere we found under southern precipices a spot where the sun had melted it away. Here we slept and my comrades woke me several times and asked whether I was not frozen—they could not close an eye, while I was tolerably warm. They shook me again before daybreak and we continued our journey, pulling our skins tightly round us. The snow was frozen very hard and had generally a rough surface, so that we passed easily over it. Our long sticks, which we frequently sharpened, here served us in good stead, as at doubtful spots we felt with them whether the snow would bear us, and no doubt we frequently crossed deep places, into which we might easily have sunk.

At eleven in the forenoon we at last scaled the highest point after excessive toil and stood on a wide snow field, which sloped down on the east to a hollow, behind which other snow mountains rose, and in the extreme distance the sky formed the background. To the south rose the white peaks of our saddle, above which extended the two mighty crests of the Bighorn. The bluish cold colour of these enormous snow domes contrasted with the warm reddish tint of the mountains and the sunlit landscape below them, and the icy peaks dazzled our eyes when we looked up at them. Before us in the west stretched out a scene which I cannot find words to describe faithfully. To the right and left on the sides of the snowy mountains which formed a semicircle we saw a sea of hills and rocks in the most eccentric shape; above them rose to an immense height the various peaks vividly illumined by the sun, and between them lay the dark shadows of the mighty glens, which were enclosed by precipices. Only rarely did the living green of foliage peep out of the desolate scene, which was slightly enlivened by the more frequent clumps of pines, and the straying glance gladly rested on the isolated patches of grass, whose fresh juicy green imparted a warmth to the landscape. At our feet we gazed at the depths, till our eyes rested on the snow-white wondrous outline of the precipices which surrounded Old Park on this side, and we followed the silvery ribbon of water that wound through it. Old Park lay like a narrow glen before us, lost in the mist and often crossed by ranges that connected the eastern and western ranges. Far away in the misty distance, above the mountain chain that borders Old Park on the west, our eyes rested on the enormous plains which sink from the Rocky Mountains to the Pacific, and in the extreme distance their outlines became blended with the sky. They seemed to be crossed by but few ranges; to the south-west we could distinguish lower chains of hills, while in the west and north-west a long dark cloud was visible, which indicated to us the snowy mountains or maritime Alps of California. So far as we could see, this country appeared to us but slightly wooded and not very well watered. The course of the Rio Colorado was alone marked by lower ranges of hills and the hue of the vegetation.

Our eyes were fixed for a long time on this grand landscape, and we found it difficult to bid it a last farewell; but the cold warned us to start, so that night might not surprise us on these inhospitable heights, on which we did not see a sign of a living creature. It was one o'clock: we once more bade adieu to the cold, desolate spot, which had afforded us this enchanting prospect, and then hastened to our last night's camping-place, where we arrived with frozen beards. We passed a very cold night here, for the wind had got up, and we felt very happy when we left the snow behind us on the following day. At noon we rested and pacified our hunger with the remainder of the raw flesh, which the condor had provided for us; then we continued our journey, and reached before evening the foot of a hill, where we found water and sufficient scrub to prepare a supper of a fat ram which we had killed on the road.

On the next day we joined our comrades again all right, found them in the best spirits, and our cattle rested and strong. Before the camp they had erected a number of small scaffolds of sticks, on which meat cut in strips was being smoked over fires, and a very large and a small bear-skin hung on the rocks proved the nature of the meat which was drying. Owl had shot close by an old she-bear and one of her cubs, whose meat our comrades were now drying for the purpose of taking with them. This was very welcome, for when a little bear-meat is roasted with dry venison, the latter becomes dainty and fat. We heartily enjoyed the tender meat of the young bear, which weighed some sixty pounds, and the fire which we had so missed for some nights. Unfortunately our salt was now out, and the same with our tobacco, while we could not expect to find in these mountains any sumach leaves which we could smoke. In a word, we were out of everything, except ammunition, for our clothes literally consisted only of deer-hide, and we merely carried with us the remains of our linen to use as bandages in the case of a wound. Still we were in good spirits and healthy as bears, and comforted ourselves with the thought that in a few months we should obtain supplies at one of the forts to the east of the Rocky Mountains.

We started on the morning after our return to camp, and went back through Old Park and up an arm of the Colorado. We followed its windings across the hills to the point where as a mountain torrent it formed the most exquisite cascades in falling over the rocks. We halted a long way up it, and though we were once compelled to quit it through the impassable nature of its banks, we sought to reach it again soon, as its crystalline waters contained delicious trout, some weighing twelve pounds, abundance of game grazed on its banks, and the latter always afforded us plenty of wood for our camp fires. Moreover, it continually formed the prettiest bathing-places, in which we refreshed ourselves morning and evening. At last, however, we were compelled to say good-bye to this pleasant friend, as it broke up into several small streams, and we ere long reached the highest point of the hill-range, which we had scarce crossed, however, ere we found on its northern side an exactly similar stream, which, instead of flowing southward to join the Pacific, runs due north and in a great curve round the black mountains on the North Platte river, and then through Missouri and Mississippi to the Gulf of Mexico. We greeted this stream with great joy, as it afforded us the same comforts as the one we had just left, and followed its course down to the spurs of the mountain chain, which we reached on the second evening, and found in its valleys a rich vegetation for these regions, which seemed, however, to be confined to the vicinity of water. The hill-side, on which we camped, was covered with oaks and pines, through which our torrent wound down to the valley in front of us, which we could survey from our elevated post. The hills gradually descended into it, and in its centre rose a conical lofty rock, whose pinnacles had exactly the shape of a ruined castle. Our stream wound round this rock, and glistened in the wood that covered its banks; we also saw a few buffalo scaling the lower rocks to crop the scanty weeds that grew among the crevices.

It was getting on for sunset, and still early enough to secure a few marrowbones from these emigrants: hence Tiger, John, and Clifton hurried off, Antonio following them on Jack. In a quarter of an hour we saw our hunters emerge from the wood at the base of the rock, and approach the buffaloes by stepping behind the stones. Light clouds of smoke rose above their heads, and the crack of their rifles reached us, while we saw one of the animals fall in a heap, and the others flying up the mountain side. Next Antonio with the mule joined our comrades, who had collected round the animal, and were busy in breaking it up. Königstein and I had meanwhile lit a roaring fire, and Mac and Owl pulled some trout out of the adjoining stream, so that, when we were all assembled again in camp, we had the prospect of a glorious supper.

The next morning we finished packing our cattle at an early hour, and were about leaving our camp, when we saw behind the rock in the valley the smoke of many fires rising, which indicated a very large Indian camp. We must employ the precaution of first finding out to what tribe they belonged, and in which direction they were going: so we rode down into the glen and concealed ourselves in the thick wood. Tiger and I then went to the rock and climbed to the top of it, whence we could survey the valley on the opposite side. Who can describe our surprise on seeing at our feet a large, animated camp, with all the signs of civilization! From the numerous gay tents pennants blew out in the fresh breeze, and between men, horses, and mules were moving in the strangest confusion. Here and there laggards crept out of the tents and ran off to the stream to remove the last traces of sleep in its clear waters. Round the fire other men, in the strangest costumes, were busied in preparing breakfast, while others were proceeding to and from the stream with horses and mules. Our amazement was great, and our joy knew no bounds. I pulled out the last remnant of a pocket handkerchief, fastened it to the end of my rifle, and then discharged both barrels, while swinging my white flag high above my head. I saw that the attention of all the occupants of the camp was directed to us, and many arms were raised pointing at us. A salvo of at least fifty shots answered my greeting, and handkerchiefs were waved in the air. We soon descended from our observatory, and hurried back to our comrades to impart the pleasant news to them, and we galloped along the stream, round the rock, and toward the camp, where our little party were received with a thundering hurrah.

In an instant we were surrounded by a crowd of curious persons, who assailed us with a thousand questions. I gave Antonio and Königstein the charge of our cattle and traps, and then went with my other friends into camp, following the eager crowd, who led us to a large marquee in the centre, from which a long white pennant floated. A man came to meet me whose features seemed familiar to me at the first glance, and on whose face I could plainly read that I produced the same impression on him. We offered each other a hand with an inquiring glance, and after the first few words of greeting, I recognised an old acquaintance, Lord S——, whom I had last seen ten years before on the east of the continent. The pleasure of meeting again was heightened by the most peculiar circumstances under which it took place.

We sat down at the fire, and I described my journey to this spot, and my plans for its continuation. A thousand questions interrupted my story, and when we reached the present moment, we leapt back to the time of our last meeting, and followed the course of my life up to the commencement of the present tour. His lordship was already acquainted with some of the details, but I had much to tell him of since the day when I bade farewell to civilization. I then heard from him in return the story of his life, which, though moving along a smoother surface, claimed my entire attention. During the period he had been back to Europe, and made a lengthened excursion to Asia; still his passion for this great, unadulterated nature had brought him back to the mountains of the New World, to bid them a last farewell, as more serious duties recalled him home. He had started from Independence, in Missouri, with a large party of friends, Europeans and Americans, and a number of voyageurs and half-breeds, engaged for the tour, in a small steamer up the Missouri, and then proceeded up the Yellowstone as far as the depth of water allowed. They landed there numerous saddle and pack animals, provisions, tents, and other traps, and had gone overland through the mountains to the banks of the Platte, which they had followed to this point round the Black Mountains. The whole company consisted of about eighty persons: they had about one hundred animals with them, most of which they purchased of Indians at the fort where they left the steamer, and had also taken a dozen of the latter into their service.

This small army offered the most curious sight I ever beheld. All sorts of dresses, from the lightly-clad savage to the most elegant gentleman were before us. Many young swells from the Eastern luxurious cities of this continent, as well as from those of the Old World, educated in ballrooms, operas, and concert rooms, had followed their fancy in the selection of their costumes, and appeared in mediæval garb, with broad-brimmed plumed hats, jerkins with slit sleeves, leathern breeches, tall Napoleon boots with enormous spurs, large gauntlets, and had put on the swords of their forefathers; others had preferred the old Spanish costume, and donned loose velvet blue or green paletots, while the hat of an Italian brigand chief, with its red-cock's feather, covered their long perfumed locks, and a broad white shirt-collar was turned down over their shoulders. The open sleeves displayed the fine linen of their shirts; wide trousers were forced into long red morocco leather boots, on which large wheeled spurs rattled, and a brace of handsomely inlaid pistols and a long dagger ornamented their belt. Others, again, had read Cooper, and chosen his heroes as their model; they were dressed in leather from head to foot, with a broad-brimmed gray hat, a long heavy hunting-knife at their side, and leaning on an enormous rifle. They seemed to envy me my shabby clothes, all stiff with blood, while their dress, which had only just left the tailor's hands, had not a spot on it. Others, again, had remained faithful to the appearance of the gentleman of the Broadway, New York, had put on a broad-brimmed hat instead of the "chimney-pot" of civilization, and went about the camp in comfortable slippers, smoking fine Havannah cigars. Only one fashion had gained the victory over the national and fancy costumes here represented, this was the beard, which had not been troubled by a razor for a long time.

We soon formed acquaintances among this medley of characters, and led a life than which a better could not be found at the Palais Royal. The most delicate wines graced our table, which was covered by artistic cooks with the daintiest dishes; we smoked the best cigars and drank the finest mocha. All these things so precious to us were rendered more agreeable by the cheerful humour that prevailed all through the camp, and was displayed in every conversation. We spent the time in firing at a mark, in riding races, in various sports in which agility was displayed, in card-playing and in dicing, in hunting, which sport, however, only appeared popular with a portion, while the rest amused themselves nearer camp. Owing to the great number of animals our new acquaintances had with them, they had not always found sufficient forage for them on the mountains, whence they had selected this rich pasturage, to give them time to rest and to enjoy a little repose themselves.

I remained with my comrades four days in camp, during which time we were favoured with the most splendid weather, and on the fifth we got ready, after breakfast, to continue our journey and bid adieu to our friends, who intended to spend some time here. My friend S—— had supplied us with all the requisite stores for the pleasant continuation of our tour, had pressed upon us many luxuries, and given us a perfectly new outfit, so that we were now better equipped than when we began our journey. Owl and Tiger were handsomely remembered, at which they felt very happy, hung themselves and their horses with numerous ornaments, and never let their looking-glasses out of their hand. S—— and several others would have been glad to buy Tiger's piebald, and offered him about 200 dollars for it, but he had no thought of entering into any bargain of the sort, and he always pretended not to hear when the subject was brought up. When we at last led our horses out of camp, S—— accompanied us with a few of his friends, while a final farewell was given us by a salvo of rifle shots. The gentlemen rode several miles with us, and then returned to their friends, accompanied by our warmest thanks and heartiest wishes for their welfare.

We were now reduced again to our own small number, but were in a very different state from that prior to our meeting with our new friends, as we had all our wants again supplied, and they now afforded us double enjoyment after the lengthened privation. Our pipes again burnt incessantly, at times we even had a cigar as a change, and at the spring we reached, brandy was often mixed with the water we drank. We halted at a very early hour, although we could easily have ridden for another hour, as we were following the river; but the supper that awaited us was too inviting for us to delay it any longer; for now once again coffee was drunk, our meat peppered and salted and biscuit eaten with it, and before going to bed a glass of grog swallowed; which comforts people cannot always value at home, but which afford great enjoyment after having been missed for so long a time.

We had again reached a valley which runs between the Rocky Mountains, and is called New Park. The mountains on both sides drew very closely together here, and at some spots hardly left space for the river to pass, which was swollen by numerous torrents, and already had a rather powerful current. It was still only a torrent, however, which dashed over large rocks, and hurried along foaming and roaring between the hills. The mountains on our right hand are called by the Indians the "Medicine Mountains." Our road here was often very fatiguing, and was rendered smooth and slippery by several violent showers; so that we were often obliged to dismount and lead our horses on the descents, for fear of them falling.

One evening we reached a rather lofty point, where we found a little grass and a few live oaks; the river rustled below us, scarce a mile distant, through the rocks, and received there a spring which ran from a small coppice near us. We had been awakened on the previous night by a sudden shower, and as our traps had been lying about us uncovered, many of them were wet through before we could get them under shelter in the darkness. As the sky was also overcast this evening, we thought it advisable to put up our small tents. After supper we gathered our traps together under the tarpaulin, on which we laid large stones, and then crept into our tents, after wishing each other good-night. The night was calm and warm, so that when Königstein lay down by my side, and fastened up the opening of our tent which faced to the north, I got up and opened it again, as it was oppressively hot in our confined space. Our conversation was but short, our tongues grew heavy; the rustling of the neighbouring stream was blended with the sound of our broken sentences, and a deep sleep carried us into the land of dreams.

An icy-damp breeze awoke me suddenly, and when I started out of my sleep the storm drove the cold rain through the entrance of the tent into my face, and violently shook its sides. I roused Königstein, and was about to jump up, when a violent blast raised the tent above us, and carried it off into the darkness, while streams of rain lashed us. All my companions shared the same fate, and ran about in the darkness seeking their blankets, hats, and articles of clothing. At the same time we heard the sound of flying horses, probably ours, which, startled by the flapping of our tents, had torn themselves loose. We ran to the spot where we had secured them, and only found Czar and John's mare, but no sign of the others except the broken lassoes. In the darkness I had thrown my large bearskin over me, and concealed my weapons under it. So I remained with Czar, turning my back to the storm, and bade him be quiet, while I saw the others running back and forwards like shadows.

The storm grew more furious still, and the powerful tornado seemed desirous of carrying away with it everything that did not bend before it. I leant my shoulder against a young oak in order to keep on my feet, but the tree often bent so low as to touch the ground with its foliage. My comrades had disappeared—at least I could not notice them anywhere, for the darkness was so dense that I could not see a yard before me. It was impossible to call to each other, as you could not even hear your own voice. At the same time the rain still poured down in almost a horizontal direction, and formed a stream round my feet. There was lightning in the north, but neither thunder nor lightning had approached us, until suddenly the eastern mountains were lit up by brilliant flashes, which displayed their white peaks, and the ground trembled beneath a tremendous clap of thunder. For more than an hour the lightning did not cease for longer than a few seconds, and the thunder roared uninterruptedly between the hills. But at last the storm moved up the valley and left an impenetrable darkness behind. We gradually came together again, and would assuredly have laughed at each other had this been the time for it, for we were wet to the skin, stood in the cold night breeze upon saturated, bottomless ground, and what was worst of all, most of our cattle had bolted. It was simply impossible to light a fire, so we made no attempt to do so, as we could not seek dry materials in the darkness. Nothing was left us but to wait quietly till day arrived, which on this occasion seemed to delay terribly.

At length the new light gleamed over the hills, and we could soon distinguish objects around. We had a melancholy prospect: here lay a wet buffalo robe, a blanket, or a leathern jacket; there some hats were half buried in the mud; farther on we saw one of our tents hanging on an oak; wherever we looked, storm and rain had left traces of their destruction. A joyous surprise was prepared for us with the return of light: we saw honest Jack grazing higher up the valley, and Königstein's cream-colour following him. Tiger and Owl soon set out to seek the other horses, which would be easily found if no accident had happened to them, and there were no thick woods in this valley to hide them from us. We fetched up Jack and the cream-colour, and while the Indians followed the trail of the horses, we sought under the stones dry grass and roots with which to light a fire, which caused us great difficulty, and only succeeded after several failures. Then we put up sticks round it in order to dry our traps, and finally looked up those which had been blown away. The articles under the tarpaulin had remained quite dry, as the water ran through the brushwood on which we had laid them, while the heavy stones kept the cover down. In time we got everything in order again, and about noon we saw our Indians coming down the valley and driving our animals before them, which they had found a long way in the mountains in two parties. During the whole day we were occupied in repairing damages. The tents had to be mended, the broken lassoes reknotted, the saddles and bridles cleaned from mud and dirt—in short, the whole day was spent in getting ready to start again. The next morning, however, we mounted again, and no one could notice that our equipment had suffered severely.

Since our leave-taking from Lord S—— and his friends about ten days had passed, during which we never went far from the Platte River, as the impassable precipices of the mountains on both sides ran down almost close to the river. At last the latter opened, the mountains on our left trended to the west, and before us was spread out an extensive and hilly tract, which, offered rather decent pasturage for these rough regions. I intended to follow the river generally to the large prairies on the east of the Rocky Mountains, in order to visit Fort Lamarie, and then proceed homewards across the open plains to the south.

It was a warm afternoon when we cut off a large bend which the river described, and riding over a grassy plain got several miles away from it. The sun shone hotly on our backs, the horses walked with drooping heads through the tall grass, and we jolted silently in our saddles, every now and then putting straight the embroidered blankets on which we sat, as folds in them become disagreeable in hot weather. I was riding on the left wing of our cavalcade, and had turned to Trusty, who was stalking behind Czar with hanging tail, when, on looking across the prairie, I fancied I saw about half a mile off two human forms conceal themselves in the grass. Without checking my horse, I called Tiger up, and imparted to him what I fancied I had seen. He advised me not to look round, as he was riding on my right hand, and, without exciting suspicion, while talking to me, could keep in sight the entire plain on our left. We had been riding on for a long time when Tiger suddenly pulled round his piebald and galloped across the prairie, in the direction where I believed I had seen the men. We stopped to look after him and watched him ride through the grass, but presently turn his horse toward us. He told me they were probably Blackfoot Indians, who were following S——'s trail, in order to steal some horses from his party. Close to the spot where he had seen one of them was a reed-covered pool, and hence it was useless to seek him, as he would have concealed himself in it. However, he was of opinion that we must be on our guard here, so that they might not get hold of any of our horses, for these Indians had eyes in the darkness, and could walk more softly than sleep.

During the following night, we again encamped on the river, and fastened our horses near camp, where Trusty mounted guard over them. He appeared extremely restless, got up several times, went growling round our camp, and barked frequently; but our rest was not otherwise disturbed. Early the next morning, as we were folding up our furs, Tiger returned to the fire saturated with dew. He had gone over the neighbourhood and said there was a number of Blackfeet close by; the dog had prevented them from approaching our camp at night; but they could not be an entire tribe, or else they would have ventured an attack by day. He had found several tracks going round our camp at some distance. Tiger told us that the Blackfeet live farther north, and only come so low down for purposes of plunder; but here they had to be on their guard against the Utahs, Sioux, Pawnees, Sacs, and Foxes, who occupied this country and lived at war with them. The Blackfeet are pursued by nearly all the other Indian tribes when they venture south, and in former years, when they prowled about the present state of Missouri, they were hunted by the first settlers there like wild beasts. The power of these Indians is very considerable, and their number is probably the largest of all the numerous tribes of natives. They live between the sources of the Missouri and Yellow-stone River, tolerate no other tribe there, and are warlike and cruel to their conquered foes. The Crows, their neighbours, are much fewer in number, but for all that oppose them in the field and wage the most sanguinary wars with them. Neither nation, however, dares to cross the Yellow-stone, without being pursued by the Indians living on the opposite side; they only do so when they have a prospect of committing a robbery without any great risk, or capturing a few scalps from their enemies.

We followed the river to the spot where the Medicine-bow River falls into it, and Tiger and Owl made an excursion along its banks, and brought in the news that some forty Blackfeet had crossed the river, probably expecting that we would follow the Platte farther up to the Black Mountains, to watch for us and attack us in the narrow passes. They told us these enemies would not leave us till we had passed that region, and we must constantly keep a watchful eye on them. We camped on this side of the Medicine-bow River, and talked over our further tour over the camp fire, and Owl was of opinion that we should do better by following the course of this river and effecting our retreat through Lamarie plains, between the Medicine and Black Mountains, as on this route we should be less troubled by Indians than on the great Eastern Prairies, and, with the exception of buffaloes and wild horses, might expect to find much more game there. We heard Tiger, who was of the same opinion, and soon agreed to follow this road.

We fished in the river till it grew quite dark, and had just put supper on the fire, when Tiger and Owl took their rifles, and, after telling us to keep a bright look-out for the Blackfeet, went up the river, and soon disappeared. I ordered Königstein to mount guard at the end of the small wood in which we had camped, at the spot where it joined the Platte, and promised to relieve him in an hour. We thus changed sentries until about eleven o'clock, when I relieved John. It was not very dark, although the moon was not shining, and sitting on the ground I could not only see across the Platte, but distinguish objects in the grass for some distance. Trusty lay by my side, with his head resting on his crossed paws; suddenly, however, he raised his nose, and I heard his low growl, which I stopped by a wave of my hand. He kept his nose turned obstinately up stream, in which direction I also kept my eyes fixed on the grass. I felt with the hand I had laid on Trusty that his attention was growing greater, for he began trembling all over, which he did when he was forced to master his growing excitement.

Still I could not distinguish anything that appeared to me strange. The grass in front of me was not tall, and there were but few patches of scrub. All at once I fancied that a bush, about fifty yards from me, had moved, but it might be imagination, as I had been gazing at it so intently. A profound silence brooded over the landscape, which was only interrupted by the continuous monotonous rustling of the river. In our camp no voice was audible, and the bright fire, which had lit up the surrounding trees and bushes, had burned down, and only indicated its position by a glimmering light. When I took my post half an hour previously Owl and Tiger had not returned, and since then I had not heard them arrive. The air was very damp and cold, and the grass around me felt quite wet. I now fancied I could be certain that the bush had moved: I rose a little and looked at it more sharply; it moved again, and a dark object, in the shape of a large stone, slowly rose out of the grass. Now I could entertain no doubt it was a living creature: but what could it be? That was a matter of indifference to me, so long as it was not either Tiger or Owl, and they would not approach our camp so cautiously and suspiciously. It could be none but a Blackfoot. I rose on one knee, cautiously lifted my rifle, and aimed as well as I could for the darkness, at the object whose indistinct outline now covered nearly the whole bush.

Bang! the flame flashed from the rifle, and a hollow plump into the river followed a few seconds later, before the smoke had risen on the damp atmosphere. I looked at the dark, shining surface of the water, and noticed that large circles surrounded a black spot, and were moving with it toward the middle of the stream. I fired my second barrel at it: I clearly saw through the gloom that the motion of the water became very violent at the moment, but then it was all over, and the next minute the current flowed on as usual, and nothing on its surface revealed what was passing in its depths. I had scarce fired the second shot when my comrades dashed up under arms. I quickly told them what had happened, and we remained under arms awaiting the return of our Indians, of whom we had as yet heard nothing. About an hour later they returned, and Tiger at once asked why we had been firing: then he told us what had happened to him, and that my shots had robbed them of several Blackfeet scalps. They had crossed the river a little higher up, at a point where it was shallow, and lay down on its banks, as they expected that the savages would return during the night to try and get hold of our horses. Shortly before I fired, Tiger had heard and seen the branches of a neighbouring bush parted, but after that all became quiet again. Tiger fancied that their number was considerable; but we had nothing more to fear from them on this night, and could go to sleep in peace. However, we posted sentries till daybreak, when I and Tiger examined the spot at which I had fired. We found that my bullet had cut away a spray in the centre of the bush, and noticed the track of an Indian, which was distinctly marked on the bank, and Tiger recognised it as that of a Blackfoot. Owl swam across the river and examined the opposite shore to see whether he had landed there, but could not discover any sign, and, pointing to the river, supposed he was sleeping under that.

We slept quietly till eight o'clock, then breakfasted, and packed our animals, so as to continue our journey on the new plan. Tiger said that the Blackfeet would be cheated out of a day, for they were awaiting us farther down the Platte, and if they had not their horses with them they could not catch us up before morning: if their number was large, however, as he believed, they had their horses with them, and would be camping in the thickets on the opposite side of Medicine-bow River. It was nearly noon when we struck camp and marched up the river. The grass was not very high, and our path slightly covered with loose stones, so that we could keep our horses at an amble, and when the sun sank behind the distant hills on our right, we had covered a distance of at least twenty-five miles. After riding past a stony knoll, round which the river described a short curve, we reached a stream flowing between deep banks, which fell into the Platte, and was densely overgrown with alders. The spot pleased us to spend the night at, and we were engaged in unpacking our cattle, when suddenly a fearful yell rang behind us, which came toward us accompanied by a dense cloud of dust. The Blackfeet! all shouted, and seized their weapons. Tiger, however, shouted to us to follow him, as he led his piebald through the alders into the stream, and the next minute all the cattle were left in charge of Antonio, who fastened them to the bushes.

We had scarce returned to the bank when a body of forty Indians dashed up to us like a tornado; lying behind their horses' necks, and covering their left side with their large shields, they allowed a very small portion of their bodies to be seen. We permitted them to come within fifty yards before we fired. The band hesitated, and we saw through the dust several horses lying on the ground, and many of the horsemen engaged in taking others up behind them, while the greater number galloped back to the hill, and uttered a frightful yell. They had not galloped far, however, when one of them, mounted on a powerful black horse, darted to their head, and casting himself in their way, swung his long lance before them. His horse reared in front of the flying horde, and the thundering voice of the leader distinctly reached us through the yelling. At the next instant the band turned back, with the warrior on the black horse in front of them. We had reloaded, and I shouted to my comrades to expend but one bullet, and reserve the other for shorter range. The savages had galloped up to within about the same distance as before, when I shouted, Fire! and aimed myself at the leader of the band. The black horse reared and fell over with its rider, while another horse fell dead by its side, whose rider ran with the speed of an arrow after his comrades, who were now flying in the utmost confusion. The rider of the black horse, however, had scarce fallen with it ere he crept from under it, and at the same instant we saw Tiger leap out of the willow bushes on the river bank, and, swinging his tomahawk, catch up the Blackfoot warrior with a few leaps. The latter fell back a pace, and threw his iron axe at Tiger with such force that, missing its mark, it flew far out into the river. Tiger now buried his axe with lightning speed in the chest of his recoiling foe, and both fell to the ground like two intertwined snakes. It was the work of a few minutes, and the yell of the flying Indians was still ringing in our ears when we dashed up to the combatants in order to help Tiger. It was no longer necessary, however, for he rose from off his lifeless foe, and setting his knee on the other's bent-back neck, he passed his knife round the head and tore off his scalp. During this time Owl had scalped the other Blackfoot, and our Indians danced frantically round the dead men, waving the reeking scalps and knives, while the blood poured down Tiger's back from a gaping wound in his left shoulder. At length they concluded their dance of victory, and then our Indians plundered their slain foes and the dead horses. The dress of these Blackfeet is made of leather, with remarkable taste, adorned with paintings and long fringes, porcupine quills, shells, scalp-locks, and coloured pebbles; the leather is smoked of a very dark hue, and gives the savages a gloomy and terrifying aspect. Their weapons are lances, bows and arrows, tomahawks, and knives; only a few have firearms.

I examined Tiger's wound, which had only cut the flesh obliquely, and was produced by his enemy's knife; while the latter had a bullet through his left thigh, a gaping wound in his chest, and a stab in his heart. Tiger had run down to the willows on the river without our noticing him after the first attack of the Blackfeet, and had thence fired at the chief, whom he afterwards killed with his knife. "Now," he said, "we can sleep; the Blackfeet have lost their head, and will go home and tell how the Delawares have some more of their scalps in their tents; their squaws will not even take their dead with them, and not let them sleep with their fathers."

We camped close to the stream, but posted sentries all through the night, as I feared lest we might have to oppose a nocturnal surprise. The night, however, passed undisturbed; but we heard incessantly a fearful yelling of wolves, which prowled round our camp, but owing to the huge fire did not dare approach the corpses, which lay not far from us in the grass. The next morning we quitted the spot, for which movement the numerous wolves were watching, and they attacked the dead Indians and horses almost before we had crossed the stream.

CHAPTER XXV
ON THE PRAIRIE

We hastened up the river for five days, during which time we crossed a number of small streams which fell into it. Then we reached the eastern spurs of the Medicine Mountains, in which the river rises and pours over the rocks in the shape of a large torrent. Here we crossed it, and following the base of these hills in the plain, we reached on the second evening a small stream, which flows for at least a hundred miles due east through this broad plain, which the Indians called Lamarie, to the Black Mountains bordering the plain, and, as Owl told us, winds through the latter till it falls into the Northern Platte to the east of Fort Lamarie. These mountains, which in height and shape exactly resemble the range from which the Bighorn rises, are to the north of that snow peak. We marched along the stream to the eastward to the Black Mountains, and then turned up an arm of it coming from the south until it was lost in the plain. We marched from here for a whole day without water, and were obliged to pass the night, too, without it or fire, as the desolate plain over which we rode showed us not a single tree. Toward evening the next day we reached a lake, which was about three miles in circumference, but its waters were slightly impregnated with salt: following its banks, however, we arrived on its western side at some clear streams of fresh water. Here we refreshed ourselves and camped, though it was early in the afternoon, and amused ourselves with shooting geese and swans. On the next evening we came to a similar lake, with fresh-water streams on its western side, so that we again had a splendid camp, and took advantage of the opportunity to bathe in the lake.

During the next day our road again ran over a desolate, melancholy plain, but toward evening we saw a low wood in the distance, and reached another arm of the river which runs through the Black Mountains to Fort Lamarie. Here we had everything we could desire, a protected camp in the wood, and a splendid trout stream, in which we refreshed ourselves and our horses. We shot several fat buffaloes, and a few black-tailed stags. The wood above us sufficed to put us in good spirits, for we were very tired of the monotonous, desolate plains over which we had been marching for a long time. Before sunset our horses neighed, and we heard them answered from, outside the wood. All at once there was a thundering burst through the low bushes, and the leader of a troop of wild horses fell in terror immediately in front of our fire, and the animals behind him one over the other, after which they got up again in the utmost fear and confusion and dashed out of the wood. The stallion was a splendid iron-grey, very powerfully built and finely shaped, and we all regretted that we were unable to take him home.

The next morning we left the river and went south, and for the whole day without finding water. The sun sank behind the hills, and nowhere was there a tree or a sign of water; the grass, too, was bad, but our cattle were very weary, and we too longed for rest. We made a poor fire of *bois de vache* and small bushes, large enough to cook our supper, then we put up our tents and secured our traps under the tarpaulin on a bed of stones, for the sky was overcast and led to expectation of rain. At nightfall it began to blow and rain, and went on the whole night till daybreak, when the clouds gathered together again, and hanging on the base of the mountains displayed the snow peaks brilliantly illumined by the sun. We quickly started, and marched from this disagreeable spot, looking for pleasanter signs ahead. At length, toward noon, wood rose again from the barren surface. We drove our animals into a quicker pace, and in a few hours were resting again on a river fringed by trees, upon glorious grass, which our starving cattle eagerly devoured. It was still very early, and we all felt inclined to go hunting, as the rain had refreshed the country, and the verdure of the forest and the meadow does the eyesight good. A few preferred fishing in the neighbouring stream; several went up the river to hunt, while I went down it, accompanied by Trusty only. I had gone about a couple of miles along the skirt of the wood when I saw something moving on the prairie behind some very low bushes. I crept cautiously up to the last bush, and before me stood, at about the distance of a hundred and twenty yards, a herd of some forty large and old giant stags. The beautiful animals—the pride of the animal world—stood in a long line before me, with their faces turned to me, and raised their powerful antlers like a forest of horns. It was a sight whose beauty only a sportsman can estimate. I lay for some minutes lost in contemplation, but when I raised my knee and rifle the whole herd turned and galloped past me. I had long had my eye on the largest stag, for its antlers rose far above the others with their broad lines. I aimed behind the shoulder and fired, heard the bullet distinctly go home, and saw, that though it was bleeding profusely, it kept up with the others. The next largest stag, being just behind this one, I fired the second barrel at it, heard the thud of the bullet again, and saw that it was mortally wounded; but it too remained in line, and I watched the stags till they disappeared a long way off in a hollow.

I loaded, and on reaching the spot where the stags were hit, Trusty at once put his nose to the blood trail and stopped, looking up at me. I made him a sign that it was all right, and when he had gone a little distance he went off slightly to the right, took up the trail of the second stag, and then again pointed with his nose to the ground, while looking at me inquiringly. I again urged him on, and he went first to one trail, then to the other, till I was able to look down into the valley, where I saw the two stags lying dead, hardly ten yards apart. I hastened up to them, and counted, on the antlers of the largest, eight-and-thirty tines, and on the smaller one six-and-twenty; the length of the two antlers was between five and six feet, and their weight between thirty and forty pounds. The antlers of this stag only differ from those of our stag through their size and the greater number of tines: the great difference between them is in the weight, as the giant stag is often double the size of ours. Both animals, it seemed, had died nearly at the same moment, for they lay side by side with their heads stretched out, as they had been running. After looking at them for awhile in delight, I broke them up, gave Trusty his share, cut out a couple of grinders as a recollection, and then went back to camp, when my comrades were equally pleased at the result of my sport. The other hunters had also been fortunate, and had killed a fat buffalo, while the anglers had pulled a number of large fish out of the river. Owl went with Antonio and Königstein to my stags, in order to fetch their skins and meat, and I requested them to bring me the antlers of the largest one, as I wished, were it possible, to carry them home. Though we liked the place so much, we left it again next morning, abundantly supplied with the best game, and Jack trotted after us with the enormous antlers on the top of his packages.

The country here became again intersected by low ranges of hills, which crossed the plain from east to west; their heights were long and barren, but the large valleys between them ornamented with small prairies and woods, in the latter of which we frequently found springs. The variety was a relief to our eyes, and offered us many a fine prospect, with the mountains approaching each other. Isolated masses of rock again rose out of these valleys, and before us in the far South were visible loftier ranges, some of them branching off from the Medicine Mountains, others from the Black Mountains. The colouring of these landscapes in the west of the continent is much warmer and more hazy than in the Eastern States, or in the countries of Old Europe. The distances, although transparent and extraordinarily distinct, float in a delicate reddish-blue tinge, in front of which the deep dark shadows and flashing lights produced by the glowing sun stand out the more powerfully. The shadows which the clouds throw on the landscape are also, like the latter, dyed with carmine and cobalt, and not, as in England, black and white, the mere sight of which produces a shudder. The streams reflect on their surface the dark ultramarine of the heavens, and the rich green of the woods and prairies loses through its countless tints and rich flora its wearisome monotony.

With every hour the beauty of the country increased, and the animal world became more animated. Countless wild horses of the most varying colours flew at our approach over the green hills, large herds of dark-haired buffalo galloped awkwardly over the wide stretches of grass, and from the stony heights the light-footed antelopes gazed down curiously at us. Up hill, down hill, we jolted in the saddles of our ambling steeds, when, on a calm warm evening toward sunset, we rode down from a grassy knoll to a stream, which was closely overhung with alder bushes, and separated the base of the hill from a wide prairie, round which it wound with numerous meanderings. Tiger was riding about forty yards ahead, and had just disappeared with his piebald in a patch of scrub, when he dashed out of the other side of it with a loud cry and an enormous grizzly bear after him. We galloped through the stream after him, while his rapid horse bounded over the grass toward us, and gained a slight advance on the grizzly. All our rifles were fired at the monster, and turning away from Tiger it came toward us with long leaps, and pursued John with an awful roar; once again our rifles cracked behind it, but the bullets did not check its clumsy but yet rapid course. John turned his mare again toward us, and had hardly joined our ranks when we fired a salvo from our revolvers at the maddened bear, and galloping after it, kept up our fire. Königstein, on the cream-colour, was the nearest to it on the left, and gave the bear a shot at short range, when the latter turned on him and smashed his broad, wooden stirrup into a thousand chips between its savage teeth. Königstein, however, had pulled his foot out and flew with his horse to our side. Again we sent a hailstorm of bullets into the broad back of the infuriated animal, upon which it sank on its hind-quarters, as a bullet had smashed its spine. Its fury and the roars it uttered were fearful, and turning in a circle on its monstrous forepaws it covered a large space around it with its blood, which streamed from its shaggy carcass.

I shouted to my friends not to fire, as I saw Tiger had dismounted and was hastily loading his rifle, and I wished to grant him the pleasure of killing the bear. He fired his bullet into its head, and then cut off its claws with great satisfaction. We took the paws, tongue, and liver of the huge animal, while Tiger rode back to the stream, and thence shouted to us to join him. We rode up, and found in the water a two-year old, very handsome chestnut horse, which the bear had captured on the prairie, and, as the trampled grass showed us, had dragged to the stream, in order to enjoy its meal without being disturbed. I took the tusks of the slain animal, and with the new matter for conversation which this fight gave us, we shortened the road to our camp, which lay in an exquisite hollow on the south side of lofty crags, under which a clear torrent rolled over loose stones that glistened like gold. They contained a substance which really resembled this metal, so that they shone through the water hurrying over them like lumps of pure gold. Some stately palms, maples, and oaks overshadowed our camp, and served as a cool retreat for the countless songsters that saluted us with their evening hymn.

It is incomprehensible why the belief prevails throughout Europe that American birds are very brilliantly plumaged, but cannot sing, while most certainly there are sweeter songsters and more varieties of them on this continent than in Europe. A single bird is wanting, the nightingale, but it is compensated a thousandfold by the mocking bird. All other classes of birds are represented, though with different and finer plumage. The belief may arise from the fact that emigrants from Europe land in the large eastern cities, and in their walks in their vicinity see no birds, from the circumstance that boys there of ten years old run about with guns and kill every bird that shows itself: and then again, these persons only seek the shade of the trees and bushes during the heat of the day, when all birds silently hide themselves from the burning sun. If they went out in the morning, however, when nature is awakening, they would hear quite as good singers as in their old home.

Before us the valley wound between partly wooded low hills, behind which the higher base now rose. For several days we marched along this valley, till on one afternoon we looked down from a hill on the blue crystalline waters of the southern Platte, which coming down from the Medicine hills, rustled through the valley at our feet. The river was large even here, and shot with the speed that characterizes the streams in this country, and with many windings between its wood-clad banks. Before us, where the river described a sharp curve, the banks were stony on both sides, and seemed from time immemorial to have been used by the inhabitants of these countries as a ford. At this moment, when probably for the first time the eyes of white men rested on this ford, a countless herd of buffaloes was occupied in crossing. They were coming southward from the mountains, and pressed shoulder to shoulder in dense masses to water in the river, while others came down the hills in a black line. The roars of these thirsty wanderers filled the air and rang through the hills in a thousand echoes. They dashed by hundreds impetuously from the high bank into the deep, rapid stream, on either side of the ford, and drifted with it into the dark overarching wood. We stopped for a long time gazing down at this scene and awaiting the end of the herd, whose head had disappeared some time previously in the valley on our left, while dense masses still continued to pour down without a check from the hills to the water. At length, at the end of an hour, only a few laggards came, after at least five thousand buffaloes had crossed the river, and yet the number of these animals is said to be quite insignificant compared with what it was twenty years ago. Who knows whether fifty years hence they will exist anywhere but in natural history? We were obliged to let the wanderers pass, as we also wanted to cross the river, though in the opposite direction, and we should have run a risk of the whole herd marching over us, had we got in their way. We now rode down into the river; but, although so great a number of huge animals had passed through it, the water was as clear and bright as if a stone had never been stirred on its bottom. We watered our cattle, and followed the path by which the buffaloes had found their way to this ford, on the supposition that they had rendered it quite passable, and that they had come from the southern prairies to which we were bound.

We had scaled the first hill, when we saw about two miles off a few buffaloes trotting towards us, which had probably lagged behind, and now wanted to catch up the herd. We rode about thirty yards off the path, to a spot where we were covered by rocks and commanded the sloping path down to the water. Ere long we heard the heavy trot of the approaching animals on the stony ground, and presently several cows, and behind them a fat old bull came past us. We all fired together, and the old bull rolled over and over down the slope, and lay dead at the bottom. We took as usual its tongue, marrowbones, and loins, and left the rest to those that came after us.

We could not have found a finer road through these hills: broad and trodden smooth, it wound along the crags, so that we were often able to advance at a quick amble. It frequently ran over dizzy precipices, whence we surveyed the pleasant valleys, whose dark shadow seemed to invite us, while the hot sun and its reflection from the bare rocks over which we were marching, was hardly rendered endurable by the fresh breeze blowing up here. We crossed a number of small streams, which came down from the western hills, and all flowed to the Platte, until at the end of a week we again reached the latter river, at the point where a large affluent, coming from the Bighorn, joined it. We appeared to be here on the last slopes of the enormous mountains, over which the snowpeak was visible in all its splendour as a farewell salutation. It rose higher above its smaller comrades, and glistened like the purest silver in the blue sky, while the edge of the mountains displayed no snow, and seemed like a thin strip of fog above the nearer hills. Eastward we noticed on the horizon of the extensive plains only low ranges of hills, while to the north the Black Mountains raised their mighty crests and a few snow-clad peaks.

We crossed this southern arm of the Platte, and camped on the other side of it, in order to grant our cattle a few days' rest there, where the most splendid grass and a cool thick wood covered its bank. The bright streams offered us the most glorious fish, which can be almost selected in these streams, as we see them swarm round the bait, and the latter can be dropped before the fish you wish to catch. The neighbourhood of our camp was enlivened by game of every description; on the slopes of the neighbouring Black Mountains we found mountain sheep and black-tailed stags; in the forests between them and the Platte the majestic giant stag was preparing for the rutting season, and with swollen neck whetting the numerous tines of its splendid antlers on the trees. The prairies near us brought to us the elegant Virginian stag and the swift, black-eyed antelope, while the buffalo incessantly passed in all directions: not far from our camp we also found a warren of those interesting little creatures, which are falsely called prairie dogs, as they do not belong to this family, but to that of the badger.

We went out and shot some dozen of these dogs, as they afford a nice dish for a change. They live in burrows under ground, which they throw up like the rabbits, and a hundred of them are frequently found close together. They are very shy, but easy to shoot, as, if you lie down for a little while in the grass, they come out of their holes and give a snapping cry, which has been falsely called barking by some naturalists. They are badgers, about fifteen inches in length, which only live on vegetables, carry a large winter stock into their subterranean houses, and form very numerous families. They frequently quit a place without any visible reason, and wander a long distance over hill and dale in order to seek a new home.

Our horses and pack-cattle were recruited, and we too had recovered from the fatigue of our journey over the last mountains; hence we set out again, and casting many a parting glance at the Bighorn, we followed the Platte in an eastern direction, till at noon we reached a well-trodden path which runs from Fort St. Brain on the southern arm of this river down to the Missouri. We crossed it, and proceeded more to the south-west, in order to escape the numerous Indian hordes going up and down this path. A few days after we crossed the hills we had seen from our last camp, and the sky now rested before us on the interminable horizon of the prairie.

For nearly a week we marched over this green plain with scarce any change in the scene. It was, however, undulating, the flora in the grass gay and varied, and a few trees afforded us shade and firewood morning and evening to prepare our meals. At length hills rose on the horizon, and we soon saw again the darker verdure of forests, which received us into their shady gloom towards evening. In this tour we were so broiled by the sun that we entered the wood with delight, and at once resolved to rest a few days here, if, as we anticipated, there was water at hand. We hurried along a buffalo path into the depths of the forest, and soon heard to our delight the rustling of a neighbouring river, whose banks we speedily reached, and it proved to be a rapidly flowing stream overhung by tall ferns. Owl told us it was one of the numerous sources of the Kansas, which runs eastward to the Missouri. "Here let us build tabernacles," we cried in one voice, but followed the path across the stream to the skirt of the wood, which was no great distance off. We unloaded our cattle in a small clearing off our path, lit a fire, and really built tabernacles, as we made a roof of bushes between several young oaks, which kept off every sunbeam, and in whose immediate vicinity were trees enough to tie up our cattle every night.

After a long ride over the open prairies of Western America the comfort of a spot like this is very great and almost indescribable. The eyes are refreshed by the rich green, after the continued view of the horizon, which is rendered still more painful by the quivering sunshine of these plains. The breeze under the trees is most refreshing, while on the prairie it is dry and oppressively hot: we felt very jolly and comfortable in our hut, roamed about the neighbourhood, which was very rich in game; went along the streams and caught magnificent trout, or destroyed colonies of bees and plundered their rich stores of honey. To the south small prairies continually alternated with narrow patches of wood, through which the streams that spring up in them run under cover to join the Kansas.

After resting our cattle for some days, I went out one morning after breakfast to hunt and have a nearer view of the country round. I rode in a southern direction, followed by Trusty, and in going off, said to my comrades that if I lost my way, I would follow the course of one of these streams till it joined the river; then I would wait till they came to me, in which they could not fail, as we knew that all these small streams joined.

In a few hours I had crossed several of these streams, and had ridden out of a wood into a small prairie glade, when suddenly a horse Indian darted toward me with a furious yell from a thicket of tall oaks and swung his bow over his head, while his long lance hung on his right arm. It was too late to dismount and make use of my rifle. I quickly drew my revolver, put Czar at a gallop, and flew towards the Indian, turning my horse to the left, as he on his right side could make less use of his bow than I could of my revolver. However, he soon perceived my object, guided his chestnut to get on my left hand, and we galloped on in the same direction some distance out of shot. Suddenly, however, he turned and dashed toward me with his bow raised over the head of his rapid steed. I too had urged Czar to his full speed, and when we were about sixty yards apart, I fired. I had not expected to hit, still it was possible, and I had five shots left in my weapon. The savage's horse leaped on one side, stumbled and fell forward on its chest. A few blows of the whip forced it to make a last effort, but it then sank lifeless under its rider, who disappeared like lightning in the not very high grass behind it.

At the moment when I saw his horse fall, I turned mine away and pulled up about one hundred yards distant. The horse lay with its back turned to me, and the Indian was concealed behind its belly. I took out my telescope to try and get a better sight of my enemy, but it was of no use, he had disappeared. All at once I saw an arrow shoot up behind the horse and fly toward me in a large curve, but I easily pulled Czar out of its way and it sank harmless by my side with its point in the grass. While the Indian was firing the arrow I distinctly saw his hands holding the bow projecting above the horse's belly. I leapt from Czar's back, threw the bridle over his shoulder, and fired with my rifle at the horse's back. I heard the thud of the bullet, but the savage did not show himself. I reloaded both rifle and revolver and walked at the same distance round the dead horse till I got to the side on which its hind-quarters lay. I could now look under its belly and saw the Indian creep under the animal's chest and roll himself up behind it in a ball: still the surface by which he was hidden was now too small to cover him entirely, and I could distinguish the upper part of his body. I fired again and noticed a quick convulsive movement on the part of the foe, but only at the moment of firing. I had recourse to my glass once more, and saw that his head was now under the horse's chest, but his legs lay behind its neck, and he was peeping at me between its forelegs. I reloaded, and now having become much calmer, I aimed again at my mark; I fired and at once saw the savage throw up his legs, then try to rise but fall back again. I drew closer to him and watched him through the glass, as he had got a little way from the horse. He did not stir and lay on his back, but he was an Indian, and such a man a white man must not trust even in death. I fired again and heard my bullet go home, but he remained motionless. After reloading, I walked with cocked rifle nearer and found that life had left him, and that he had my second bullet in his right hip, the third in his head over the right ear, and the last in his chest, while I found one bullet in the horse's chest and another in its back. He was a man of about thirty years of age, tall and powerfully built, of a very dark colour and with sharply marked features; his remarkably long hair hung wildly round his head, with two eagle plumes thrust into the topknot, while his neck was decorated with a necklace of bears' claws, and his arms with brass rings. The lower part of his face and the eyelids ruddled with vermilion, and his forehead and cheeks painted black, gave him a terrific, uncomfortable aspect, which was heightened by the dazzlingly white teeth visible between his drawn-back lips. I only gazed for a few minutes at the corpse, took his bow and quiver of arrows, hung them on my horse and speedily beat a retreat, as the comrades of the dead man were certainly not far off, and might very easily be on the road to the spot, guided by my shots. I rode back on my trail and soon reached camp, when I told my friends what had happened.

Tiger was out hunting and not yet returned. I ordered a rapid start, had the horses packed and everything ready to be off. We had scarce completed our preparations when Tiger, bathed in perspiration, came back along my track, and said he had heard my shots, followed their direction, and found the Indian and his horse. He was a Pawnee, whose tribe was certainly close at hand, and when his companions missed him they would seek him and easily find us too, in which case we should run a great danger, as they were brave men. He quickly packed his horse, and in a few minutes we left camp. Tiger rode ahead into the stream, and we followed him, riding singly down the water, which offered us no obstacles beyond here and there a fallen tree, as it ran over pebbles, was nowhere deep, and had flat banks. Evening arrived, and the sun was already low on the western horizon. We marched almost constantly in the stream till we found on its right bank a wide plain covered with pebbles, when we turned off to the south at a right angle. We reached on the other side of the plain a similar stream, which was also overshadowed by trees, entered a thicket and dismounted to let our horses graze without unsaddling them, and to await nightfall. The moon was already up, and though her light did not brilliantly illumine the country, it was sufficiently strong to enable us to distinguish objects at a slight distance. We then left our hiding-place, marched out of the thicket into the prairie, and urged our horses on at a quick pace. Without interruption, we hurried on through the silence of the night, which was only disturbed by the howling of the countless wolves and the roar of the buffaloes we put up, until shortly before daybreak the moon withdrew her light from us and the darkness did not allow us to advance. We sat down on the damp grass round our cattle and waited till the first new light appeared on the eastern horizon, then we remounted and hurried on toward a distant strip of wood which rose before us on the prairie. The sun was standing high in the heavens when we reached it and led our wearied animals to a stream. Here we unsaddled and let them graze, hobbled, in a small glade, while we prepared breakfast at a small fire.

We were very tired and after the meal could hardly keep awake. We posted sentries in turn to watch the plain behind us, and kept lively by smoking and telling stories. Our cattle wanted sleep more than grass, and we were sorry at being obliged to saddle them after a short rest, but Tiger and Owl insisted on our going on, as we were certainly pursued by the Pawnees, and could only escape them by keeping the start we had on them.

It was hardly noon when we started again and spurred our horses on toward the southern prairie. They only moved because they felt the sharp steel in their sides, and we were obliged to lead the mules by lassos and appoint a man to drive them, as they refused to follow. The heat was oppressive, there was not a breath of air, and the plants on the plain we crossed hung their leaves in exhaustion, an incessant buzzing of the insects in the grass filled the motionless air, and a trembling dazzling light lay on the wide expanse around us. The sweat ran in streams from our cattle, and was mixed with the blood which the countless musquitos sucked from their coat, so that under their belly their colour could not be distinguished. But not noticing their sufferings or fatigue, we urged them on and looked back at the distant horizon to see whether our pursuers appeared on it, till the sun sank and in the distance a wood rose, which crossed the prairie to the east like a mist. Tiger said that we should be safe there; this was the wood running along the Arkansas, and the horses of the Pawnees could not go so far without a rest. The sun mercifully withdrew its beams, and the moon's cool light showed us our road, when we expended the last strength of our cattle and so reached the forest.

We had ridden for over fifty hours since yesterday morning, a greater part of the distance without any path, through rather tall grass and over stony soil. On the whole route we had been exposed to the burning sun, and only once had been able to cool our fevered lips at a stream. For our cattle, it is true, we had more frequently found water, though only standing rain, which collects in large hollows on the prairie, but at this season is more mud than water; at the same time it is almost boiled by the sun, and if it can keep a man alive it does not refresh him. We as well as our cattle were utterly exhausted to such a degree that we would incur any danger for a few hours' rest. We rode into the wood and followed a buffalo path, but had not ridden far when Tiger, who was ahead, stopped, saying he had lost the path and could go no farther. The foliage over us was so thick that only here and there the moon's pale light stole through it, and only a few leaves and small spots on the branches glistened like silver in the obscurity. We turned our horses in all directions seeking the path, but after going a few yards were continually stopped by the hanging creepers. Tiger now leapt from his horse and sought in the darkness dry grass, which he twisted into a torch and came to me to light it. It soon spread a light around, and while I held it up Tiger collected a larger stock of dry grass and made a thicker torch, which we lit, and soon found an issue from this impenetrable thicket.

We soon reached a small arm of the Arkansas, on whose fresh, cool water we and our cattle fell insanely. We now lit a fire, though there was no grass for the cattle near at hand, as the small, open spot on the bank of the rushing stream was surrounded by a dense wall of forest. At this moment, however, rest was more necessary than food, and our cattle had scarce been freed from their load when they all sank on the ground and fell into a deep sleep; we did the same, and, after drinking several draughts, fell back on our saddles and forgot that we still stood a risk of being caught up by the Pawnees. We had collected our fire into a small pile, so that it only coaled, and spread no light over the crests of the tall trees, which might possibly have been noticed from the prairie. We slept without moving a limb till the turkeys in our neighbourhood awoke us, and, though Tiger and Owl protested most strongly against it, we shot four of the birds, resolved to defend ourselves to the best of our ability if the shots betrayed us to our pursuers.

Tiger now mounted his piebald, rode through the river, and soon disappeared in the forest on the other bank, where he sought pasture for our cattle. In half an hour he returned and told us that between this wood and the Arkansas there was a fine prairie, on which we should find excellent grass for them. We followed him across the river and out of the wood to a small glade, which was overshadowed by close-growing trees. Here we camped and prepared breakfast, while our cattle greedily browsed on the fresh, dewy grass. We rested here till the sun cast the shadow of the forest far across the prairie; then we set out again and rode to the Arkansas, which here rolls its foaming waters between low banks. We reached the opposite forest and rode into its cool shade before sunset, so that the last beams still lighted us as we marched over the next prairie and hurried to a low scrub, from whose centre several tremendously tall poplars rose and announced water near their roots.

The sun had just set when we came to a stream running toward the Arkansas, and covered on this side with bushes, while on the other the most splendid grass hung over its crystalline waters. We watered our cattle and then rode down stream on the other side, as the pasturage seemed more luxuriant lower down. In a few minutes we reached a small cascade, where the stream fell over rocks about ten feet, and below this fall formed a deep basin, whose bottom was also composed of stone slabs, and on one side was overhung by rock strata about twenty feet in height, which covered a considerable space near the basin, whose bottom and sides also consisted of bare stone. We camped on the top of this overhanging ledge, as a number of medlar-trees grew there, to which we could fasten our horses at night round the camp, and at the same time the richest grass grew all around. We unsaddled, hobbled the horses in the grass, lit a fire, and put the supper before it, and then went to bathe in the basin under the rock. After we had cooled and refreshed ourselves we supped and then prepared our resting-place; but John took his weapons and skins and said he would sleep on the stream under the crag, as it was much cooler and pleasanter there, and he should not feel the heavy dew so much as in the grass. We wished him pleasant dreams and shouted to him not to let himself be devoured by a bear.

We had fastened up our horses, and had fallen into a deep sleep, when the sharp crack of a rifle aroused us, and we all leapt up, arms in hand. At the same moment a second shot was fired below us on the water. We were only a few yards from the edge of the crack, and on hurrying there saw an enormous panther slowly walking among the low bushes on the opposite bank, and looking over at us. We showered bullets upon it, and induced it to hasten its pace till it disappeared like a shadow in the mist. Now John ran up to us with his baggage, and told us he had accidentally waked up. He fancied he heard a growling; rose on his arm, and recognised the moonlit shape of a panther walking towards him hesitatingly, with lashing tail, round the basin. He quickly seized his rifle—fired one barrel at it, and gave it the second in the water, into which it leapt. Providence had aroused him, for before we could have hurried to his help from above the brute would probably have killed him, and we might very easily have known nothing of it till we found our comrade's lacerated body on the next morning. However, we soon forgot this incident, and slept till dawn woke us and showed us the grass around wet as if from a shower, while a thick fog brooded over the flat country. We led our horses out to graze, put our breakfast to cook, and then I went with John and Tiger, accompanied by Trusty, to the spot on the opposite bank, where the panther had been standing when we fired at it. We found here a quantity of hair, and soon after blood, which increased with every step, and presently came to a spot where the jaguar had halted and covered a large space with its blood. We went about a hundred yards farther when Trusty stopped, looked round at me, and then into the bushes with his tail erect. I called him to me, and crept cautiously to the spot, when I saw the panther lying under the roots of an old poplar, with its head turned towards me, and showing its teeth. I shot it through the skull, and Owl took off its fine coat to prepare it for John, who wished to preserve it in memory of the danger to which he had been exposed during this night.

CHAPTER XXVI
THE COMANCHES

Our route ran from here through the most pleasing and rich countries, crossed by numerous streams running eastward. Generally this country had the character of the prairie; it was undulating, and covered with fine grass; the hills and woods on the streams gave it variety, so that the wearied eye did not stray over interminable plains, seeking in vain for a resting-place. Prairies alternated with coppices and patches of forest oak, and here and there an isolated hill rose, which gave the country greater diversity. The grass, though rather tall, was fresh and juicy, and hence did not greatly impede our horses, while it rendered it easy for us to stalk game, large quantities of which we found here. We had been marching for nearly a month through this pleasant region to the South, and had crossed the Red Arm as well as several other affluents of the Arkansas, when one evening we reached the Saline. It was fringed with forests, which were much thicker and richer than those farther to the North, and offered us splendid wild plums as refreshment when we rode through.

We crossed the river, and went through the wood on its south side, and had just unsaddled our horses and picketed them in the prairie, when suddenly several hundred horse Indians came round the nearest angle in the wood, and halted a few yards from us, while we gazed at each other in amazement. At the head of them rode a single Indian, with a smoking piece of wood, who at the sight of us gave a piercing yell. We saw that great excitement was produced in the ranks of the caravan, and that the men collected in the fore ground, while the squaws and children hurried to the rear, and hastily drew back the numerous pack animals. We, too, ran at full speed to our horses, and were removing them to the bushes, when Tiger shouted to me that they were Comanches. The name at once tranquillized me, and I told him I believed they would do nothing hostile to us when they heard my name. He went towards the savages, and shouted my name to them, upon which they raised loud cries, and an old man, on a large mule, trotted towards us, in whom I recognised my friend Pahajuka. He was followed by his squaw, and both testified their joy at seeing me. The whole band was now coming towards us, when Pahajuka checked them in a loud voice and with commanding gestures. They turned away, and disappeared again soon after round the angle of the wood. He told me his people were impudent, and would rob us if he did not keep them away, and for that reason he had ordered them to camp lower down the river. Both the old folks dismounted, and sat down on their buffalo robes, while Antonio lighted a fire before them. I sat down with them, and gave them a couple of cigars. We prepared our supper, which my savage friends shared and enjoyed, and the squaw gave full vent to her eloquence. She told me they were going to the sources of the Puerco on the western side of the Sacramento Mountains, where a great council of all the Comanche tribes was about to be held. They invited me to go there, but I declined, as in spite of the friendship of these two, I did not care to trust myself among so many savages.

Gradually several men, with their squaws and children, crept up and camped curiously round our fire. Their number quickly increased, more and more of them crawled through the bushes and sat down around us, till it appeared that the whole tribe was collected. They pressed round our baggage, and I was obliged to call to Antonio and Königstein to keep a sharp eye on it, as I saw they were beginning to examine it. Suddenly old Pahajuka leapt up, and in a furious voice shouted some words we did not understand to the intruders, upon which the whole band disappeared again in the bushes, except a very pretty girl of about sixteen, whom the chief introduced to me as his granddaughter. She was a nice creature, gracefully formed, with a remarkably pretty head, from which a great mass of glossy black hair floated loosely over her shoulders. Her finely-chiselled, slightly aquiline, nose, her small mouth with its pearly teeth, and the modest, shy glance of her large black eyes, would have rendered her a perfect beauty had her skin been white, but even with her dark complexion she was handsome, and her appearance produced an extremely pleasant impression. The leathern petticoat which hung from her hips was finished with considerable taste and exquisitely painted; her finely-formed long neck was adorned by a necklace of white beads, and on her plump, graceful arms she had a number of polished brass rings. Her father, Pahajuka's son, so the old squaw told us, was shot in a foray in Mexico, and the old people had adopted her as their daughter. I was sorry that I had nothing with me to make her a present of, but I promised her lots of pretty things if she would visit me at home with the old folks, and the latter promised to do so.

The moon was up, and my guests rose to mount their mules, in which I assisted the squaw. I wished to accompany them to their camp. They rode in front and I followed with their daughter Tahtoweja (Antelope) along the skirt of the wood, and reached the camp not long after them, which consisted of some forty large tents of white buffalo hides, which were put up in two long rows and formed a wide street, on both sides of which the fires were burning in front of the tents. Pahajuka dismounted in the middle of this street, and his squaw was leading his horses away when I reached the first tents with the young Indian girl, and the old chief's thundering voice rolled along the camp, while he walked quickly up and down the tents with the most animated gestures. My companion pulled me back by the hand when I was going up to him, and led me aside behind the first tent, where she sat down and peeped round it at him, while I noticed that all the Indians had crept into their tents and only popped their heads out. For half an hour the old fellow stormed up and down the camp, during which time no other sound was heard, and not one of the Indians ventured to come out of the tents. All at once he came up to me as calmly and pleasantly as if he had not uttered an angry word, took me by the hand, and led me to his fire, where I was obliged to sit down. He told me he had been giving his people a reproof for the impudence with which they had forced themselves into my camp, so that they might learn how to behave with white friends. I remained with them a long while, and listened to the animated, sensible stories of the old squaw, which were at times interrupted by a reproving look from Pahajuka, when he fancied she was more lively than propriety admitted, and that her remarks slightly wandered from the literal truth; then, however, she bent over him, laughingly pressed his head to her bosom, and patted him on the back with her hand till he freed himself from her affection.

Tahtoweja too became more lively, took part in the conversation, and laughingly supported the old lady in her amicable dispute with Pahajuka. At the same time she became quite impatient when the interpreter did not express her remarks quickly enough, and tried by signs and gestures to make up for his omissions or incorrect rendering. Her language was quick and fiery, her large eyes, in which the flame of our fire was mirrored, flashed with the stream of her eloquence, and her little hands or fingers sought to render her meaning clearer, and in all these movements there was extraordinary power, decision, and grace. So soon, however, as she ceased speaking, she sat motionless, looking down or attentively listening to the remarks of her foster parents, while her dark eyes were fixed on them. She sat slightly back from the fire, so that the outline of her dark form was blended with the obscure background, and the small fire only lit up her eyes and her beautiful teeth when speaking, by which her appearance acquired a peculiar and mysterious charm.

It was late, and except our little party there was not an open eye in camp. I got up, offered my hand to my hosts, wished them good night, and when I put my hand to Tahtoweja she sprang up and laughing pointed in the direction of my camp, that she would accompany me, and at the same time gave the old squaw an inquiring glance. The latter nodded her assent, adding that she would accompany me too, but her feet were no longer so light as those of Antelope, and so the latter passed her graceful arm through mine and walked with me along the forest through the dewy grass. The distance was only a few hundred yards, and when we turned round the angle of the wood our camp was blazing brightly, and lit up my still waking comrades who were sitting round it smoking. Here Tahtoweja stopped, pressed my hands kindly while wishing me good night, and flew through the light mist back to her camp.

The next morning before daybreak Pahajuka with his squaw and pretty daughter joined us. The latter ran up to me with the pleasantest morning greeting, took the pipe from my mouth, and placing it between her cherry lips, sat down among tiger skins by the fire, making me a sign to do the same. We prepared as good a breakfast as our means allowed in honour of our guests, served up the last of our biscuit and handed round afterwards some Madeira which I owed to the kindness of Lord S——. After our friends had enjoyed themselves thoroughly, they returned to their camp to prepare for a start, for, as Pahajuka told me, they wished on this day to reach the northern arm of Canadian River, between which and the stream on which we now were, no water was to be found. I went across with them to see the large tents loaded, while my comrades packed our animals, for, as our road ran in the same direction. I wished to accompany our savage friends. When we arrived in camp we found perfect quietude there, the various families were lying round the fires in front of the tents engaged in breakfasting, while the children were amusing themselves in the long tent street with shooting arrows, throwing stones, wrestling, and running races, in which they were observed, praised or blamed by their parents. Pahajuka stopped at the first tent and shouted a few words I did not understand, upon hearing which all the squaws hurriedly rose and set to work striking the large tents. The latter are about fourteen feet high, pointed at the top, and some twenty feet in diameter on the ground. There are openings above on the sides which can be pulled open in the direction of the wind to let the smoke out when the weather is cold and the fire is lit in the middle of the tent. The buffalo hides of which the tents are composed are tanned white, and adorned inside and out with paintings. They are very thickly sewn so that no rain can penetrate, and in winter when the fire is burning the interior is very warm and cozy.

In a quarter of an hour all the tents had disappeared, and at the spot where they had stood lay bundles bound with straps. The squaws came up with the horses and mules, hung on each side of them a very long tent pole which was allowed to trail behind, and a few feet from the end fastened cross bars, on which they placed the tents, buffalo hides, cooking utensils, and all their traps, and then seated either themselves or their children atop, while others mounted horses or mules, and took two or three or even four children up with them. While the girls and squaws were performing this operation the warriors lay smoking round the fire, and only rose when their horses and weapons were brought to them. In less than half an hour everything was ready for a start, and one of the Indians took some firebrands of musquito wood, which keeps alight for a very long time, and rode ahead of the party southward, while I, accompanied by Pahajuka, his squaw, and Tahtoweja, returned to my camp and mounted Czar, and we then followed the Indians.

It was a glorious day: the sharp breeze rendered the heat endurable, while clouds every now and then obscured the sun. We rode sharply on without a check, as the distance to the appointed camping-place was over sixty miles. Still our horses did not object to it, as we followed the track of the Indians, and their numerous cattle formed a smooth road, and they often made the last ride at the head of the file, so as not to fatigue individual horses too much. Our road ran over an open prairie, and the sky line soon formed the horizon. The grass around us glittered in the darkest green, which in the distance grew lighter and lighter, till at the extreme point of sight it melted away into the blue colour of the sky. Flowers of the most varied hues sprang up out of the rich verdure, and for a long distance dyed various spots on the prairie with their prevailing colour. Pahajuka and his squaw trotted in front of us on their capital mules, while Tahtoweja kept her stag-like little pony at an amble by my side, and took all possible trouble to keep up a conversation with me by means of signs. On her saddle lay several folded hides, on which she sat like a cushion, and her little feet were thrust into wooden stirrups on either side of her horse's neck. She frequently swung her small, graceful leather-woven whip over her horse's head, and spoke to it in her sweet voice, while pulling up its head with the bridle.

Without resting we rode the whole day, and had only now and then opportunity to water our horses at standing pools, till the sun sank beneath the western prairie, and we could scarce recognise to the south the blue outline of the woods on Canadian River. Darkness very rapidly spread over the plain around us, while the sky was still red over the departed sun, and in the east a pale yellow patch on the horizon announced the rising moon. Our horses had fallen into a swinging walk, when the new light appeared above the prairie and rose like a glowing ball above us, while the clouds were gradually lit up by its silvery light. A fiery shower of fire-flies glistened over the extensive plain, and in front of us lightning flashes in the distant southern heavens every now and then displayed to us the dark contour of the forest which we were approaching. It was not far from ten o'clock when we unloaded our wearied animals on the skirt of the forest near the long-looked for river, and camped close to our savage friends. After supper no long time was granted to conversation, for each soon sought his bed to rest after the exertions of the ride. The next morning Pahajuka, his squaw, and daughter, again shared our breakfast, and then prepared to go on, while we resolved to rest for the day. The two old people were very sorry at being obliged to leave us, but promised, without fail, to come to my house after the great council on Puerco River and remain some time. Tahtoweja tried by laughing to hide the tears which glistened in her long lashes as I helped her on her pony and bade her good-bye. She gave me a small leathern pocket very artistically worked in beads which hung from her belt, while she was unable for her sobs to utter the words she wished to say. She pointed to my eyes, then to the parcel in my hand, laid her little hand on her heart, and said—Tahtoweja. Once again she offered me her hand, and then hastened to join her grandparents, who were already leading the file behind the fire-bearer.

Carrying fire from one camp to the other appears to be a custom peculiar to most of the savage tribes in this country. They halt on the last elevation, whence they can look back at the deserted spot, lay a still smoking brand on the ground, wave a farewell across, and then try, by swinging and blowing the brand, to keep it alight as long as possible: on a long ride they naturally do not bring it burning into the new camp.

We halted this day on the northern Canadian River in order to rest our cattle, which had the most splendid pasture here, and the next morning marched south again. Toward evening we reached a spring which ran out of a low range of hills. Here we found a pleasant camping spot, and followed the course of this stream on the following day to the Southern Canadian River, on whose bank we unsaddled, after crossing it with much difficulty. From this point we altered our course, as we went up stream, in order to reach its springs, the southernmost of which well up in the Sacramento Mountains, at the point where the latter form a low pass which separates them from the mountain chain which runs parallel with the Puerco river, in nearly a southern direction, to the San Saba Mountains, and form an extensive rich valley between themselves and the former river. On the western side of the Puerco, between it and the Rio Grande, with which it also runs parallel, again rise large ranges, forming beautiful valleys toward both rivers, until the former river falls into the Rio Grande at the western end of the San Saba Mountains. All these rich regions on both sides of the Puerco as far as the Rio Grande and the western settlements in Texas, the Comanches and Mescaleros regard as their property, and only tolerate there a few of the civilized tribes, such as the Delawares, Kickapoos, &c., because they fear them, and do not care to be engaged in war with them.

This district is indubitably by far the finest in the whole of the States, as regards richness of soil and climate, as here tropical and northern vegetation are blended. The banana, the cocoa-nut, the orange, the plum, the apple, and the cherry flourish, and vines spread over all the woods: the soil in the valleys is extraordinarily rich and productive during the whole year. The pasturage is incomparable, and cannot be equalled in the whole world: it is covered with the splendid musquito grass, which remains green and juicy in winter as in summer, and sooner or later these valleys will support as many domestic animals instead of the countless herds of wild creatures now living there. The climate is magnificent; the great summer heat is rendered endurable by the cooling winds from the Gulf of Mexico, while the winter has no long lasting rain, and a very slight frost is only felt rarely, just before daybreak. There is no visible cause for diseases, as there are no swamps, and the forests as well as the prairies consist of undulating land, from which the water left by heavy showers or inundations of the rivers quickly recedes. The region is abundantly traversed by the clearest streams, which well up in the neighbouring granite mountains, and through their remarkably rapid fall render it an easy task to irrigate the surrounding land should ever a drought occur. The great variety of plains, hills, mountains, and the most luxuriant vegetation in the virgin forests as well as on the plains, impart to these regions remarkable picturesque attractions which are heightened by the transparency of the atmosphere, the dark blue sky, and the peculiar light effects.

Our road now ran along the south side of the Canadian River to the west, and in a few days the Sacramento Mountains rose before us. We reached an affluent of this river, on which some miles farther up the iron stone was said to lie with which Tiger told us the god of hunting had killed a Weico. As it would not take us very far out of our course if we rode to it, I requested Tiger to lead us to it. Before sunset we reached a prairie, round which the little wooded stream ran in a semicircle, and saw in the centre of it the stone rising about three feet out of the short grass. It was a meteorite of enormous size; its circumference on the plane measured twelve feet, and it did not rest on rock; it must have sunk a great distance into the ground, although the latter is excessively hard on the prairie. It had considerable magnetic power, was of a dark rust colour, and so hard that it cost us great difficulty to knock off a few splinters with the back of our axes. It is certainly the largest stone of this sort in existence—at least the largest I know are much smaller, and it would repay the trouble and expense to fetch it from this desert and convey it to some museum.

We slept here for the night, and had to hear several times the story of the Weico who was slain with this stone. The next morning we left the river, marching westward along the mountains, and camped again on the banks of Canadian River. For about a week we followed this course, to the spurs of the Sacramento Mountains, where we left the river, and went along the former to the south, until in a fortnight we reached the sources of the Red River, which flow from the eastern slopes of these mountains. We rode up them to their source among the granite rocks, where we found at a considerable height a splendid camping place, on which we found the remains of several Indian camps, made by foot Indians, who do not carry large tents with them. They consisted of long thin sticks, four or six of which were crossed and had both ends stuck in the ground; over these sticks they hang skins, and thus obtain a decent shelter against rain and cold. A much-trodden path led on the north side of this stream to the camp, and from here ran up to the saddle of the hill, and thence, as Owl and Tiger told us, down it to the south, over the San Saba range, to the sources of the Rio de las Mires, which stream falls into the Gulf of Mexico at Corpus Christi. This is one of the oldest connecting paths of the Indians between the northern lands of the Rocky Mountains and the Gulf, and proves by the depth it is worn in the rock that it has been used since the earliest period by these wanderers as well as the four-footed denizens of the desert.

The springs at which we camped welled up under immense granite crags, which rose in terraces, and formed in front of them a small basin in which they collected and flowed in a rivulet through the plain on which our cattle were grazing, and thence to the wide prairies which we had recently crossed. Around us lay large masses of rock, which had probably fallen from the heights, between which the path wound upwards. On the east we gazed at the immense plains through which Canadian River marked its course by the rich woods that overshadowed it, and at our feet we looked into savage gorges, from which here and there small patches of grass and scrub peeped out, and a few enormous cypresses raised their gigantic branches, inviting the wanderer in these deserts to enjoy a fresh draught in their shade, as these noble trees only flourish in the vicinity of water.

Day had scarce broken on the next morning, when we prepared breakfast, and the sun had not risen over the eastern horizon, and the valleys were still covered with mist, when we were already mounted and going up the path, to take advantage of the cool of the morning, as during the day we might calculate on great heat upon these barren rocks. The morning was splendid. The fresh, cool mountain breeze refreshed us, and every plant, every blade of grass between the rocks seemed to enjoy the treat. We had ascended a considerable height when the sun spread its beams over the earth. Our path ascended from hill to hill, till at about ten o'clock we reached a barren table-land, which in some parts was broad and others narrow, and overshadowed by crags. The landscape on either side of us was remarkably fine, and frequently the crags in our immediate vicinity offered very pretty pictures. When we drew near the western slopes, we looked down into luxuriant valleys on both sides of the Puerco, as far as the hilly range which divided that river from the Rio Grande, or a distance of from 150 to 200 miles. Farther south, in the valley on this side of the river, was an isolated mountain, whose peak ascended to the clouds, and which the Indians called the Guadaloupe Mountain. When our road ran nearer the eastern slopes, or the plateau along which we were riding became narrower, our eyes rested on the rich grasslands to the south of the river in the vicinity of the Salt Lake we had passed on our journey, as well as on the numerous streams which spring up on the eastern side of our mountains, and flow, some to the Brazos, others to the Colorado. It was now very hot, however, in spite of the violent breeze; but a rest without any shade could not refresh us. The stony strata along which we rode, and which at times were deeply trodden in, reflected the sunbeams and rendered the heat almost unendurable; our animals dripped with perspiration, and trotted on with hanging heads, as if anxious to get away from this glowing surface. Nowhere, however, did we see a spot to receive us in its shade, as the sun was vertical, and the few lofty rocks we passed cast no shadow. No path ran on either side downwards, which might afford us hopes of reaching water, and the few cypresses which indicated it to us were too far down in the bottoms for us to attempt to get to them. Our cattle became more and more tired, and at last hardly able to move, when the sun had sunk a long way on the western horizon. We halted several times in the shadow of large rocks to let our cattle breathe, and gave them the juicy pear-shaped fruit of the cactus, which grew here abundantly, and they eagerly devoured it. My comrades also ate them contrary to my advice, and several of them became very unwell in consequence. Such a rest could not do us much good, and so we continually urged our horses on, till after passing about sunset between tremendous crags, we found a broad path, which soon wound down the eastern slope, when about a mile farther on we saw a copse of low cypresses. With great delight we accepted their invitation, and followed the path which ran into a small glen, where we found good grass and splendid spring-water.

Here, too, we found the traces of several Indian camps, some of which seemed to be quite recent. The few halting-places in the vicinity of this mountain path are well known to the savages who go over these mountains, and are used by them like hotels by travellers in the civilized world. We kept up a large fire during the night, as we here heard for the first time the howls of the jaguars rising from the valley to us, so soon as darkness lay over the earth. We allowed our cattle to graze till far into the night, when they lay down, and we brought them near our fire and slept quietly till dawn.

The sun had scarce risen, when we left this spot and hastened back to the road across the ridge. Our cattle walked quickly along the path in the cool morning breeze, and at about nine o'clock Guadaloupe hills lay to the north-west, while the western mountains on the opposite side of the Puerco opened, and allowed us a view through a broad pass of the Rio Grande and Paso del Norté. This is the only easily accessible pass through the Cordilleras, through which, too, ere many years elapse, the locomotive will snort from the Atlantic to the Pacific. Between this pass and the mountains on which we were standing, stretched out the rich green valleys on both sides of the Puerco, and through it we saw in the extreme distance the blue contour of the mountain ranges beyond the Rio Grande. Though it was so grand up here, we longed to be down below on the banks of the Puerco, and resolved to seize the first opportunity of descending afforded us by a direct path. During the whole day, however, we only found indistinct traces where buffaloes had descended the western slopes, till at about four P.M. we found a very practicable path, which crossed ours from east to west, and which we went down. It was at places so steep that we were obliged to lead our horses, and the latter slipped down on their hind-quarters after us: then again it wound round crags, past precipices, and between isolated peaks, up hill and down, until about sunset we reached, greatly fatigued, a rivulet, upon which our cattle greedily fell. The path ran down from the spring, and we followed it for about half an hour, till about nightfall we reached a small leafy coppice, in which we camped. Tiger and Owl were of opinion that the path led down to the valley, as it ran past the springs, and because a path corresponding with it had run down the eastern side of the mountains.

The next morning we ate our last meat at a very early breakfast, and Tiger saddled his horse to make certain whither the path ran, and also to try and shoot a deer or an antelope, of which there were large numbers on these mountains. During this time we wished to let our cattle graze and recover, as they greatly needed rest; and in the event of our being obliged to ride back to the ridge, we wished to halt here till the next day. The sun had just risen when Tiger left us. We lay in the shade of the closely-growing elms and poplars, and were drinking coffee at noon, as Tiger had not yet returned, when we suddenly heard the footsteps of a horse beneath us, and directly after saw the piebald come round the precipice. Our surprise was great, however, on seeing that the horse's handsome white seemed dyed quite red on the neck and breast, and Tiger too, when he drew nearer, was quite bloody. I hurried toward him, and saw, to my terror, that he had serious wounds on his left shoulder, and that the blood covered his arm and the whole of his left side. I took his rifle, helped him off his horse, and went back with him into the shade of the elms, while Antonio looked after the piebald. Tiger now told us he had been riding about three miles down the stream through a small coppice when suddenly an immense jaguar leapt at his horse's neck, but at the same instant he buried his hunting-knife between the beast's ribs. At this moment he slipped off his terrified rearing horse— the jaguar buried its claws in his right shoulder, while he dealt it several stabs, and it then fell dead. The piebald bolted down the stream as fast as his legs would carry him over the stones, and Tiger believed that he should never see him again when he noticed him on a bleak crag: he shouted to him from a distance, and the faithful creature at once hurried up to him. He then washed his own and the horse's wounds, and returned to us, suffering great pain. He had four wounds on his shoulder, close together, as if cut with a knife, and which ran about four inches down his arm. The foremost was so deep that I was obliged to sew it up. I bandaged him as well as I could, laid all the rags we possessed in a moist state on the wound, and made him moisten them pretty frequently in the neighbouring stream. Then I examined the poor piebald, who had on his back four deep wounds from the jaguar's fangs, and several injuries on the neck from the claws; still none appeared dangerous, and though the throat swelled considerably, constant washing soon produced an alleviation.

Owl now went up the hills in search of game, while I proceeded down the stream with Antonio and Königstein to fetch the jaguar's hide. We reached the scene of action, where the jaguar lay outstretched on the bank, and the ground was trampled by the horse's hoofs; the animal had five knife stabs near the heart, and the earth and grass around were dyed with its blood, while we were able to follow the blood-stained track of Tiger and the piebald down the stream. My two comrades at once set to work removing the splendid skin, while I followed the path for the purpose of procuring meat.

I had gone some distance without getting within shot, though I frequently saw game, and the low position of the sun warned me to commence my return to camp, I was following a small affluent of the stream, which came down from the hills a little more to the south, in order not to return by the same road I had come, when I suddenly heard about half a mile off a roar that exactly resembled that of a lion. I ran in the direction whence the sound came, and soon saw on the bank of the stream two giant stags engaged in a most furious contest and surrounded by a herd of does, and further on some large stags on the watch, I ran up within forty yards of them unnoticed, while with their huge antlers intertwined they butted each other, and frequently sank on their knees. I shot the largest, which fell, and its enemy at once buried its tines in the flanks of its overpowered foe, not suspecting that the same rifle which had slain its opponent still held a deadly bullet in readiness. I could easily have killed it, but preferred a fawn, which was standing no great distance off, and killed it. I now got up behind the rocks to reload, and the startled herd darted off to the mountains. I went up to the stag, which had two-and-twenty tines, and was very plump; after which I hurried to reach camp before it grew dark, and met Owl, who had shot nothing. As we had nothing left to eat, we at once started with Jack to fetch in the game, taking some firebrands of pine-wood as torches. The night was dark, but the torchlight illumined all the objects around the more distinctly in consequence. Antonio walked in front, I followed with Trusty, and Königstein, with Jack, formed the rear. We soon reached the stags, and loaded Jack with a large supply of meat, with which we arrived in camp about ten o'clock. Our hunger was great, as we had eaten nothing since morning, and we sat till a late hour round the fire turning our spits. Tiger was much better; the pain was reduced, and the swelling of the wounds was slight. The next morning, however, as the bandages had not been wetted during his sleep, his arm was very stiff, while the pain was greater, and hence I resolved to stop where we were at least for the day.

It was scarce daylight when I took my weapons and went to pay another visit to the rutting stags, John accompanying me. The morning was cool, and the dew lay in heavy pearls on grass and stones, the valleys below us were still veiled in mist, and large white clouds hung on the hill-sides. We reached the spot where I had shot the stags, and heard thence the roars of the animals echoing through the valleys. They were standing, however, rather higher up the stream, as they probably remembered my last night's visit. We pressed through the tall ferns, from which the dew dripped upon us like rain, and reached a plateau that hung over a dizzy precipice. Here stood the game, and nearest to us an old stag, which had its proud antlers thrown back, its thick swollen neck outstretched, and was roaring furiously. All around the other stags responded from the hills, and we listened for a long time to the concert of these jealous lovers ere we thought of hunting them. As it was the first giant stag John had had a chance of firing at, I readily granted him the first shot, and allowed him to stalk the stag. The majestic animal, hit by my comrade's deadly bullet, fell on its knee in the midst of a roar, raised its head once or twice, and then fell lifeless on the scanty grass that covered the rock. John could not master his delight, and ran up to the stag, by doing which he put an end to our sport here for this morning, as all the deer flew at the sight of him. The stag had six-and-twenty tines, and a pair of colossal antlers, whose ends were like shovels. We broke it up, threw the paunch over the precipice, and hoisted John's white handkerchief near it in order to keep beasts of prey aloof.

It was still very early, the first sunbeams were just illumining the highest points of the steep precipice on the opposite side of the abyss on which we were standing, and the cool breeze was too refreshing for us to think of hurrying back to camp. We followed the plateau therefore, from which the opposite one continually retired, until the gorge widened into a rocky glen, from which colossal masses of stone rose in wild confusion. Far down the valley, at the point where it trended to the east, round the opposite hill side, we distinctly noticed a path which ran along the base of the mountains, and was probably the continuation of the one on which we were camped. As we still heard numerous stags roaring we advanced till we were able to look down into the valley on the east, and follow our path for a long distance through it. We stopped to gaze at the wondrous forms of the mountains. I took out my telescope, looked at the path, and saw a long way off dark forms moving among the rocks, which I soon discovered to be a large party of horse Indians. No doubt but the path they were marching along was ours, and they would be in our camp in less than an hour, while we had a good half hour's walk to it. We therefore turned and hurried at full speed to join our friends.

CHAPTER XXVII
HOME AGAIN

Tiger advised us to saddle at once, while he and Owl carefully removed everything that could betray our recent presence here. All the logs were carried into the stream in a deer hide, the horse excreta and scraps of food hidden in the neighbouring bushes, and after giving our camp the appearance as if its occupants had left it some days previously, we led our horses over the firm stones down to the stream where I had shot the stag on the previous evening, and then along it till we could survey our path from a distance of about two miles from camp. Here we led our cattle into a coppice where they were hidden from the Indians by the bushes and rocks. Ere long the latter marched up the path. Tiger recognised them as Apaches who were probably on the road to the eastern trading ports of the United States, as they had their squaws and children and large bales of hides with them. We let them pass in peace. We then rode down the stream to the path and put our horses at a sharp amble in the direction from which the Indians had just arrived. The path led us round many blocks of granite into the glen, down into which we had gazed that morning while stag hunting. John looked up at the overhanging crag, on which his stag and pocket-handkerchief were, but could not see it from here, and only regretted that he could not take the antlers with him as a memento. He spoke about it several times, and said he would willingly give ten dollars to have them. On this Owl rode up to him and said he would procure them for him by the evening, after which he turned off into the rocks. He shouted something to Tiger that we did not understand and disappeared, while we soon reached the spot where the valley turned to the east. On both sides of it rose the barren mountains, and only an isolated yucca or mimosa grew out of the crevices. The valley itself, here about two miles in width, was covered with loose stones, and only from time to time did we notice on the stream that wound through it a small clump of trees or patch of grass. In spite of the great heat we hurried on till the sun was rather low, and the mountain wall that closed the extremity of the valley cast a long shadow into it. From here it trended to the south-west. The crags that enclosed it sank, and we looked down into the valleys of the Puerco River, between which and us lay smaller hills and mounds frequently covered with forest. When the sun sank behind the southern pillar of the mountain gate in front of Paso del Norté, the Diablo Mountains, we unpacked at the first wood we reached after leaving the glen, and camped on the bank of the stream which we had followed nearly all through it. It was one of the numerous exquisite points we had found during our tour, and the wonderful evening light did much to heighten its beauty.

We had lit our fire under the dark foliage of the oaks and thus illumined the surrounding scenery, when Trusty rose from my side, walked a few paces toward the pass and began growling. I called him to me coaxingly and bad him lie down by my side, and at this moment we heard the sound of a horse rapidly approaching us from the valley. We knew it was Owl, but for all that every one seized his rifle and awaited the arrival. Our friend soon rode up to the fire, took the enormous antlers with the entire head of the stag off his horse, silently laid them and the handkerchief before John, led his horse into the grass, and lay down on his buffalo robe near the fire without saying a word. I asked him whether he had seen anything of Indians, upon which he stated that he had left his horse in the glen and gone up alone to the stag: after cutting off its head and taking the handkerchief he went to our camping place and ascended the nearest hill whence he could have an outlook. The whole party of Indians were quietly camping on the spot, and at least a dozen columns of smoke were rising from it.

We cut the antlers off the head and put them with the skull bone to dry at the fire, and then got supper ready, while Owl turned the stag's tongue on a spit. In the morning the familiar notes of awakening turkeys aroused us again once more. After a long time we cheerily seized our rifles and hurried down the stream toward them to the spot where large peccan-nut trees enthralled them by the rich crop of nuts. We behaved most unmercifully to these dainty birds, and when we returned to camp had a perfect hill of them lying before us. We set to work roasting and frying, in which we were greatly aided by the extraordinary quantity of delicate fat which these birds have in autumn. The remaining turkeys were cleaned, rubbed with salt, and wild pepper, which is very common in the woods at this season, and packed on the mules; we then continued our journey down through the hills to the long looked for valley of the Puerco.

Our road was very fatiguing, and we were frequently obliged to dismount and lead our horses down the steep slopes; at the same time the path was covered with small sharp stones, which rendered going down hill still more wearisome to the cattle, and it often ran over loose blocks of stone, where they ran a great risk of breaking their legs. Still all went well, and toward evening we rode out between the last hills into the fresh verdure of the Puerco valley, and camped on the stream whose course we had been following for some days, and which here ran as a small river to the Puerco. We preferred riding down the valley along the hills, in order to keep out of the way of the wandering Indians who generally marched up and down the river, and whose number was large, especially now, as all the tribes of the Comanches and their relatives were *en route* for the great council at the sources of this river. Then, again, we could calculate on finding more game on this side of the extensive valley, and had only one disadvantage, that we must at times go without water. Nature everywhere showed us that we were approaching home: the prairie was again ornamented with the gorgeous flora which had so often delighted us there; the sky above us was darker, and, in the distance, more hazy than in the north, and a warmer life seemed to be stirring in everything. Still the vegetation, especially that of the woods, did not bear the peculiar southern character which is so striking at our home. We started very early, rode till far into the evening, and rested, when we could manage it, at noon in some shadow, for the heat was most oppressive from eleven till three. Moreover, we were in the moon's first quarter, which lighted us a little when the sunshine had departed, and enabled us to employ the cool of the evening on these smooth plains in pushing on.

We marched, thus without halting for about a week along the hills, during which the mountain chains on the west of the Puerco constantly drew nearer to us and contracted the valley. We had followed our course one whole morning without finding water, till about two o'clock p.m., when the heat became unendurable, and we looked out ahead for some shadow in which we could rest for a few hours. At length we caught sight of a clump of trees, and to our indescribable joy we saw distinctly that they were poplars which retained their fresh foliage, an infallible sign that there was water near; for such trees often stand in pools, and when the water dries up their leaves turn yellow and fall off. We urged our cattle on in order to reach the trees as speedily as possible, for now that we might expect shadow, and probably water, we felt the sun's heat doubly. On these plains objects are seen so clearly and distinctly for incredible distances, that you often deceive yourself, and such was the case with these poplars; we constantly believed that we must reach them in a quarter of an hour, and yet hours passed ere we really arrived. We hastened into the thick shade of the old trees, and I can scarce describe the cheerful feeling that possessed us all on seeing close to them, instead of a pool of muddy slime, two ponds of the clearest, freshest spring water, one of which the poplars overshadowed with their long branches. The cattle were quickly unloaded, and rolling themselves on the grass they dried their wet backs, while we, reclining on the turf, inhaled the cooler air. The pools, like the mountain-springs near my house, had no visible connexion with any other water, but for all that retained their freshness, though almost constantly exposed to the burning sun.

We lay without stirring, so as to avoid any movement which might have impeded our rapid cooling: not a breath of air stirred, the easily-agitated leaves of the poplars hung motionless from the long stalks, while over the water lay that quivering dazzling glow which announces the highest degree of heat. The insect world alone seemed to revel in this heat, and filled the air with an uninterrupted monotonous buzz, like that which a patient hears in his fever dreams. Near me there rose from the roots of an old poplar a chameleon, which probably found it too warm. This wondrous lizard glistened and sparkled with a thousand hues, puffed up the large orange-coloured bladder under its chin, and displayed every tint, as if illumined by a variegated light in its inside: it sat motionless, with widely-opened mouth, fixing its large golden eyes on me, as if asking whether I would leave it the cool spot it so enjoyed? I lay with my head on the roots of a poplar quite still, so as to be able to gaze at the beautiful creature for as long a time as possible; then my eyes turned from it to the ponds whose surface dazzlingly reflected the sunlight, but quickly returned to the blessed shade which we and our cattle were enjoying.

I accidentally looked again toward the sparkling water and noticed a trunk of a tree in the middle of it, which I had not seen a few moments previously. What could have raised it from the bottom of the pond to the surface? I sat up a little and saw a second and a third emerge by its side: I did not stir, but continued to gaze, and in ten minutes the pools were covered with old wood. I cried in a low voice to Tiger to look, but he had scarce done so ere he laughed, and said they were alligators enjoying the sunshine. The surface of both pools was literally covered with these monsters, mostly of a large size. I cried to my comrades to take their rifles, quietly aim at their heads, and fire when I gave the signal. I did so; our guns exploded simultaneously, and the water spirted up furiously, and bedewed the grass for a long way round. Only two of the monsters remained in sight, shooting backwards and forwards in the water, and beating their tails so furiously that the spray dashed over us. At this moment Antonio came up with a lasso, and in an instant threw the noose over one of the furious creatures. We all ran with the end of the rope over the grass, and dragged the alligator on land, when it snapped savagely around with its fearful jaws, and lashed its tail. We now set to work with pistols, and ere long its head had so many holes in it that it could not move its dangerous jaws. Its comrade was still swimming quietly on the top of the water, so we fetched it out too on to the grass, when it behaved as furiously as the first, but we soon put an end to its fun. They were two gigantic animals, nearly sixteen feet long, and their throats were armed with rows of terrible teeth, some of which we all took as a memento.

It is a riddle to me how the creatures got here, for the nearest stream was many miles away, while they never quit the banks of the water in which they live, and are as awkward as tortoises ashore, so that a land journey was impossible. But even assuming that one of the creatures had strayed and reached this spot after a long wandering, it could not be assumed that hundreds of them had emigrated together to a spot so distant from their element. Another question presented itself which was more easy to answer, however, and which was settled before our departure—on what such large creatures lived here? They were supplied by the unfortunate inhabitants of this country, who came many miles to this spot in order to quench their burning thirst at these glorious springs, and strengthen their wearied limbs, during which they were dragged under by the watchful monsters, and torn to pieces by thousands of teeth. I am convinced that even a buffalo, in spite of its gigantic strength, would be overpowered and killed by these monsters, if, fatigued by a long journey over the prairie, it ran into their ponds to cool itself.

The sun was near the hills, we had satisfied our hunger with turkey breasts and venison, and were ready to leave this pleasant spot, when Königstein slit up an alligator with his hunting knife and drew out of the belly of one some deer feet, and then out of the other the leg of a turkey. We would gladly have extirpated the whole nest of disgusting monsters, but not one of them was now visible, and the evening sun played as cheerily on the surface of the water, as if no horrors and dangers were concealed beneath it. We watered our horses once again and then trotted on in order to cover a good bit of ground, for the nearer we got to our home, the greater grew our longing for it and all the friends whom we had left there.

We continued our journey for about a week, and crossed a number of small streams, which ran into the Puerco, till one noon we reached another rivulet, on whose shady bank we resolved to rest. From this point we surveyed in the south a large forest which ran across our road from the eastern mountains to the Puerco, while we saw above it distant ranges of mountains running in the same direction, which we saluted as the San Saba Mountains. These were the only ranges that separated us from home, and full of desire of them as old friends, we saddled toward evening, and at midnight entered the forest, which we had seen before us ever since our midday halt. The moon had hitherto distinctly shown us the buffalo paths, but here her rule was at an end, and only now and then did a ray fall through the lofty masses of foliage which now roofed us over. We stopped on a very trampled path, which we could not follow, however, through the forest, for even if our cattle kept the road, the creepers hanging over it rendered our progress difficult. Our cattle were very thirsty, and as we had no doubt of finding water in the forest depths, we resolved to try and reach it. We dismounted, gathered dry grass, out of which Owl and Tiger twisted torches, one of which we lit, and then pressed on, leading our horses. We had not gone more than one hundred yards into the forest when Tiger cried that he was at the river, and shortly after we led our thirsty horses down the bank and refreshed them in the cool stream: we filled our gourds and returned by the same road to the prairie, where we fastened up our cattle in the grass and lit our fire. As the horses were very hungry we did not drive them out of the grass, but set a sentry over them who was relieved every half hour. At daybreak we shot turkeys in the wood for breakfast, bathed in the adjoining river, and then fetched up the sleep we had lost in the night.

We stopped here till about 3 P.M., and then continued our journey southward. As the banks of the stream were very steep here, we were delayed a little till we had all our baggage across, but then rode for two hours without a halt through the glorious shade of the forest, in whose gloom only now and then a bright yellow patch was lit up by the inquisitive sunbeams. We felt here as much at home as on the Leone or the Mustang, and the conversation throughout the whole day turned upon home and our friends there, for nature all around offered pictures of those regions. The trunks of the trees here rose again side by side; from their lofty branches llianas covered with gayest hues swung across, and under the evergreen bushes the flowers displayed their brightest colours. The parrots with their lustrous plumages hung high above us on the branches head downward, and innumerable bright red cardinals flew like live coals through the dark foliage. Here a proud stag with mighty antlers peered out from a cozy glade, and there a timid antelope fled with its two fawns behind it through the thicket. When we rode through the last clumps and reached the prairie on the other side of the wood, the sunbeams were falling on it obliquely, and we did not miss the delightful shade so much as we should have done had we exposed ourselves to the sun a few hours earlier. We rode sharply, and at about 9 P.M. unsaddled at the foot of the San Saba Mountains, and camped on a torrent that ran down thence to the Puerco.

The next morning we followed the stream to the river, and about noon reached the principal Indian path that led from these valleys over the San Saba Mountains, and greatly facilitated our passage over them. On the third morning we looked down on the hills near our home, on which we camped the same evening. The next day we reached Turkey Creek at sunset, and would assuredly not have camped, but ridden home without resting had not our cattle been so fatigued. It was very late ere we thought of lying down to rest, and even then the conversation was carried on for a long time. After the old fashion the turkeys announced to us that day was breaking. On this occasion, however, we did not shoot any, but each breakfasted quickly and got ready for going home. A little more attention was paid this day to our costume; although we could not make much of it with the greatest skill, still we looked altogether tidier when we left camp, and each galloped on to be the first. I was obliged to hint that we still had a long way to go, and ought not to begin with galloping. The journey to-day seemed very long to us, although our horses advanced sturdily, as if they too noticed that we were going home. At about ten o'clock we made a half-way halt and let our cattle rest for a few hours, while we lit a fire at the same spot where we had made coffee at the beginning of our journey, and drank it again: at about two o'clock, however, we saddled and spread over the baggage of the mules the finest jaguar skins, above which the two splendid stags' heads were displayed.

We were still busy with our horses, when suddenly Jack kicked up behind, gave a few springs, and then trotted along the path that led to the Leone. He would not be deprived of the pleasure of being first, for so soon as we approached him he doubled his pace, and even galloped when it appeared necessary. All our cattle now plainly showed that they knew they were near home, and could not be held in. Long before sunset we passed through the wood on the Leone, and entered the prairie below the Fort, where we fired all our shots. We were greeted from the Fort in the same way, and its inhabitants ran out to meet us and overwhelm us with congratulations. Everything was as before, except that another good harvest had been got in, that horses, cattle, pigs, and dogs had multiplied, and that numerous new settlers had arrived both north and south.

John was impatient to get home, and left me no time to change my clothes, as I wished to accompany him. I therefore saddled Fancy, left Königstein to look after Czar and Trusty, and rode with my companion toward Mustang River. From a distance we could see that the Lasars had built a large new house with glass windows and galleries, whose whitewashed walls glistened through the gloom. We had reloaded and announced our return to our friends some distance off. Soon after we saw white handkerchiefs waving, light dresses hurrying out of the garden gate, and old and young, black and white, hurried to meet us and welcomed us with expressions of joy and congratulations. I had to apologize for my dress and retire, but I was obliged to stay to supper, which meal we took under the verandah, and after it we sat in the garden before the house, where the perfumes of splendid flowers surrounded us, which, illumined by the moonbeams, formed graceful groups around us. The bottles went so rapidly the while, that I thought it advisable to seek my homeward road before I had any difficulty in finding it.

It was about midnight when I reached the Fort, where I found everybody up and also cheered by wine, for I had ordered Königstein, when I rode away, to give them a treat. I, however, soon sought my bed-room with Trusty, and slept with open doors and windows till the sun stood high in the heavens. I hastened down to the river, and after a bathe the old trunks were opened and the garb of olden times was taken out.

Some weeks passed ere I was quite at home again; all the works looked after, others to be undertaken arranged, and repairs and improvements carried out. I frequently came across the Lasars; visited, with the old gentleman, the new settlers in the neighbourhood; consulted with him about making roads and bridges, and was appealed to by him in any important undertakings in his private affairs. Although we now felt no alarm about the Indians coming to the numerous new settlements, their friendly visits now grew wearisome and disagreeable. Every moment a new tribe arrived, of whom we had scarce heard, to make friendship with us and receive presents. Something must be given them, else we ran a risk that they would take it out on our cattle, or fire the prairie when a violent wind was blowing, or take some other revenge which would do more injury than the value of the presents. They no longer ventured on open hostilities within range of our settlements; to such only the more distant squatters were exposed, who lived nearer to the desert.

Shortly after our return, arrived a Mr. White, from Virginia, with his wife, two sons of twelve and fourteen years of age, and two younger daughters. He applied to Lasar and myself to show him a good bit of land on which he could settle. The people pleased us, they were friendly and honest, lived on good terms together, as we noticed on our frequent visits to their camp on the Leone, and were the right sort to defy such a mode of life. Lasar and I resolved to take them under our wing, and induced them to settle at our old camping place on Turkey Creek, for which purpose we set out early one morning with them, Lasar ordering twenty negroes to come with us and prepare an abode for the new-comers. We built for them there in a few days a neat double blockhouse, that is to say, two houses about twenty yards apart, over which and the space between one long roof was thrown. Then we surrounded the house with a palisade, in which they could lock their cattle at night, and fitted for them a lot of wood, with which they could fence in a garden. Lasar gave them a handsome cow, and I gave them a breeding sow, some fowls, and maize to eat and to sow for the coming spring. White was one of those resolute, unswerving men, who, after struggling for a long time with misfortune in the civilized world, turn their attention to the western deserts, where they try to extort from fate what has been refused to them elsewhere. With his peculiar energy and restless execution of everything he had once undertaken, he set to work in his new home, in order, as soon as possible, to lay the foundation of his own and his family's future prosperity; but unfortunately he was only able to see the foundation, for the garden was hardly fenced in and the maize field taken in hand, ere he fell ill, and a violent fever carried him off in a few days. His eldest son, Charles, rode over to me to bring me the melancholy news, and tell me that his mother wished to speak to me. I rode across the next morning with Königstein and a negro. The widow was sitting inconsolably by the side of her dead husband, without any plan for the future; and on my entrance pointed—with sobs, and unable to utter a word—to the dead body. I at once ordered the negro to dig a grave, and buried the poor fellow; after which I sat down by the widow's side, and tried to give her some consolation by offering her my assistance. I proposed to her to settle near me till her sons were old enough to look after their present farm. But she was of opinion that they were able to do so already, although not strong enough to do the heavy field work, such as clearing the land from bushes and trees as well as felling and clearing the wood itself. If this could be done for her, she would not leave the spot, as her lads could plough and use the pick, while both fired a rifle as well as any frontierman; and she, too, if it came to the point, knew how to use her husband's fowling-piece. I made every possible objection to her plan of living here alone, but promised my help and Lasar's if she insisted on adhering to it.

The next morning I said good-bye to the woman, who was determined to stop here, and promised to send her help to prepare her garden and fence, and bring her a few trifles for her comfort. I got home at an early hour, and rode in the evening to Lasar's to tell him what had happened. The old gentleman at once declared that he would send John off the next morning with the requisite number of slaves to arrange everything for the widow, and all the members of the family vied with each other in displaying their sympathy by sending articles of clothing and stores of every description. In a week everything was in order at White's—the garden was laid out, and a field of five acres prepared for planting with maize, beans, gourds, and potatoes. The best varieties of vegetables were sown in the garden, and seeds of all sorts given to the widow. The woman had for the present only to keep the garden in order, while the sons procured game, which they could shoot at times from their own door, for all her other wants were amply supplied.

Thus peace and contentment soon returned to this house, and the love of her children restored Mrs. White the activity and determination which the loss of her husband had palsied. Dawn found her busy with domestic duties— cleaning the rooms, dressing her daughters, milking the cows, preparing breakfast, salting and drying game, in short, with all sorts of occupations; after that she was seen sitting in the shadow of the roof between the houses, cleansing and spinning cotton to make clothes for her children, while the two little girls sported around her, and the sons were busy in the garden or hunting close at hand. She could recall them at any moment by sounding an immense cow-horn which hung in the passage between the two houses, near the door of the keeping-room.

Shortly after peace had settled down again on this solitary abode, the widow was seated as usual in the cool passage with her daughters, while her second son, Ben, had gone to the spring to fetch water, and Charles had gone into the neighbouring wood with his rifle. All at once the very sharp dogs which guarded the family made an unusual disturbance and ran barking across the yard that surrounded the house. Mrs. White jumped up and saw several Indians standing in front of the nearest wood, and then retire into it again directly after. She seized the horn, sounded it with all her might, then ran into the room and took down her deceased husband's fowling-piece that was loaded with slugs, with a resolution and courage such as has grown almost entirely strange to the feminine sex in civilization, and is only found on rare occasions on its outermost frontier on this continent. In a few minutes Ben ran up and found his mother already behind the palisade with the gun in her hand. "Quick, Ben, your rifle!" she cried to her twelve year old son; "but don't forget your bullet, boy;" and then blew the horn again. The dogs now came in again, and Mrs. White closed the hole in the fence through which they passed. All at once a frightful yell was heard from the wood, and from its gloom sprang a swarm of some thirty red-skinned fiends, who dashed over the grass toward the house with an awful war-cry. "Don't fire, Ben, till I have loaded again!" Mrs. White cried, and then rapidly discharged both barrels, sending some forty leaden pellets among the charging horde. The effect of the two shots at hardly fifty yards distance was so tremendous that the horde darted in all directions as if struck by lightning, and eight remained on the grass while the others ran howling to the wood. "Fire, Ben!" Mrs. White cried to her son, who had thrust his rifle through the palisades, while she poured a handful of slugs down her gun, and placed two cotton wads upon them. Ben fired into the thickest of the fugitives, and one of them fell with his feet in the air, while the yells of the others filled the air. "I have hit, mother," the boy said, as he poured fresh powder down the barrel. "Bravo, Ben! but where is Charles? He ought to have been here by this time, as he has not been gone long. Run into the house and have a look at Fanny and Bessie, but come back again directly." Thus Mrs. White called to her son while she was hurriedly making cotton wads, which she moistened with her lips, and threw back her long raven hair which hung over her shoulders. "Mother, Charles is coming with Kitty!" Ben cried, as he ran out of the house and hurried to the hind part of the fence to open the gate for their cow Kitty, which was trotting over the grass in front of Charles. The latter had heard the horn and the shots and yells of the Indians as he hurried home, had come across Kitty, and had driven her home.

Everything was quiet, and the Indians did not make the slightest sound. Charles and his mother secured the two fence gates with logs of wood, and then the mother went to her young children, leaving her sons orders to call her if they saw anything of the Indians. The day passed without the savages making a fresh attack on the settlement; but the greater on that account grew the widow's alarm, lest they should take advantage of the night to satiate their vengeance. Toward evening, she bade her sons lie down and sleep, so that they could keep awake during the night, while she kept guard in front of the house. The sun set and darkness was lying over the country, when Mrs. White and her two sons took their places behind the palisade, and carefully surveyed the open prairie. It was about nine o'clock, when they saw the light of a fire coming through the wood, rapidly grow larger, and presently appear on its outermost edge. Again the fearful yell was raised, with which the savages always accompany their attack, and the light moved from the forest over the grass. A dark object moved across the plain toward the house, and the light shone out on both sides of it. The object slowly drew nearer, and Mrs. White soon saw that it was a framework of bushes behind which the Indians were concealed, and pushing it before them. This leafy wall had advanced within twenty yards, when Charley and Ben fired at it, and the groans of the wounded were distinctly heard amid the yells of the assailants. For all that, the wall moved slowly forward, and in a few minutes leaned against the corner of the palisade, after which flames suddenly darted up and set the fence on fire. The savages had brought a heap of dry wood with them behind the screen, piled it up against the palisade and kindled it, after which they ran back about forty yards and lay down flat in the grass.

The space behind the fence round the house was now so brilliantly illumined that Mrs. White feared lest the savages might fire arrows through the palisades at her boys; hence she retired with them into the house, and went up under the roof, whither she took her daughters, too, while the dogs ran furiously along the palisade. Then she raised several of the shingles with which the roof was covered, and placed others under them, so that she could survey the brilliantly-lighted prairie, where she saw the Indians lying in the short grass. At the same instant, however, sparks fell down from the roof, for the savages had fired a number of burning arrows, which set fire to the dry shingle roof of cedar-wood. An inhuman yell of joy from the savages greeted the first flash of the flames, which soon ascended with a crackling sound. "Charles, the axe!" Mrs. White shrieked to her son, while she thrust her double-barrel through the roof and fired at a group of savages lying together in the grass, who doubtless fancied themselves safe from the besieged. The unhurt men leaped up with a yell and darted back to the wood, while the second barrel was fired after them, and again brought down several. Charles handed his mother the axe, with which she soon made a hole in the roof and pulled out the blazing shingles, so that the fire was extinguished in a few moments. Then she ran with axe and gun down into the yard, reloaded, and checked the fire at the palisades, which, as there was no wind, spread very slowly and was speedily put out. The corner of the palisade was certainly burnt down, and there was a large opening in it, while outside a large heap of burning coals remained from the fire. Mrs. White, with her sons' help, pulled the small cart which had conveyed their little property hither into the opening, and then filled up all the gaps with logs of firewood. The night was passed under arms, and when dawn lit up the country the heroic woman looked out of the roof at the battle-field in front of her fortress without being able to see a trace of Indians. The savages had carried off the corpses of their comrades in the darkness, and had probably departed with them in the night to let them rest with their fathers; for the Indians take the dead bodies of their friends with them and carry them hundreds of miles to the burial-place of the tribe.

Late on the following night the barking of my dogs awoke me, and when I shouted out of the fort, asking who was there, Charles White announced himself and told me what had happened. I had his wearied horse looked after, gave him a bed, and early next morning rode with him to Lasar, to consult with the latter what was to be done. This humane man soon formed a resolution, and told me he would let a faithful old negro, who was not of much use to him, live at Mrs. White's. He could sow a bit of land with cotton, the proceeds of which would be his own, and the family would have a protector in him, as he was an excellent shot and a fearless, determined man. Within an hour, we were mounted and rode past my fort, in order to fetch Owl and Tiger. We arrived in the evening at White's, where we saw the damage done by the savages, and then heard the story from Mrs. White's own lips, on which occasion she praised Ben's bravery, who during the narration stood by his mother's side with her arm thrown round him. The woman was most grateful for our kindness and sympathy, and said that, with the help of the old negro, Primus, she would withstand a whole Indian tribe. Primus remained there, and this settlement was really never again disquieted by Indians. It was, however, less the presence of the negro that made them refrain from hostilities, than Mrs. White's heroic defence. At a later date, Indians told me that the aggressors were Mescaleros, and Mrs. White fired so many bullets among them all at once, as if the storm-god had been scattering a hail-storm on the earth. Since then an Indian was hardly ever seen there. Such atrocities often happened at the outermost settlements, while very possibly the same Indians who committed them came to us as friends and were dismissed with presents and assurances of amity.

CHAPTER XXVIII
INDIAN BEAUTIES

Shortly after the occurrence on Turkey Creek, I was sitting one afternoon in the verandah before my house and drinking coffee, when I saw a long way down the prairie a cloud of dust coming down the river. Curious as to who it could be, I went into the house and fetched my telescope. I saw three Indians on horseback, a man in front, and two squaws following him. They rode very fast, in spite of the great heat, and soon came up the hill to the Fort. I went out to them, and all three came through the palisade gate, and pulled up in front of my house. The warrior leapt from his horse, while the two girls remained seated on theirs. He told me in English that a tribe of Indians wished to make friendship with me, and the chief had sent to inquire whether he would be allowed to pay me a visit with his people. I asked him to what nation they belonged, which question appeared, as it seemed, to be disagreeable to him, and he passed it over in silence. He then said something to the two girls which I did not understand, and then told me they were Mescaleros, but not of those who made the attack on Mrs. White. The chief of the latter was no good friend of the white men; but the father of these two girls was a very good friend, and hence he wished to come and tell me so himself. I replied, that I should be glad to see him here, and invited the girls to drink coffee with me, which invitation they did not at once accept, but, with their elbows resting on their horses' necks, gazed at me curiously, and then took side glances through the open door of my house at the interior. I offered them cigars, and took a lucifer match out of my box, the lighting of which surprised them immensely. I lighted my cigar at it first, and then handed it to them, and they loudly expressed their satisfaction at the excellence of the tobacco. I then took a drink of coffee, and handed the cup to one of the girls, who first examined it curiously all round, and then raised it to her lips to taste the contents. She had scarce tasted it, however, when she emptied the cup at a draught, and gave it back to me, with an intimation that I should give her sister some. I gave her a full cup, too; she emptied it at a draught and asked for more, so that in a few minutes my whole supply of coffee was expended. I gave them cakes, which they ate with equal appetite, and then went into the house to fetch a bottle of sweet Spanish wine. I poured out a glass, tasted, and handed it to one of the Indian girls, but she declined it, and after saying a few words to the man, their glances lost the calmness and merriment which they had gradually assumed.

I emptied the glass and placed it on the table, without again offering them wine, but handed them a light for their cigars, which had gone out. After a while the man asked me whether it was fire-water the bottle contained, and when I replied in the negative, and assured him it was capital wine, he said that one of the girls wished to taste it. I filled the glass, put it to my lips, and handed it to her on the horse: she raised it to her lips rather timidly, but drank the wine off at a draught so soon as she had once tasted it. Her eyes beamed with joy, and as she sat up on her horse, and passed her hand from her neck over her breast and stomach, she said, with an expression of delight, "Bueno," and handed me the glass back with a sign to give her some more. I filled it again, but gave it to her sister, who was looking on silently but eagerly. She, too, liked the wine, and emptied the glass, which I set on the table. At this moment both girls leapt from their horses, gave the bridles to the Indian with a disdainful gesture, while one of them told him imperiously to take the horses to graze; I at least concluded so from the gestures with which she accompanied her words, and from his at once going off with the horses. The speaker then turned to me with a most gracious smile, and, after throwing a contemptuous glance at the man, said to me "Mexicano," and now it became clear to me that he was a slave, probably stolen by this Indian tribe when a boy.

The two young savages now ran up to the verandah in front of my house, and I saw for the first time properly what remarkably pretty visitors I had; for both girls had been so crouching on their horses that but little of their figure could be seen. The one who seemed to me the younger, was very tall, slim, and most beautifully formed; her shape was elegant, but round and full, and her bones so delicate, that the comparison between horse and deer involuntarily occurred to me; her hands and feet, like those of all Indians, were very small, and so gracefully shaped that the white colour was not missed. On proportionately broad shoulders and a plump, round neck, she carried her head freely, and her demeanour proved that she was perfectly well satisfied with herself. Her glossy black silky hair hung, fastened together on the left side of her head with a strip of vermilion leather, for a length of four feet over her shoulders, and on the top of the red fillet floated by the side of her head a round bush of countless feathers of the most brilliant colours, which heaved up and down at every movement. Her fine lofty forehead was adorned by sharply-cut, glistening eyebrows, beneath which black eyes flashed; but their wild expression was toned down by the shadow of long eyelashes, and only in moments of excitement did the passionate look return to them. The small, pretty nose turned up slightly at the end, and gave a saucy look to the face, while the laughing, fresh, half-parted mouth, with its full cherry lips, cut in the shape of a Cupid's bow, heightened the expression. When the laughing lips parted they displayed the most beautiful and regular teeth, and in the peach-coloured cheeks were two deep dimples. At the same time her mien was elegant, her movements were rapid but graceful, and her whole appearance was full of young life, unchecked and wild, but attractive and pleasant. Her dark colour passed easily from light brown to olive, and announced that under it dwelt those warm feelings which are only born under a hot sun.

Though the interpreter was absent, our conversation now went on better than before, as the eyes of the Indian girl and her gestures rendered a dictionary quite unnecessary. She quickly disposed of another glass of wine, and would certainly have drunk a good deal more, had I not filled the glass again and handed it to her sister, and then locked the bottle up in a cupboard. The sister displayed less of the passionate Indian blood; she was quieter in her movements, and though she, too, frequently opened her mouth to smile, she did not burst into a loud laugh, and while the former looked all around, the eyes of the quieter girl were fixed the more firmly on the object she was surveying. She was shorter than her younger sister, but much plumper, more of a Titian's beauty, had also splendid hair, arranged in the same fashion, coal-black, but smaller flashing eyes, a graceful aquiline nose, and a smaller mouth. Her colour was rather darker than that of her sister, and it was doubtful whether a dazzling white or this transparent brown was the more beautiful colour for the skin.

The name of the elder sister, who was about nineteen years of age, was Cachakia (sparkling star), while the younger was called Pahnawhay (fire), and had not seen more than sixteen summers. The costume of these two savage beauties was much alike. Over their shoulders hung a handsomely painted, costly dressed deer-hide, in the centre of which was a long slit, through which they thrust head and neck. This mantilla was ornamented all round with a fine long leathern fringe, to whose ends glistening stones and shells were attached; it hung lower down before and behind, and left the pretty round arms at liberty. Round their hips was a petticoat, also of leather, adorned with long fringe, and handsomely painted in colours, while the leathern trousers were also decorated at the sides with similar fringe. Their little feet were thrust into deer-hide shoes, also ornamented with, stones, shells, and fringe.

Pahnawhay was the first to run up into the gallery; at each step she rose on her feet as if walking on whalebone, while Cachakia came on with a quieter but scarce audible step. Both sate down at the table, and the younger sister took the wine-glass and drained it, while making me signs to give her more wine. I made her understand that she had better not drink any more, as it might send her to sleep; but I would give them some more before they rode away. Pahnawhay had looked for a long time curiously at my room; at last she jumped up and ran to the door, and leaning against the lintel, thrust her head in as far as she could. With a loud cry of amazement she sprang back several steps, clapped her hands, and, with a beaming face, said something to her sister, and then ran back to the door. I went into the room, and made her a sign to follow me; but she only took one step across the threshold, looked around her in amazement, and then cried to her sister to come, who, however, did not obey her. I now went to Cachakia, took her by the hand, and led her into the room, where I made her sit down in my large rocking-chair. The admiration and surprise of the two girls were extraordinary; they remained for a long time motionless and silent, looking from one object to the other, until Pahnawhay first found her speech again. Running to my bed, she drew a red blanket from under the jaguar skin, that served as counterpane, and hung it proudly over her shoulders. As she had not yet noticed my large looking-glass, I led her in front of it, and a loud cry of surprise burst from her pretty mouth. She turned round before it, and at last ran up and from it with the most graceful movements, while Cachakia looked at her in silence, but showed by her flashing eyes that she would like to be in her place. I now led her in front of the mirror, took a bright silk handkerchief from a chair, bound it round her thick hair under the tuft of feathers, and made her understand that it was hers. I then took another blue and yellow one out of the chest of drawers, and fastened it round Pahnawhay's hair, for I knew if I did not it would be all over with her good temper.

Everything in the room was now examined, and if possible handled, and I had to explain its use. Cachakia too became gradually more animated and took a greater share in the conversation, always trying to make me understand that her sister knew too little and her chatter was not worthy of attention. Everything pleased her, and when she saw anything she wished particularly to have, she made me understand that we would swap, but never said what she intended to give me in exchange. Still I could not help giving both a number of trifles, such as knives, thimbles, needles, cotton, and sewing-silk, and I was very glad when the negroes came and announced that the dinner I had ordered for my guests was on the table, through which their desires took a different direction. I conducted them to the dining-room, and was obliged to dine with them again in order to show them the use of knife and fork, which they, however, soon laid aside and employed their little fingers instead. They liked everything, but the pudding most, and when coffee and cakes were again served, it seemed as if they intended making a separate meal of them. After dinner I gave them cigars and intended to keep them in this room till they rode off, but they soon got up, and after pointing round the room and saying with a dissatisfied expression, "no bueno," they walked off straight to my house. Whether I would or no, I was obliged to admit them, and Cachakia was now the first to nestle up to me and point with her little hand to the wine-glass, while she looked up at me with her sparkling black eyes and laughingly displayed two rows of pearly teeth. I could not possibly refuse her, and when I had filled the glass to the brim she raised the golden liquid to her lips and drank it to the last drop. Pahnawhay also drank a glass, but then I locked the bottle up again, and in spite of Cachakia's languishing looks and her sister's more stormy requests I did not take it out again.

Pahnawhay had again taken the red blanket from my bed and walked round me praising it loudly, while I was sitting by Cachakia, but she seemed not to have the courage to ask me for it. I noticed her embarrassment, and as I had long wished to have a dress like these girls were wearing, I pointed when she again stood before me to the various articles of her costume, then to the woollen blanket, and made the sign of exchange. As if the greatest piece of good fortune had happened to her, she fell back a step and repeated my signs inquiringly as if not believing her luck, and when I again affirmed it, she threw off in a few moments all her clothing, folded herself in the blanket, and stretching out her arm under it, carefully laid her leathern dress on my bed. I was so surprised at this instantaneous metamorphosis that at the first moment I did not think how Cachakia would be humiliated by it; but Pahnawhay pointed to her, and said I must give her a blanket as well. In truth the thermometer had already fallen in the eyes of my pretty neighbour, so I got up quickly and opened a chest in which I had several blankets, but not a red one; however, there were five blue ones among them, which pleased Cachakia remarkably, and in an equally short period her dress was also lying on my bed, and she was seated, highly delighted, in the Turkey blue blanket in my rocking chair smoking her cigar.

The sun had already set, and darkness was spreading over the landscape, when my princesses trotted out proudly into the prairie, wrapped in their blankets, with an assurance that they would return early the next morning with the whole tribe. At an early hour I had a very large kettle of coffee made and extra bread baked before the cattle were driven out to pasture, a fat ox was driven into the enclosure, the dogs were chained up, and I ordered my men to keep the Fort closed, as the Indians whom I wished to enter it would be led through my house, which stood at the south-eastern angle, and had an entrance through the palisade.

At the appointed hour we saw the party of Indians coming down the river, and soon halt in front of my fence. I went out, received the chief with the usual ceremony, and saluted his two daughters who on this day only wore snow-white bran-new petticoats, painted in the brightest colours with very considerable taste. They wore necklaces of very handsome beads, earrings of the same material hung down on their shoulders, and their round arms were ornamented with flashing brass rings, while a new long tuft of feathers of the most brilliant hues was planted on the left side of the head. They left the blankets, which had hung loosely on their shoulders while riding, on their horses, and the latter were led off by the Mexican slave. After this both girls, but Cachakia not so quickly as her sister, hurried to me, and we exchanged the usual signs of good-will in the customary fashion; they pressed my hands, wound their pretty arms around me, and would assuredly have kissed me were not this mark of affection quite unknown to the Indians, and would have seemed to them highly ridiculous. After the first greetings they pointed to their father and then to my house, saying "Vino," and making the sign of drinking. The chief was a man of about fifty years of age, about six feet high, with broad shoulders, and arched chest, regular handsome features, straight nose, sharp black eyes, lofty forehead, and—a rarity among the Indians—a heavy moustache twisted into points. He had a haughty, imposing mien, and something very determined in his appearance, which was however kindly and hearty, so that we fraternized in a few moments. I proposed to lead him and his daughters to my house, but he turned to his tribe and said something I did not understand, upon which two men stepped out of the mob and joined us. We reached the gallery in front of my house to which I had had all my chairs carried, in order, if possible, to keep the interior clear for the curious guests. I made them sit down at table, and handed the chief the pipe I had myself lighted; he passed it to his neighbours, and so it went the round; while the two girls swung themselves in the rocking chair or the hammock hung up in the gallery, and smoked cigars. After the calumet of peace had passed round, the chief informed me of the purpose of his visit, to make peace with me, and introduced the other two Indians to me as the Chief of Peace and the Sage in Council, in which the Mexican acted as interpreter. Dinner was now served, the chief employing knife and fork as I did, while the two others used their fingers. Pahnawhay had fetched a buffalo robe out of the house and laid it on the ground, and sat upon it with her sister to have her dinner. I handed them the plates of food, but they returned me the knives and forks, saying it was easier work with their fingers. They amused themselves famously on their buffalo hide, and teazed each other with the heartiest merriment, for which their father gave them several warnings, to which they responded with a laugh. The chief now explained to me that many tribes of his nation entertained hostile feelings against the white men, but he hoped they would soon see it was to their advantage to enter into friendly relations with them, and that his tribe from henceforth would never commit any act of hostility against us.

We had finished dinner, and I told the chief that I now wished to give his men their dinner, on which he rose and said that he had better be present or else no order would be kept. We went out in front of the palisade after I had locked my house door, unseen by the two girls, and had the caldron of coffee, sweetened with honey and mixed with milk, brought out, as well as the bread, which last the chief distributed among the various families, telling them to use in coffee-drinking their own utensils, which consisted of shells, horns, and cocoa-nuts. There were above two hundred souls in camp, though among them all were only forty warriors.

I now showed the chief the fat ox, which I had shut up in the cow's milking enclosure, remarking at the same time that I intended to give it to his people, and asked whether it should be shot now, to which he assented. Königstein brought me a rifle and I shot the ox through the skull, after which some of the Indians skinned and carried the joints to camp. Ere long some thirty fires were lighted, round which the Indians lay and roasted the meat, while constantly running to the coffee-caldron to fill their vessels.

I was standing and admiring the appetites of these people, when Cachakia thrust her arm through mine and affectionately tried to induce me to go to my house with her to open the door, which, as she made me signs, she could not manage. I told her I would wait for her father, so that he might drink coffee with us. I walked through the groups of Indians to him, with my young lady friend hanging tightly on my arm. These Mescalero Indians were certainly the least civilized I had as yet seen: their dress consisted of leathern breech-clouts fastened round their hips, and large, strangely-painted dressed buffalo-hides. In the whole camp, however, I found nothing emanating from white men. On all their faces something shy, mistrustful, and savage could be noticed, which is not generally the case with other tribes. The people were, on the average, not very tall, but sturdy and broad-shouldered, and well fed; the women, however, were nearly all good looking, and I do not remember having seen so many pretty Indian girls together as in this camp. As we walked from fire to fire, which appeared to please the savages, Pahnawhay dashed every now and then like a young filly through the grass to my side. It had taken too long to open the house, and she now hung on my other arm, and pulled my beard as a punishment for having kept her waiting so long. I told her I was waiting for her father, she could go and bring him to my house while I went on in front with Cachakia. On arriving, my companion could not at all understand in what way the door was closed so tightly, and was quite surprised when I opened it with the key. She wished to try the experiment herself, and said she would keep the key so as to let herself in when she pleased, and it was not till I made her understand that in that case I could not open the house without her, that she returned it to me.

I now took my guitar from its case, and sitting down on my bed, let my fingers stray over the strings. Cachakia stood with widely-opened eyes and mouth before me, and became quite beside herself when I began playing. With one leap she sat cross-legged on the bed behind me, and peeping over my right shoulder, watched my performance. She was really delighted at the music, attempted to play the guitar herself, and became very angry and impatient when she could not manage it. At last Pahnawhay arrived with her father and the two ministers: we again took our seats in the verandah, and I ordered the coffee and cake, which my guests tremendously enjoyed, then I gave them all cigars to smoke, after which the chief told me that his people were well satisfied, were very good friends of mine, and would remain so. I took him to the arms-case in my house to let him see my weapons, about fifty first-rate implements. They did not fail to arouse my guest's admiration, and when we returned to the gallery I took a revolver, and at about one hundred yards put a bullet into a young tree, not nearly so wide as a man, and then fired the other five rounds in rapid succession. After this I placed in a few seconds a fresh cylinder in the lieu of the discharged one and fired the six rounds with equal rapidity, remarking the while that I could go on firing thus uninterruptedly. This weapon excited my guest's attention in the highest degree, and he looked at it for a long time with the greatest astonishment, and declared with the utmost seriousness that it was the grandest medicine he had ever seen. I made him a present of a very pretty hunting-knife, whose handle was composed of a roe-foot mounted with a silver shoe: his joy at it was childish, and in his excitement he assured me that he would lift the hair of the first enemy he conquered with it: this knife was also a great medicine.

The girls now left me no peace. I must fetch wine, which the three men at first looked at very suspiciously, but on my assurance that it was not fire-water, they tasted it, and drank with great satisfaction. When I carried the bottle back to the cupboard I filled a glass and put it on the table, making Cachakia a sign that it was for her, but at the same time I laid my finger on my lip so that she might not let the others know it, as I did not wish to open a fresh bottle, and this one was nearly empty. She understood me perfectly well, and as a proof nodded to me when I came out of the house, while a quiet smile played round her little mouth. I returned to my seat, and she carelessly rose, walked into my room, took the glass from the table, and gave me a nod unseen by the others, as she slowly drank the contents. Then she walked back into the gallery carelessly and sat down with us, like a person who is proud at having been preferred; but she cast her eyes down, as their sparkle might betray her.

Evening arrived; we supped, and when the moon had fully risen, went out to the Indian camp, as the chief wished to spend the night with his men, because the latter might be alarmed about him if he slept in the Fort with me. We had hardly reached the first fire, when we heard a fearful row at the other end of the camp, and the chief ran with his two colleagues in the direction of it. I was anxious about what was going on there, and hastened after them, accompanied by the two Indian girls. Two young men had quarrelled, and were engaged in a violent dispute when we came up, while the voices of the chief and his colleagues were raised to a loud key. Suddenly, however, the two men rushed to different fires, seized their bows and arrows, flew about a hundred yards apart into the prairie, and in a few minutes disappeared from sight. The chief shouted after them, but no one pursued them. The Mexican was standing not far from us at the next fire, and I called him up to give me an explanation of the disturbance. Pahnawhay, however, explained to me with a few very intelligible signs, that the two young men loved the same girl, and she had given her affection to both, upon which they quarrelled, and had run off to kill one another. The Mexican confirmed this statement, on which I asked why no one tried to prevent it, but I received the laughing reply, as if the thing were self-evident, that this was impossible.

A number of Indians had by this time collected round one of the fires, and Cachakia, taking me by the arm, drew me to it, when we saw a weeping and loudly lamenting girl seated with her head between her knees, with dishevelled hair almost concealing the whole of her person. This was the sweetheart of the two jealous knights, one of whom had probably by this time the deadly arrow in his heart. We were standing by the side of the unhappy girl, when a frightful yell echoed far across the moonlit prairie, the war-cry of the combatants, who had now met in open fight, as they had not been able, probably, to discern each other by crawling through the grass. The first note scarce reached us ere the weeping girl sprang up, threw back her hair, and hurling back the people standing round her, ran off with a shrill scream and disappeared. A deadly silence set in, as everybody expected to hear at the next moment that the fire was over; and all looking in the direction where the girl had disappeared, seemed to be anxiously holding their breath. At this moment the girl's piercing scream rang through the night air, and immediately after a fearful yell that pierced the marrow, and was answered by all the occupants of the camp pretty nearly. It seemed as if the latter had only been waiting for this signal, for now a number of men and squaws, some of whom held firebrands, ran off, and we could see these fires collected into a point far away. Cachakia said to me, "He is dead," and pressed her head down with her right hand to the left side, and closed her eyes. We soon saw the light moving towards us, until we could at length distinguish the separate torches, and the procession marched into camp. Four Indians bore the bloody corpse of the murdered man to the first fire, and laid it on the ground. I took a torch to see whether life still remained, but the last spark had disappeared. On his left side, near the heart, gaped three fearful wounds, which almost divided the chest in two parts, and his hair was bound into a mass by the curdled blood, while his head was cleft with a tomahawk. The Indians only take a scalp when it belongs to an enemy of their tribe. He was carried to the middle of the camp and covered with a buffalo robe. I asked Cachakia what would become of the other man and the girl? and she told me that the warrior must fly within four and twenty hours, and keep away till he had made it up with the dead man's relations, or otherwise they would take his life in return. Thus time was allowed him to fetch his traps, and if he came into camp during the period, he would not be molested, but after that he would be nowhere safe from them.

The chief now held a council with the relations of the dead man, which was just ended, when the victor's sweetheart appeared, silently led his horses to his fire, packed all his traps on them, and then went out into the night again without a word, while no one in camp appeared to have noticed her, although she walked openly towards the blazing fires. Indians do not consider it any harm for a girl to be a coquette, but they punish the infidelity of a wife, and frequently with death; but it is more common for the husband to cut off her nose, which indulgence is chiefly occasioned by the squaws being a portion of the husband's fortune, as he is obliged to buy them, employs them as servants and labourers, and can sell them again for ever, or for a time, as he pleases. I missed in this tribe more female noses than in any other I had seen.

In a very short time all became quiet again in camp, as if nothing extraordinary had happened; and after I had sat for a while with the chief, I wished him good-night, and was accompanied home by Cachakia, which attention appears to be one of the forms of politeness on the part of the savages; and even though the home of a parting guest is a long way from their camp, they always accompany him to the last highest point, whence they can look back on their camp.

Day was hardly dawned when I opened my door, and stepped out into the gallery to greet the fresh morning. In the Indian camp all appeared to be still resting except a few forms moving about in it. I saw through my glass that they had with them a horse and a mule, and ere long an Indian mounted the latter, and two others raised something that was wrapped in a large buffalo hide up to him. Then another Indian mounted the horse, and they went off up the river with the mule in front. I conjectured that it was the corpse of the murdered man which the two were carrying to the burial-place of the tribe, and found my supposition confirmed when I entered the camp. I had another caldron of coffee and a great quantity of maize bread carried to the camp, invited the chief, and his two councillors of state, and his daughters to breakfast, after which he told me that our friendship was now eternally concluded, and that he would depart with an easy mind. I made him a number of trifling presents, such as blankets, tobacco, looking-glasses, vermilion, &c.; gave the daughters several keepsakes as well, and my guests quitted me apparently remarkably well satisfied.

During the two days Owl and Tiger had not shown themselves, as the Delawares, though not open enemies, are not on very friendly terms with the Mescaleros, and so they went off hunting. Owl had received his wages long before, but still remained with us, as he seemed to enjoy himself, in which our cooking played a great part; but he now came one morning to me, and said the time had arrived when he promised to join his family, and so he must leave us, as he did not wish to render his friends alarmed about his safety. He rode to Lasar's and took his leave, when he received handsome presents: I, too, gave him numerous trifles for his fidelity and devotedness, and he went off, accompanied by Tiger, promising to pay me a visit very shortly.

CHAPTER XXIX
THE SILVER MINE

It was now the busiest time in the fields. The storms had blown down a great number of huge dried trunks standing in the fields, which had to be cut up and rolled away, which business was one of our hardest jobs. Moreover, I had the field enlarged, fenced in a very large extent of land, part prairie part forest, where I could turn my mares and colts out, and on rainy days had wood felled to let it dry, and afterwards employ it for building purposes. Axe and plough were equally active on the Mustang, and on many smaller streams in the vicinity, where civilization had set its foot. Thus whole patches of forest disappeared before man's busy hand, and the soil was robbed of its natural protection: the roots were turned up to be burnt or rot, and the earth was thus forced to receive and generate seeds foreign to it. The prairies, which a few years back had only been traversed by the desert animals, were now inhabited by herds of tame domestic creatures attached to a home, and the traveller's ear in these regions was no longer startled by hearing the unexpected sound of a cattle bell.

But nature will not allow laws to be prescribed to her without taking vengeance, or have changes made in her domestic arrangements forcibly by human hands. With the felling of forests and the turning up of the soil she sends diseases which check her insulter in the work he has begun, and punish him for his audacious inroads. It usually takes half a century ere nature is appeased and ceases to contend in this way with the mortals who trouble her; at least in Continental North America the diseases produced in this way usually increase for thirty years, and decrease for so long a period, until they entirely cease. This is the case with the interior, but not in the cities, where other relations occur in proportion with their expansion. At my settlement there had been for many years no malady, save those caused by external injuries; but now one or the other frequently complained of ague, bilious fever, flux, &c., and we often cursed the time when we saw the first white face settle amid our solitudes. At Lasar's matters were proportionately worse, for a hundred negroes would be down at the same time. For my part I had as yet been spared, while all my companions had been ill.

It was a very hot day when I rode to the nearest town, as usual only provided with a blanket, and during the nights lay by my fire in the open air with it pulled over me. I remained several days in town, and during the period felt a never-before-known ailing, and a reduction of my strength. My business being ended, I rode off about noon to reach the next house, whose inhabitants were friends of mine. I arrived there about an hour before sundown, but found the family in a great state of disorder, as the head of it had just died of a violent attack of fever. Although I felt very unwell, I did not like to be troublesome to the family, and rode on after a short halt. My illness increased with every quarter of an hour; at one moment I shook with cold, at another I felt as if I were being burned alive, and my head ached as if it would burst. I rode on, although I could hardly sit my horse, and at last tottered in the saddle, quite incapable of thinking; at the same time an indescribable burning thirst tortured me, and my tongue seemed to cleave to my roof, while I had a singing in my ears, as if there were thousands of grasshoppers inside my head.

It was nearly dark when I reached the middle of a very wide plain, that was covered with fine, very white sand, and in which the horse at every step sank above the hocks. I could no longer remain in the saddle; dismounted; sat down on the red-hot sand, fell back, and became perfectly unconscious: presently I fell into a profound sleep, from which I did not wake till the next morning. I looked around in surprise, and it was some time ere I could remember what had brought me here. I jumped up, and Trusty the faithful leapt barking around me, but I did not see Czar. My feet would hardly carry me, and my head was as heavy as if I had lead inside it. I looked for my horse's track, dragged myself along it, and to my great consolation saw the faithful creature in a hollow, nibbling some cactuses, and saddled and bridled as I had left him on the previous evening. I got on to his back with difficulty, and turned him in the direction of home. Thirst now began to grow unendurable. The sun burst forth, and poured its burning beams upon me with such fury, that I fancied I should never be able to reach a pool, about five-and-twenty miles distant, which contained the only water in the neighbourhood. This pond was at last the only thought of which I was capable; at the same time my head threatened to burst, and the fever shook me mercilessly. My horse walked along the familiar path through the heat, and bore me, when the sun was vertical, down a sand-hill to the edge of the pond, where I sank powerless, and crawled to the water in order to moisten my burning lips. But it was no water, but a thick, dark red mud, which was nearly boiling, and in which buffaloes had been wallowing very shortly before. No matter, I lay with my mouth over the thick fluid, and swallowed as much of it as I could. It was really a comfort, for the dryness of my throat

The Backwoodsman | 293

was removed; but my helplessness was so great that I could not resolve to leave the spot, though I lay exposed to the burning sun on the hot sand, and was only a short distance from shady trees.

I lay as I was, and had but one thought that the sun must kill me here, but still I could not muster up the courage to go away. At length, toward evening, when the sun was lower, the terrible fever gave way a little. I crept slowly into the shade, and soon was asleep under the tree. It was quite dark when I awoke, and though very faint, my head was clearer. I went up to Czar, who had been grazing by my side all this time, got into the saddle, and continued my journey, on which the pleasant light of the new moon lit me, and the cool evening breeze refreshed me. I rode till ten o'clock, when I reached the Lynx Spring, which I had christened after one of those animals that I had found dead here many years ago, and whose water was the best for miles around. I was quickly off Czar's back among the roots of the magnolia, beneath which the spring bubbled up, and I drank as if I should never be satisfied. I had a biscuit and a paper of coarse sugar about me. This was my supper and I washed it down with the pure fluid. I felt much refreshed, drew many a deep breath in the powerful breeze, and gazed at the patches of light around me which were thrown by the moon through the dense foliage, and through the violent motion of the leaves trembled and continually altered their shape. It was a very dangerous spot, as this water was the only spring for miles round, and wandering Indians often select it as their destination after travelling for a day through the desolate, waterless sand-plains; but I would not have ridden away even if I had been compelled to defend myself against a whole tribe. I had a few good cigars about me and lit one, which I smoked leaning against a tree, and, as I fancied, inhaling fresh strength at every breath.

It was about midnight when I set out to reach a camping-place at which I should not be so threatened as at the present one, and after filling my gourd with water I rode away, faintly lighted by the waning moon. I knew the road thoroughly, and the outline of the trees was sufficient to enable me to keep my course. I could, if my horse went at any pace, reach within an hour a well-known camping-place at which I had passed many a night, and which lay but a little way off my route. It certainly had no water, but excellent grass for my horse, and hence various sorts of game could generally be found there. The main point was, that it lay some distance from the principal Indian path and was tolerably concealed, so that a fire could be lighted there without any great risk of being seen from a distance. It soon became very dark after the moon had sunk behind the hills in front of me, and I was obliged to yield the reins to Czar, and leave it to him to find the road, while I sent Trusty on a little way ahead to make certain there was no danger. Every now and then, however, I saw by familiar clumps of trees or knolls that I was still on the right track, and I approached my destination rather quickly, considering the circumstances. The country through which I rode consisted more or less of sandy hills, covered with isolated black oaks, without any scrub, under which grew a very tall grass, disliked by cattle, which had now entirely decayed. So far as I could judge in the darkness, I was no longer any great distance from my camping-place, for I saw in a hollow on my left a wood running along my route, and which I knew to be a swampy patch, in which all the rain-water of the neighbourhood collected. On my saddle hung several new tin cups and a coffee-pot of the same material, which rattled at every movement of my horse and thus produced a ringing sound which could be heard for some distance. I dismounted and twined dry grass between them to keep them quiet.

I had just remounted my horse and was riding up a hill, when suddenly bright flames sprang up not far behind the latter and illumined the whole country around. In terror I stopped my horse, and saw in a few minutes that not only on the right of the hill the flames rose to the branches of the surrounding oaks, but that the fire was spreading with extraordinary fury on my right and in my rear. There was only one opening in this circle of fire on my right, near the swamp. I turned Czar round and galloped through the low oaks and tall grass toward the valley, in which I was obliged to trust to the safe foothold of my horse, as I could not see a sign of a path. The wind luckily was not very violent, or else I could not have escaped; as it was, I reached the wood before the fire darted down into the bottom behind me. I stood here on moist ground, between green bushes which the flames could not reach, and saw that they had fired the oaks and converted each of them into a fiery pyramid. The whole country ahead of me was now a mass of fire, whose tongues rose over fifty feet, in which the flames of the trees could be recognised by their dark red hue, while above them the ruddy clouds of smoke rose to the sky. Ere long, however, the burning oaks stood alone like pillars of fire on the denuded knolls, and the sparks flew out of them with a terrible roaring and crackling. I stood before this fire till day broke and showed me the black skeletons of the still burning trees, and the dark smoke-clouds rising above them. Ere long, only small flames crept round the bare trunks. I mounted my horse to get away from this scene of conflagration and rode up the wood, being obliged frequently to draw nearer to the burning trees to escape the swampy ground, until at last I was compelled to pass through the fire, owing to the impassable nature of the ground. The smoke, the black ash, and the heat were almost unendurable, and frequently heavy branches fell close to me. I rode as sharply as I could, and in an hour reached an open burnt clearing, where I was once more able to draw fresh breath. The fire had undoubtedly been lit simultaneously at different points for the purpose of burning me by the Indians, but none of them had ventured on to the prairie leading down to the bottom, as I could see over it, and if a fire had been lit there, I could have detected the culprits.

I hurried along in the refreshing morning breeze, and arrived about noon at a stream, on whose bank I turned into the adjoining wood, and granted my horse and myself a rest. On the road I had shot a turkey, which pacified my hunger and Trusty's, and I strengthened myself by a sound sleep, from which I did not awake till evening. During the whole day I had felt tolerably well, but looked with terror for the next, as I must expect that my fever would return every second day, so I rode till a rather late hour in order to reach a camp where I was tolerably certain I could pass the day without disturbance. Before I rode off, I dug up some roots of the tulip-tree and chewed them, swallowing the juice, till I reached camp. These roots are one of the best remedies against fever which nature offers in these regions. I slept till the sun disturbed me, and woke with aching head and weary limbs. I took Czar to graze, and then lay down on my blankets, after placing my gourd full of fresh water by my side. The attack of fever was not very violent: about 2 P.M. I was able to continue my journey, and slept that night on an affluent of the Mustang. The next morning I mounted at an early hour, in order to reach the Fort as soon as possible, and made Czar step out, as I felt very well.

About ten o'clock I rode through a prairie which ran down to the Mustang, which here an insignificant stream, flowed between high banks over loose pebbles, and was only deep at isolated spots. The prairie was covered with clumps of tall cactus and sunflowers, and I was riding between some of them when a large stag got up before me and stopped a little way ahead. I turned Czar half round and shot the stag, which fell, but got up again and ran off to the Mustang. As I saw that it was very sick, I sent Trusty after it, who soon disappeared with it in a thicket, and I had scarcely reloaded when I heard his hoarse bark and recognised by its tone that he was occupied with something else than the stag. I went up the wood as fast as Czar could carry me, leapt off and ran through the bushes to the bank where I heard Trusty's voice. A mortal terror assailed me on seeing Trusty in shallow water near a deep spot, with his left hind leg in the jaw of an alligator, whose skull he was smashing with his teeth, though this did not make it open its clenched teeth. I sprang at one bound into the river, in order to prevent the horrible brute from reaching deep water, to which it was retreating and was only a few feet from it. I sprang on the beast's back, held it between my knees tightly, and lifted it into the shallow water while it lashed its tail madly. I now pulled out a revolver, held it against the hinge of the jawbone, and fired one bullet after the other till the bones were splintered and the lower jaw fell off, liberating Trusty from his arrest. I examined him and found that his leg bone was not injured, though the flesh had suffered severely: at the same time he was losing much blood and appeared to be enduring great pain. The stag lay close to the scene of contest, so I drew it ashore and cut off the haunches; then I fetched Czar, bound one of them on either side of the saddle, packed a lot of bushes on the lot and spread my blanket over them, on which I raised Trusty, after I had bound up his wounds as well as I could with wet pocket handkerchiefs. I reached home in the afternoon, and at once made a decoction of the roots of the tulip and pomegranate and willow bark, in order to check the fever, which it soon effected, combined with a strict regimen.

Though these illnesses may usually be checked so easily, their frequent return affects the body greatly, and makes it more and more susceptible to injurious climates and atmospheric influences, so that the slightest change is often sufficient to bring back the fever. Still, all the diseases produced in these regions by an alteration in the surface of the ground are less dangerous than in any other part of the United States, which may be chiefly ascribed to the free unimpeded motion of the air, and the fact of no large swamps or standing waters existing here.

Tiger returned, after accompanying his friend to the Puerco River, whence the latter travelled on alone to Santa Fé, at which place he had promised to meet his friends about this time. My young Indian friend now complained very often that I allowed him to ride out hunting alone, which was most disagreeable to him, as I did not permit him to take Trusty, who was of such great value in the bear hunts, which are principally carried on at this season. I had certainly placed Leo, an excellent dog, at his service, but he was only half the value of Trusty. One evening Tiger returned from hunting, and told me that he knew where a very large bear was sleeping, but it would be difficult to get at it, as it was living in an old cypress that grew in the middle of the river and was too large to fell. He described the spot to me, and I at once recognised the tree. We talked about the matter at supper, and resolved to make an attempt to get hold of the sleeper on the next day.

On the following morning we put our weapons, axes, and dinner in the canoe and floated down the river in it. It was carried along by the current like a dart, so that we were obliged to steer very carefully between the numerous rocks. In an hour we stopped at the cypress, which was nearly six feet in diameter. We cut down some saplings on the bank, conveyed them to one side of the tree, and fastened them together so as to form a raft on which we could stand; we then placed the canoe on the other side of the tree, and set to work with our axes felling it. In addition to Tiger and myself, Königstein and Antonio had come, so that one of us was always able to rest. About noon we had got some distance through the tree, and as we had heard nothing of the bear, we began greatly to doubt whether it was in it; but Tiger insisted, in spite of our laughter and chaff, that it was sleeping there. We dined, drank the health of the occupant of the tree, and then set to work again. In a few hours the supports of the tree became so weak that it was time to take precautions lest it should fall on us. We had hewn it on the side of the raft, toward which it naturally hung, and we now all proceeded to our canoe and held ourselves in readiness to push off at any moment. We gave the tree a few more cuts, and ere long we heard the first sound of cracking in its wood. We were certain that it could only fall over the raft, and the only danger was that it might slip backwards from the stump, in which case we might easily be sunk. A couple more blows and the lofty crown of the cypress bent more over the raft, one more stroke and it groaned and cracked at its base: we pushed off, and with a frightful crash it fell into the river and splashed up the water so high that we were completely wet through, while the splinters and broken branches flew in all directions. We involuntarily held our heads down into the boat, which was raised a great height by the waves; but after the first oscillation, we all burst into a hearty laugh and mockingly asked Tiger, "Where is our bear?" At the same moment, however, the bear leapt out of the middle of the splinters covering the surface of the river, and while the water poured down and prevented it from seeing, it laid its huge fore-paws on the floating pieces of wood and sought a support, by means of which it could lift itself out of the disagreeable element. "The bear!" everybody shouted, and we seized our rifles and fired at it. At the moment when it reached the stern of our boat and was trying to get into it by means of its paws, Königstein ran at the brute with his sharp axe and buried it deep in the skull of the enormous animal, and then drove into its carcase the bent iron point of the boat-hook to prevent it from sinking. We pulled quickly ashore, where we hauled in our quarry with lassos.

Antonio ran back to the Fort and fetched our cart with two mules, with which he joined us before sunset. With the help of the animals we pulled first the bear and then the canoe on land, rolled the former into the cart, then raised the canoe on the back of it, where we secured it, and so drove back to the Fort, with the stern of our boat trailing along the grass. The bear gave us a large quantity of splendid fat, and its smoked flesh long supplied our table.

We and our friends on the Mustang now rarely visited the districts lying beyond the distance of a day's journey, as our domestic duties kept us more or less constantly at our settlements; but we became all the better acquainted with our immediate neighbourhood, and on our hunting excursions learnt every path and locality. I had found but a few miles from us the traces of an old Spanish settlement, and the remains of a forge, whence I concluded that the precious metals had been found here, and that they still existed in the vicinity. Old Lasar was a man of most enterprising spirit, and as he had more working power at his command than he could employ profitably on his cultivated ground, he always desired some other speculation by which he could derive greater profit from his slaves. A silver or gold mine was always one of his favourite schemes, and he quickly turned the conversation to the subject, expressing an opinion that the mountains near us certainly contained the precious metals. He came to me one day greatly excited, and told me with great mystery that an Indian had been to him and told him under a promise of the profoundest secrecy, that he knew a spot where the old Spaniards worked silver mines, and offered to show it to him if he would promise to hold his tongue as to whom he obtained his information from, as the Indians would certainly kill him if they discovered that he had revealed the spot. Lasar stated that he had told the Indian to return in eight days, when he would ride with him, and reward him if he really pointed out the silver mine. The old gentleman then begged me to join him on this excursion, on which he only intended to take his son John. I promised to do so, and when the appointed day arrived, I rode over to Lasar's, accompanied by Trusty, and found the Indian there, whom I took for a Mescalero, though he stated himself to be a Shawnee.

We left Lasar's settlement at noon, rode west toward the Rio Grande, and crossed the hills on that river by a path which I had not known before. We passed the night on the banks of this river, and on the next morning proceeded into the hills in a south-west direction. The path, to the great comfort of our horses, wound along the hill-sides without crossing any steep ascents, and our Indian guide appeared quite at home here, for he often left the main path and followed scarce visible tracks, which always brought us back sooner or later to the main path, while we had escaped a steep hill or a thick cedar coppice. We found here, too, though many miles farther south, traces of the forest fire which Tiger and I had occasioned against our will, and many bare knolls rose between the cedar woods which had been robbed on that occasion of their leafy covering. We passed the third night on the western slopes of these hills, and on the next day reached their spurs, whence we looked down on a very extensive plain, which appeared to be excellently watered, and displayed a rich tropical vegetation in its summer garb. Although these plants, which belong to the real tropical region, especially the varieties of the palm, do not attain such luxuriance and such gigantic size as they do farther south, they still grow in these protected valleys very powerfully, and surprise the traveller by their foreign but agreeable appearance. We marched through the valley, and camped for the night at the foot of the hills bordering it on the west, not far from which spot was said to be the ancient mine to which the Indian promised to lead us on the following morning.

It was one of those mild southern spring nights when man feels beneath the star-enamelled vault of heaven that he is nowhere better in health or stronger than in the open air. The odour of the flowers had sunk upon the earth with the motionless air, and the glistening insect world sparkled and flashed like streams of diamonds from the dark shade of the evergreen shiny foliage. Lying round our small camp-fire, we were soon lulled to sleep by the feathered songsters of the night, among which the mocking-bird appealing to its mate was the most remarkable, and we negligently allowed the last flames to die out; but at a late hour we were startled by the roar of a jaguar close to us, and on awaking we recognised the sound of flying horses. We ran to our cattle, and only found Czar and John's mare, snorting and dragging at their bonds, while the Indian's horse and Lasar's mule had bolted, and we heard Trusty barking down the glen. We quickly blew up our fire, and threw fresh wood on it; but the damage was done, and we might reckon with certainty on the loss of one if not both beasts. We spent the rest of the night on the watch, and just as day dawned, and we had breakfasted I rode accompanied by Trusty, down the glen, while John and the Indian proceeded to the mountains in search of our fugitives. Only Lasar remained in camp, as walking through the grass was too fatiguing for him. I followed the foot of the hills, along which ran a stream overshadowed by yuccas, tree-like aloes, gigantic cactuses, palms and mimosas, and had ridden about four miles, following the tracking dog, when the latter showed me on the clayey bank on which no grass grew the hoofmarks of our mule and the imprints of a jaguar running down to the stream. Not long after, on riding round a projecting clump of shrubs, I noticed in the grass Lasar's mule, and upon it an enormous jaguar, which appeared to be asleep, as its golden-spotted body lay stretched out and motionless. I led Czar back into the bushes, and then crept down the stream nearer to the beast of prey, until I concealed myself within shot in a tuft of old mimosa trees, from which I could survey it. Laying my rifle on a low branch, I aimed at the centre of the brute's back, which was turned toward me, as its head rested on the mule. I fired, the jaguar sprang up, but fell on its side immediately, and while uttering an awful roar, looked about the valley in search of its assailant. It was unable to rise on its hind-legs, and strove to drag itself on its forepaws to the adjacent water. I had reloaded in the meantime, and stepped out of my hiding-place on to the grass plot. The jaguar now saw me, its fury increased with every step I took, and dragging itself toward me it made the hills ring with its savage roars. I walked pretty nearly up to it, and put an end to its life with a bullet through the head; then I went to Lasar's mule, whose belly was slit up, and one of its legs devoured. The jaguar must have caught it up while running, for on its croup I found numerous wounds where the beast had buried its claws.

After taking the animal's skin, I rode back to camp, and bore Lasar the sad news, which painfully affected him, as this mule was a favourite of the whole family, and its loss the more grieved him, because it belonged to his wife, and was always ridden by her. It was not to be helped, however, and so when John and the Indian returned with the horse, we started for the silver mine. Lasar saddled the Indian's horse and rode it, while the latter walked ahead of us.

In about two hours we really arrived at an old deserted shaft, into which we were able to go about fifty paces; then, however, it was blocked up, and any farther advance was impossible. In it we saw a number of scattered pieces of ore, and also found several of them under the turf at the entrance of the shaft, which proved that a long time must have elapsed since any works had gone on here. We took a good deal of the ore with us, and after carefully noticing the bearings of the place, we rode back to the valley, from time to time making a sketch of the localities, so that we might find them again hereafter. On our homeward road the Indian guided us on foot, so that we did not progress so rapidly: but for all that we got back without any misadventure, and produced great grief in Lasar's family by the announcement of the death of the faithful mule. The old gentleman was determined to take the requisite steps next year with the Mexican Government to buy the land on which the silver mine was, and then set to work on it.

A few days after my return to the Fort, I was surprised by an unexpected visit from my old acquaintance Warden, whom I had not seen for a long time, and who declared that he could no longer resist the desire of seeing me again. He had been living principally on the western side of the Cordilleras, and during his perilous hunting expeditions on the Gela and the Rio Colorado had got as far as the Gulf of California. His powerful horse had been killed there in a skirmish with the Apaches, and he had saved his own life under the greatest dangers, after the savages had incessantly pursued him for several weeks. We again sat till far into the night, and listened to the interesting stories of this daring man who had gained nothing by all his privations, fatigue, and frightful perils, except the recollection of them, but had thus perfectly carried out his sole object. As before, he remained some weeks with us; but then he felt compelled to leave this quiet life, which he could not endure. He saddled his horse, in order to continue his solitary life. On parting I made him a present of a brace of pistols, for which he was most grateful, and he galloped over the prairie and disappeared from my sight on the horizon. It was the last time I saw or heard of him. I often asked western hunters about him, but none could give me any news of him, and in all probability he at last met the fate, which he seemed to desire and seek, a solitary death in the desert.

CHAPTER XXX
THE PURSUIT

Lasar and I were occupied for several weeks on the settlement of Messrs. Clifton and MacDonnell and a Mr. Wilson. The latter had arrived from Georgia with a considerable fortune and numerous negroes, and the three young men settled together on Turkey Creek, in the neighbourhood of Widow White. We helped them by word and deed, and in a short time a very large lot of ground was cleared and sown with maize, although it was late in the year for it, and a large garden laid out, and the necessary buildings erected at a spot where very recently an axe had never been laid against a tree, or a plough had turned a furrow in the earth. The three young men set eagerly about the heavy work which such a new settlement demands, and were busy the whole day in the garden or the field, or else in felling wood. While doing so, they often forgot that they and not we were now living on the outermost Indian frontier, and constantly went from home unarmed. They went into the woods with an axe to fell trees, or rode without any weapons into the prairie, to drive home their milch kine, or fetch their draught oxen. Lasar and I had frequently blamed them for this negligence, but it was of no use, and often when we visited them, one or the other was away from home unarmed; while we, during the years, that we had no neighbours, when working in the field, chained up our dogs round it, in order to be informed of the approach of stalking Indians, and carried our rifles either on the plough or on our backs, they ploughed and worked for days without a dog or any other weapon but their hands. Their dwelling stood on the south bank of the river where it joined the prairie; but they had their field on the northern side in a wood, which extended for a considerable distance.

At an early hour one morning they all three crossed the river with a few negroes, in order to thin the growing maize crop, which operation is generally performed in the morning, as you are obliged to stoop constantly, which is very fatiguing in the hot sun. All three took their weapons into the field, and rested them against the fence, as they thought it too much trouble to carry them on their backs. They followed the rows of maize, one behind the other, from one end of the field to the other, and were again nearing the spot where they had placed their rifles, when suddenly some fifty Indians dashed over the fence with a loud war yell and attacked them. They could not think of flight, as the Indians surrounded them before they could recover from their first terror. Resistance was equally impossible, as they were quite unarmed, and hence the sole chance of escape lay in the mercy of the barbarians to whom they surrendered. The two negroes were accidentally at the other end of the field, and, at the first glimpse of the Indians, leapt over the fence into the woods, to save themselves by hiding in its recesses; on looking round, they saw that each of the three young men was surrounded by a party of Indians busied in tying his arms behind his back. They ran through the wood to the river, swam across it, and on reaching the houses, leapt with the other negroes on horses and mules, fled with the utmost speed toward the south across the prairie, and reached my Fort before sunset, horrified and half frightened to death.

The terrible news aroused all my people. I at once sent a negro to Lasar's to tell him of what had happened, and at the same time beg him to join me as speedily as possible, in order to pursue the Indians, and, if possible, save the prisoners, during which time we made our preparations for immediate departure. I had provisions got ready and packed on a mule, which this time was not faithful Jack, as he had been galled by a badly fastened saddle; after this a stock of ammunition was laid in, and we sat down to supper, which meal we had hardly finished when our friends from Mustang Creek, eight in number, galloped over the prairie, led by old Lasar himself, who was fire and flame, and vowed revenge like the youngest of us. Tiger, Antonio, Königstein, and one of the colonists of the name of Lambert, accompanied me, and we were soon urging our horses at full speed through the gloomy forest.

Tiger led our party, who trotted on as long as the moonlight lasted, but then fell into a walk, and towards morning reached the deserted blockhouses of the prisoners. We expected that the Indians would have burnt them down, but found them uninjured, which proved to us in what haste they must have departed with their quarry. We rode through the river into the wood, and found the spot where the savages had lifted their prisoners over the fence, and led them to its northern end. Here we found the traces of numerous horses galloping in the direction of the northern mountains. Tiger examined all the signs very carefully, and after we had followed the trail for about an hour, dismounted and sought about in the grass. Ere long he stretched out his arms and parted fingers to the north and north-west, and told me that the fellows we were pursuing had divided here, and were pursuing different routes, which fact I was also able to recognise after a slight investigation. I asked Tiger what we were to do, but he laughed, and joining his hands together and pointing to the north, he stated that the Indians would come together again on the other side of the mountains in two days.

We now followed a trail which ran along a deeply-trodden buffalo-path, and reached before sunset a spot in a valley covered with isolated rocks, trees, and bushes, which was bordered on both sides by steep hills. Here Tiger suddenly stopped and leapt from his horse. I rode up to him, and he showed me on the bare rocks that several horses had left the track and turned off to the left down the glen. He showed me several pebbles which had been turned over by the horses, and on the rocks the graze of their hoofs, as well as here and there a trampled leaf or a broken blade of grass. He followed this trail carefully, and requested me to follow him, while making a sign to the others to remain on the path. A few thousand yards farther on the track wound between large masses of stone till we reached a clearing, on the other side of which we found signs of an extinguished fire near a spring. Tiger picked up a blackened bit of wood and showed me by rubbing it with his finger that the wood was still wet, and hence, as it lay in the open sunshine, must have gone out shortly before. He now begged me to call up our comrades, so that we might rest ourselves and our tired horses here for a little while. I rode up to them, and when we returned to Tiger, he showed us behind the spring the shambles where one of the unhappy prisoners had ended his life. On a large flat stone we saw a quantity of curdled, half-dry blood, and behind it lay the entrails of a man. Round the stone we found marks of boot-heels, which had probably belonged to the murdered man, and had been put on by one of the savages. Our fury against them was terrible, and we would gladly have pursued them without resting had our horses been able to carry us, but they were too tired, and greatly required a rest.

We supped, and slept till near day, and by dawn we were following the trail again, along the path which we had quitted on the previous evening. Without halting longer than was necessary, we rode hard all day through the most impassable regions of the San Saba mountains, and reached in the evening the prairies on their north side. We were still on the same trail, which had been made by five or six horses, and unsaddled when the sun had long disappeared behind the hill, and Tiger was unable to follow the trail. We had ridden very sharply, so that our horses would hardly touch the good fodder here offered them, and we had no sooner watered them in an adjacent stream, than they lay down in the grass with a long breath and fell asleep. We did not tie them up, so that they might graze directly they awoke, but kept up a good fire the whole night, and posted a sentinel.

At daybreak we were *en route* again and hurrying after Tiger, who led us along the foot of the mountains. About noon we rode through one of the streams that flow into the Colorado, and found in the wood on its bank a deserted camp, from which the fugitives could not be gone long, as the bushes and weeds trampled by the horses were not dry yet. We merely watered our horses and then urged them on, for Tiger believed that we must catch up the Indians that same evening, as their horses were tired and did not raise their feet high from the ground. Evening arrived, and in the distance another forest rose out of the prairie, which we reached with night; but our foe had gone farther on, and we were compelled to halt again, as we could not follow their trail. Our guide consoled us with the morrow, and said their horses could not last out any longer. We rode the whole day, however, without seeing anything of the Indians, save the track of their horses. About sunset we rode into another forest, in which we hoped to find running water: we soon halted on its bank and noticed on the other side the last camping-place of the Indians, for several of their fires were still burning, and Tiger said that they now supposed themselves out of danger and would not ride so fast. We crossed the stream, in order to occupy the deserted camp, but had scarce reached it when Tiger called to me and pointed to a young tree, with a smooth shining bark, the lower part of which was dyed with blood. He told me that one of the white men had been murdered here: the Indians had tied him up to the tree and fired arrows at him, and the bark displayed numerous marks of their points. At the height of a man the tree was sprinkled with blood, and over it we found a deep cut, which appeared to have been made by a tomahawk. The Indians seemed to have come together again here, for a number of fires had been lighted, and the trampled ground indicated a large troop of horses. We all insisted on riding on at once, but Tiger reminded us that it was impossible to follow the trail, and by overriding it we might easily lose much time, and give the cannibals a chance of escape.

Our impatience had attained the highest pitch, all were ready to start, but it was still too dark: we stood by our grazing cattle and counted the minutes till dawn appeared, and allowed us to see the track of our enemies once more. Then we hastened on, and joyfully greeted every thicket in front of us, as we hoped to find the cannibals in it and be able to take vengeance on them for our friends. Our hopes were frequently disappointed, and the sun was approaching the western hills when we still urged on our awfully tired horses, following the trail of the Indian horses, which could not possibly be far from us, as their excreta on the path plainly indicated. Once again a wood rose before us on the prairie, but it was still so distant that we could not hope to reach it before dark. Tiger told me that we must either ride very sharply so as to reach the wood by daylight, or camp on this side and approach the wood at dawn, as we should get the worst of it if we came upon the savages in the darkness. We resolved on the former course, and collected the last strength of our animals. Spurring and flogging we went on at a trot or a gallop, as if certain of reaching our destination to-day. One of our friends might possibly be saved by a few minutes' sharp riding, and so we paid no heed to the fatigue and pace of our horses. We rapidly approached the wood, but so did the sun the hills, which soon spread their lengthened shadow over the plain. The country before us became more uneven and covered with large blocks of stones, and here and there rose an isolated clump of trees and bushes, while the forest appeared to be half an hour's ride distant. The darker it grew the sharper we rode, and we dashed at a gallop between the rocks toward a patch of young oaks, with Tiger some distance ahead of us. While galloping round some rocks I saw him suddenly turn his piebald towards us and halt in the clump of trees, which we reached in a few minutes, and Tiger informed us that the savages were sleeping no great distance ahead on the barren bank of a river.

Our excitement was frightful; trembling with eagerness we fastened our steaming horses to the long branches of the young oaks, thrust our holster pistols in our belts, and advanced, leaving Antonio with the horses, silently and noiselessly after Tiger, when it had been arranged that I should give the signal for a general attack by firing first. The moon was high but lighted us poorly; the daylight, however, had not quite faded away when we emerged from the rocks and reached a small knoll, over which we saw almost invisible columns of smoke rising at various points. We spread out here in a long line, and crept up the hill, covered by some isolated rocks. When we reached the top, we saw the savages about thirty yards from us collected round several fires. A deadly silence brooded over the slightly illumined landscape, which was only broken by the rustling of the rapid stream, on whose banks the Indians were encamped. The glow of the fires cast a dark red reflection over the brown bodies of the reclining savages sufficient to enable us to see them more distinctly, while the light of the moon illumined the sights on our rifles.

All our barrels were pointed at the cannibals, and we could hear our hearts beating, while they did not suspect the approaching vengeance, and were most of them asleep. The wide chest of one of the ruffians was lit up by the fire right in front of me, while he was gazing into the ashes with his head resting on his right arm. The sight of my rifle was pointed at his heart when I pulled trigger. At the same moment the rifles of all my comrades cracked, and directly after we fired our second barrels among the rising Indians, who for a moment raised their war yell, but then fled in great confusion and dashed into the river, beneath the fire of our revolvers and pistols. In this faintly lighted scene of fury and terror, the long red and white striped silk handkerchief on Tiger's head waved, the broad blade of his heavy knife glistened in his right hand, his shrill voice filled the ears of the cannibals with the war cry of the Delawares, and immediately after the first shot he flew, worthy of his name, among them, and spread death among their ranks. Trusty, too, forgot his usual obedience, and pinned one of the savages by the throat who had fired an arrow at him; he killed the Indian in a few minutes, and then dragged him about in the grass, satiating his fury. In a short time the battle field was deserted by the enemy, with the exception of two-and-twenty killed and wounded they left on it, the latter of whom Tiger soon sent to join the former with his tomahawk. His war axe flew from skull to skull, and with every blow drove a soul out of its earthly tenement, after which he raised the hair of several whom he had killed in action.

The fight was hardly over, when a familiar voice called several of our names, especially Lasar's, mine, and Tiger's. It came from a little way off the camp and reached us but faintly. We ran in the direction, and to our joyful surprise found MacDonnell bound hand and foot lying on the grass behind a rock. His bonds were quickly cut, but he was unable to get up; we bore him to the nearest fire, blew it into a bright flame, and now looked at the death-like face of our poor friend, who since his captivity had endured death in a thousand shapes, and envied his two comrades their release from torture. He was so fatigued that he was unable to sit up. The joy at our appearance, and the fear lest we might go away again without finding him, had given him the strength to raise his voice, but now a greater faintness naturally set in, and he could scarce make signs to us to give him water. The fresh draught was handed him, then we laid him on a bed made of buffalo skin and left him to sleep, which, with the consciousness that he was saved and among friends, did him more good than anything else we could have offered him. The large fire lit up the plain around us, and displayed the victims we had sacrificed to the blood of our friends: farther on it shone on the great number of utterly exhausted Indian horses, most of which were lying fastened to lassos among the large stones in the grass. Although we did not apprehend any attack from the fugitive savages, many of whom had doubtless killed themselves by leaping off the high banks into the river which dashed over rocks, and who too possessed no weapons that could be dangerous to us, we still posted sentries on both sides of the camp, and lit large fires in order to be able to watch the horses, as it was very probable that the Indians would attempt to recover them toward morning, after the moon had gone down. Our own horses we tied up in the grass close to camp, and then lay down by turns to rest as far as our state of excitement permitted it.

Morning dawned without our having been disturbed, and with the growing light we began to survey the field of battle and investigate the details of the events of last evening. The savages were a tribe of Mescaleros, and as we afterwards learned the same who had made the attack on Mrs. White a few months before. Among the dead was their chief, who had been killed by the first shot fired, which was the principal reason why the assailed did not offer a greater resistance, for they only discharged a few arrows, one of which hit Trusty, while another passed through Königstein's thigh. The weapons lay scattered about the battle-field. On the lofty bank were distinct signs where the fugitives had leapt off it; but we found below no signs of them on the rocks jutting out of the river, as they had apparently fallen into the deep water between them. For all that, there was no doubt but that many had not reached the opposite bank alive, for the stream was too rapid for a man to swim across it.

Our friend MacDonnell still lay motionless asleep, and we did not disturb him. It was bright daylight when John Lasar summoned us to the fires of the savages, where we found the roasted and partially-gnawn bones of one of the murdered men, while Königstein discovered other remains of the dead bodies behind a rock. At about ten o'clock, MacDonnell woke and felt greatly strengthened; we gave him food and a cup of wine to drink, but he was very weak and terribly excited, so that we prohibited him from talking about his own sufferings or those of his own comrades. About noon, we prepared to start and carry off the horses, of which we had captured forty-six, among them being several first-rate animals. Tiger at once sought out the leader of the troop, an old mare, whose head and tail were hung with all sorts of ornaments, and so soon as he led it away all the others would follow it. He bound the mare to a tree, let loose the other horses and wound the lassos round their necks, upon which they all collected round the old mare. We then saddled our horses, selected the best saddle of the savages, very handsome Mexican one, for MacDonnell, put it on one of the captured horses which appeared good-tempered and safe, and covered it with a buffalo hide, a large quantity of which we also found, then we lifted our suffering friend on the horse. Tiger marched ahead of us, leading the mare behind us by a lasso and followed by all the Indian horses, while we rode behind and drove on the laggards. Thus we rode slowly to the south, and camped at sunset in a narrow strip of wood on a stream, where we found good pasture for the numerous horses. We merely fastened up the leading mare and our own cattle near the fire. MacDonnell rapidly recovered; the ride had done him good, and he was now able to walk again. We made him a soft bed by the side of the fire, and he told us the chief events of his captivity.

No sooner had the savages seized the three young men in the field than they bound them, lifted them over the fence, and then carried them to their horses. Here three Indians took them before them, and the whole band flew out of the wood into the prairie, where the savages soon halted and went off in different directions. MacDonnell was taken off to the right with ten horsemen, while Lyons followed the path, and Clifton was carried to the left. The savages rode without halting all that day and the next night with MacDonnell, without giving him water or food, until they allowed their horses to graze for a few hours the next morning, when they gave him some roast meat. Then they hurried on with him again, and only stopped to water their horses, until the latter, toward evening, refused to go any farther, in spite of the incessant blows. They unsaddled in a wood by a stream, and roasted meat at a fire, after laying him with his feet bound among the bushes. His hands had swollen through the bonds, and pained him terribly, but his complaints and groans were unheeded by the cannibals, and it was only after long entreaty that they gave him a drink of water. Toward morning, they rode on, and reached in a few hours a river, on whose bank they unsaddled in a thick wood, and rested with the utmost carelessness, while he was placed with his back against a tree near the fire.

Soon after, another troop of Indians came up, and MacDonnell recognised the man who had given orders at the outset, and whom he took for the chief. He was now wearing a portion of Lyons' clothes and had put on his boots. This savage brought his horse to the fire, and to his horror, MacDonnell saw the severed limbs of his unhappy companion hanging from the saddle, which the Indians now unfastened and threw near the fire. The savages then gathered together and the chief placed bits of the flesh of the unfortunate Lyons on spits and devoured them when roasted. The Indians seemed to pay no attention to MacDonnell, but to listen to every sound, and several times the chief laid his ear on the ground in order to hear more distinctly. Ere long, other Indians arrived, and at noon the last of them with Clifton. He looked at MacDonnell inquiringly, but neither had the heart to utter a word. Clifton's feet were also bound, and he was placed against a tree, while all the savages lay around the fire and talked with much animation, pointing first to Mac and then to Clifton. At last the chief stretched out his hand toward Clifton and said several words in a commanding voice, upon which several men leaped up, carried the prisoner to a tree a little lower down the wood, and fastened him to it in a standing position with leathern thongs. Most of the young Indians, in the meanwhile, assembled with bows and arrows about fifty yards from Clifton, and awaited the chief's signal to commence firing. The signal was given, and the first arrow was buried in the entrails of the unhappy victim, whose cries of agony made the forest ring. Thus one fired after the other, till Clifton's whole body was pierced with arrows and his head hung down. Upon which the chief leapt up, swung his tomahawk over his head, and hurled it at the murdered man. It flew into the tree close to Clifton's head and remained imbedded. The chief went up to Clifton, plucked the hatchet out of the tree, and buried it deeply in the unhappy man's skull. After this the cannibals fell upon the corpse, which they cut up and each carried a piece to the fire. MacDonnell witnessed the whole fearful scene, and now the chief came up to him and said something he did not understand, while pointing to the north, whence Mac assumed that the same fate awaited him farther on in that direction. The savages started again ere long and rode by shorter stages to the camp where we surprised them, and where they had arrived but a few hours before us.

This description had recalled to Mac's mind all the scenes of horror, and he fell back exhausted on his bed. We restored him with a little wine-and-water, and begged him to hold his tongue and rest while we got supper ready and looked after the horses. During the night we posted four sentries and lit up the Indian horses with large fires. It passed without disturbance, and the next morning we continued our progress to the south. We now made but short marches, as our own horses were very tired, but the captured ones were so exhausted that we could hardly drive them on with long sticks. We on several occasions unsaddled at noon because we found good pasturage on water, and rested till the next morning, so that we might not have to spend the night at a worse spot.

One evening we found ourselves in the middle of an open prairie, on which only isolated mosquito trees could be seen, and camped at a spot where there were several ponds, and an old fallen mosquito-tree lay, which, judging from the fire marks, had offered burning materials to earlier travellers across this plain. The nearest woods to the south lay on the remotest horizon on the San Saba Mountains, and we did not calculate on reaching them till the next day. We lay in a hollow of the prairie, between two small elevations, and fastened our riding-horses and the leading mare to lassos driven into the ground, while the captured horses grazed on the bottom. The evening was splendid, and as Mac was all right again, we were in the best spirits. After supper the conversation turned on the captured horses, and we resolved to throw dice for them. The mare was allotted to me without throwing, as I gave up my chance of all the rest. Ere long all the horses had owners. Antonio and Lambert resolved to try theirs the next morning, as they were not very well mounted, and everybody praised the good qualities of his horse, and expounded how the animals must be treated and ridden to make first-raters of them. Thus the night arrived, during which we again posted sentries on the nearest mounds, but it passed without any alarm. Day dawned; we blew up our fire and got breakfast ready, while the horses were grazing around us. The sun rose while we were lying carelessly on our buffalo robes round the fire and drinking coffee, when suddenly a fearful yell reached our ears over the next height, and a band of thirty horse Indians thundered down the hill-side towards us, waving in one hand their buffalo-robes over their heads, shaking in the other tin pots, gourds, and buffalo-bladders filled with pebbles, and uttering the strangest and most awful yells. In an instant the troop passed us, and dashed right through our fire and camp. They went over us like a tornado, and our terrified horses, which had torn themselves loose, dashed over the prairie in front of them, trailing the broken lassos after them. Before we had seized our rifles, the Indians were so far off that the bullets we sent after them produced no effect, and we silently stared after them till they disappeared from sight over the last rising ground on the prairie. We asked each other, with our eyes, what was to be done, but no one was yet able to speak, the fright and the heavy loss had fallen upon us too unexpectedly, and it was long ere we could think of the immediate future: at length all eyes were turned to me, as if I could help them. This confidence restored my power of speech, and I told my companions in misfortune that I was able to lead them home without horses, and that MacDonnell's life was worth more than our animals.

I had hardly spoken to this effect, when Königstein shouted to me, and pointed in the direction where the horses had disappeared; and though it was so far off, I recognised Czar and the cream colour flying over the prairie, pursued by five Indians. I ran towards them as fast as my legs would carry me, and fired a bullet at the Indians long out of range, but which they must have heard "pinging," for they gave up their pursuit and merely fired a few harmless arrows after the horses, which now dashed up to me and stopped panting and snorting. Czar came up to me and laid his head on my shoulders while looking round in wild terror after his pursuers. I led him into camp, where both the horses were greeted with loud shouts of joy. We now held a grand council, and soon agreed to cache our baggage in a hollow near at hand, cover it with turf, and then start for home on foot, in which, of course, we could only cover short distances; at the same time we arranged that Mr. Lasar should ride the cream colour, and Mac Czar, while we also packed our food on the animals.

The whole day passed before we had cached our baggage, so that we slept another night at this inhospitable spot. The next morning we saddled and packed, and after carefully taking the direction of the nearest tree with the compass, we began our wearisome journey. On reaching the tree we blazed it with a knife, and then started for another, and so on, carefully marking each, so that we might be able to find our way back to our traps from tree to tree. The road to the San Saba Mountains through the tall prairie grass was one of the unpleasantest I ever followed. There, however, the ground, though hilly and stony, was still adapted for human feet, and we soon grew accustomed to walking. Tiger had not a word to say for himself, he was revolving vengeance on the Lepans, who had stolen his faithful piebald, and swore that the Delawares should take many of their scalps in return.

After several weeks of unspeakable fatigue and privation, we at length arrived one evening at Widow White's, who received us with great cordiality and delight. We at once sent her son to the Fort to fetch riding horses for all of us, as we had had quite enough walking, and stopped the while with our kind hostess. Late the next evening the long-looked-for horses arrived from the Leone; we let them rest for the night, and on the next morning said good-bye to the widow, and started for home, which we reached at an early hour and found horses there for Lasar and his companions to carry them at once to Mustang River. The loss of Lasar's handsome horse and of John's mare again caused fresh sorrow in the family, with whom they had been favourites; but I willingly put up with the loss of my two horses and mules, and considered myself remarkably fortunate in recovering Czar and the cream colour. The last lesson which we gave the Mescaleros seemed to have had an intimidating effect on the Indians generally, as we neither saw nor heard anything of them for several months.

Tiger, during this period, rode a splendid black horse of mine, which I had been always obliged to leave at home, as it was too timid and impetuous for hunting purposes. Now that it was ridden daily, it became a first-rate horse, and Tiger often said that it was better than his piebald. Great was my surprise when Tiger knocked me up early one morning, and on going out of my house I saw the piebald quietly grazing: on waking Tiger had found it tied up in front of his tent, and told me that the Lepans were frightened, because his tribe would come in the autumn and learn their hostile behaviour. With a sad look he remarked that he would now be obliged to give me back the black horse, he supposed, and was quite beside himself with joy when I told him that I made him a present of it.

In the course of the summer friendly Indians visited me, but never stopped long, and gave me to understand that I lived too much among the white men. It would be much better for me to move nearer to them and then they would visit me more frequently. Thus arrived one evening just before sunset my old friend Pahajuka, accompanied by his good old squaw, and his granddaughter, and a few Comanches. The joy of the old folk was great, and they said that had not the white men blocked the road to me, they would willingly stay some time with me, but as it was we were daily more separated. Tahtoweja said nothing, but her black eyes plainly expressed that she too felt happy at being with me again. She could not in her silent admiration gaze sufficiently at the decorations of my room; and for hours she would gaze at the pictures on the walls, or turn over the sketches in my portfolio, when business prevented me from being with her. Music seemed to be her delight, and she often came late at night into the gallery and begged me to play the guitar, when she seemed to fall into a happy dreamy state and entirely forget the world. She too begged me to come away from among the pale faces and settle nearer to them: the Comanches loved me more than they did. The people remained some weeks with me, but one morning they came into my room, and the old lady said with tears, that this was the last visit they would pay me, as the road to me was growing too narrow. I was obliged to promise them a visit at the parts where the buffalo still grazed, and the antelopes and stags had not so many feet as here.

After breakfast I saddled Czar and rode with my guests to the mountain springs, where we spent the night, and the next morning we took leave of one another. I promised to join them the next winter on the Puerco, when a great council of the Comanches was to take place. They often looked with tears in their eyes in the direction of the Fort: then they offered me their hand once again and rode off, never again to cross the threshold of my house, to which they were so attached.

Tiger too seemed dissatisfied at the new settlements, and could not understand how people could have an objection to his pulling down the fences and riding across the fields to save distance. They had also forbidden him taking dry corn leaves for his horse out of the stacks, or fastening his piebald to the grand stockade in front of the house, while he went in to beg a drink of water. What I had long foreseen happened, he was beginning to feel the trammels of civilization and wrestled against them, while its comforts still attracted him. Shortly after Pahajuka's departure Tiger's tribe arrived in the neighbourhood of the Fort, and the chief paid me a visit with several of his warriors. He told me that Tiger wished to go home with them, in order to see his relations and return to me in the following spring. Though I felt sorry for it, I saw that he could not remain much longer in our settlement without parting from us on unfriendly terms: hence I offered no objection, and on the day of their departure I accompanied them as far as Widow White's, as I wanted to pay a visit to Mac on Mustang River. I took a hearty farewell of Tiger, as I was really attached to him, and he was obliged to promise me a visit ere long.

The next day I rode to MacDonnell's, when I found everything prospering. His field had produced a rich maize crop, and was now covered with beans, potatoes, melons, gourds, &c. His orchard already contained fine young trees; his garden supplied him and his negroes with magnificent vegetables. The yard round his house was crowded with poultry of every description, and the interior of his blockhouse was very neat and tidy. A large new patchwork quilt was thrown on his bed; over the mantelpiece was a handsome looking-glass, and by its side hung the framed portraits of three men, which are very frequently found in frontier houses, and by which the Americans do not pay themselves the worst compliment. They represent the greatest, the best, and the most useful men of our century—Washington, Alexander von Humboldt and Liebig.

The now frequently traversed road from Turkey Creek to the Leone shortened the distance between the two rivers much, as the greater portion of it could be galloped over. I reached the Fort again at an early hour, and helped Königstein in his preparations for a start on the next morning. He was going with Antonio, Lambert, and several pack animals to fetch our saddles and traps, which we cached after the loss of our cattle in the prairie to the north of the San Saba Mountains.

Although we are still living on the frontier of the desert, we have now in front of us a line of settlements facing the Indians, which keep off us the ordinary dangers of a frontier life; and we are rarely reminded by the personal appearance of these savages in our vicinity, that their hunting-grounds are not a great distance from us.